CW01623318

For World Book Day
2023

Best wishes

Peter Handley

A-P reckons he has joked enough now about bygone schoolmasters, ungrateful employers and flaky redundancies. None of that really matters today.

Surely what matters now is turning the tide against the criminals who are keenly trying to steal whole countries (including our own) and dealing with the bloodthirsty few who have actually managed to grab one.

Isn't it time to act before those guys manage to steal the whole planet, or destroy what's left of it?

Tabarin

How Danny Rook ran into an old shipmate, got properly Shanghai-ed, continued to feel expendable – and finally quit

A P Handley

THE REAL PRESS
www.therealpress.co.uk

Published in 2022 by the Real Press.
www.therealpress.co.uk

ISBN (print) 978-1912119387
ISBN (ebooks) 978-1912119981

Cover illustration: 'Operation Tabarin:
The *William Scoresby* and S.S. *Fitzroy* in Whalers Bay, Deception Island, February 1944'
(A watercolour painting by Mark Myers, PPRSMA, F/ASMA)

To my agent, Emma, who laboured tirelessly to get my work into print, and to Clip & Sue, who caused all this.

About Secret History

Studying history, we sometimes come to a point where the provable facts run out, and then pick up again on the other side.

The genre of *Secret History* – which is fiction, after all – invites readers to think about the previously untold story and perhaps to wonder whether it could be true.

At its core, *Secret History* deals with real people, real times, a wealth of established facts, and a skeleton in the cupboard that fits the facts... It's just that nobody has ever rattled those bones before. The point of Secret History is the secret. By the end of the story, the secret has to remain buried, known only to a select few – and the reader, of course. But although the secret doesn't *change* anything, it certainly might *explain* something...

In the end, who can disprove a story that has never been chronicled in the media or documented in the archives, when all other details appear to be established facts?

Acknowledgements

Following the official launch of *Bunkeya* and *Pedro Miguel*, and hard on the heels of *Kola*, welcome to this – the fourth episode in the Danny Rook saga. Once again, I am grateful to David Boyle and the people at The Real Press for having confidence both in me, and in Danny's ability to put a different slant on Cold War history.

Now that the official inquiries have been held, and the important people have been found virtually blameless, once again it's time the underlings had their say.

CONTENTS

Historical context

Throughout the 1930s, Argentina had maintained a diplomatic rivalry with the United States, convinced that her traditional customers in Europe would always be more important than those in a pan-American market that was sure to be dominated by the USA. Hardly had war been declared in Europe when, in November 1939, it was reported that Argentina – perhaps concluding that Britain was doomed – had formed a committee to rouse public opinion over the 'recovery' of the Falkland Islands. Others less committed to totalitarianism thought differently and, in 1940, a Pro-Ally Committee began offering support to Britain.

After Pearl Harbor, Argentina was openly at odds with the United States, having remained detached from the total of nine other countries of the Americas that had followed Roosevelt's lead and declared war on Germany. At the time, Argentina maintained a questionable neutrality in which its armed forces paraded around in coal-scuttle helmets, the foreign press was censored, and such a poor watch was maintained over paroled internees from the sunken German "pocket battleship", *Admiral Graf Spee*, that many sailors had managed to escape, and had re-joined the Kriegsmarine.

In January 1943, the Argentine government attempted to convince the population that Britain fully supported her neutrality. She refused to correct that impression, even when the Foreign Office delivered a strongly-worded statement. In early June, President Castillo was deposed in a military coup, but hopes of a change in Argentina's posture were short-lived. A second coup took place in February 1944; President

Ramirez was deposed, and the pro-Axis government of General Farrell was installed.

The year 1944 progressed. Even though the United States maintained an embassy in Buenos Aires, she had not recognised the new regime, a position that continued to be justified by events. Whipped up by the openly pro-Nazi radio and press in Argentina, anti-Jewish riots occurred in Buenos Aires in June, and the pro-Axis Minister of War (Colonel Juan Peron) was appointed vice-president. The US ambassador was recalled at the end of June and, by July, Britain had recalled her ambassador too.

Although Argentina lifted press censorship, the measure only lasted for six weeks before being re-imposed in September. Also in that month, when nations worldwide were lining up to declare that Nazis leaders and war criminals would be denied refuge, Argentina could at first only manage a woolly press statement. Though this was later beefed-up, the government's promises must have been made with its fingers crossed behind its back. The fact is that both Adolf Eichmann and Josef Mengele lived in Buenos Aires after the war; Eichmann was of course kidnapped in May 1960, spirited away to Israel, tried and executed.

At the end of September 1944, President Roosevelt spoke out against the pro-Nazi intrigues and propaganda put out by the Argentine government, a paradox (he said) when the majority of the population of Argentina wanted to be governed democratically rather than by military dictators.

The above are matters of historical accuracy, intended to give the reader a little background information. You will come across some of it again later in this story, in words spoken by Rodger Winn and Victor Marchesi. And frankly, if there isn't a statue of Rodger Winn somewhere in Britain, you would be right to think it a gross omission.

But we need to take an even-handed view. It should not be forgotten that several thousand Argentinean volunteers served with the allied forces during World War II. When the outcome of the war was beyond doubt, Argentina finally declared war on Nazi Germany on 27 March, 1945. Clearly, this was all that was required to finish the job, because six weeks later, Germany surrendered.

Moving from the 1940s to 1982 and the Falklands War... Today, even 40 years after that brief and bloody conflict, it is perhaps too early to arrive at a balanced opinion of those times.

Some say that the Falklands were an embarrassment to successive British governments which were forced to defend a remote, sparsely-populated settlement which was largely 'owned' by commercial companies that administered the islands pretty much as they pleased.

For a time in the 1960s there was scope to believe that Argentine governments had begun to adopt a softly-softly approach in an attempt to woo the hearts of the islanders. For example, ten years before the conflict, a Falkland islander told me how, in the years after World War II, and with no proper hospital on the islands, patients who suffered a medical emergency were often evacuated to Argentina on a humanitarian flight aboard one of that country's flying-boats.

It might even have been possible to negotiate away sovereignty, had Argentina's penchant for dictatorships not run so close to the surface. Unfortunately, dictators nearly always need to divert the eyes of the populace away from the shabby state of affairs at home. So, at the difficult time of the *desaparecidos* in Argentina, no better distraction could have presented itself to that reckless criminal regime, other than the Falklands – and no better example could have been put before the islanders to make them want to remain British subjects.

Equally, history may conclude that not only dictators but prime ministers, too, can find themselves gambling with people's lives over the very same adventure. Setting aside the heroism of 1982, which must not be denied, perhaps the very best result of the conflict so far has been that it gave a nudge back in the direction of democracy for those potential abductees, the every-day citizens of a nation on the edge of distress.

Finally and briefly, I wish I could have known Victor Marchesi for longer. Although he was clearly a man who knew how to keep his mouth shut, and would not easily have volunteered material for book such as this, Vic's life would have made a gripping biography. For example, not many people get to have their exploits celebrated on a postage stamp. But as you can see, Vic did – along with his ship, HMS *William Scoresby* – on a £2.50 commemorative stamp issued back in 2008 by the British Antarctic Territory.

As you read on, perhaps you will agree that, in the circumstances, for Vic to have his face on a postage stamp was doubly fitting.

Reproduced with the kind permission of the Government of The British Antarctic Territory

APH
November 2022

German military ranks

The first part of this book is set in 1944. Because you're going to meet a number of German military officers on the first page, and because their military ranks may not be familiar to everyone, I have set out a ranking structure below. I hope it will help to compare the relevant German ranks with the equivalent allied or NATO ranks; these may be more familiar to many. Because this section attempts to acquaint you with part of the Wehrmacht rank structure, I have not given these ranks further emphasis in the story, although some other less-familiar German words have been italicised.

For the sake of clarity, the word 'Wehrmacht', sometimes taken to mean 'the army of Nazi Germany', actually encompasses all three services – the Heer (i.e., the army), the Kriegsmarine (the navy) and the Luftwaffe (the air force).

Starting with the Heer:

Generalfeldmarschall, normally abbreviated to **Feldmarschall**, is equivalent to a NATO field marshal (or 5-star general). Although this was the highest rank in the German army of World War II, Hitler was persuaded by Hermann Göring, who had an insatiable lust for power, to appoint his deputy to the rank of Reichsmarschall – effectively a 6-star general.

Generaloberst is equivalent to a British general (crossed sword and baton, crown, pip) or a US 4-star general. Don't be confused by the ending '-oberst'. It doesn't mean 'colonel', but more accurately 'upper' or 'superior'.

At this point, comparisons can get a little difficult since a 3-star general in the Heer normally headed a corps, or a particular branch of the army (for example, General der Panzertruppe). This results in the next two ranks being displaced from their apparent US and British counterparts. So:

Generalleutnant, which clearly translates as 'lieutenant-general' was actually equivalent to a 2-star general (i.e., a major-general).

Generalmajor, which appears to translate as 'major-general' was equivalent to a 1-star general (or brigadier).

Oberstleutnant translates as lieutenant-colonel.

Turning to the Kriegsmarine:

Großadmiral, which translates as 'Grand Admiral' would be equivalent to an admiral of the fleet (or a field marshal in the allied armies). Hitler promoted Karl Dönitz to grand admiral in 1943 when he succeeded Erich Raeder as the head of the Kriegsmarine. Großadmiral is therefore a 5-star rank.

Konteradmiral is a 2-star rank, equivalent to a British or US rear-admiral. Below flag rank, we have:

Kapitän zur See (or, more commonly, just **Kapitän**) was the highest senior officer rank in the Kriegsmarine and was the direct equivalent of an allied naval captain. Likewise, the next two lower naval ranks, **Fregattenkapitän** and **Korvettenkapitän** corresponded to the allied naval commander and lieutenant commander (equivalent to lieutenant-colonel and major in the army).

Oberleutnant zur See was equivalent to a 'full' lieutenant in the allied navies, i.e., one rank above a sub-lieutenant.

Obermaat was a petty officer rank, equivalent to the allied sergeant.

Part One – Winn

(I)

Thursday 20 July, 1944
East Prussia

Generalmajor Walther Scherff sat on the grass, his ears ringing from the blast. He glanced to his left. There lay Generaloberst Korten of the Luftwaffe, conscious but in a bad way. To his right sat Generalleutnant Heusinger, shaking with shock, his uniform ripped to shreds, his scalp covered in blood and his eyes wild with fear.

Still dazed, Scherff moved his hand up to feel his own scalp. It felt sticky, painful and oddly remote. He lowered his hand again, looked down, and found his fingers charred, bloody and unresponsive. Korten was moaning now. It looked as though he had been wounded by flying splinters. Scherff coughed but brought up no blood. He hoped he was in a better state than Korten.

The Fuhrer appeared from out of the building, his arms draped across the shoulders of Feldmarschall Keitel and Lingen, his servant. What in God's name had just happened? An air-raid? Thank the Lord that Hitler had survived. They were supposed to be discussing the losses on the eastern front. Everyone had tried to suggest the situation was unsustainable, but Hitler had demanded they should fight to the last man.

A stretcher party galloped up to their small group. The medical orderly began assessing Korten, poor bastard. A second orderly lit two cigarettes. Holding Heusinger by the chin, he poked one between the General's lips. He held out the second cigarette for Scherff but noticed his fingers. The orderly looked more closely at Scherff's face then eased the cigarette between the least-burned part of his lips. Scherff sucked hard, inhaled deeply, then gave a series of slow wheezy coughs, puffing out air and smoke from the corner of his mouth so as not to drop the cigarette.

He looked around, for the first time beginning to count the survivors. Nobody from Hitler's personal bodyguard appeared to have been hurt. As far as he could see, the white-coated waiters and those wearing SS Security Service uniforms were untouched too. It was only officers of the High Command who had been wounded – those who had been in the conference room.

SS uniforms were starting to flood the place now. Scherff shook his head and tried to think. No air-raids had ever got as far as the *Wolfsschanze* and anyway, there was a steel-reinforced concrete cap over the conference suite. They said the roof was two metres thick. No damage to the other buildings, only the conference centre, where the windows had all been blown out. Out, not in. Unlikely, then, that it had been a near-miss in a daylight raid by the US Army Air Force. Someone must have smuggled a bomb into the room. Scherff turned again towards Korten, drawn by the ghastly image of the penetrating splinter wounds. The table... there must have been a bomb under the table.

"Stumpy. That's who," said Heusinger.

"What?"

"You asked me, 'Who could have done this?' So I told you: Stumpy." Scherff didn't remember having spoken. Obviously Heusinger's cigarette must be helping. He wasn't quivering so badly. He had stammered slightly, but was interacting again, recovering quickly. They don't make you a general just for knowing how to use the correct cutlery. "Stumpy. Remember? He came back from the *kackstuhl*, then a couple of minutes later he was called away to the telephone. He'll be gone now."

"Yes... Him." It sounded logical. "And he left his briefcase in the room, too."

"Crazy. They make you leave your pistol outside the door but they never look in your briefcase." Heusinger coughed on the tobacco smoke. "Stupid."

"I saw your adjutant nudge Stumpy's briefcase aside, out of the way, against the table-leg."

"Brandt? Yes, I reckon he'll be dead meat now." Heusinger seemed dissociated from the event, lacking any sentiment. "He probably took the full force."

Hitler, Keitel and Lingen, surrounded by SS troopers, were just vanishing into the underground bunker. The Fuhrer was waving his left arm, walking with a bit of a stagger, but looking virtually unharmed apart from his tattered trousers. Imagine if he hadn't survived. What then?

"Stumpy must have had help, though," said Scherff. "He couldn't make a bomb all on his own. I mean – he can't even cut up his food properly. Who do you reckon?"

"Who? I'd want to be talking to Himmler for a start. He wasn't here, was he?"

"No, but he hasn't come to a military strategy meeting for a long time."

"Perfect excuse..."

"But wider than that. Think about it. Who's got most to gain from killing the Fuhrer? You know... Stalin? Churchill? Roosevelt?"

"There you go, Scherff, thinking like a bloody historian again. All of them, I'd say – devious bastards. If any one of those three swallowed a nail, he'd shit a screw." Heusinger was trying to get to his feet. "Time to get organised," he said. The medical orderly interrupted, asking him to lie down on the stretcher, telling him he needed to get his burns dressed.

Heusinger was still good for a parting shot, though. "You might think you'd got a deal... But none of those bastards would stick to it."

"Yes. Right. See you in hospital." Scherff waved a swollen hand as the stretcher-party, still trying to make the protesting Heusinger lie flat, hefted him off the ground and bore him away. "You'll be okay," he called, then added softly: "once you've had a good sleep."

Scherff's mind had stopped buzzing and started to focus. A conspiracy, then... Military minds. So obviously they wouldn't try something like this without a proper plan. He guessed they would have told themselves they were acting in Germany's best interests. Whoever was in charge must also have convinced the plotters they could reach a peace agreement with either Roosevelt or Churchill. Anyone could see that with things going so badly in the east, the key to Germany's survival lay in ceasing resistance in the west and joining forces with the Americans and the British Empire. Only then could they hope to stop Stalin's tanks rolling through Poland and East Prussia.

At the speed they were going, the Russians could be on Denmark's North Sea coast by Christmas. Who had more to gain if Hitler wasn't taking the decisions any longer? Scherff had no feeling in his fingers, so he spat out the cigarette butt. Who? Churchill or Roosevelt?

Early August, 1944
Rastenburg Hospital

Hitler paused at Scherff's bedside. The Fuhrer held his left arm across his stomach, clutching his right arm above the elbow to help raise that shoulder. His right-hand side still hadn't properly recovered.

"General Scherff!" The patient stiffened as if on parade. "I have decided to award a special medal to the survivors. You'll have something extra to write in your history book now, won't you?"

"*Jawohl, mein Fuhrer*. I'm so glad you survived." Hitler inclined his head a little to his right, to favour his left ear. He made it look more like a gracious acknowledgement than an admission of hearing-loss on his right. He smelled vaguely of some sort of liniment and had a plug of cotton wool in the right ear, nursing a burst eardrum.

"You see? God, and my stars have preserved me. Together we shall achieve even greater glory for the Reich."

Scherff felt sceptical about either the involvement of the Almighty, or the influence of any protective astrological force. He felt fortunate to be plastered in burn-ointment and mummified in bandages, because even if the briefest of doubts had flickered across his face, nobody would notice. He would need to be careful to keep any hesitancy out of his aching voice, though.

"The chief traitors have already been executed," said Hitler. Scherff thought that was significant. Hitler couldn't even bear to use von Stauffenberg's name. "General Heusinger tells me you think the Russians were behind this conspiracy."

"If that was my first thought, I've had time to think again."

"Churchill, then?"

"As *you* know, only too well, one has to understand the motive first, *mein Fuhrer*." Scherff knew he would have to take it further, but delicately. "Before he died, did von Stauffenberg say what he wanted to achieve?"

'Before he died' – what total *Schnickschnack*. 'Whilst he was being tortured and before he was shot' would have been more accurate. Scherff noticed that Hitler was trembling a little. He hoped it was either the drugs or the aftermath of the bomb, not something personal. Nothing concentrates the mind of a tyrant so much as the realisation that his own henchmen are trying to kill him, and Scherff was keen not to be suspected of belonging to the plotters.

"The plan appears to have been to make peace with the English-speaking ruffians in the west and turn together against the Mongol hordes from the east. Their hope was to destroy Stalin before the winter. They were mistaken. What will preserve the Reich is total victory. We shall fight on."

The man was mad. He would be taking extra shots of Eukodol now because of the pain. Scherff wondered whether it was the drug that was causing him to be blind to reason.

"That means Churchill can't be behind it, *mein Fuhrer*. He's clever enough to see the consequences of turning on the Soviets. In five minutes, he'd be a victim of his own propaganda. Remember how he built Stalin up when times were really bad for the English?" Scherff had not spoken so many words for days. His throat felt sore, his voice rasping. "If Churchill turns against Russia now, he knows the miners and the factory workers will paralyse England. There'd probably be a mutiny in the army as well. Not Churchill. Besides, England is bankrupt, so the old man has to follow America's orders now." It was getting painful to talk. Scherff knew that Hitler had other officers to see. He hoped the conversation would be over quickly.

"You suspect Roosevelt, then?"

"It's logical. He's dying. He doesn't care a pinch of sand for the British or their Empire. And he wants to rescue his reputation so history will see him as the president who avenged Pearl Harbor, not the one who let it happen. He doesn't believe in 'Germany first' any longer." Speaking, stretching the burnt skin on his face, was making Scherff's whole scalp, forehead and cheeks throb. Hitler waited for him to say more. "FDR trusts Stalin to finish the job and doesn't care if Montgomery and Patton never get as far as the Belgian border. He wants to concentrate on Japan. Before it's too late for him personally, I mean."

"That was my assessment too." Hitler's chin rose by a millimetre or two and he adopted a haughty expression. "But by contrast, I did not need time to think. History will not be kind to an indecisive leader – you should know this. We shall have to teach the Americans a lesson."

His voice had begun to rise and he was starting to clench his right hand into a fist. "What we must do – it came to me straight away." But then the man seemed to remember where he was, and that a dramatic outburst would be inappropriate. He patted the starched sheets as if it were they that needed sympathy and reassurance. "Come and see me when you feel well enough." Then he twisted a little awkwardly and made to step away but, appearing to think again, turned back to address Scherff.

"The Americans. So poorly equipped. Do you know? None of their troops that drowned in the marshes of the Douve, or got washed ashore on the Cotentin peninsula or captured around Sainte-Mère-Église – none of them even carried a gas mask." Then he shuffled away, slightly stooped, to visit Oberstleutnant Heinrich Borgmann, his adjutant.

'The man must be insane,' thought Scherff, 'if he plans to gas the Americans when they get to the German border.' With Germany fighting on all sides, their arrival seemed inevitable. The only question was when.

August, 1944
Howaldtswerken AG Shipyard, Hamburg

After her launch, U-1226, a Type IX U-boat, had completed preliminary trials in November 1943, before being handed over to the Kriegsmarine for acceptance testing. By August 1944 no active patrols had been undertaken and the boat had returned to dock to fit a snorkel which would allow the diesel engines to run while the submarine (except, of course, for the head of the snorkel tube) was under water. The submarine's commander, Oberleutnant zur See August-Wilhelm Claussen was sitting outside the office of the Korvettenkapitän appointed to look after the affairs of U-Boat Flotilla 2 in Hamburg. A severe-looking fraulein from the Kriegsmarine Auxiliaries called him inside.

Claussen's first impression was that the Korvettenkapitän looked anxious to relieve himself, though whether of a responsibility or a surfeit of ersatz coffee remained to be revealed.

"I'll come straight to the point," the officer said, before adding with a grimace, "...As far as I can." He waved a sheet of paper. "This has come down from the B.d.U.[1] but it started life at the Fuhrer's headquarters. I'm ordered to find a suitable U-boat for a secret mission, a long-range mission, to transport *something* – I'm not aware what – to a location – I'm not told where – and hand it over to *somebody* – God knows who. Are you following me so far?"

"Er... yes, I think so." At the mention of the Fuhrer, Claussen had not known whether he should have leapt to his feet and stood like a statue until the briefing was over. But it seemed likely that the Kapitän had finished already. "I'm sure this is an honour, sir. That is, if U-1226 is the boat that has been chosen for this operation."

"How much longer are you likely to be in dock?"

"Work should be completed in a couple of days, but if it's urgent, maybe you could speak to the yard? They're complaining about losing time because of the bombing. When they're done, we still have to get the snorkel acceptance-tested, of course..."

---

[1] B.d.U. - *Befehlshaber der Unterseeboote:* U-Boat High Command

"I wouldn't trust that thing. If it fractures under water, your diesels will suck all the air out of your boat before you know it. The pressure will force the seawater in so fast, you'll be on your way to the bottom before you've had time to ring 'Stop Engines'."

"They've told me not to exceed 5 knots submerged, so the tube doesn't get bent, Kapitän."

"See? Even the people who invented it don't trust it!"

This exchange left Claussen uncertain. It felt disloyal to question the fitting of a piece of tactical equipment intended to increase his chances of remaining below the surface, undetected. He decided to press on.

"Then there's hydrophone and noise tests. And stores, of course – we aren't stored for a sea patrol yet."

"How long altogether before you can go deep-sea?"

"Provided there aren't any last-minute repairs, I'd say three weeks. But that's a minimum as long as everything else goes smoothly. I don't want to make difficulties, especially now you've given me the opportunity to serve the Fuhrer, mein Kapitän, but if it's urgent then maybe some other boat..."

"There is no other boat – not in one piece, anyway. You're all I've got now that Brest and Lorient are cut off."

"Could you get the yard to prioritise my boat a bit more highly then?" Claussen had been trying to contain his curiosity, not wishing to invite a rebuke, but he still dared to insert a slight interrogative tone. "Obviously this mission must be urgent..." In the space of his two-minute interview he had persuaded himself that he was entitled to know a little more, but so far, his subtle hints had failed to work. He tried again. "I presume that's all you can tell me, Herr Kapitän?"

Evidently displeased, the Korvettenkapitän thrust the paper forward. "Read it for yourself. Apparently, you'll get sealed orders at Kiel when you top-off with bunker oil and fresh stores. I know nothing more." He stood. "That will be all Oberleutnant." Claussen stood too and they exchanged Hitler salutes.

Paris

In August 1944 there could be found several dozen Royal Marine commandoes and specialist officers from naval intelligence who had a good claim to being the first Allied troops to enter Paris. That, of course, was what 30th Assault Unit had been set up to do – to get in ahead of the front line and seize as many German documents and artefacts as possible, before either the rightful owners destroyed them, or looters (from whoever's side) got to them.

When 30AU arrived at the Kriegsmarine headquarters, the Germans were not quite ready to surrender. For about 90 minutes, presumably the time required to destroy the remainder of the most sensitive documents, the occupants maintained a creditable armed resistance and then abruptly gave up. Not surprisingly, thereafter, the site and its contents proved disappointing. So, with the prisoners under American guard and over 50 other suspicious places in their 'black book' to investigate, 30AU re-formed into a couple of squads and spread out.

The unit heading northeast along the Boulevard Lannes enjoyed better luck at 43 Avenue Maréchal Fayolle, a Kriegsmarine communications centre. When the squad arrived, they discovered with relief that there seemed to be no Germans in sight. Instead, a motley group of Frenchmen had taken possession. 30AU therefore deduced that their opponents had fled before completing the task of destroying everything of value.

Because the vengeful Parisians lacked the means to cause much damage to the sturdy iron-framed apparatus (apparently built to last well into the second century of the thousand-year Reich) they had searched instead for combustible material. With as much patriotic enthusiasm and as little organisational talent or forethought as might be expected, the citizens were discovered joyfully attempting to finish the work that the Germans had failed to complete. 30AU made a forceful intervention, put a stop to the mayhem and set about rescuing as much paper from the conflagration as possible. The intelligence officers had quickly knuckled down to sifting through their haul when there came a shout.

"Oy! Halt! Halt, you bugger! Halten-Sie! Handy hock!"

The shouting was followed by the sound of two pairs of feet, one shod more heavily than the other, and repeated cries of 'Halt!'. The disturbance lasted no longer than fifteen seconds.

A lieutenant-commander, RNVR, peered over the banisters of one of the building's internal staircases. "What's all the row?"

"He wouldn't stop, sir. I warned him."

"Couldn't you have taken him prisoner, Causley?"

"He was already at the bottom of the stairs so I had to jump on him."

"Where from?"

"Where you're standing, sir."

"That's twelve feet up, man!"

"Not so much of a drop if you land on his shoulders, sir. Soft enough. Only the same as parachute training"

"It's him I'm bothered about, not you. He might have told us something. He's not going to do that now is he, with his head all cocked over sideways?"

"Sorry sir. I wasn't thinking. I reckon it was all that champagne last night." That was probably true. By 1941, the hoteliers and café owners had squirreled away the best champagne, taking to heart Churchill's promise of liberation, and anticipating the need for something with which to celebrate when that great day came. On the previous evening, neither their lavish hospitality nor the gratitude of the ladies had distinguished between officers or enlisted men. "Anyway, he shouldn't have struggled," added Causley.

"Couldn't you have just knocked him out or something?"

"Sorry sir, they never taught us how to half-kill a Jerry. All or nothing, it was."

It was clear that continuing the inquest would be futile and would distract attention from the real priorities. "Where did he spring from?"

"That door on your starboard side, sir."

"Well don't just loll about down there, Causley. Make yourself useful. Come back up here and let's have a look." The officer drew his pistol.

"Just a mo'. I'll go in first, if you don't mind, sir."

A short while later, after the officer and his bodyguard, temporary corporal Causley, RM, had stamped out the flames, the officer spoke.

"It's a good job you spotted him." He brandished the contents of a manila envelope. "This is bloody gold-dust." Causley raised an eyebrow. "It's an order from Adolf, no less, to Grand Admiral Dönitz." The officer carried on reading, then gave a low whistle of astonishment and fluttered one of the papers. "See this? It's ordering U-Boat flotilla 2 to prepare a vessel at Kiel so it can transport a nasty surprise for use against the Americans." The officer was enjoying the moment. "And do you know what else?"

"No idea, sir."

"They don't sound too happy about it." He held out another page and pointed to some pencilled scribblings. "Someone here thinks Adolf's gone potty."

"Huh," scoffed Causley. A Royal Marine for almost five years and still only aged 21, he felt entitled to his opinion.

"Well, it's taken a bleedin' long time for the penny to drop, sir."

≈

Many of the documents captured at Avenue Maréchal Fayolle were the same revision-levels as copies seized in the American sector at Cherbourg a couple of weeks earlier. But that just seemed to prove that the Nazis no longer had time to initiate action. They had become reactive. They were on the back foot.

In due course, the Intelligence Officer made up a shipment of the most important treasure and consigned it to Bletchley Park. Amongst the haul were copies of the full seven-volume set of naval code books, including the latest versions of such things as the short signal code book and the complete list of naval three-letter call-signs. But the papers that more accurately described Chancellor Hitler's unwelcome gift to the Americans were half-charred, crumbling and, by the time they reached England, almost illegible.

Thursday 21 September, 1944
Kiel Naval Dockyard, Germany

A flat-bed lorry that had driven from the secure compound at walking pace and under heavy guard, halted alongside U-1226, five metres from the edge of the dock wall. More for the purpose of being seen to do a proper job than to counter any threat, unlikely as such a thing seemed, the troops formed a semi-circle, enclosing the lorry. They held their weapons at the ready as two civilian labourers, matured before the Kaiser's war and probably now grandfathers, climbed out of the cab onto the damp dockyard cobblestones.

The workers began to un-lash the wires securing the lorry's only cargo, a single white-wood crate, perhaps 60 centimetres square at the ends and about 2 metres in length. Because most of the dockside cranes had been destroyed in bombing raids, a mobile crane eased into the space between the dock wall and the lorry, and made ready for the lift.

Aboard U-1226, a party of sailors had already assembled around the forward torpedo hatch. Within ten minutes at the most, the crate had been off-loaded from the lorry, lowered gently into the U-boat and manoeuvred into the torpedo compartment. Oberleutnant Claussen signed receipts in triplicate, after which the troops, workers and lorry disappeared to fulfil other tasks.

"Just make sure nobody goes near it, sir," said the clerk in charge of the paperwork. He pointed to a warning notice, stencilled on the crate. "Let alone tries to open it."

"What's in it?"

The clerk shuddered, turned his lips into the shape of a trumpet-bell and made a sucking sound. "Secret, sir." But Claussen could tell from his face and tone of voice that the man knew. Those sorts of people always did. The clerk changed the subject. "Message from the dockyard super, sir. Wants to see you urgently. Maybe he can tell you."

After making sure that his new cargo was properly secured so that it would not break free once the boat was at sea, Claussen inspected his uniform, keen to appear as smart as possible. Then he donned an oilskin to protect himself against the day's persistent drizzle, and set out on the short walk to the office of Kapitän Mohr, the dockyard superintendent.

The interview was inexplicably brusque. Claussen felt Mohr's manner had the flavour of disapproval about it. But he imagined Mohr was probably just having a bad day, forced to dance to whatever tune some admiral was playing that morning. However, as a motivational exercise, particularly from an experienced combat officer who should have known better, Claussen felt uninspired by the superintendent's treatment. What the hell had he done to deserve such a reception?

When he opened his orders, although they seemed quite simple, they were no real help. He was to put to sea the following day, carry out a few short working-up exercises and arrive at Horten, on the west side of Oslofjord by the 26th.

U-1226 proceeded via the swept channel and made her way north, as close to the Swedish coast as possible, to avoid the allied minefields. All Norwegian ports had been mined too, and needed to be swept regularly. U-1226 survived her short cruise and berthed at Horten to wait for further orders. On the evening of the 30th, a meal was about to be served when Claussen was ordered to prepare the boat for sea and proceed to Kristiansand for additional stores. He decided the meal had priority and allowed the crew to finish eating, before he called every man to his station. Then they cast off and sailed out into the Skagerrak. U-1226 made an uneventful passage at 14 knots on the surface, arriving at dawn, but no fresh orders turned up. Worse, Claussen failed to get any sense out of the Kriegsmarine port captain, who knew nothing about any planned operations. Things changed on October 4, when the boat was ordered to Stavanger.

This involved a slightly longer passage, although Claussen was still able to make the whole voyage on the surface and in darkness. The trouble was that they didn't want anything to do with U-1226 at Stavanger either and hurried him along to Bergen, where the boat arrived on the 6th.

On the afternoon of October 7, an officer and four men from the Marine *Küstenpolizei* accompanied three civilian passengers on board. The police officer asked Claussen to sign a receipt for the passengers and then produced two Kriegsmarine envelopes, labelled 'A' and 'C', and a stiff tube wrapped in brown paper, labelled 'B'. He requested Claussen to open envelope A, and to sign, once again, that he had received three items, opened the first and understood what he was required to do. The administrative process of multiple form-filling, copies to be filed, and signatures duly witnessed was comfortingly normal. By contrast, the contents of envelope A, though easy to understand, seemed quite irregular, if not downright unhelpful:

1. Fahren Sie sofort zu Marinequadratkarte HJ11 [Heinrich-Julius-Eins-Eins], wo Sie Umschlag B öffnen sollen.
2. Seien Sie am obergenannten Ziel spätestens um 12.00 Uhr, Sonntag, dem 19. November 1944.
3. Meiden Sie jeden Kontakt mit dem Feind.
4. Position alle 72 Stunden melden.
5. Versuche den Kupferzylinder zu öffnen sind strengstens untersagt.

Claussen understood his mission to be secret and so the third instruction about avoiding contact with the enemy was unquestionable, as was the fourth – reporting contact every 72 hours. As to the fifth instruction, Mohr had declined to say what was inside the wooden box. Now Claussen knew a fraction more. Because he had been warned at Kiel about the danger from the contents of the crate and because its markings carried a hint of mystery, for the time-being, he was happy to suppress his curiosity and accept the order not to attempt to open the 'copper cylinder'. Whether or not Mohr knew what was in the cylinder, Claussen hoped that one of the other envelopes would contain greater detail.

Of more immediate concern was the location of ocean square HJ11. For one thing, he would need to plot a course to make sure that U-1226 met the requirement to arrive before November 19. However, this much was clear from familiarity with the charts – *Großquadrat* HJ lay nowhere near Norway. Once the *Küstenpolizei* had gone away, Claussen squeezed into the submarine's chart room and began to leaf through a folio of large-scale oceanic charts. Although it did not take long to discover where he had been ordered to go, the destination caused Claussen to scratch his chin for a good half minute, wondering why.

Once darkness had fallen on the 7th, in company with two escorting *Schnellbooten*, Claussen piloted U-1226 south of the island of Askøy then turned north, using the sheltered channel leading to the North Sea. At 5:30 a.m. on the 8th the signal station on Fedje Island flashed the information that a Luftwaffe patrol had reported no surface targets, and so U-1226 and her escorts set a course north-westwards. They aimed to stay well clear of the coast and make a surface passage to reduce the risk of being snared by enemy sonar. Royal Navy submarines were known to lurk in the inshore waters for the chance of picking off a transport vessel or perhaps even a U-boat.

Once clear of Fedje, the sea surface was choppy and cold, so it was only possible to maintain a speed of 10 knots. Any faster than this caused such volumes of sea-spray from waves breaking over the bows that visibility was severely restricted. Quite apart from the unpleasantness of having frigid salt water continually flung back into his face as he peered over the rim of the fin, Claussen needed the lookouts to maintain a proper watch. They couldn't risk being surprised by the Royal Navy and forced to fight before the voyage had even begun. By 8 a.m. Claussen judged that they had moved sufficiently far out to sea, so he signalled the escorts to make a course-change. Accordingly, with the horizon clear, as far as he could tell in the dim and misty half-light, the three vessels altered course to 350°.

The more northerly course brought the direction of the sea-waves onto the port beam and so ought to have permitted an increase in speed. Unfortunately, after dawn the westerly breeze grew to force 5 or 6, so that just as much spray curled aft as the wind snatched it up and hurled it into numb, frozen faces. U-1226 was forced to reduce speed to 9 knots.

Just before 5 p.m., now again in darkness, Claussen called for the snorkel tube to be hauled into the vertical position. The escorts would soon be turning back and, once alone, if he were forced to dive, he wanted to have the choice of proceeding on either battery power or diesels.

When the U-boat sailors had secured the snorkel, the escorts drew close alongside U-1226. Crew members from both torpedo boats gathered along the rails for a formal salute, dipping their ensigns before giving the U-boat a cheer. Then, with a last wave, they peeled away into the night.

Claussen had already been busy with his charts. For the first time he felt that the voyage aboard this, his first real command, had properly begun. He ordered a new course of 300°, heading for a waypoint that he felt would give him sufficient clearance from the extensive minefields protecting the gaps between Iceland, the Faeroes and the Shetlands. He also needed to avoid any possible Arctic convoys outward-bound from east coast ports of North America. This whole sea area had become a death trap for U-boats.

The Allies now had complete air superiority too. Claussen made sure that the 'Naxos' gear was turned on and ordered that the operator be relieved every two hours. He didn't want anybody falling asleep on the job. The latest version of the equipment should give him a healthy chance of detecting airborne radar signals. If alerted, he could cut the main engines, dive to maintain a greater degree of safety, and proceed on battery power until the threat had departed.

Monday 9 October, 1944
Yokosuka, Japan

The Imperial Japanese Navy's submarine I-8 (the 'lucky' I-8) arrived at the naval dockyard, inbound from Singapore after a cruise in the Indian Ocean. 'Lucky' because, a year before, the I-8 had completed a voyage to France and returned with the outgoing Japanese naval attachés from Paris and Berlin, together with a consignment of newly-developed drugs, and an arsenal of the latest advanced German weapons technology, all made freely available between Axis partners.

For the past two months, the plan had been that as soon as possible, the I-8 would leave Yokosuka and sail to an agreed location to make a secret rendezvous with a German U-boat. She would then return to Japan with yet another valuable strategic cargo.

Europäisches Nordmeer

Aboard U-1226, it seemed the Naxos receiver hardly ever stayed silent. One of the helmsmen had complained that the thing was chirping all the time, like a flock of sparrows in a bush. But the device was clearly doing its job, warning of radar signals from approaching ships and aircraft. Whenever possible Claussen tried to stay near the surface and use the snorkel, but frequently he was forced to dive deeper and proceed on battery power. The hydrophone operator often reported propeller noise from multiple surface vessels, so it felt prudent to stop engines for two or three minutes every half hour, to listen and assess the situation. Claussen knew he must avoid leaving even the smallest wake, so he made sure that the boat was virtually stopped before he dared to raise the navigation periscope for a look around. This made for slow progress, but the whole idea was to keep everyone alive. Whatever the crew thought about his caution, his orders were to steer clear of the enemy. The mission had been sanctioned by Hitler himself, so the objective must be more important than taking pot-shots at shipping.

On the 11th, the time came to report the boat's position. Well before leaving Kiel, Claussen had listened to the gossip between U-boat commanders fortunate enough to have survived their latest cruise. The talk often turned to how much more frequently Allied aircraft or warships were able to pounce. Suspicion had grown that the Allies had somehow cracked Kriegsmarine codes, and were using U-boat position reports to ambush them. Now, with the Allies fighting their way through northern Europe, commanders reckoned it was certain that Enigma machines, code books and daily setting tables would have been captured. Having encountered so much Allied naval activity already, Claussen could only agree. The evidence that Kriegsmarine codes were compromised was undeniable.

In private, one U-boat commander had urged Claussen only to report an approximate position, rather than advise his exact latitude and longitude. His recommendation was to work back from the boat's daily noon position and advise what it would have been at noon, Berlin time. By the time U-1226 was west of Ireland that would mean an error of at least two hours. But Claussen wasn't convinced. That particular commander had been showing signs of stress – involuntary jerky movements of his head, chain smoking and excessive drinking. Two hours submerged at 5 knots was a mere 10 miles, or 3 minutes' flying time for a patrol aircraft. If the codes had been penetrated, that left no safety margin at all.

Claussen had a better idea. His orders directed him to *Planquadrat* HJ11 – hardly pinpoint accuracy, just a rough guide to get him heading in the right direction. Map squares were 54 sea-miles from north to south, so he calculated that even if the British were able to decipher instantly what square he was in, they would need either a vast armada of ships and aircraft or an extreme fluke to track him down in 3,000 square miles of ocean. So, if it was good enough for the B.d.U., it was good enough for Wilhelm Claussen. He would report his positions with the same lack of precision.

Accordingly, once he had calculated the noon position, he consulted the table of position-offsets, applied the daily correction to further confuse the enemy and scrambled his message through the boat's Enigma machine. With all those measures, it felt impossible that the Allies could locate him there, passing through square AE68. Pleased and comforted at his deception, he passed the signal to the wireless operator for transmission.

On the 14th Claussen calculated his noon position as being in square AE87. Three days later, U-1226 had advanced to square AL91.

By this point Claussen had become concerned about his boat's slow progress. The cause was simple to understand. His destination required him to cross every east-west shipping route in the north Atlantic, but the Naxos receiver was keeping him below the surface for the majority of the daylight hours. And of course, the shipyard in Hamburg had advised him not to exceed 5 knots submerged, for fear of fracturing the snorkel. Any faster would be reckless. Advancing slowly was inevitable.

What seemed curious, however, was that there had been no criticism from B.d.U. Nobody had queried either his imprecise method of position reporting or indeed his apparent lack of drive. In his favour, Claussen figured that once U-1226 got south of the sea-lanes that funnelled into the English Channel and the Mediterranean, he would have a better chance of pushing ahead more rapidly. Maybe B.d.U. agreed. Or maybe they were deliberately leaving him alone, refraining from unnecessary radio traffic to minimise the risk that the Allies could home in on his radio transmissions.

By October 20, Claussen advised that U-1226 was located in a chart square, over 450 miles west of Cape Finisterre. But although the wireless operator listened for messages at the scheduled times, B.d.U. still had nothing to say about their sluggish pace.

On the 23rd Claussen reported his position over 700 miles west of Gibraltar.

(II)

Friday 27 October, 1944
Admiralty Citadel, Whitehall

A year before, Lieutenant-Commander Fleming had confided to a friend that when the war was over, he intended to retire to Jamaica, build his own house and write novels. Had he been trying to avoid a literary cliché that morning, he might well have been struggling to re-phrase the notion of his heart skipping a beat. In any event, his heart certainly followed any brief hiatus with a number of pounding thumps. He took in several deep breaths to steady it, but his shock discovery did not prevent the colour of embarrassment rising to his cheeks, and flowing as far as the tips of his ears. His forehead became distinctly warm and moist.

Oh God! This was serious. He looked again in horror at the single sheet of paper. His first instinct was to wonder how he might cover his mistake. But in the next instant he realised that somebody, somewhere, would either already know or be likely to find out; 30AU for instance. Although he was no longer responsible for them, he still felt as though they were his boys. Their lives had been at stake gaining the intelligence in the first place. It would never do to sweep this matter under the carpet. Besides, it could be *bloody* important.

It was clear what had happened. The only thing a gentleman could to do was to own up and attempt to play a creditable part in rectifying matters. Gentleman or not though, his best policy might be to find someone other than his commanding officer, the Director of Naval Intelligence, to whom to confess.

≈

Fleming, outwardly his normal nonchalant self, descended to the basement and knocked on the door of the Submarine Tracking Room, a core function of the Operational Intelligence Centre. He waited to be let in. Security was always tight.

"Anyone seen Commander Winn?" The male officers carried on doing whatever they had been doing before he arrived. Fleming had been Admiral Godfrey's protégé, but now that Rushbrooke was in charge, he no longer enjoyed as much influence.

A sub-lieutenant, WRNS, handled the uncomfortable moment. "I think *Captain* Winn left about five minutes ago with the DDO, sir."

Fleming thanked the Wren. Careful to avoid showing signs of panic, he turned around and set off in the direction of Captain Lloyd's office. Frank Lloyd, the Deputy Director of Operations, a man for whom Rodger Winn could do no wrong. As he came within sight of the office, Fleming noticed that its door stood open, so he continued past, flicking an over-the-shoulder glance into the room. Lloyd and Winn sat on opposite sides of the desk, examining some paperwork.

Winn was a very focussed officer who used every second wisely; he never rambled off the subject. Taking into account what the Wren had said, Fleming figured that the meeting might end soon. He halted at a notice board a little way along the corridor and pretended to read the signals in the hope of catching Winn before his loitering became obvious. Time ticked on. Fleming gravitated to browsing through the daily orders before being reduced, in desperation, to studying the Atlantic weather forecast. His vigil was finally rewarded when Winn came out of Lloyd's office and headed away from him, back in the direction of the Tracking Room. Crippled by polio, Winn never moved anywhere quickly, so Fleming was easily able to draw alongside him.

"Rodger! Glad I found you. Could you spare me a few minutes? Something rather urgent has reared up and bitten me, I'm afraid." Although he might have thought that with this initial approach, he had handled the worst part, the scrap of paper still troubled his conscience, leaving him a little agitated.

Perceptive both by nature and training, Winn turned and looked him in the eye. He had spent the previous five years worming his way into Admiral Dönitz's thought processes. He had replicated a Tracking Room that functioned so similarly to Dönitz's U-boat war room that some said Rodger Winn could take over the *Befehlshaber der Unterseeboote* just by changing his uniform. Winn knew most of what Dönitz knew. He read the Admiral's signals on the day they were sent. He even knew when the Admiral caught a cold. Winn narrowed his left eye by a fraction. "Let's find somewhere quiet, Ian," he said.

"I'd decided to have a bit of a tidy-out," Fleming began. "Now I'm not in charge of 30AU any longer, I've got a bit more time to sort things out. Then, this morning, the latest list of promotions landed on my desk." He shook his head. "Well, I'm not interested in how many snotties have been made up to subs and how many subs are now lieutenants." He had recovered somewhat, and easily slipped into his prepared excuse. "And I was just about to throw it in the bin when I thought I probably hadn't thrown out last month's promotion list either. But when I looked for it in my filing tray, I had a bit of a shock."

Fleming knew very well that, before hostilities, Winn had enjoyed a highly effective career as a barrister. What he failed to quite appreciate was that it takes a very accomplished liar to sit in front of a King's Counsel and get away with a half-truth. Winn made no reply, wondering perhaps whether

Fleming might yet condemn himself, without cross-examination.

"All I can suppose is that after I'd read this summary report from Paris, I must have picked up this envelope..." he dangled a large brown envelope, "and the gummy side of the flap must have been underneath and it stuck to this report. The envelope went into the filing-tray, and the Paris paper that should have gone into the action-tray, er... went with it." He spread his arms apologetically. "And there it stayed till about fifteen minutes ago."

"I see."

"And there's me, wondering why I hadn't heard any more about this... Not that I necessarily would do, but..." He flexed his left hand and slanted his head to one side with an ostentatious sigh, a theatrical mannerism adopted from a socialite acquaintance. It normally brought about Fleming's intended outcome – extracting an excessive favour or deflecting all but the most furious wrath. "I'm sorry, Rodger. You should have seen this a month ago... I came to find you as soon as I could." He placed the envelope, with the page still attached, into Winn's hand.

Winn examined the gummed strip, then gently peeled the two items apart. "Saucer stain," he said. Fleming wrinkled his brow. "What you're saying is the saucer must have been damp and made the flap sticky. That's why this piece of paper went into the filing-tray, attached to the envelope, instead of into the action-tray."

"Sorry, Rodger."

"A clear desk policy, Ian." Winn skewered Fleming with an accusing stare. "That's what you need to employ. That was the first thing I learned in chambers. By the time you leave the office, there should be no paper on your desk. The majority of your paperwork should be handled once and once only. Acted upon, delegated, filed or sent for destruction, but only handled once. Wasn't it the same at your family's bank?"

"I dare say it was supposed to be," said Fleming. "But whenever I managed to half-clear my desk, some blighter would come along and tip another cart-load of paper onto it."

The corners of Winn's mouth twitched, as if he were on the point of pinning on a weary expression. Instead, he asked what Fleming had madc of the despatch from Paris.

"What caught my eye first were the comments in pencil. Somebody in the Kriegsmarine being bold enough to write a thing like that: 'The Fuhrer must be mad.' Astonishing."

"Whom the gods would destroy..."

"Madness. Yes, I know... I can't decide whether to be encouraged or worried that the other side is finally reaching the same conclusion as us."

Winn's nature was to want to move things along. "Do you feel that's the nub of the matter, Ian? Hitler's mental state? It's hardly a revelation."

Fleming stopped to consider. "I'm not sure I do, Rodger. It's important, but it's only a circumstance. He's clearly been doolally for a long time. Something must have tipped him over the edge, though. But you need to read the rest of it."

Winn tilted his head back and stared at Fleming for a moment through his boiler-rim spectacle lenses. "You're very tense this morning, Ian."

Fleming puffed. Although he tried to look relaxed, he remained a little flustered. Winn bent over his desk and began to absorb the contents of the paper. Shortly, he looked up again, intrigued. "What do you make of this unspecified *Vergeltungswaffen*? A new V-weapon, perhaps? A 'revenge' weapon, but revenge for what? And why the Americans?"

"I really don't know. I suppose he feels they're to blame for something. Look – whatever he's planning, it involves U-boat Command – that's why I came to find you."

"This pencilled scribble... I don't think it means 'angry-mad.' Surely it's 'insane-mad'."

"Yes, I agree. And this scheme doesn't just involve one of Dönitz's submarines." Fleming wagged a finger at the papers in Winn's hand. "It's this Japanese one as well. The I-8."

"Help me with this then, Ian. You're an inventive soul. Put yourself in Hitler's shoes. To start with, your inner voice tells you what a great leader you are. You see things clearly that are a mystery to others. It used to be the case that nobody ever argued with you. Has some brave soul stood up to you and told you 'no'? Would that be enough, or has something odd suddenly happened to make you start foaming at the mouth?"

"Surely, if it was personal anger... Bang! He'd just have whoever-it-was shot, wouldn't he? And, all right, he's facing military reversal on all sides, but his first reversal came in '42. Essentially, he's dealing with a familiar situation – just a lot more serious. He may not see it that way. He may not like it. But would it drive him insane?"

"Maybe it's not irrational insanity... What about wickedly insane – criminal insanity?"

"Well, yes... Especially if he's plotting something evil. That would fit."

"He's lashing out. He wants to punish somebody. Get even. Whatever's caused it, he's not thinking logically. It could be something we might think quite trivial. Or worse – a total misconception." Winn struck his fist on the desk. "Come on, Ian. Imagine you're Hitler. You're upset... Livid. But something has happened and you've convinced yourself it was the work of the Americans. Think!" Winn now levelled a finger at Fleming and emphasised his next few words by beating time with it. "What could the Americans have done to Hitler for him to want revenge?"

"Perhaps it's because they've joined in a war against him."

"And?"

"Just like they did in 1917."

"And?"

"They're bombing Germany every day. They've invaded Normandy."

"Us too. Stick with the bombing."

"Er... No matter how many aircraft the Luftwaffe shoots down, more turn up the next day." Struggling, Fleming raised his eyes to the ceiling. "German civilians are dying. Production is falling."

Winn thrust his chin forward and gave Fleming come-on hand signals. "Keep going."

"Er... Stalag Lufts – dozens of them, full of RAF and American airmen. Er... I don't know, Rodger. What?"

"Hmm... American airmen." Winn mused. "Good suggestion. Schmidt, Schultz and God-knows-what. A sprinkling of German names, Ian. No longer just your British Tom, Dick and Harry, Smith, Jones and How's-your-father RAF airmen." Winn swept his right arm through the air. "Think about the Supreme Allied Commander. Eisenhower – another German surname. German ancestry and, to Hitler, they're all fighting on the wrong side. How would he feel about that?"

"He'd call them traitors, Rodger. To him and the Reich."

"But it's not just American traitors. What about the home-grown ones?"

"Christ, Rodger! They tried to kill him a couple of months ago, didn't they? The bomb plot! I'll bet you're right. The bomb plot." Fleming frowned and massaged his chin in thought. "German-born traitors trying to kill him. That'd make anybody mad. But that's no reason to see an American hand in it..."

"Forget logic. He's mad, remember? And what does Hitler do with traitors?"

"Enough, Rodger." Fleming sat back and held up a hand. "That'll be it. Von Stauffenberg has pushed him over the edge, hasn't he? I'll bet old Adolf's ears must have been ringing for a month afterwards. No wonder he's crackers."

"But is *that* the nub of the matter?"

"No it damned-well isn't, is it? I see it now. It's a possible cause, that's all. It's what he does next that's at the heart of all this. Not cause, but effect. Consequences."

"So again – what is he going to do to the traitorous Americans?"

"He'll want to do something bloody nasty I expect, Rodger."

The war had hardened a great many people, so no shuddering ensued, nor facial expressions of distaste. Just two temporarily uniformed civilians staring stony-faced at each other, forced for the past five years to confront ever-growing levels of callous human brutality.

Fleming continued to develop his deductions, barely lightening the gloom. "No need to bother with the Geneva Conventions... Or the rules of war. Nothing stands in the way of a madman, does it?" Winn let him ponder for a few moments. "But the fact that it's a submarine... It's telling us a great deal isn't it?"

"Certainly."

"Hitler wouldn't need a submarine if he wanted to kill great swathes of Patton's soldiers in France or Belgium. So, this revenge that he wants to inflict on America can't be in the European theatre."

"Well, you're making an assumption that he wants to kill, which is almost certainly true, and kill soldiers, which may not be true. But don't forget the Japanese connection."

Fleming leaned forward across Winn's desk and tapped the paper. "You're suggesting he's giving them a weapon to use against the Americans, out east, aren't you?"

"Maybe out east, maybe not. But something nasty, as you said."

"Not rockets or bombs though. You can't carry much cargo in a submarine."

"There's always paper. You could get a lot of plans and drawings and technical instructions inside a U-boat. Samples, too... Prototype weapons, if you broke them down into bits and pieces..."

"True, but kit like that isn't any use to the Japanese now. They're retreating too, and they haven't got a land base close enough to the USA to rain down rockets on places like Seattle or San Francisco." The only move that Winn made was a slight arching of one eyebrow. "Bloody hell, Rodger! You're not thinking he'd use one of his new poison gases, are you?" Winn didn't move a muscle. "Not that? What then? Disease? Anthrax or the plague or some awful thing? Or something we don't even know about yet?"

"Why not, if he's desperate? The man's a psychopath. Feeling evil. Wanting revenge... And his scientists are second to none."

"No, hold on a minute... Suppose it was germs. Suppose it wasn't out east. Suppose he wanted to release a cloud of anthrax over New York or Washington. Well, he could do that without any help from Japan, couldn't he? His U-boats have been working off the eastern seaboard for a couple of years already."

"Fair assumption. Except that the I-8 is big enough to carry a seaplane. They could launch it a hundred miles offshore, fly in, surprise everybody and spray this stuff from the air."

"Ah, but what evidence have we got that he's tested it anywhere? None. If he means business, you'd expect him to want some guarantee that it'd work. And launching a seaplane... It'll be winter soon – the sea could be too rough.

No. A plane is too easily detected – too easy to shoot down." Fleming was now playing to one of his strengths – thinking up irregular ways to exploit the enemy's weaknesses, although in this case the roles were reversed. "Another thing... He'd be too dependent on wind direction to disperse the germs. All that trouble and perhaps only twenty or thirty percent chance of getting through and no idea whether it'd work. Not worth it." Winn remained silent; Fleming thought for a few more seconds. "Same odds for California. Not worth it. Besides, it's just inviting retaliation in kind. Escalation, probably."

"If this means you're ruling out a slapdash attempt to infect American civilians, you're back to military targets. Soldiers and sailors again."

"Tactically useless. Germs and bugs won't kill troops on the battlefield. Not straight away." With an obvious sense of realisation and dread, Fleming then added, "Which brings us back to gas."

Winn slapped his hands down on the desk and sat back. "There you are, Ian. You've solved half the puzzle. It's a fair bet that Hitler has taken it into his crazy head that he has to punish America for something, possibly the bomb plot. And if your captured papers from Paris are correct, the Grand Admiral has assigned a U-boat to this horrible scheme..."

Fleming interrupted. "You think he's sending plans to the Japanese High Command so they can manufacture one of his new poison gases."

"He's probably included a sample, too..."

"You said, 'solved half'. What's the other half of the puzzle?"

"Location... Where he wants them to use the damnable stuff." Winn rested his forearms on the desk to help shift his weight and ease the pain. When he spoke again there was a hint of anger in his voice. "And of course, by now it's probably at sea, heading for this bloody rendezvous with the Japanese." Winn drew in a noisy lungful of air. Heightened by the ache in his twisted joints, his annoyance at the delay that Fleming had caused was clear to see.

"Yes, of course."

Winn's sudden change of mood caught Fleming off guard. For a moment, an element of contrition was forced to compete with astonishment at the speed and certainty with which Winn had announced his conclusions. Although they seemed to be his own conclusions too, Fleming imagined there could be a thousand other explanations. In the mental whirl he made the mistake of trying to deflect Winn's displeasure.

"Look," said Fleming, "all that sounds terribly logical, but it's total supposition, isn't it?"

"No Ian, what I do is *not* supposition." Winn's eyes narrowed. "It's painstaking analysis of the available facts, followed by an informed forecast of likely outcomes, ranked by probability. And I'm pretty successful, most of the time."

"Sorry Rodger. I didn't mean to be rude, but what we've just conjured up – what we're trying to do is to get inside *Hitler's* head – a madman – not Dönitz."

"Well, all right. We've cooked up one potential operation between ourselves in ten minutes. But whether we're anywhere close to the truth or miles away from it, it's missing the point. Your Paris paper tells us something nasty is about to happen. That's the crux of this matter. So we've got to find this U-boat before it finds the I-8. And we've got to obliterate one or both of 'em."

"Yes..."

Although it was clear that the meeting was effectively over, Fleming sat still, feeling unsettled. He needed to salvage something from the situation, rather than leave under the cloud of Winn's disapproval.

"How would you guess they're going to use this stuff then, Rodger?"

"Like I said, it's of secondary importance. Stopping it happening is the priority. Try answering your own question. How do *you* think he wants to use it?"

"I don't know. Maybe Hitler thinks the Japs can gas thousands of U.S. Marines on each new Pacific island, as they race up the beach. Mass slaughter." Fleming needed no help to see the implications of such a strategy. "But it would only work once. The American public wouldn't stand for loss of life of such a loathsome kind. Hitler would be opening up a home-based front – political pressure."

"Nice way of prolonging the war, though, while the Allies work out a way to get round the problem," said Winn. "Suppose FDR diverted some forces away from Europe. Excellent way of taking some of the heat off Germany." Winn had been holding a pencil. He turned it point-upwards, tapped the blunt end on his desk to show that the subject was now closed, and put it away in a beer glass placed close to the edge of his desk. He leaned forward confidentially. "Stopping him, Ian. That's what's important. We know he's planning to do something. We may not know exactly what or where, but..." It was unlike Winn to leave a sentence hanging, but it was clear what needed to be done; Fleming had achieved his objective.

"Yes, right enough, Rodger. Can I leave it in your capable hands now?"

"Thank you, yes. I'll handle it from now on." However, it seemed he wasn't quite ready to let Fleming off the hook. "All the same, I wish I'd known about these papers a month ago."

"Yes... Sorry." Fleming had the tact to hang his head a little. "Silly mistake."

"Very."

Fleming started to rise from his seat. However, in many cases, when Winn could tell that a reprimand had hit home and there was hope that a lesson had been learned the hard way, he refrained from further punishment. It was highly effective. Having confronted the accused with the charges against him and found him guilty, the change from menace to business-like normality frequently left the offender grateful for what mercy had been shown to him, and determined to do better.

Winn waited until Fleming was on his feet. "How's your German these days, Ian?"

"Not much call for it lately." He sniffed. "But I can still manage the documents. Why?"

"Intercepted a signal. Wondered what you might make of it."

"Go on."

"On the 23rd, a U-boat was reporting machinery problems from south of Iceland. Huff-Duff confirms that's the area where the transmission came from. Sounds quite genuine on the face of it. Apparently, the snorkel had failed, or got blocked – could have sucked in some floating Sargasso weed or something. They used a technical term: '*Backbordzwilling unklar*'. What do you think it could mean?"

Fleming pulled a face. "At first sight it's too unspecific to have much meaning."

"Unspecific?"

"Vague at the best... It could translate as 'port-side twin doubtful', but does he mean his port-side twin main diesel engine, the port half of his twin rudder? What?"

"I don't know. It worries me. Translated literally, it seems to have no real implication." Winn smiled. "You might say it's er... '*unklar*' itself. I thought perhaps it might have a different colloquial meaning. I wondered if you'd ever come across it before."

"No, never. Did anything come of this snorkel malfunction?"

"B.d.U. didn't offer any help with the 'twin' problem. They just told him to keep trying to clear the snorkel, but to keep it raised at all costs. They wanted him to head off to the south of marine area AK and act as a weather-reporting station."

"What's your take on it?"

"On the face of it, it's a bit dismissive; not very helpful. But on the other hand, it could be Dönitz trying to be cunning again. Intentionally misleading."

"Tempting us? Offering us a bit of bait?" Fleming was aware of Dönitz's periodic attempts to prove that Enigma was still fit for purpose, in the face of suspicions expressed by many in the Kriegsmarine that the system had been penetrated. "I suppose he's hoping we'll use the Intelligence to start hunting for a crippled U-boat, limping south..."

"Yes, maybe. But the story lacks credibility. What they'd be asking us to believe is there's a boat-load of engineers out there – *German* engineers, mark you – descendants of the people who actually invented the internal combustion engine – and these poor people can't unblock a pipe or mend a diesel motor."

"You refused to bite?"

"Exactly. If Dönitz remains happy believing that whenever we get lucky, it's through an informer, that's fine by me. The signs are he's still unwilling to believe we've cracked Enigma." Winn's face almost glowed under an expression of great pleasure. "As long as he's content to turn the Kriegsmarine upside down looking for spies, that's an own-goal for us. We just hope it'll last."

Fleming became focused. "You think there's more to it, though."

"If your Paris stuff is correct, as I said, it's almost certain that the German boat has been at sea for a while. Dönitz will be wanting to protect it – to lure us away."

"And what made you suspicious about it?"

"Because it appears there are two of them with the same callsign." Fleming's head snapped backwards in disbelief. Winn continued. "We think we're getting short, coded transmissions – less than a dozen letters – from the real boat, U-1226, every three days. Nothing except his position. And because of the level at which he's reporting it, it's only accurate to the nearest fifty miles or so. But then there's this second signal from the north Atlantic, burbling on about snorkel problems."

"Presumably you've eliminated other possibilities, like similar call signs or transcription errors from the Y stations? It's definitely an attempt at misdirection?"

"I'm quite convinced. Starting on the 23rd, U-boat Command kept trying to contact the decoy U-1226. She never replied. No surprise there. But I know Dönitz. I reckon he's hedging his bets."

"How do you mean?"

"If we ignore the bait, he'll take it for granted that he's been right all along – that Enigma is secure. With luck, maybe he'll assume we know nothing about this operation either. But assumptions are always dangerous... And you'll never convince a believer that he's wrong."

"You're hoping he'll think the real U-1226 is no more vulnerable than any other U-boat."

"Even less, because they're playing a cautious game."

"And if he's wrong?"

"If we *are* reading his signals, he's already primed us with a plausible explanation. Just in case we've cracked Enigma, he's trying to make us believe this boat has suffered catastrophic snorkel problems. If he can convince us she's sunk, we'll stop being interested in her. This whole thing is too fishy for my liking."

"When did we last hear from the real U-1226, then? Where was she?"

"Yesterday she reported position from a beautifully empty section of ocean, 500 miles southwest of the Canaries. And one more thing. Yesterday too, the B.d.U. scaled down its attempts to contact the red herring – the fellow reporting the faulty snorkel."

Fleming let out a low whistle. "Bloody hell, Rodger!"

"Yes, but I think he's tried to be too smart this time. I think he's given the game away."

When Winn got back to the Tracking Room, he drew aside his second in command.

"Mr Beesly," he said. "Do you remember the I-8?"

Indeed he did. "Arrived in Brest at the end of August forty-three and left again in October, sir. Huge thing. Brought a new type of Japanese torpedo, a new seaplane and relief naval attachés for the Japanese embassies in Berlin and Paris. Big propaganda coup for the Axis. I recall we had to lean on the editors to keep it out of the newspapers."

"Yes, well it could be heading this way again. Another *Yanagi* exchange mission."

"Hmmm! I wouldn't be too sure. The Intelligence is that the I-8 is heading in the opposite direction – on her way back to Japan – may even be there already. She's been busy sinking tonnage in the Indian Ocean. Committing atrocities, too."

Winn tutted and shook his head. "All right, but this Intelligence came from 30AU. They picked up some papers back in August... Named the I-8 in a mission to meet a German U-boat to transfer some rather horrid cargo. I don't care so much whether the Japanese half of the mission is or isn't the I-8, but see what you can find out, eh?"

"Will do."

"Meanwhile, there's one of Dönitz's U-boats already at sea, expecting to rendezvous with some Japanese sub' or other. I suspect it's U-1226 but I want a special meeting of the Intelligence group in fifteen minutes to see if we can come up with any other candidates. Once we've pulled this apart, I'll take it to the DNI."

When temporary Captain Winn RNVR asked for a confidential meeting with the Director of Naval Intelligence, there was never any question of delay. Winn briefed Rushbrooke about the Paris document and about Fleming's careless part in imposing a considerable delay in taking action against the German mission. Then it was time to discuss strategy.

"The thing is," said Winn, "everything I've learned about Karl Dönitz makes me think a revenge operation goes against his principles. He'll be torn between obeying the Fuhrer's orders, and some other personal course of action that he may not initially be able to put his finger on. This late in the war, the writing is on the wall. The question he faces is whether to shoot himself now, to avoid doing something that'll condemn his name for ever... Or he could carry out his orders and shoot himself just before the Allies capture him... Or he could carry out his orders and risk being hanged as a war criminal... Or something else."

"What do you think that might be?"

"He's a formidable opponent. If he was a Royal Navy admiral, we'd have showered him in decorations long ago. But this scheme of Hitler's... It isn't Dönitz's way of fighting a war. He has his own code of honour. I think he'll be struggling with the only real option open to him." Rushbrooke knew better than to guess. "I think he'll follow orders and let the mission go ahead... But if his conscience wins the battle, and I hope it will, he'll find a way of turning

King's evidence and 'shopping' the whole show to us – as I'm sure they still say in my former profession."

"There's a lot of 'might maybe possibly perhaps' about this, though isn't there?"

"Over a significant portion of it, yes, but Japanese involvement is key. We can't be sure if it really is a plan to divert American attention from Europe, but it very well could be... We certainly don't know where or when Hitler wants the Japanese to use this ghastly weapon. But the thing is, we know enough to realise we have to stop this U-boat."

"As you say. And it's a pity we didn't know about it earlier."

"We've still got time to rescue the situation, sir. We're pretty certain we know the particular German U-boat that's involved, and we know fairly accurately where she is. Right now, she's heading south. If she then turns east, there should be a good chance to sink her as she rounds the Cape of Good Hope."

In case the Admiral had not yet appreciated the further consequences, Winn proceeded to spell them out. "Only there's another angle to this. Quite apart from the threat to the 'Germany First' principle if U.S. troops get transferred to another theatre, this delay is down to us. If thousands of U.S. Marines die a horrible death, and it could have been prevented, Uncle Sam's finger will be pointing straight at us."

Rushbrooke gave a grunt of cynical understanding. "You're saying this makes it a political problem as well as a naval one."

"Yes sir. That's why I thought you'd want to check with the Prime Minister. Do we keep quiet and sink her ourselves? Or do we let the Americans know, make it a joint effort, and risk exposing the fact that we pretty much messed it up for a couple of months when Jerry made us a present of the papers in Paris? In either event, Winston needs to know."

≈

Newly returned from Moscow, by way of Cairo and Rome, Churchill had plunged back into Parliamentary matters with great energy, buoyed up, no doubt, by the satisfactory course of the war. Clearly, he also felt that he had achieved near-unanimity from his conferences with Averell Harriman, standing in for President Roosevelt, and with Marshall Stalin. The Prime Minister had spent a busy morning making a detailed statement to the House about his trip abroad. He then allowed himself a well-lubricated lunch to celebrate, followed by a long-deferred rest. During the late afternoon he received word that the DNI wanted to see him and would bring Captain Winn. Because Churchill still loved to involve himself in naval matters, especially the more cloak-and-dagger kind, he agreed to see the delegation at 5:30 p.m.

Although the Submarine Tracking Room used its own specially-printed Admiralty charts, overlaid with Kriegsmarine map squares, Rushbrooke had brought along a set of captured German charts of the north and south Atlantic to add authenticity and also to excite the Prime Minister. Winn, tired from his long day and leaning on a table to support his twisted frame, had been taking Churchill through the history of position reports sent by U-1226 and deciphered at Bletchley Park. He placed a finger on the chart.

"Yesterday, Prime Minister, U-1226 was located just here, in Kriegsmarine square DT16. She has crossed a whole series of shipping lanes without incident and reached relatively quiet waters. This will permit an increase in speed, sir. The indication is that she has also changed course."

"Ever vigilant, Captain Winn. What global backwater do your deliberations now suggest that this Nazi U-boat is seeking to infest?"

Rushbrooke was determined not to be left out. "It all depends on when she altered course, Prime Minister.

Presently she seems to be heading for the Brazilian coast. It's hard to tell. She's probably zig-zagging, which makes her destination a bit more difficult to predict."

"What's this then? Privileged Nazi rats leaving the sinking ship and heading for a new life in South America?"

"No, I don't think so. At least not in Brazil, a declared ally. That's not to say it won't happen elsewhere in South America. The point is this, Prime Minister: we have Intelligence to suggest that U-1226 is scheduled to rendezvous with a Japanese submarine. We know the Germans and the Japanese have exchanged scientific information before... Also, special equipment, strategic supplies and so forth. We think this could be another one of those missions – transfer of weapons technology – not fugitives."

"Exchanging goods in a South American port? I don't think so, Admiral." The great man shook his head, then continued in a growl. "Even the Argentine is teetering away from the Axis now. If they allowed something like this to happen, it would be as good as a declaration of war. They wouldn't dare."

"I quite agree sir, but it wouldn't stop these two subs finding a nice remote inlet somewhere and doing the dirty deed there in secret – or in some calm tropical waters a couple of hundred miles off the Brazilian coast."

Churchill gave an intimidating grunt that seemed to convey his opinion that the whole scheme was a hare-brained fabrication and that Rushbrooke was wasting his time. "What do you think, Winn?"

Winn, however, had survived bad-tempered grunts from the most irascible members of the judiciary and was not to be cowed. "A strong possibility, Prime Minister, is that this latest position could be a feint to keep U-1226 clear of the main shipping lanes before she makes a turn southeast to head round the Cape and into the Indian Ocean. A rendezvous at Penang or Singapore. This, after all, is what they've done a number of times already."

The mention of two former Royal Navy bases now under Japanese control, and from which German U-boats and surface raiders were known to operate worsened Churchill's mood.

"Since the Nazis and the Japanese have a history of these exchanges, this appears to be nothing new." Churchill now scowled at Winn. "I trust therefore that you are about to disclose to me the additional import – not to say, the *impact* of this suspected rendezvous?"

"Prime Minister, the matter to which Admiral Rushbrooke wanted to draw to your attention is the political implication of how Hitler wants to use the substance, the weapon, the technology that we suspect may be on board this German submarine. And because the Admiral's business is sinking enemy ships and your business is, with respect sir, the conduct of the war, of relations with our allies, of government and politics... we stand before you now, ready to provide you with enough information to make your decision."

Churchill turned back to Rushbrooke and raised his chin. "Then tell me, Admiral, just what is this so-called political implication?"

So Rushbrooke told him.

Still lying on Churchill's desk was a copy of his notes for the speech that he had given in the House of Commons that morning. When Rushbrooke had finished explaining the naval options open to him to assist in resolving the political situation caused by the U-1226 operation, Churchill reached for his notes and spoke.

"You will be aware that the Hitler bomb plot had its origins in the realisation amongst many holding high office in Nazi Germany that the days of '*Das Reich*' were numbered and that the arrival of Marshall Stalin's armies on German territory would precipitate a bloodbath of proportions never before witnessed in human history. You are also party to the knowledge that we have been approached in secret and on more than one occasion on a subject taking many forms, one of which involves British and American connivance at a Nazi capitulation in the west. This would enable the Wehrmacht to switch bodily to its eastern front to hold back Stalin, and then surrender at a strategically opportune moment before Christmas and so preserve as much of Germany from butchery as possible. In Moscow, I was called upon to give an undertaking that there will be no one-sided deals with Hitler, an assurance that has also been sworn by Marshall Stalin and our American allies."

Churchill adjusted his spectacles and ruffled his notes. "This morning, in the House, I had these opening remarks to make, which in view of your urgent desire to see me, and the matter now before us, are words that I can justifiably claim to be prophetic..." Churchill looked down at his papers and began to quote. "I said, 'The enemy has two hopes. The first is that by lengthening the struggle he may wear down our resolution; the second (and more important) hope is that division will arise between the three great Powers by whom he is assailed, and whose continued union spells his doom. His hope is that there will be some rift in this alliance; that the Russians may go this way, the British and Americans that; that quarrels may arise about the Balkans or the Baltic, about Poland or Hungary, which he hopes will impair the union of our councils and, consequently, the symmetry and momentum of our converging advance. *There* is the enemy's great hope. It is to deprive that hope of all foundation and reality that our efforts must ceaselessly be bent.' Therefore Admiral, it is our duty to strike down and defeat any attempt to drive a wedge between the Allies. This Nazi death-boat must be destroyed."

Churchill then put his notes back on the desk. "However, Admiral, it is clear that the delay introduced by this man, Fleming, places us in an awkward and serious position. It appears to me that there is an advantage in that many days must still elapse before this U-boat makes her passage around the Cape, and that this gives us time to prepare a trap for her: mines, nets, torpedo aircraft, depth-charges, secret systems and weapons lying as yet untested in our arsenals. There is time to lay the most extensive and inescapable trap for this vessel skulking beneath the waves with its damnable cargo. Whatever is needed must be flown to Cape Town without delay. And when we can confirm that we have sunk this fellow, we may, with some joy, let our allies know that there is one less U-boat in existence... But we shall never tell them how much we knew about its mission... Or when we knew it.

"The cost of bringing the United States into the European war will have to be paid by the British taxpayer – the money men in Washington have made sure of that – and the pain will be felt in the loss of our Empire. But this is as nothing compared with the cost in additional blood of having the United States divert its forces to the Pacific before Nazi Germany is brought to its knees and has surrendered... That exsanguination would, for generations to come, bring intolerable suffering to all the peoples of Europe."

Rushbrooke appeared to believe that he had been given his orders and began to rise from his seat. However, Churchill had not quite finished.

"Admiral, while I was in Moscow, Marshall Stalin chided me, provoked me indeed, for Britain's lack of zeal in ridding the world of this Nazi scourge. 'What have you done?' he asked. 'What have you given? All you have given is speeches. America – what have they done? All they have given is their money – loaned at interest. But Russia has given her blood.'

We on this island know his accusations to be false. The conduct of this war is advanced daily with the unselfish acts of English-speaking men and women, far and wide." Churchill held up a finger. "Let the obliteration of this U-boat be one more such act. But let no whisper of this operation ever come to the ears of any of their generals or political operators in Washington. We will destroy this dirty, dastardly, death-dealing demon. We shall do this ourselves and never count the cost."

Rushbrooke was now on his feet. "Make it so, Admiral. Make it so."

"Aye aye, sir," said Rushbrooke.

"Thank you, Prime Minister," said Winn, conscious that although he wore naval uniform, salt water would never flow through his veins, and therefore traditional naval jargon or terminology ought to be used sparingly.

Rushbrooke and Winn turned to leave, but Churchill had one more subject on his mind.

"And what of Fleming?"

Rushbrooke halted, inclining his head towards Churchill.

The old man continued. "The fellow has slipped up badly. Had his mistake not been discovered, the consequences would have been incalculable."

"Yes sir."

"I never liked the man... Or his methods... The man is a gigolo."

"I'm sure some would agree with you, sir. But Admiral Godfrey did appreciate the way in which he raised the profile of Naval Intelligence with the people who matter... And at the time when it mattered most."

"Perhaps so. But this Lothario, this debauched libertine was operating horizontally! Not with the people who matter, but pillow talk with the *wives* of the people who matter."

Rushbrooke declined to remind Churchill that it had been a mightily effective strategy. “Leave it to me, Prime Minister. I believe I have the perfect solution.”

As Churchill’s two visitors climbed back into their car to return to the Citadel, Rushbrooke turned to Winn and said: “Rodger, this is serious. Even if you or I have to sell our soul to the Devil himself, we must find out what Hitler has got hidden away on that U-boat and what he intends to do with it.” He then faced forward again. After a moment he added: “Whatever it is, we must also sink that boat and seal the fate of every man on board.”

U-1226: 350 Miles Southwest of Cape Verde Islands

By October 29, the Naxos equipment had been silent for days and the hydrophone operator only reported faint sounds from shipping that was clearly a long way away. Claussen was pleased with the performance of his crew, so he stopped engines and gave permission for the men to enjoy a splash in the warm blue waters. At the same time as the men were plunging from the becalmed boat, he was busy operating his sextant.

Having spent ten minutes calculating the boat’s position, Claussen gave a chit to the wireless operator, trusting him to encipher a short signal reporting their location in *Planquadrat* EH64, duly offset. After that, he threw off his clothes, jumped into the water too, and challenged Obermaat Klein to a swimming race round their cramped and malodorous war canoe.

Thursday 2 November, 1944

Admiralty Citadel

Rodger Winn had finished briefing the DNI about the previous day's deciphered position for U-1226. He felt that it was still too early to tell whether the U-boat was heading south east for the Cape of Good Hope. It was equally possible the boat's captain intended to maintain a healthy distance from the Brazilian ports of Natal and Recife before heading south or south west, for a rendezvous at sea.

"What else do we know about these buggers then, Rodger?"

"We read a diplomatic cable yesterday. I've brought a translation with me." Winn took two pieces of paper from the satchel that he habitually carried over his shoulder to keep his hands and arms free for operating his crutches. "Purple code, sir, so a routine break. Pat Beesly was right about the I-8. This signal is from naval High Command in Tokyo letting their attaché in Berlin know that the I-8 won't be available." He kept the original and handed over the translation page, allowing Rushbrooke time to read it.

When the DNI had finished, he leaned his elbows on the desk in an inverted V, clasped his fingers together and rested his chin on his thumbs. After a few seconds he spoke. "Arrived Yokosuka October 9th. Undergoing dockyard conversion... What do you make of all this mumbo-jumbo about manned suicide torpedoes?"

"What it says about structural conversion to carry those things is irrelevant as far as we're concerned. All right, it's a reasonable excuse for not using her to rendezvous with U-1226. And of course, it tells us the Japs are getting more desperate as the net closes in on them. We know that there was a general order on the 13th, pulling back all available submarines to deny Philippine waters to the US task forces.

It all fits in." Winn changed to a more confidential tone, careful to avoid sounding too professorial. "But you see, they've given us a clue about what was intended between the I-8 and U-1226. There in the second half of their telegram. Size..."

"I know. I remember this I-8 was a whopper."

"Yes. A good fifty percent longer than a Jerry Type IX U-boat like the one we're worrying about. But that's the point. What if the Japs have had another think and decided that the I-8 is too long for what they'd planned, or possibly too deep a draught? What if it's a rendezvous up some creek or other, and they've realised she won't make it into the place they'd originally chosen?"

The fresh implications struck Rushbrooke, causing an audible intake of breath. "Goodness, Roger! Two scenarios pretty-much eliminated at a single stroke. No exchange out at sea; no dirty work in a neutral port."

"Yes, that's our thinking, sir. We reckon they planned for their little assignation to be in some sheltered bay or, more likely, a river inlet. But they might just have been a bit too cunning. They've ended up choosing somewhere that's got too many tight turns before they arrive at a jetty or a suitable anchorage. And what the Japs are implying is that the I-8 couldn't have safely squeezed herself round those bends."

"Hmmm..." Rushbrooke leaned back in his chair. "I just hope that's not one deduction too many, that's all." For a few seconds he became detached, as if considering the options. When he surfaced, he seemed more thoughtful. "Who's the Japanese naval attaché in Berlin?"

"Rear Admiral Kojima Hideo, sir. Arrived earlier this year on the I-29."

"Yes... Admiral Hideo. I don't think I've ever met him. Pity."

"Might have been useful, sir."

"Well, Rodger... Obviously, his embassy has some work to do. First, they've got to get this telegram decoded. Second, decide what to do and think up some good excuses. And third, get an audience for Hideo with the Grand Admiral." Admiral Rushbrooke still appeared to be musing but, as he spoke, he began to smile. "What do you think, Rodger? Maybe this news has arrived on my desk even before Dönitz's, eh?"

"We try to do our best, sir." Winn never liked to milk a compliment.

"Next move?"

"You'll see they're not saying they won't make the rendezvous, sir. Just that it'll have to be one of their smaller boats. Which means the operation is still going ahead – but delayed."

"And since you haven't told me yet what's on board the U-1226, I presume we're still in the dark?"

"Only what we'd speculated before, sir. But it won't be the old standard stuff – chlorine or mustard gas." Winn gritted his teeth. "Something far more deadly, I'm afraid."

U-1226: Crossing The Line

After weeks of slow progress, Claussen had taken advantage of the calm seas and the absence of enemy ships or aircraft, and had called for increased engine revolutions. Following his noon sight, he discovered that by midday on the 2nd (Berlin time) they had already crossed the line at longitude 29° 52' west, and were officially in the southern hemisphere.

After weeks of tension and confinement, he worried about the impression that his three passengers might get if King Neptune crawled aboard and incited his men to wreak havoc throughout the boat. He decided to have a word with Obermaat Klein.

"Hans, I've noticed the way you handle the young ones. They respect you."

"Thank you, Herr Oberleutnant. All I do is try to tell them important things in interesting ways. It seems to work. They've got a lot to learn. I've always found that young people learn faster if they can be helped to enjoy it."

"Hans, we have some important passengers." Klein acknowledged with a bow of his head. "They may also be very influential, so they deserve our respect. I don't want any bad reports to find their way back to the Fatherland."

"Has somebody behaved badly?"

"No, but for the sake of the crew it wouldn't be right to ignore that we are now in the southern hemisphere. We have crossed the line, Hans. We ought to hold a ceremony... but not a boisterous one. Do you see what I mean?"

Klein nodded and risked a smile. "I guess we must both have heard tales of what can happen. I wouldn't want any of my young sailors to offend the scientists."

"Do you have anything to suggest?"

"Perhaps if I took the part of Neptune, Herr Oberleutnant? No engine oil, no galley slop-bucket, no painful scrubbing. Maybe just a tot of Schnapps to welcome everyone to my kingdom."

"And perhaps also, Neptune's blessing for our mission?"

And so, because the majority of Claussen's crew, himself included, were first-timers south of the equator, all novices assembled on the forward casing and toasted the sea god by passing a bottle of Schnapps from hand to lips along the line. Seeing this, the three passengers (who had clearly heard the same tales as Claussen and Klein, and were somewhat apprehensive as a result) formed up along with the crew. Indeed, it was necessary to send for two more bottles before all of Neptune's latest recruits were able to call themselves proper mariners, with the freedom to sail every one of the seven seas, whenever they wished.

Claussen's calculations also contained a welcome surprise. Over the preceding 24 hours, U-1226 had made a full 14 knots, although when he showed this information to the chief engineer, his delight was tempered by news of an unexpected problem. The surface temperature of the seawater had risen to 25°, and because this water was used to cool the boat's main engines, the machinery showed signs of overheating.

After the ceremony, and once back on the fin with the lookouts, to acknowledge the great surge in speed, Claussen turned his hat round so that the peak lay over the nape of his neck. Then he spread his legs wide, leaned forward, threw both arms out, left and right, and, as if gripping the handlebars of an imaginary motorcycle, he twisted the throttle. Finally, narrowing his eyes, he glared at the far horizon with predatory determination and imitated the growl of a motorcycle engine.

The lookouts roared with laughter at the pantomime, and loved him for it.

(III)

'Koralle' U-Boat Headquarters, Bernau

In January 1943, *Großadmiral* Dönitz had appointed his friend and confidant, *Konteradmiral* Eberhard Godt, to command the U-Boat division of the Kriegsmarine. By November 1944, this was effectively the only remaining fighting arm of the German Navy. On the morning of Friday 3rd, Dönitz came to see Godt on a serious matter. He began by showing Godt a copy of a Japanese telegram.

"This arrived on my desk yesterday. It's a de-crypt of a diplomatic cable to Koji."

It didn't take long for Godt to read the translation. He placed it on the gold-inlaid surface of his desk and smoothed it down. "Has he asked to see you?"

"Not yet."

"They still think their systems are secure, then." Lately Godt had become cynical about the professionalism of the Imperial Japanese Navy. However, Dönitz clearly viewed this new development as worrying, so, adopting the humourless manner of a pox doctor, Godt played it safe. "Do you want to treat this as good news or bad news?"

"I haven't decided." Donitz sucked his teeth. The mariners had known one another for long enough to appreciate that they were both holding back substantial irritation with the Japanese. "I'm wondering what to tell the Fuhrer."

"You know, Karl, this place stinks of cigarette smoke today. I really do need a walk."

"Yes... You should tell them to open a few windows. I don't get enough exercise either."

≈

The sight of two Admirals strolling through the narrow parkland, a former moat that surrounded Bernau's town walls, caused the occasional person who was taking the air that morning and could not make a hasty detour, to stand aside like a sentry. Other passers-by bowed their heads out of respect, their behaviour harking back to the ingrained courtesies of the Kaiser's Germany, forty years before. The trim figure of Karl Dönitz made him immediately recognisable. Although his eyes were shaded by the gold-encrusted visor of his high-peaked cap, they had never lost their penetrating quality. His loyal staff boasted that he would still be the first to spot the masthead of a ship, hull-down on the horizon, twenty sea-miles away, or a loafing sailor hiding behind a ventilator cowl, craftily seizing the chance for a smoke... Or the first to notice that initial flicker of an impending lie.

"You were never happy about this mission," said Godt. "I could tell. But the Fuhrer had decreed it. There was nothing any of us could do. All the same, I can't think of anybody who had any enthusiasm for it."

"No." Dönitz seemed introspective. Then, "Even though this filthy weapon would not be used in German hands, the thought that the Kriegsmarine had played a part in deploying it gave me an ache here." He touched his greatcoat above his heart, then deepened his voice and touched his temple. "And a constant worry here... It would have been better if..." But whatever that thought had been, the rest of it never reached his lips.

Perhaps Godt understood. "Oberleutnant Claussen is good. So far, he's avoided enemy contact, just as he was ordered to do."

"Was there any evidence that the Allies swallowed that story about the blocked snorkel?"

Godt pretended to be startled. "This isn't Karl Dönitz before me, is it? Yesterday you thought Enigma was safe. Today you're implying the Allies might be reading our messages..." He looked sideways and smiled. "Just like we're reading the Japanese cables. All this is worrying you, isn't it?"

"Perhaps."

"For what it's worth I don't think they paid any special attention either before or after we... er... *lost* U-1226."

"You still believe they haven't broken Enigma?"

"I didn't say that, Karl... But no I don't, not for certain. The boys who make it home again – well, when we debrief them, you can't ignore what they say. Sometimes enemy warships or aircraft just seem to spring out of nowhere and attack our boats, like..." He struggled with the simile. "...Well, it's like nothing we've ever known. It's starting to feel too well-planned, too well-rehearsed. Think about the accuracy of positioning. Think about the frequency of attack. That isn't just luck. Not every time."

Although autumn was not yet deeply entrenched, some trees had had a poor season. Most of the crisp brown leaves and diseased yellow ones had already fallen. The pair walked on in the dank silence. Dönitz broke it first.

"This makes a mess of the schedule. With the Japanese having to detail a smaller boat to make the voyage, it means Claussen is going to arrive at the rendezvous well ahead of them."

"His orders already cover that," said Godt. "He knows what to do if the I-8 isn't there. Do you think we really need to tell him, right now, that they're sending a different boat?"

"We have to consider the scientists. They'll have to wait ashore for much longer than we expected. He needs to tell them that much, at least."

"Yes, I suppose that's true. We could cover that in a blind broadcast, though... So he doesn't have to break radio silence."

"I know." Dönitz kicked at a fallen twig, staring at his toecaps as he did so, plodding gently onward. "But we're not getting a full daily report from him, are we? Position, course, speed, fuel consumption. We excused him from all of that. The Fuhrer's getting anxious to see some progress. Once I tell him about this delay, he'll want to know the full details."

"I know he will, Karl. But even though everyone agrees it's mathematically impossible for the Allies to be reading our messages, if they really are and if Claussen breaks radio silence, we could be sending fifty or sixty men to the bottom."

"I still think we need those reports." Dönitz halted so that Godt would stop too, enabling him to look into his subordinate's eyes. "Between you and me, Eberhard, hasn't Germany done enough? This weapon is too much. It'll only invite reprisal with something similar. There's no honour in being the first to use something like this on an Aryan race that looks pretty much the same as you and me. It was a mistake in the last war. Remember?"

"There's no honour in disobeying our orders either, Karl. Besides, what we're sending is only a tiny sample."

"And the instructions for making it. And the scientists who know how to produce it." Distaste was on Dönitz's lips. "The Fuhrer's orders! We should be thankful he didn't think of sending out one of the replenishment submarines with fifty or a hundred tonnes of that stuff on board."

Godt tilted his head, then massaged his jaw. "On the other hand, three months have passed since the Fuhrer thought up this idea. We ought to assess Claussen's progress... I mean, review the plan, in case Hitler wants to know. Obviously, if this Japanese problem threatens the mission, we might need to modify Claussen's orders."

"Indeed so," said Dönitz. "I haven't mentioned this before, but if we should need to justify anything, there's already an open file at the archives. Schloss Tambach holds every detail about this operation. Everything we've done complies with the Fuhrer's orders. We can prove that if necessary."

"...And, by implication, it'll be clear what we *haven't* done, too?"

Dönitz faced forward along the path and re-commenced his slow march. After about 50 paces he spoke. "There seems to be no point in keeping secrets from Claussen any longer. I suggest we send a detailed signal as soon as possible. Authorise him to open envelopes B and C. Ensure the contents are seen only by himself, of course. Tell him that the I-8 won't be there to meet him – that there's been a delay – that the Japanese will be sending a smaller boat." Godt had fished a notebook and a pencil from inside his jacket pocket and was writing rapidly.

Dönitz paused, waiting for him to finish. "And ask him, if it were to become necessary, whether he has enough fuel to reach Penang. Just use the *Großquadrat* name, not the actual place. I'm sure it's *Großquadrat* Ludwig-Friedrich; check that."

"Yes, I'll fix that," said Godt. He faced his commander. "For the record, my opinion is that because circumstances have changed, these actions are operationally necessary." He gave Dönitz an encouraging smile "I just wanted to be sure we both thought the same. It's clear to me this isn't disobeying the Fuhrer's orders, or even re-interpreting them."

"Tell Claussen I want a full reply, Eberhard. And so he can carry out his orders with proper efficiency, tell him to ask any questions that he feels relevant to his mission."

"Jawohl, Herr *Großadmiral*. Heil Hitler!"

Saturday 4 November, 1944

Rushbrooke knew that Winn laboured harder than was healthy for him, so he had found a way to relieve some of the pressure by making use of Fleming to chase down any information that might help to prove the exact nature of the weapon that the Nazis planned to offer to the Japanese. He had told Fleming he wanted an answer by 9 a.m. on Monday.

Conscious of his deadline, Fleming had studied the U-1226 file and found a fragment of new information which had trickled in from the Norwegian Resistance. Sadly, it seemed to contribute almost nothing: U-1226 had left her berth at Bergen during the night of the 7/8 October. But the Norwegian angle set him thinking. He spoke to a colleague to ask how he should go about contacting the section dealing with Scottish and Norwegian fishermen operating out of Shetland. One could never tell; they might know something.

There was nothing more to be gained by studying the file, so he decided to return it to the tracking room. Once he had gained admission, he found Winn examining the latest decrypted position report from U-1226. At noon, the boat had been in square FK51, a little farther east than it had been three days before, and much farther south. If this told Winn little, it told Fleming even less.

There had been a general assumption that the U-boat was zigzagging towards the Cape and would suffer its fate there. However, Winn was not yet totally convinced. Taking account of the Intelligence about the I-8, his suspicion had grown that the rendezvous might lie in some river inlet or estuary, or even an island in the South Atlantic. On present indications it seemed impossible to tell which way she was really heading, other than generally southwards. Winn told Fleming he needed one more position report so that he could join up the dots and be more specific about the two submarines' common destination. However, if U-1226 followed the normal pattern, he couldn't expect another message until Tuesday 7th.

Fleming returned to his desk in Room 39, right next to the green baize-covered door leading to Admiral Rushbrooke's private office. During the afternoon, following his colleague's advice, he had asked the telephone operator to put him through to the headquarters of the oddly-named 'Shetland Bus' at Scalloway, a fishing harbour a quarter of an hour's drive from Lerwick. The idea seemed nothing but a distraction, driven by impatience at the stagnant situation. He had no great expectation of making fresh progress. In any case, he imagined that the telephone connection would probably take the rest of the evening to sort out, and that getting hold of the right person on a cold weekend in November would be next to impossible. Then, as he sat brooding beneath a descending cloud of Virginia tobacco smoke, his phone rang.

"You're through to Scalloway, sir."

Fleming clapped the instrument to his left ear, cupping his hand around the earpiece to concentrate its sound. He leaned forward across his desk. "Hello, this is Commander Fleming at the Admiralty in London. To whom am I speaking?"

"Lieutenant Dalebø, Royal Norwegian Naval Special Intelligence Unit here, sir."

"I asked to speak to somebody who might know anything about recent German submarine movements out of Bergen. Would that be you?"

The lilting voice replied. "Yes, sir. I hope I can help you. What do you want to know?"

"U-1226," said Fleming. "I believe that particular boat left Bergen on October the seventh, during the night. That's all I really know, although I have some later position reports from a boat using her call sign as she headed south through the

Atlantic. I wonder how much you know. The names of any of her people? The destination? Any cargo? Anything at all?"

"Sir, I already sent some information earlier today. I think I ought not to say any more in case this is just an ordinary telephone line. It's just that you and I have never spoken before."

"Damn it, Lieutenant, I'm the personal assistant to the Director of Naval Intelligence. I need to know what you sent."

"Sir, I can tell you what time I sent it, if that helps you to find what I sent."

Although Fleming's business was secrecy, he didn't like being a victim of it, particularly when the difficulty was inflicted by his own side. The knowledge that Dalebø was acting correctly failed to improve his temper. "Do that. If you won't help, I'll have to trace it at this end, myself."

A thought occurred to him, although he failed to limit the cynicism in his voice. "If I find it and I've got any questions, will you help me then, or will you make me get Admiral Rushbrooke out of bed... Or Churchill, perhaps?"

"Oh no, sir. If I know we have a secure connection I will help. Very glad to help."

Fleming hesitated. He could escalate the problem, but resolving the issue himself could take a lot less of his precious time. "When did you send it, Lieutenant?"

"I sent my message at 18:27 GMT today."

Fleming discovered that the message had been marked for the attention of his colleague, who by then had left the building and returned to his lodgings. It contained information said to have come from a female Norwegian cleaner who worked for the *Küstenpolizei* in Bergen. During her evening shift she had noticed the signed receipts for some civilian personnel embarked aboard U-1226, and had attempted to memorise the three names. By the time she had left the police station and been able to write down the names, she remembered that two of the people had the title 'professor' but could not remember which two. The names were, she said, Thiessen, Neumann and either Fischer or Fleischer... or perhaps Fleischmann.

Fleming phoned his request through to the card-index repository. He hoped there was somebody competent on duty that evening. It took until midnight to get a partial answer.

"Two professors name of Thiessen, sir but one of them is 82."

"Forget him," said Fleming. "The other one. What's his subject?"

"Oriental studies, sir. Spoke at Oxford in 1934 and '36."

"Specialisms? Languages, that sort of thing?"

"Chinese art and pottery. Er... Also expert in Sanskrit, speaks Japanese, written a..."

"That's him. I'll need full details, please. Next?"

"Not so promising, sir. Neumann, Fischer, Fleischer and that – they're all common surnames. I've picked out all the doctors and professors, but there's well over fifty." The speaker did not sound keen. "Well over. Could be nearly a hundred."

"Doesn't make it any less important. Why don't you read the names on the cards and tell me what their jobs are? Scientists and engineers, I'll be interested. Professors of agriculture, less so."

"Well all right, sir. Here we go then. Doctor Otto Fischer, Professor of Dentistry."

"No."

"Doctor Rudolf Fischer, Roman History."

"No..."

Monday 6 November

Rushbrooke's timekeeping was precise – a welcome courtesy. He invited Fleming to inform him about progress over the weekend.

"On Saturday night I got a lead from the 'Shetland Bus', sir. Obviously, it takes a while for the information to get over here, but we received news that the U-1226 had embarked three passengers. Even included some possible names." The DNI appeared pleased. "There's a good chance – better than good, perhaps – that one of them is a Professor Thiessen. He speaks Japanese. Essential part of the team, I'd say."

"Agreed."

"The others, we're not so sure about. There wasn't total certainty about the names but we've ended up with about twenty possibles. I've had their life stories sent over. I'm combing through them, looking for any links or patterns..."

"Let me stop you there, Fleming. I want you to do something for me."

"Sir? I think I ought to stick with this for the time being. Apart from Rodger, nobody, other than you or I, is in the picture."

"That's all right. I'll take responsibility for this now."

"Are you relieving me, sir?"

"You've been under a lot of strain. I want you to take two weeks' leave."

"Sir, I'm afraid I must protest. There's absolutely nothing wrong with me."

"This isn't about your health."

"Performance is it then? I was very disappointed when you took 30AU off me..."

"Different times, different needs, Fleming. By then the planning and the training were all done. 30AU had stopped being an administrative operation. They were fighting their way through to the intelligence targets that *you* had specified.

It needed different talents – a fighting officer. I'm sure Admiral Godfrey would have done the same."

"And now you're taking me off this. What have I done?"

"You haven't *done* anything. But you're wasted here, now. Any semi-decent police inspector could co-ordinate this current U-boat problem."

Fleming raised his eyebrows and listened hard. He was astute enough to realise from these words that opportunities still existed; his naval career might have some distance yet to run.

"This U-1226 is a case in point," continued Rushbrooke. "I'd love to know what she's carrying. I'm quite interested in who might be on board. But the navy is going to sink her. Believe me we are. It's an old-fashioned naval problem now. Find her. Sink her. And worry about any dead professors afterwards. People are sick of this war, Fleming. We need to end it and end it soon. Jerry's on the run. We need to roll him up and squat on as much of Europe as we can before Stalin gets his hands on it."

"And me?"

"I've got a new job for you. I want you to go out to the Far East and Australia. Sydney. There's a new C-in-C Pacific Fleet, Sir Bruce Fraser. Going to need a hand."

"Doing what?"

"What you've done best. I want you to put together a counterpart of 30AU for Fraser. He'll need it when we take back Singapore and Hong Kong and so forth. You're already half up-to-speed with these Japanese submarines. I-8 and that... There'll be a lot of their kit we'll be interested in."

"I see, sir."

"Two weeks' leave. Think who you'll need on your staff. If it's a reasonable list, I'll sign the papers and you can get moving."

"Sydney?"

"Eventually. Kandy or Trincomalee for starters, I should think. You've got a brother over there, unless I'm mistaken? Maybe see him for Christmas." Rushbrooke looked up and smiled. "Think of us back here in the fog."

'So that was it,' thought Fleming. Once the Admiral had started laying it on three inches thick and promising him Christmas up in the hills in Ceylon, he knew he was beaten and it was time to go. He could see what the DNI was afraid of. It was an American war now. The Axis would be defeated, just as Churchill had promised. But the Yanks had a stranglehold on the press and would win the war on land, sea, and in the air – and on Wall Street just as much as in Hollywood.

Fleming also knew that Rushbrooke had become disillusioned with the US Navy's concept of sharing intelligence. If the Japs had got something that Britain wanted to benefit from, the only way to have a chance of sharing it properly was to grab it first. The other way round – we'd never see stem nor stern of it. Clearly, once the surrender was signed, it would be 'to the victor the spoils'. An eastern 30AU made a lot of sense.

Tuesday 7 November

Rushbrooke had asked Winn to brief him daily on the U-1226 situation. What seemed clear was that Dönitz still believed Enigma to be secure. Concealed in Winn's satchel lay the text of a lengthy blind broadcast, repeated at intervals, that had been transmitted to a previously unseen 3-letter callsign, one not included in the latest captured *Marinefunknamenliste* codebooks. The use of new code letters looked like another trick. Allied photo-reconnaissance was so widespread that Room 39 had known for at least three weeks that no unidentified Kriegsmarine vessels had been completed or left port on their maiden voyages.

“Summarise the situation again for me, Rodger.”

Winn briefly mentioned the size of the I-8 and how the working assumption made it seem more likely that the original intended rendezvous with the U-1226 would be in some remote inlet, or perhaps a South Atlantic island.

“I can hear it in your voice, Rodger. Something’s changed.”

“Yes sir. Today we intercepted a transmission to what we’re sure must be U-1226: ‘Can you reach major square LF without taking additional fuel? If so, what would be your ETA?’ Square LF, as I’m sure you’re aware, extends from close to where the Siamese border strikes the Andaman Sea, and down the Malacca Strait, about as far as Port Dickson. Not quite to Singapore, but it still includes Penang.”

“Using a second call-sign... Logical deception, I suppose. Your analysis?”

“There must be some form of time pressure. I’d suggest Hitler is getting anxious to see progress on his scheme. With these Japanese delays, maybe the Kriegsmarine is coming to the rescue. They’re thinking about pushing the rendezvous site closer to Japan.”

“So if U-1226 confirms he can make it, we swing into action off the Cape and hit him with everything we’ve got.”

“Precisely, sir.”

“Could he make it without refuelling?”

“He should do. We haven’t deciphered an acknowledgement from him yet, so we haven’t got his latest 72-hour position report either. But he ought to be able to make it to Penang, with all the slow-steaming he’s been forced to do. That’s a long-range submarine, he’s got there.” Winn repacked his satchel but made no move to leave the Admiral’s office. There seemed to be something on his mind.

“You’re looking a bit smug today, Rodger... Anything else I should know about?”

"You'll remember Fleming discovered that Professor Thiessen speaks Japanese? He thinks he's narrowed down the other two passengers now. Neumann and Fischer. Intelligence knows about two particular people with those names. They're German chemical engineers who've been involved in the manufacture of poison gas."

"Hell, Rodger. It's certainly coming together, isn't it?"

"I'm afraid so. Remember what some Jerry wrote on that Paris document? 'The Fuhrer must be mad'. Nutty as a fruit cake, I'd say." Winn reached for his crutches.

But now it was Rushbrooke who hadn't finished. "Rodger," he said. "One more thing."

"Sir?"

"There'll be no need to keep Commander Fleming informed about any of your work from now on. He's on embarkation leave. Off to India in a fortnight."

Others might have attempted a riposte, but Winn merely nodded and uttered a curt, "Sir."

"And Rodger... Until we've dealt with this bloody U-boat, report everything directly to me. My deputy's got enough to do, so you come straight to me. Understood?"

"Sir."

U-1226: Marinequadratkarte FQ86

When the wireless operator had first handed the signal to Claussen, the wordiness of it gave him rather a shock. His first thought was that the message might contain the long-expected dressing down for his slow progress during the earlier stages of the voyage.

He felt annoyed. That would be typical of a desk-tied officer – to wait until things had improved and then censure him for something that had happened well before. As a result of these mixed emotions of anticipation and resentment, Claussen twice made mistakes in his use of the Enigma apparatus, and had to reset the whole thing and re-start the process for a third time.

When he had finally deciphered the message, his first thoughts were confused. He had not expected a rendezvous with the Japanese. All he knew about was an imprecise destination in an area of ocean greater than 50 miles across. Now, he was told, this Japanese submarine, the I-8, the object of the mission, wouldn't even turn up on time. At least that took the pressure off arriving at HJ11 by November 19.

There was some compensation. Having been given permission to open his secret orders, he could satisfy his month-long curiosity. And at the same time, he might get a better understanding of any other implications lying half-buried in the message. He extracted *Umschlag C* from his safe. Because the size of *Umschlag B* made it too big for his safe, he had stored it under his bunk. He had always suspected that, being tubular, it would contain a rolled-up navigation chart, although it was heavily weighted in case it needed to be thrown overboard in an emergency.

Claussen snipped through the string that bound Envelope B, peeling away the loops of tape and sealing wax and the brown paper wrapping. As he had predicted, the package was a cardboard cylinder, but there was an envelope curled around it, also labelled '*Umschlag B*'. Far from predictably, the tube contained a British Admiralty chart. Claussen opened the envelope and scanned the contents at speed.

> Chilean waters...
> Lat. 53-20-00 south. Long. 72-48-51 west...
> Arrival by November 23...
> Permission to contact the Embassy in
> Buenos Aires...

The British chart covered those exact waters. *Umschlag C*, also weighted, was quite specific about the passengers and what to do if the I-8 wasn't at the rendezvous, but it told him nothing about what was inside the mysterious copper cylinder. However, Claussen was shocked to find that his new orders gave him permission, once the mission was complete, to surrender to the Argentinean authorities. Surrender!

His immediate thoughts were utterly cynical. 'Thank you very much,' he thought. 'Thank you for this great opportunity to send back such a lengthy reply that enemy direction-finding stations will be able to locate my transmission with great accuracy. Thank you. Just like the boys back at Kiel had said, the British will be able to fly right down my throat and make me and my crew yet another monument to the perpetual stupidity of the men in charge.' And what was all this rubbish about working out an ETA for *Großquadrat* LF when *Umschlag B* had just given him his exact destination? Because he had been on the point of enciphering his three-day position report, he engaged in a brief personal mutiny and set aside the task. He needed time to think.

Claussen could see that he would need to brief his passengers about their destination, although he wondered whether at least one of them might already know it. This could also give him the opportunity to probe for more information about the copper cylinder. Unless the passengers appeared to know a good reason why not, he would consider whether he could get away with invoking total radio silence, because there was one very important reason to keep quiet...

Let the B.d.U. work out his ETA at *Großquadrat* LF if they wanted. They weren't so ignorant that his timing and their estimate would differ by more than half a day. But if he could convince his passengers and crew that he had just received secret orders about their mission which also imposed a complete blackout on all outgoing signals, there was a far greater chance of following the spirit of his new orders, whilst at the same time remaining undetected... And alive!

(IV)

Wednesday 8 November, 1944

It had been clear from the start of the voyage that Professor Thiessen always deferred to Professor Neumann. Neumann and Doctor Fischer could often be found examining blueprint plans together or leafing through weighty textbooks, some pages of which were stained yellow, blue, or a kind of browny-purple from contact with substances about which Claussen felt ignorance could be a blessing.

It was obvious that Neumann was the senior man, but when the blueprints were spread over a bunk or the mess table, it was also apparent from the way in which Doctor Fischer tapped the plans with his pencil that he had the more practical engineering brain. Presumably, Neumann had the edge in theory. And the subject that occupied almost every waking hour for Neumann and Fischer was chemistry. Thiessen had long since excused himself from the discussions and spent most of his time writing. Perhaps, thought Claussen, he was drafting his next academic work. Since Neumann and Fischer were inseparable, Claussen decided that his next step should be a confidential word with both of them.

"Gentlemen?" Fischer stopped in mid-sentence and they both looked up from the plans. "I have received a coded signal from B.d.U. Naturally some of it must remain secret, but some of it relates to our mission." Claussen felt pleased that the deep-rooted German respect for authority had operated, giving him their full attention. Because the three of them were alone in the forward sleeping quarters, Claussen cocked his head sideways towards the bow torpedo compartment. "Is there anybody working up there? Anyone who might hear us?

"We've been here for at least an hour," said Fischer. "Nobody has passed us, so I'm pretty sure there isn't anybody up there."

Glancing alternately at the two scientists, Claussen asked, "Can I check how much both of you knew about our mission and destination before we left Norway?"

"Yes, of course. I suppose we both knew a great deal."

"What about Professor Thiessen? How much does he know?"

"He only knows that he's here to translate for us – to make sure it goes well when we meet the Japanese submarine."

"Very good. The fewer people who know, the better." Although they were alone, Claussen lowered his voice. "How accurately do you know our destination?"

"We know the exact place," said Neumann. "We know what to expect. We know we might have to wait for a few days for the Japanese to arrive."

"You knew more than I did, then. The B.d.U. has only just radioed and given me permission to open the second and third envelopes – the detailed orders."

"I don't understand that. Why should it be secret? You are the captain, after all."

Claussen tried to make light of it. "I just follow orders, Herr Professor." The two chemical engineers had not been at all reticent, so it felt easy to slip into the first of the important questions that was worrying him. "Tell me, was anything ever mentioned about a destination in Malaya? Penang, for instance?" The pair looked puzzled, and each shook his head. "Or about surrendering?"

"Ah," said Neumann. "I've been prepared for you to ask me about that."

"Perhaps now would be a good time for an answer?"

"They gave me two special radio frequency crystals. When the time came, I was going to hand them over, so you could communicate with the embassy."

Clearly, Neumann knew everything, including their potential surrender. Why had the B.d.U. kept quiet about that, and these special wireless arrangements? Claussen played along. "In Buenos Aires?"

"Yes. Something about the crystals being cut to operate in a different part of the waveband so it would be less likely that the British or the Americans might intercept any of our wireless transmissions. Less likely they could trace where we were, as well."

"That's interesting. Except that I've just been ordered to keep radio silence."

"I suppose that won't matter for a few days."

That made yet another statement from Neumann that Claussen could not quite rationalise. "You said, 'when the time came', Professor. As far as I know, radio silence means just that. I can't even let my wireless operator tune-up his equipment for a test. What kind of a time did you mean? Why would anything change after a couple of days?"

"Well, obviously I can't order you to send any messages, but I was told to contact the embassy a week or ten days before we got to the destination. They might be holding special orders for us."

"Like what?"

"Anything to do with the I-8, maybe."

"Or the war," said Fischer. "What if the Japanese have surrendered? It's been a month since we left Norway, with no news. If they've capitulated there'd be no point carrying on. I expect B.d.U. tried to think of every contingency. If we couldn't make it back to Germany, entering a neutral port might be the correct thing to do... Even surrendering to the

British, if that was appropriate." He paused for a few seconds. "Or we might need to tell B.d.U. something about the cargo."

Neumann choked off a chuckle. "I don't know about that. If anything had happened to it, we'd be dead already."

Claussen jumped in quickly. "It's gas, then?"

"We aren't allowed to discuss it, but we prefer to think of it as an 'agent'."

"Well, that's the only confirmation I need..."

"Captain, it's better not to ask too many questions. As you said a minute ago, the fewer people who know, the better."

"I see." But Claussen's curiosity was not quite satisfied. "Does it have a name, this gas?"

Neumann's face betrayed his realisation that by making only a modest admission he had gone too far. "A chemical name, and a formula of course... And a code name. But really, I can't say any more."

"That's all right, Professor – I'm not going to tell anyone. I think I'd better take charge of those wireless crystals now, though – just in case I change my mind and decide we can contact the embassy."

"Of course. I'll get them right away."

Claussen thanked Neumann, clicked his heels, flung up a Hitler salute and turned to go. As he left, he figured the news that the I-8 wouldn't be meeting them could wait for a few more days. He needed time to do some more thinking. For now, he intended to have a word with the wireless operator and reinforce the message that the only source of outbound messages must remain himself. There must be no special treatment for friendly passengers.

Claussen found the wireless operator sweltering amongst the knobs, dials, switches and cables in what had almost become an oven in its own right, next to the galley. The poor fellow had stripped down to what was virtually a loincloth.

"You look like you're about to die of heatstroke," said Claussen. "Leave all that. Come out on deck and take a breather. Come and talk to me." The lad needed no persuasion. Claussen led the operator aft of the fin and together they leaned on the port safety rail, gazing out to the east.

"That was a hell of a message to decipher," Claussen began. "I must be getting rusty. Had to start afresh a couple of times."

"Yes, skip. It *was* a pretty long one, wasn't it?"

Claussen agreed, then took Neumann's crystals out of his pocket and held them out to the young man – two small metallic cases, rather like miniature Zippo lighters in shape and lustre. Each had two pins protruding from the bottom of the case. Clearly, they were designed to plug into some piece of electronic equipment.

"Ever seen anything like this before?"

The operator knew instantly. "Crystals for the h.f. transmitter," he said. "Should have the frequency stamped on the case somewhere." Claussen started to examine them; the operator looked nervous. "If they're important, sir, I should put them back in your pocket in case they slip into the water." He smiled to indicate to Claussen that he didn't mean to be insubordinate. "They won't float, skip."

Claussen returned the crystals to his pocket. "Professor Neumann gave them to me a couple of minutes ago... So we can contact the embassy in Buenos Aires. It's a pity, because part of that long message ordered us to keep radio silence."

"Oh, I see."

"That means no more position reports. That's why I didn't give you one yesterday." The operator nodded. "And no testing the transmitter. No tuning it up just to see how much smoke you can get out of it." The operator sniggered. "No crafty messages to any of your girlfriends, and definitely no messages sent as a favour for Neumann or the others."

"No, skip."

"I'll keep these crystals locked in my safe, for now." Claussen changed the subject. "Tell me – what's the latest rumour about where we're going?"

The wireless operator gave Claussen a sideways glance. "Rumours, skip? Not in this boat... But if you're asking me to start one, I could make out a hell of a good case for Penang."

"Coconuts... All the bananas you can eat..." Claussen laughed. "It wouldn't seem right." They fell silent, lulled by the sound of the foaming white bubbles bursting to the surface all along the side of the boat, both men daydreaming while the vessel cut through a sea of the deepest blue from which the occasional flying fish glided away, at right angles to their course.

Although the boat was now practically due east of Rio de Janeiro, a haze had descended – a rarity for the time of year in that latitude. With visibility hovering around 5 nautical miles, the lookouts were nervous of being taken by surprise by the sudden appearance of a merchant ship. The Naxos would have warned of enemy radar signals, but an unescorted allied merchantman was a distinct possibility. Allied captains, homeward bound from Australia or New Zealand via the Cape Horn route would have been keeping well to the east of the normal shipping lanes for fear of encountering a German raider or wolf-pack. Now it was the predatory U-boat proceeding on the surface that needed to avoid meeting a merchant ship.

The irony of having the tables turned on him had not escaped Claussen. As to their speed, Claussen had called for engine revolutions to give him a speed of ten knots, although he stopped engines every two hours so that the hydrophone operator could listen for possible propeller or machinery noise coming from well beyond their five-mile visual range.

After a while, Claussen broke the silence. “What’s that Berlin naval transmitter like, now Paris is off the air? Powerful enough to reach us out here?”

“Oh it’s powerful enough, skip – reasonable signal strength. But it was a lot harder to get through when I sent that last report a few days ago.”

“With radio silence as well, I guess we’re pretty much out of contact, then?”

“Not quite, skip. I can still receive the blind broadcasts, and I could still get a message off at the right time of day if you wanted.”

“How you know what frequency to use – it’s all a mystery to me.”

“It’s not that hard to grasp. As you get farther away from home, you need to use a higher and higher frequency – a shorter wavelength. And of course, there’s times of day when you can’t get through at all.”

“And those gaps last for longer the farther away you get, I suppose.”

“Well, partly, yes. But it’s like everything, skip. It shouldn’t be, but it is. It’s just what the operators at home get used to. Plenty of strong signals all the time from boats in the Atlantic or the Mediterranean.” He sounded wistful. “But it just feels like sometimes they aren’t listening for boats farther away like us.”

“Isn’t reception better at night?”

“Yes, but you can hear a lot more stations. That’s the problem. Everybody’s signals interfere with everyone else’s.”

“You must need to be a bit lucky to get through.”

“Lucky... Tricky... Skilful. All three, sometimes.”

Saturday 11 November, 1944
Admiralty, London

8 p.m., and Rodger Winn was worried. After the Y-stations had failed to intercept a position report, or anything else from U-1226 on the 7th, he had been awaiting the report due on the 10th. With no deciphered data yet to hand, he had back-tracked through Bletchley Park to find out whether there had been any hold-up in the delivery of intercepts from the listening stations, but they told him no transcripts were missing.

Now more anxious, he conferred with Peter Kemp, in charge of the high frequency direction-finding service to check whether anything, even a transmitter test, had been detected in the South Atlantic east of Brazil. Once again, there was nothing to report. Something was seriously wrong. Winn had no option other than to call Admiral Rushbrooke and let him know. Because it was unusual for Winn to need help, the DNI said he would drop what he was doing and return to the Citadel.

In the Tracking Room, Rushbrooke, Winn and Kemp were studying the South Atlantic plot, with a copy of the weather-routeing chart for November open on one side and an Admiralty chart overlaid with Kriegsmarine map squares on the other. Winn was briefing his colleagues.

"The last two position reports that we are aware of for U-1226 gave his position on the 1st in square ER73 – I've shaded it in – and on the 4th in square FK51, also shaded. Peter, I think you'd confirm that the Huff-Duff triangulation agrees with the deciphered message?" Kemp verified that it did. "Since then, we expected a position report on the 7th – and didn't get it – and another one around 24 hours ago on the 10th. We didn't get that one either."

Rushbrooke interrupted. "Could the Yanks have found him just by chance and sunk him, and forgotten to tell us? Or maybe he's had an accident with his snorkel and sunk himself?"

"Highly unlikely that he's fallen victim to an allied warship, sir. There are no reports of any engagements in that area. But I'd submit that we cannot – dare not – assume that he's suffered an accident. Not without concrete proof."

"What's your appreciation of his likely destination now?"

"Not much has changed, sir. As you know, B.d.U. asked him if he could make it to the Malacca Strait. Certainly you can see the trend. The sequence of shaded squares points to that as a destination, via the Cape. The farther he goes though, the less likely it is that he'd try for an exchange of cargo with the Japanese at sea. Too rough, too dangerous, too risky that the cargo could slip into the water and disappear for ever. You'll recall our early favourite was always a sly rendezvous in some sheltered bay or inlet. The worry is we don't think he's sent a message to the B.d.U., saying when he'll arrive off the Malayan coast. But even though he hasn't acknowledged, the safe bet looks like an exchange on Japanese-held territory in the Far East. That still has to be the marginal favourite."

"I can't see you've got much else to go on, Rodger," said Kemp.

"All the same, I'd like to remind everyone it's Dönitz we're dealing with here," said Winn. "I think it's time to weigh up the options."

But Rushbrooke was the man with the years of seagoing experience. He looked eager to show what he could do with a chart ruler and a pair of dividers. "Let's have a look at the charts," he said. For the best part of two minutes, he pored over the weather-routeing chart, uttering the occasional 'hmmm', before asking a question.

"What sort of a speed has Fritz been making, Rodger?"

"Well, over those last few days, we reckon he's had a couple of runs at around 14 knots. But then, there hasn't been much for him to worry about lately. Calm seas; no surface ships; no air patrols. In the North Atlantic, he had to keep below the surface, operating with the snorkel, we suspect. For days on end, we reckon he was limited to below 5 knots. Then 7's, 8's and 9's when he worked his way south of the shipping lanes."

"Pretty much what I'd expect, Rodger. Not a bad tactical operation, if a bit sneaky. But let me ask you this..." Rushbrooke pointed to the chain of remote islands in the centre of the ocean. "What's the chances of him making his way to Ascension, Saint Helena or Tristan and finding a lee there to exchange cargo with the Japanese?"

"Less than one in a hundred, I'd say. We've got to remember this all started when 30AU captured a load of documents in August. Unless this was an extremely long-running and well-planned operation, I can't believe Jerry meant for us to snatch them. After all, one of their chaps was killed trying to set fire to them. And those documents all pointed to a rendezvous with the I-8. It all ties in when we take into account the cable to the Japanese naval attaché." Kemp and Rushbrooke seemed to agree, nodding or giving the occasional throaty grunt.

Winn still held the floor, and continued. "But my man Beesly says there's no sign of a replacement Japanese submarine heading beyond Singapore into the Indian Ocean to meet U-1226. It explains this business about the Jerries asking the sub' if he could go the whole way to major square LF, presumably meaning Penang. The inference is that Hitler must still want this operation to go ahead, so this boat is heading farther east than originally intended, to make up for poor efficiency from the Japs. If he only goes as far as, say, St

Helena, it's taking a huge chunk out of the time to bring off the operation. Plus, of course, all three islands belong to the Crown. He can't take the risk of being spotted."

"Good. Exactly what I thought."

"Then there's the three passengers. One Japanese linguist and two chemists. It fits in with what the captured documents said about Hitler's nasty surprise for the Americans. And of course, there were also reports of the Fuhrer bragging to *Il Duce* about a deadly war gas."

"Right! We've ruled out a rendezvous at sea or near one of these islands then. As you say, Penang has to be the bookies' favourite. Now look here." Rushbrooke tapped a finger on the weather chart again. "This position on the 4th is a couple of hundred miles east of Recife. Now, here's the great circle routeing from Recife to Cape Town, marked in red, just to the south of him." He traced a finger along a gently-curved line pre-printed on the chart. "Just over 3,300 miles, it says. Now obviously, he's going to want to steer clear of the shipping lanes to Cape Town, but at 10 knots, that's 330 hours, or almost 14 days. He could be rounding Cape Agulhas on the 18th. That's a week from today, gentlemen."

"That's what was worrying me," said Winn. "I wanted one more position report, to be certain which way he was heading after FK51. But we didn't get it."

"Or the next one," said Kemp.

"Which is why," said Rushbrooke, "I'm going to get into a huddle with the Foreign Branch ACNS and his DDO, and take it straight to Cunningham. Then it's up to him what he tells Winston, eh?"

The talk of great names excited Kemp's curiosity. "Out of interest, sir, what would you do if you were First Sea Lord, and something like this landed on your desk?"

"Well, Peter, if my arse was going to be the one getting the kicking when this all turned into one big SNAFU, I'd pull back everything I've got in the South Atlantic and the southern Indian Ocean. I'd rally all ships on Cape Agulhas, and in view of what's at stake here, I'd make sure we sink that bastard so he doesn't get anywhere near Penang with whatever he's carrying." Rushbrooke straightened up and appeared ready to leave the Tracking Room. "Any more questions, gentlemen?" Then he looked directly at Winn. "Anything we might have missed, Rodger?"

"No. We'd be fools to do anything different." Winn was obviously in pain. He eased himself into a chair. "But if Dönitz is behind this, it all seems a bit too straightforward. It isn't his style. I keep trying to spot how he's trying to con us, but I just can't see it."

"Well, what I'd recommend is you sleep on it, then when your mind is fresh, go through it again. But it's out of our hands now. We're not going to solve this problem by behaving like English country gentlemen. It's about to turn nasty. It'll soon be time for the killing to start."

When Rushbrooke had left, Kemp turned to Winn. "Rodger," he said. "While the boss was talking tactics, I did a rough calculation. If U-1226 can spin up the revolutions to cruise at 16 knots, he could be there as early as the 13th. That's bloody Monday!"

Winn gave a soft, slow groan of pain. Each long day and the struggle against constant muscle fatigue ate into his strength. The cold of November was also dragging him down, harder to tolerate as the years progressed. "Rubbish, Peter! He'd burn too much fuel. He still has to make it to Penang." He seemed to realise he had spoken sharply and that Kemp was not at fault. "Sorry, Peter. Get one of your chaps to find an officer who can work out the distance from FK51 to a point 25 miles south of Cape Agulhas, then calculate a set of ETAs at speeds between 7 and 16 knots. Highlight the 8.5 knot estimate and we'll discuss it with the DNI tomorrow. I'm off home. I've got to get to bed."

Kemp acknowledged. Winn had been ill through overwork once before and nobody wanted to see it happen again. "You're still worried, aren't you, Rodger?"

"Yes, bloody worried. This Nazi operation is evil and it's real. And those last two positions supposedly leading us eastward towards the Cape look to me like a decoy." Winn fixed his colleague with a stare like a searchlight. "And when you throw in this confounded new twist – radio silence – it's got Karl Dönitz written all over it. If he'd written a personal handbook on deception, this'd be straight out of chapter one."

Sunday 12 November, 1944

Rushbrooke had called a meeting with the Assistant Chief of Naval Staff (Foreign); the Director of Naval Operations had hooked up via the telephone. Foreign Branch had no better suggestion than to concentrate forces off South Africa and annihilate U-1226 by massive weight of numbers. After the meeting, the ACNS took Rushbrooke aside and reminded him of Winn's physical frailty and that, once before when Winn had been under tremendous pressure, his health had broken down. The two of them decided that it might help if some proper American coffee was available, served in china cups, to present a relaxed tone for their coming discussion with him.

"I don't know, Rodger," said Rushbrooke with a wink and a comic leer. "I seem to remember you thought Dönitz would eventually come to his senses and find a way to turn this U-1226 over to us. I'm still waiting. All I ask is 'when'?"

"I think he tried. I think all that nonsense about *Großquadrat* LF might have been the Grand Admiral's attempt to get his U-boat commander to give himself away to us. It would have worked if he'd replied with a long message full of questions, his ETA and so forth."

"Oh," said Rushbrooke. "Hadn't thought of that one."

"Cannon fodder," said the ACNS. "Sometimes you..."

"Well Dönitz might have got something out of it too," said Winn. "If we'd wiped out U-1226 just after this chap made a long radio transmission, it would have shown him just how powerful Huff-Duff has grown; how far-reaching. He'd have reacted though; changed his tactics. Far more radio blackouts. That would make *all* his U-boats harder to find."

Rushbrooke leaned forward and offered Winn another biscuit. "You think this U-boat commander is a bit of a clever bugger then, do you? You think he's weighed up the odds and decided that the risk of replying to the B.d.U. and giving away his position isn't worth it. He's decided to carry out Hitler's orders in silence and argue about it afterwards."

"Why not? If it was me, I'd fake a fault in my radio transmitter for a week or so. By the time he gets home again, if he ever does, there'll be far more to worry about than convening a court martial. Even if he was lying to cover up disobeying a lawful command, they could never prove it."

"More likely they'd just shoot him. Do we know his name – the boat's commander?"

"We're pretty sure it's an Oberleutnant zur See August-Wilhelm Claussen."

"Party member? Loyal Nazi?"

"Not sure, but clearly he's a trusted German officer, sir. He'll always do what he's been ordered to do. Also, if he thinks he's on a personal mission for the Fuhrer, he's likely to be blind to anything else. For him it's not only his duty; it'll be a matter of honour."

"How do we stop him then, Rodger?"

Winn sniffed. "You time-served regular navy chaps don't need wavy navy blokes like me to tell you how to stop him. But if Peter and I can find him for you, that's our job."

"All right. What'll Dönitz do now, do you think?"

"He might send another message. Different. Something that Claussen would be obliged to acknowledge. Think of it this way. You've only got to read some of the debriefs. Growing numbers of captured Kriegsmarine officers are convinced Enigma is penetrated. If Dönitz can catch us out responding tactically to something specific in a message that ought to have been secure, he's got his proof that we've broken it. He'll be betting on a 'heads I win, tails you lose' situation."

"Meanwhile Claussen doesn't look like he's going to give himself away as easily as all that." Rushbrooke fiddled with his cup for a second or two. "Where do you think this fellow's going to turn up?"

"It all points to Penang."

"Come on, Rodger. You don't believe that. If not there – where?"

"The Argentine." The ACNS raised his eyebrows and gave Rushbrooke the sort of look that conveyed cause for concern over Winn's sanity. "I mean it, Admiral. I'm deadly serious. You asked – I answered. It's about the only other place he can go."

"Yes, but..."

"Think about it. I put it to you that since D-Day, Britain and the United States have withdrawn their ambassadors from the Argentine due to constant overt support for the Axis by President Farrell and this other Nazi – the Minister of War and now Vice President – Colonel Perón. In August, Perón admitted that the country's military strength had doubled since last year's revolution – and he's still recruiting. The country is in dispute with our ally, Brazil."

"Yes, but..."

"I put it to you that there has been incitement against the Jews. Press censorship was lifted and then re-applied six weeks later but there are still Nazi newspapers and a Nazi wireless station operating there in total freedom."

"That may be so but..."

"I put it to you as naval officers that since 1940 the country has connived at allowing the escape of officers and crew supposedly interned after the *Graf Spee* was scuttled. In fact we are now recapturing officers from sinking U-boats – officers who formerly served on board that vessel during the battle of the River Plate. I put it to you, sir, that it would be a wise and prudent course of action if you were to telegraph our naval attaché in Buenos Aires and ask him to make discreet enquiries regarding the whereabouts of the remaining *Graf Spee* officers and crew. Any concentration of supposedly paroled or loosely-guarded Germans in the south of the country should be viewed with suspicion. Bear in mind that the U-1226 could be there in perhaps a week. Nor must you forget that our favourite was always a rendezvous up some God-damned creek, many of which, I am sure, may be found in Patagonia."

Rushbrooke and the ACNS turned open-mouthed towards one another, but Winn had plenty more to say.

"I put it to you that repeatedly since September, Argentina has been forced to deny plans to accommodate Nazi war criminals after the war, this denial being as big an admission of actual policy as you'll ever see. But remember! This isn't just my opinion but also that of Mister Cordell Hull, the US Secretary of State and President Roosevelt, who refers to an 'Argentine paradox'. Finally, I would remind you that deposed ex-President, General Rawson, who was favourably disposed towards the Allies, was recently arrested. Oh, and by the way – none of this is remotely secret. It's all there in

The Times in black and white for anyone to read." Winn drew breath, but it appeared that his superior officers were so taken aback by his assault that no pertinent rejoinder occurred to them.

"Grand Admiral Dönitz has laid it all out for you, gentlemen. All fingers point to Penang. And as naval officers, the two of you, together with the First Sea Lord, the Vice Chief, the rest of the Assistant Chiefs and Directors of Naval Operations – you would all be traitors to tradition if you ignored the disappointingly flimsy evidence. Gentlemen, any court martial would absolve you from blame if you decided to look no further. Let it be Cape Agulhas. From the middle of square FK51 to a point 25 miles south of that promontory, maintaining an average speed of eight-and-a-half knots, U-1226 will arrive at oh-six forty-one on the morning of the twentieth" Winn raised one finger. "But for my part, I suspect there's something fishy going on. So my money will be going on a rendezvous half way up some remote inlet in the Argentinean half of Tierra del Fuego."

Winn had finished. He gave a cheerful smile to both officers, slapped a hand down on Rushbrooke's desk and used it to help himself struggle to his feet.

"Nice coffee, Admiral."

It would have been wrong to gloat, but as Winn pitched and rolled his way along the deep corridors of the Admiralty Citadel he wore a smile and scarcely noticed his pain. It felt good to have quashed Rushbrooke and the ACNS, if only temporarily. He had left them goggling and gaping like a pair of overgrown codfish. His talent for a dramatic performance in the courtroom had not deserted him. It did no harm to show his superior officers that he could still 'cut the mustard'.

The courtroom analogy was not quite appropriate though, for if Claussen was on trial it was not for some crime he had already committed, but for something he was about to do.

The debate was less to do with guilt or innocence and more about where the sentence would be carried out. Without question, Winn's imaginary naval jury would find Claussen guilty, even though the evidence was all circumstantial. Such a court would convict on the basis of two position reports and the suspicion of being about to transfer poison gas technology to the Japanese. If it took place, the death sentence would be carried out off the South African coast in a few days' time, in perhaps one of the most one-sided naval battles in history. Winn had even told them that this was what he expected they would decide to do.

But what he hoped they might yet understand (and which had formed the basis for his anticipating the Kriegsmarine's strategy through four years of war) was that Dönitz was reliably unpredictable. While feinting to the right, the man could easily duck to the left, under the Allies' guard. What was needed was some better evidence. And there was one avenue that, although it had yielded little in the past, might yet hold some promise.

Winn tried to contact Beesly at home by telephone, but was told that his deputy would not return for a few hours; Patrick had gone to take Sunday tea with a maiden aunt. Winn pulled a memo pad towards him, took the top off his fountain pen and began to write.

Patrick. *Sunday 12th, 13:15 p.m.*

I am sending this to your home by despatch rider so that you can give some thought to it before our driver arrives on Monday morning. We can discuss it as we travel in, but I want you to make this your <u>*TOP PRIORITY*</u>*.*

Up to now, we have reacted to the content of the occasional diplomatic telegram, but (I confess) I have not paid too much attention to the processes by which they arrived in the Tracking Room. (Better sources of information about U-Boats always seemed to exist.)

I believe the Reich's Diplomatic Service enciphers its telegrams using something called Grundverfahren. I think we call it 'GEC' but with the Anglo-Saxon gift for ridiculing our enemies we have nicknamed it 'Floradora'. I don't know much more about it, except that we cracked it some time in '43. I don't even know whether it depends on Enigma.

What I require you to do is to pull as many strings as possible and find out:
(a) how B.P. receives its raw diplomatic information;
(b) typical daily traffic volumes;
(c) typical time taken to decipher messages;
(d) how many beat the system and can't be cracked, etc.

Also, I urgently require to see all relevant German diplomatic traffic that has been exchanged, starting 24hrs before U-1226 went off track on 4th November through to to-day, to continue for the next two weeks (minimum). 'Relevant' means all Auswärtiges Amt traffic to or from Buenos Aires, Montevideo, Asunción and Santiago de Chile. (I am presuming the German Embassy in Rio closed in summer '42 when Brazil declared for the Allies. If B.P. knows differently, I shall require to see Rio telegrams too.)

...I may hang for this but I am convinced Claussen is heading for South America!

Winn

(V)

Monday 13 November
London

Patrick Beesly was something of an academic, so he welcomed the opportunity of performing some valuable research into a new subject. Obtaining an overview of Floradora took him until mid-afternoon and required train journeys to and from Bletchley Park. On returning to the Admiralty and seeking out Winn, his breathless excitement was almost as spirited as a schoolboy's.

"Apparently 'Floradora' is a sort of double-additive cipher system," he said, "with two random starting points taken from ten thousand lines of code, protected by changing the indicator keys every one or two days." It sounded like he was repeating a speech that he had learned by heart. Mercifully, as soon as the script ran out, he became his normal self again. "The chap started explaining it all to me but he cut it short when he saw me go glassy-eyed. When I told them what you wanted, I got a really weird reaction. It sounded for a minute as if he was going to accuse me of wasting their time by asking for the impossible. I thought I was going to get torn off a strip."

However, it was clear to Winn, from Beesly's enthusiasm alone, that his deputy's day had been profitably spent. "Oh, they're normally far more polite than that, Patrick," he said.

"Indeed they were. But, 'Rio? Buenos Aires?' the chap barked at me, as if they were the last places on Earth. Only it wasn't anger – he was completely bowled over by the irony of it. Apparently, working in those two embassies were two of the most useless cipher clerks in the whole German

Diplomatic Service." Beesly paused, hands on hips, enjoying the comedy of the moment. "It seems these two lazy buggers must have been particularly badly affected by the Latin temperament. They thought they'd save time by always using a couple of favourite pre-determined coding additives, and this gave the Yanks their way in. They broke a few lines and then – God knows how – they used some sort of calculating machine to try the known lines against incoming messages... I think that's the way it went, anyhow."

He became more business-like again. "But the point is that Floradora is broken. We can read almost everything they send, more or less on the day they send it. And because of the B.A. connection, the chaps at B.P. would be over the moon to see their diplomatic intelligence used against that particular outpost of the Master Race."

"Good news for a change. But the important thing is, when might we expect to see the first batch of telegrams to and from Buenos Aires and the other South American embassies?"

"Well we agreed Brazil was too far back in history to be useful in the present case, but Argentina is a different kettle of fish. Apparently, we've been on high alert, monitoring B.A. from Montevideo for a while." Beesly lowered his voice and adopted a confidential tone. "There's a particularly useful girl there, a German speaker who keeps all the code books locked up, and does all the deciphering. This means the local team can do a speedy first pass through the telegrams and react more quickly to anything with any particular significance for the region. But they'd be delighted to help. B.P. can send the first batch of stuff over tomorrow. And this girl – she really sounds to be on the ball – she'll watch particularly for anything about U-boats, interned Nazi sailors or coastal operations in remote places."

“Thank you, Patrick. I’m pleased. You’ve done well.” But Winn remained a little subdued, an aura that Beesly didn’t fail to notice.

“Are you all right, sir? Not coming down with a dose of the ’flu or anything?”

“No, it’s nothing like that. The thing is, this is one occasion when I hope I’m wrong.”

“Sir?”

“If the admirals are right, everybody on U-1226 will probably meet his maker off the South African coast a week or so from today.” Beesly gave Winn a worried look. “Don’t worry, Patrick. I haven’t turned into a pacifist or a Nazi sympathiser.” Winn set his jaw and lowered his brow. “The only real clue we’ve got is the one about Penang, and so Claussen’s only logical route is round the cape – the South African way. The admirals’ minds are made up – in fact I reckon they’d all be keel-hauled if they did anything different. So, they’re going in hard. They’re pulling in everything they’ve got, from a thousand miles in every direction.”

Beesly saw it straight away. “Oh I see! Leaving nothing in reserve if or when Claussen pops up in a completely different spot – like your favourite – Tierra del Fuego.”

“Yes Patrick. All the navy’s eggs are in one basket. That’s why I hope the admirals are right... Not me.”

40°45' South, 41°19.5' West

U-1226 had penetrated the ‘roaring forties’, and although better visibility had returned once more, the greater swell and wave height permitted no increase in speed. All three passengers had begun to suffer from seasickness, forcing Neumann to plead with Claussen to find some respite. Claussen’s reaction was to urge his supernumeraries to spend more time perched with his lookouts at the top of the fin, feeling the wind and the salt spray in their faces. However, this cure only worked for the time that they were enjoying the fresh air and the distant horizon. Once they clambered below again, the stink of shit, sweat and sauerkraut proved too much to bear, and the minute that the first man retched, the stench of fresh vomit caused the other two to heave up in sympathy.

Petty Officer (second class) Klein introduced the gentlemen to the submariners' solution, a slop bucket half-full of water, with a centimetre film of diesel oil on top into which he invited his patients to throw up, on the principle that the heavier components would sink to the bottom and the oil would prevent the smell reaching the air. But it wasn't just the nauseous odour, it was the sight and sound that were infectious too.

Eventually (and grudgingly) Claussen decreased engine revolutions to reduce the boat's pitching motion. He knew that after any more than 48 hours of violent seasickness his passengers would be hospital cases and the mission would have to be aborted as a failure. In truth, he didn't mind reducing speed. For one thing, he was no longer under pressure to arrive at square HJ11 by the 19th. For another, his noon calculations put the boat south of a particular line marked on the weather routeing chart. The line read 'EXTREME ICEBERG LIMIT'. He didn't want to meet one of those at 14 knots in the dark.

Tuesday 14 November
Cabinet War Rooms, Whitehall

The Prime Minister had requested the First Sea Lord and the DNI to attend in person, to provide him with a situation report and the latest plans for the destruction of U-1226.

"This naval operation is turning into a veritable Colossus. A Titan, Admiral Cunningham."

"There can be no guarantee of success with a small force, Prime Minister."

"You miss my point. Will not our Allies, when they discover the scale of this undertaking, of which currently they know nothing and in which they have not been invited to participate, be initially somewhat piqued and, in times to come, succumb to ever greater curiosity regarding the reasons for our secrecy?"

"We have deliberately kept external communications low-key by not giving this operation an official name, Prime Minister. Once the kill is confirmed, one hopes to reassign the majority of vessels to their duties without any fuss. One prays that the list of vessels that become a casualty will be short and entirely one-sided."

"You hope to keep everything quiet?"

"Just so, Prime Minister."

"And Captain Winn. What does he think of it all?"

Cunningham's intake of breath had something in the nature of an impatient sigh about it.

"Meaning nothing against his reputation, Prime Minister, but he's less inclined to believe the U-boat's destination to be Penang... Er, despite the evidence of the position reports. He seems to think that Admiral Dönitz is playing us along. He fancies Tierra del Fuego, I understand. Tomorrow it may be South Georgia or the South Sandwich Islands – possibly even the Falklands themselves."

"Each of those being territories to which the Argentine has recently laid claim."

"But as a neutral, Prime Minister, even if Argentina had occupied every one of those islands without affecting their neutrality – and I can't see how – they would still be bound by the provisions of the Hague Convention, 1907. They would be under a duty not to permit Nazi Germany or Japan to violate its neutrality by an act such as this – the transfer from one belligerent power to another of a new and fearsome weapon of war."

"The word you omit, Admiral, is 'knowingly'. Article 1 protects the neutral. It would be up to any complainant to prove that the neutral had *knowingly* violated the Convention. The administration of the more far-flung coves and creeks at the tip of South America can surely be said to be so far beyond the day-to-day competence of the Government in Buenos Aires, that one would struggle to use Article 1 as a pretext for any action against these bandits."

"Yes, but..."

"...Article 5 – Using neutral ports or waters as a base for naval operations against one's adversaries. Hopeless! If the United States is seen as the adversary, then by any calculation America must be at least five thousand miles away." Churchill's voice rose. "Tierra del Fuego is hardly the ideal base for mounting a naval campaign against that great country!"

"You are particularly well-informed about the Convention, Prime Minister."

"I should think so! I was serving as First Lord of the Admiralty when you were still a Lieutenant-Commander in HMS *Scorpion*. I know every word of the damned Convention."

"But in any event the Convention would hold that U-1226, and whatever Japanese submarine is able to make it to the rendezvous, may only remain in an Argentinean port or roadstead for a maximum of 24 hours."

"For a piece of infernal work with a rope and a block and tackle that wouldn't trouble a one-armed Spanish sea cook for more than half an hour. And how is one even to become aware of it? Ridiculous. Don't trouble me with toothless remedies, Admiral." Churchill glowered; a pugilist threatening his opponent. However, he was only just getting started. "How about another consolation to the collaborator: Article 8, Admiral Cunningham? What have you to say about this? 'A neutral Government is bound to employ the means at its disposal to prevent the fitting out or arming of any vessel within its jurisdiction which it has reason to believe is intended to cruise, or engage in hostile operations, against a Power with which that Government is at peace.' How do you suppose the words 'reason to believe' are to be interpreted in the case of a duplicitous regime that routinely denies all knowledge of this or that or the other?"

"I do see your point, sir."

"Or Article 18? 'Belligerent warships may not make use of neutral ports, roadsteads, or territorial waters for replenishing or increasing their supplies of war material or their armament...' If our good friend Winn is correct, what chance have we to catch the enemy exchanging this evil arsenal, when half our fleet is massing at Simonstown?"

"Prime Minister, every other one of these exchange missions has taken place on the enemy's own soil or captured territory –"

"– Ha! Those that you know about, Admiral."

"Admittedly, yes – those that we know about. However, no mission has involved a neutral country, and as such the Hague Convention has no bearing..."

"...God damn the Hague Convention! What good is it to us, faced with such a partisan neutral as the Argentine?" Churchill shook his finger in the face of the Admiral of the Fleet. "I tell you, sir. Neutrality in war is like baking a cake from a mis-remembered recipe. Too little principle, not enough honesty, too much fear and a surfeit of greed; few of those at the table are likely to find the result to their taste." The quivering jowls made it clear that should Winn be right and the navy wrong, the Prime Minister would stand first in line as the chief critic of any unpalatable consequences. "And what of our loyal Falkland Islands?"

"I believe you will find, sir, that the build-up of naval forces off South Africa does not detract from the defence of the Falklands, which is more than adequate in the circumstances."

Churchill grumbled and grunted, making intimidating use of the phlegm in his throat. "Cannot any vessels be turned around, in order to picket the waters of the continental shelf between our steadfast Falkland Islands and this so-called 'Land of Fire'?"

"I believe it would be unwise, Prime Minister. It would be likely to leave a gap in what you might term a picket, but which I regard as our line of battle. The order of battle is already drawn up in preparation for deployment south of Cape Agulhas." Churchill stayed silent and appeared to be sulking. "Prime Minister, I do not want this fish to slip through the net."

"Then catch it, Admiral. Gut it, fillet it and bring me its head on a platter. Good night to you, sir."

In single file, Cunningham and Rushbrooke stepped from the building into the open air and negotiated the narrow corridor in the double-banked sandbag redoubt that sheltered the Horse Guards Road entrance. The military sentries came to attention as the admirals emerged. From force of habit, both old seafarers looked up at the sky as they felt the first breath of wind on their cheeks.

"I'm glad he didn't press any harder into our measures for protecting the Falkland Islands," said Rushbrooke.

"If he had, I was prepared to make as much as possible about the battalion we've got down there. Yorkshire lads, I think." For a moment, Cunningham seemed amused. "Should be used to the sight of thousands of sheep, anyway."

Rushbrooke caught the mood. "Sufficient to deter any stupid moves by South American dictators, I should have thought... The soldiers, not the sheep." They both snorted softly.

"At a push, I suppose I could have made up some waffle about the shore base at HMS *Pursuivant*. I didn't want to have to admit to being practically defenceless down there."

"We aren't though. Not quite, anyway. There's Operation Tabarin."

"Best not to have brought that up. Churchill was against the idea from the start. What was his objection? Didn't want to upset Roosevelt by defending against a neutral in America's self-awarded sphere of influence, or some such nonsense. Sod-all consideration for the poor bloody crown colonists living there, though. These warlords are always insensitive of other men's lives." The remark needed a few moments to lose its bite. "Anyway, if it wasn't for the navy's appreciation of the risks there'd be no troops down there at all. No – he's too exposed – never admits his mistakes. He'd never have been the first to mention Tabarin."

Rushbrooke failed to quite appreciate the politics of the situation. Clearly, both Churchill and Cunningham had been reluctant to refer to the secret operation. As far as Rushbrooke was concerned though, one reason it had been conceived, as Cunningham had said, was to counter any risk of invasion by Argentina, or anyone else... Rather like now. He made a non-committal rejoinder. "43, wasn't it?"

The two strolled on in silence, crossing Horse Guards Parade towards the Admiralty buildings. Although a full minute had elapsed since the last remark, Cunningham spoke again as if making a direct response. "Just one bloody boat down there... And we're lucky not to have lost the whole crew on their way south, as I understand it. No... Dragging up Tabarin wouldn't have gone down well with the Old Man."

"You're right," said Rushbrooke, hoping that would mark the end of the matter.

With the threat of a German invasion of Britain now reduced to a statistical joke, the Home Guard sentries and patrols in central London had recently been stood down. The parade ground was quiet – empty except for a few parked official cars and the motorcycles of despatch riders on the night shift. Another minute passed.

"You're right," said Rushbrooke again. "HMS *William Scoresby*. Best not to have said anything... She doesn't even carry any armament now."

Churchill's mood and the underlying politics had soured the evening. Rushbrooke, something of a peacemaker, felt it would have been wrong to end on this rather depressing note, so he cast around for a suitable afterthought.

"I think I'll look in on the Tracking Room before I turn in. See what's going on. See if there's any news of 1226."

"I'll join you if I may, Eddie."

Friday 17 November
49°07' South, 51°25' West

In the hierarchy of Neumann's thoughts, almost certainly the second most important was the desire never again to be obliged to yodel into the slop bucket. Whenever the underlying maritime conditions made this more likely, and because he and his colleagues had been given permission in those circumstances to come out into the air, he did so.

That morning, the boat's pitching had been accompanied by a disturbing judder which did little for his wellbeing. Fortunately, once out in the daylight with a visible horizon to steady him, he quickly regained a measure of control. The turgid feeling between his temples and the churning above his diaphragm subsided and he was able to take notice of his surroundings.

The swell was long and from a little to the left of their course – was that port or starboard? Occasional sea waves were breaking white. Low clouds covered a good three quarters of the sky but there were still patches of blue. He had been told that this was a good thing; high cloud could sometimes bring bad weather on the following day.

He and Fischer had resolved most of their outstanding mission-related issues, so Neumann had a little time to call his own. He engaged one of the lookouts in conversation, asking why the boat seemed keen to shake itself apart.

"It's when the propeller comes out of the water, sir. With this swell, when the bow dips the stern pops up, so the screw is only partly covered by water."

Neumann absorbed this information. His scientific mind analysed what the effects of this might be. "I suppose what happens then," said Neumann, "is that the engine races faster or the blades of the propeller slap the surface of the sea, or something."

"It's too complicated for me, sir. No point worrying about it. I just watch the horizon."

So Neumann watched the horizon too for a little while. Then he watched the wake as it slipped down the side of the boat until he felt himself staring unblinking at it, virtually hypnotised, almost drawn over the rail and into the water. Then he thought he saw a seabird some distance away, disappearing into the trough between swell waves, so he tried to concentrate on that, waiting for it to flash into view again. Some time later – he had quite lost track of time – Claussen appeared through the fin hatchway and began to busy himself with his sextant. It felt to be nowhere near noon. Navigation by spherical trigonometry was not one of the subjects that fascinated him, but the activity made him think.

“*Herr Kapitan*,” said Neumann later as a conversational opener, “You seemed to be taking your noon sight rather early today.”

Claussen enjoyed the compliment – Neumann using his courtesy title, rather than his rank. “Yes, Professor. Unfortunately, there isn’t an unbreakable rule that says the sun always shines at noon. On overcast days like today, just in case the sun forgets its obligations, it’s a good idea to get a position line before noon. That’s what I was doing.”

“I see. It made me think...”

“What did it make you think, Professor?”

“For one thing, I’m pleased the crew still don’t appear to know where we’re going. From what they told me a few days ago, they seem to think we’re heading for Penang... You and I know differently, of course. Look – I’m sorry you didn’t know that Fischer and I were aware of your orders. However, I don’t wish to harbour any secrets. I know that you’ve been told to arrive in a certain ocean square by Sunday the 19th. That’s only two days away.”

Neumann paused for a moment as if giving Claussen a chance to anticipate all the questions that flowed from his remark, and then to provide answers. But Claussen simply nodded.

“My question then is this: Shall we arrive on schedule? If so, I think we need to contact the embassy to check the status of our mission.” Claussen had stopped nodding. “If not, however, we need to contact the embassy for the same reason and also to advise them how far behind schedule we might be.”

“Thank you, Professor. You may appreciate my difficulty, perhaps. The B.d.U. has directed me to avoid making any wireless transmissions, but here you are, asking me to disregard that order.”

“Are you refusing to help?”

"Not in those exact terms, no. If you were to put together a short signal and submit it to me, I could start by checking that it wouldn't compromise our security. Naturally I couldn't permit a signal to be sent un-enciphered, so you would need to tell me what cipher to use. For instance, I presume there is a naval attaché at the embassy. Does he use a naval enigma machine? If my assumptions are incorrect, what cipher should I use instead?"

Neumann's face had changed slowly from evident scepticism, and now registered something more like relief at Claussen's apparent willingness to co-operate. But Claussen had more to say.

"This isn't all, Professor. I imagine you must have a schedule of watchkeeping times and wireless frequencies specifying when the embassy will be listening for us. The problem is, if I agree to transmit one short message, that won't be the end of it, will it? There'll be a reply. More questions. Then another reply. If the Allies home-in on any one of our wireless transmissions, not only will the mission fail, but every one of us will be dead, too. All because of a single message."

"I understand, *Herr Kapitan*, but I also have my orders."

London

Rear-Admiral Rushbrooke replaced the handset of one of the six telephones that sat on the table to the left of his desk. Exactly who had direct responsibility for the *William Scoresby* was a debatable point. However, the ACNS (Foreign) had agreed that if a signal could be sent, underwritten by the two of them, then there could be little argument. Rushbrooke called across to his secretary.

"Miss Cameron, I'd like you to take an urgent signal." She picked up her pad and a pencil. "Urgent. Cable to the British Ambassador, Montevideo, for the naval attaché, whoever he is at the moment. Begins. 'If HMS *William Scoresby* – S, C, O, R, E, S, B, Y – is not already at Port Stanley, she is to be recalled there without delay to await further orders.' Ends. Turn that into a proper signal, run it past Reggie, code it up and bash it out on the cable, not the diplomatic wireless service, if you'd be so kind."

"Very good sir."

A small but necessary step. It wouldn't hurt to have the *Scoresby* ready to transport a few pongoes around the islands if Winn was right and Claussen turned up in some remote bay on West Falkland or wherever. For sure, the bloody Falkland Islands Company wouldn't want to risk damaging one of their vessels by ferrying the Army around the coast.

"Thank you. If there's any way of getting Montevideo to find the best compromise between secrecy and urgency, I'd appreciate that. Apparently, there isn't a cable link from there to Stanley. Shows what an out-of-the-way place it is." His own words caused the admiral to begin to appreciate Winn's concern. If Dönitz had wanted to choose a remote spot to exchange cargo, there could be few places more isolated. He considered whether, on his next visit to the Tracking Room, he might pick up a pair of dividers and roughly step off the distance from Port Stanley to the South American coast. Just to get an idea. Just in case.

By the time it was dark, Rushbrooke had gained another worry. After days of leaving Claussen to manage his own affairs, the low frequency Kriegsmarine transmitter had started broadcasting to the boat again. Winn sent along the translation. It gave away nothing:

```
IMPERATIVE YOU ADVISE ETA AT
WAYPOINT GIVEN IN UMSCHLAG A
ALSO AT FINAL DESTINATION AS
GIVEN IN UMSCHLAG B STOP
```

URGENTLY REQUIRE INDICATION OF CONDITION OF CARGO STOP REPORT ANY ISSUES ENDS

U-1226

Enciphered telegrams from B.d.U. were the very last thing Claussen wanted. Because the latest one contained far fewer code groups than the previous mammoth message, he hoped it would not cause him too many problems. To his relief he managed to decipher it in one pass. However, not long after he had written out the text, Neumann appeared with his own message for transmission to the embassy. Claussen took one look and refused to consider it.

"Brevity, Professor. Cut it down by half, and I'll see what can be done." Whilst that might not curb Neumann's impatience, it might at least secure one of them a night's rest.

Saturday 18 November
51°14' South, 54°05' West

Neumann, like almost everybody else on board, only had an inexact notion of where U-1226 actually was. The accurate information was known to just two people – Claussen and his second in command. Neumann saw the point. If the boat had been attacked and there had been any survivors, although their destination would no longer matter in terms of a mission thwarted, the intelligence might somehow still be of use to the enemy.

In basic terms, however, he could deduce what everybody else was already speculating about. Over the last month the weather had got warmer then started to cool off. The seas had been rough to begin with, then blissfully calm and were now lumpy again. Enemy shipping had been all around them at first, but lately nothing had forced them to dive down deep. But those who knew a little geography, together with the helmsmen and those privileged to have spent time sheltering behind the rim of the fin on lookout duty, not to mention those intellectuals who remembered that the sun rose in the east and set in the west, had all got their heads together. There was no doubt about it. Their course was roughly southwest. And that meant they were now in the South Atlantic heading for Cape Horn. This seemed a roundabout route to take if their destination was still Penang.

Neumann decided it was better to let Claussen work out a noon position, before asking him again for permission to contact the embassy in Buenos Aires. However, when approached, Claussen agreed to explain everything to him with the aid of the navigation chart. It seemed like progress.

First, Claussen explained that U-boat commanders believed the Allies must have seized plenty of Kriegsmarine codebooks during the campaign in France, and had probably got their hands on naval Enigma machines too, after capturing Channel ports. Also, if the Allies were as good as Germany at determining the bearing of radio signals, even from short messages, then things were somewhat worse. With German territory shrinking and the Allies occupying land from Iceland to the Caribbean to the coast of Africa, they would be able to get a very accurate idea of a U-boat's position simply because they could get so many more wide-spread cross bearings.

Forced to confront this obvious truth, Neumann hunched his shoulders. Clearly, Claussen was building a case for turning down his request to contact the embassy. Anticipating refusal, Neumann's lips turned white as he compressed them into a line.

Claussen then fished out a large-scale chart of the South Atlantic and showed Neumann the course line, including the alterations that U-1226 had made since the beginning of the month. He pointed out the overlaid map squares and explained how, all along, he had been reporting only an approximate position to make it harder for the Allies to locate him.

"Now look," said Claussen, tapping the chart. "There's our position on the 1st, and a few hundred miles farther on – here, on the 4th. Aside from Berlin – I hope – that's all anybody knows, except for me, my second in command and now, you. But if you were the British or the Americans, and you'd cracked our codes, and you saw those two positions, what would you think?"

"It looks like we're heading..." Neumann seemed to be working out a compass direction. "Southeast. In fact, more southerly than southeast."

"Right. So it does. But for the last two weeks, I haven't sent any position reports at all. Any navigator seeing those positions might easily think that I'm steering clear of the shipping lanes off Brazil and making as much distance south-southeast as I can, thus saving time on a passage around the southern tip of Africa." He paused. Neumann seemed fascinated by this depiction of their voyage. "That's my little trick. If the British are watching, I want them to feel pleased with themselves for working out that my destination lies to the east."

"I see. Very clever."

"Now look at today's position..." Claussen pointed his pencil at the chart. "...And tell me what you see."

Neumann added his finger to the chart. "These islands seem very close."

"Very close and very British. Port Stanley, here, is now less than 140 miles away and getting closer." There was plenty of time. Claussen allowed Neumann a generous helping of it before appearing to change the subject. "In the Kriegsmarine, we make a serious study of history. These islands were the site of a naval battle during the Kaiser's war. On the 8th of

December, 1914, a German squadron commanded by Admiral Graf von Spee was defeated by ships of the Royal Navy which, unknown to the Admiral, were already inside the enclosed harbour at Port Stanley. When Graf von Spee tried to enter the bay and the firing began, our fleet couldn't turn around and reverse their course. It was a great loss."

"Oh yes," said Neumann. "I think I remember."

"Well, Professor. Neither you nor I nor anybody on this boat knows whether there's another Royal Navy squadron hiding behind that headland. But we can expect the place to be fortified. The last thing I want to do is let my wireless operator tune up his equipment and start sending a long message to Buenos Aires, because my feeling is that there will be British ears listening just here." He tapped the chart again. "And because we shall be getting closer for the next 24 hours – tomorrow we shall come within 100 miles of Port Stanley – you can see how nervous it makes me feel."

But Neumann was still anxious about their progress. "When should we get to HJ11 and alter course?"

Claussen shrugged. "Some time on Monday."

"I can see it's some way beyond Port Stanley. How far?"

Claussen picked up a pair of brass dividers, stepped off two days' sailing, then roughly measured the return distance to Port Stanley. "Say, just over 200 miles by noon on Monday."

"But a day late. They ought to be told."

"It isn't a serious problem, Professor. I've received a message to say the I-8 won't be meeting us on schedule. They've decided to send a different boat. That means the Japanese will arrive even later than us."

Whilst Claussen was torn between duty and caution, Neumann had his orders too. Like every faithful German, his instinct was to follow them.

"Could we do a deal?" Neumann tried to make it sound man-to-man.

"What do you mean?"

"Send a message. Short. Maybe like this: 'Umschlag A waypoint ETA noon 20th. Cargo A1.' Say nothing about when we're going to get to the rendezvous. If they want to know, they could easily work it out, couldn't they? If the wireless operator thinks this is a good time to transmit it, do it now before we get much closer. If the operator at the embassy isn't keeping his schedule properly, and we don't get through in – say – under 2 minutes, give up for a little while. Let your operator choose a different time – better conditions, a better chance. One more attempt, and if he can't get through, give up until the 20th."

"What's this deal?"

"Do this. We both satisfy the people who wrote the orders. When I get to Japan, I send a message to Admiral Dönitz to say how helpful you were. It ought to get you an award – the *Kriegsverdienstkreuz*, at least."

Claussen began to roll up the charts. "Deal," he said. Then he called out to his wireless operator. "Funky! Get in here. We've got a message to send."

(VI)

Sunday 19 November
The Admiralty

Another long day prepared to merge into the next, unnoticed by Rushbrooke, Winn and Kemp. Although it was late, this failed to diminish their admiration for the dedication shown by the British Embassy in Montevideo, whose interception of all diplomatic wireless traffic to Berlin (and the miracle of Floradora) had given the navy its opportunity.

Whichever clerk in Buenos Aires had originated the message had given away more than he could have imagined. Trusting in the impenetrability of his systems, he had added a preamble stating the source of the information being forwarded. Then, properly, he repeated the U-boat's short signal, with the boat's ETA and the tantalising reference to the cargo. That confirmation of identity was almost the answer to Winn's prayers. Almost.

"Well Rodger," said Rushbrooke. "I've got to hand it to you. You said to expect Claussen off the Cape on the 20th and you appear to be right. But I believe you predicted breakfast time, and he's saying he'll be altering course at this waypoint around lunchtime." He gave a great grin. Morale at the Intelligence Centre had taken a boost. "Rodger! You're adrift by a whole morning. Do buck up and try a bit harder next time."

Rushbrooke laughed. Winn smiled too. The hunt had reached its final stage. Oberleutnant Claussen could have no idea of the weight of high explosive that awaited him. The Nazi had less than 24 hours to live, and when the fateful moment arrived, Hitler's nasty surprise would sink to the bottom with him.

"Bobby Burnett's squadron has been in position for a couple of days now," continued Rushbrooke. "They reckon their hydrophones will hear Claussen coming from a hundred miles away. More, maybe. He's had it, Rodger. Good work!"

Kemp agreed. "Yes, damned good work, Rodger. You must be feeling chuffed."

"Thanks, yes, but I'm still not totally happy. I'm a bit anxious about a couple of things. For instance, the cover story; I'm worried that it looks a bit thin. I've had more time to think about it and I can't see it convincing the Americans... If we ever needed to, that is."

"Oh, I don't think that's fair, Rodger," said Kemp. "I think my boys did a good job of faking the Huff-Duff record log. That intercept by the Freetown station on the 18th – well, it's a work of pure artistry."

"But that's the point, Peter. We can't afford to leave any holes in our evidence, especially if they point the wrong way. If, for any reason, the Americans become interested in what happened, why, and importantly, *when*, before we sank Claussen, this forged Huff-Duff log might look suspicious. Any doubt might lead them to discover the real facts about 1226. Facts that we wanted to hush up in the first place."

"Rodger may have a point, Peter," said Rushbrooke. He turned to Winn. "But surely this stuff from the Jerry embassy in B.A. fills in any remaining gaps?"

"Thank you, sir. That's exactly my point. I know I fully concurred with the cover story when it was all we had, but in the light of today's intercepts I think it becomes harder to explain. We can't be seen to be acting on earlier Huff-Duff evidence which we've fabricated, whilst there appears to be more reliable evidence coming in later from Montevideo."

"Hmmm," mused Rushbrooke. "I think I see what you're saying." He put on an earnest look, as if he had realised this problem all along, then turned to Kemp. "Peter? You'd better see what you can do about retracting those Huff-Duff records."

"Thank you," said Winn. "I must say, as evidence goes, it's not bad. But it's not watertight. There's a big assumption in the middle of it, and that's my second concern."

"Look Rodger, old chap," said Rushbrooke. "I know you held out for Tierra del Fuego, but I just wonder if you've got too close to Dönitz. Instead of you getting into his mind, he's got into yours. Claussen is as good as done for. Accept it and move on, there's a good chap."

"I'm not pouring cold water over the navy's plans, Admiral. I just don't want us to get caught out. We mustn't leave any more holes."

Perhaps Rushbrooke remembered how effectively Winn was always able to state his case; it would do no harm to listen. "All right, Rodger. Have your say. What's this big assumption, then?"

"Well, sir... I can see that a wireless message from the South Atlantic has a long signal path to Berlin. Certainly, over that distance, Claussen's signals would become very weak. Far easier for him if he can relay through a station closer to him, like B.A. Now, I admit we purposely started analysing diplomatic traffic when I was looking for a South American link. It was my call and it paid off with this intercept. I ought to feel pleased. But..."

"You worry too much, Rodger."

"Right now, that's my job sir. What's worrying me is this: Even though we went back over everything sent between B.A. and Berlin, right from the time Claussen went off the plot, we found nothing. This message from their embassy is the first we've received." Winn spread his arms, inviting the admiral to understand his concerns. "Right now, we're feeling very confident, but this was just a lucky break. Does Claussen's message tell us categorically where this waypoint is? No. It doesn't."

"But –"

"– But nothing. We're latching on and assuming he's still heading southeast, heading for Cape Agulhas because the date matches and it suits us to assume that. By tomorrow I may be proved wrong. Believe me, I hope so. But right now, without more proof, that's still circumstantial evidence."

"But it mentions the cargo..."

"And we still don't know what that is. We're pretty sure there's two top Nazi scientists and a Japanese linguist on board. Once again we're assuming, because it's convenient to do so, that when they say 'cargo', they mean a quantity of poison gas, not the scientists, or something else we don't know about. And naturally Berlin is interested to know whether it's still viable. But we don't have any proof that such a specific cargo was ever loaded. It's an assumption. And that makes it circumstantial evidence again."

"I do understand what you're driving at, Rodger," said Rushbrooke. "And if it's any consolation, I won't sleep easy in my bed either – not until we get confirmation that 1226 is definitely sunk with all hands."

Kemp had been shifting awkwardly in his seat. "That's right," he said, giving Winn a conciliatory smile, no doubt hoping that he might begin to build a bridge between Rushbrooke's reliance on statistical probabilities and Winn's search for absolute proof. "But it's the consequences that bother me."

Rushbrooke jumped on the remark. "They bother us all, right on up to Churchill."

But Kemp was not to be squashed. "Indeed so. But just in case Rodger's right, it wouldn't hurt to think about what we do if Claussen doesn't turn up on time – or turns up somewhere else. There's too much riding on this to leave anything to chance." He went wolf-eyed and harsh-voiced. "Pardon me if I seem callous, but I want this man dead and Hitler's dreadful weapon destroyed." Then in a more muted tone, "If I thought it was right, I'd be praying for that."

At the idea of divine intervention, all fell silent.

Eventually, Winn coughed and broke the spell. "It's a war," he said. "Best not to pray for other men to die. Just ask God to help you see what's evil and if he thinks it's right, give you the power to help bring an end to it. I can't fight, but I can think, weigh the evidence, influence others. I say Hitler is evil and what Claussen has been ordered to do is evil, too. Maybe in another life Claussen could have been a saint... But in this life, he's a sinner. The only way out is for him to die – and everyone else on that damned U-boat. And until he *is* dead, I shall be on his tail." Then he added, "And if I'm wrong, then God will be on mine."

"Well said, Rodger. I think that probably goes for us all."

"Thank you, Admiral. And I know it's only a small thing, but that message doesn't quite answer everything that B.d.U. asked in their blind broadcast." He fell silent for a moment, affected by the sudden sombre mood. "Claussen's message didn't give his position. No grid-square. That's the first time he's done that."

Monday 20 November
Submarine Tracking Room, The Admiralty Citadel

To witness Claussen's demise, the Royal Navy's top brass had assembled, displaying enough gold braid to re-stock a naval outfitter for the next couple of years. Admiral of the Fleet, Sir Andrew Cunningham, could bear it no longer and voiced everyone's concerns.

"Are you sure there's still nothing?"

"Absolutely sure, sir," replied the lieutenant, WRNS.

"But he was supposed to cross our path three bloody hours ago."

"I know, sir." She had heard far worse language.

By 3:45 p.m. Winn had had enough. In the imperfect world of disbelief, assumption, and missing evidence, no plan would be ideal. But that was not an excuse for having no plan.

"Gentlemen!" Winn rapped the plotting table with a brass paperweight. "If I may be so bold, I have a suggestion to make." It would have been a brave man who told him to keep quiet. All eyes turned towards him, then to Cunningham.

"Blaze away, Rodger."

"Gentlemen, you all know how deeply interested the Prime Minister is in this er... *operation* without a name. So far, he has left us alone. I submit that the last thing any of us wants is for him to walk through that door now, find us in disarray and demand to take charge." By the vehemence of the invective that greeted this statement, it was clear that Winn had summed up the mood flawlessly.

"I have no wish to insult anyone's intelligence – I'm sure we all see it the same way – but in order to deal with U-1226, first we have to find it." The notion was so obvious that Winn knew he needed to move straight from talking about their situation into the solution. "What I propose is that we spend no more than ten minutes listing the broad possibilities about where Claussen might be and what he may be up to, before assigning each one to a senior officer. The objective must be to chase down the merits of each option and any evidence that suggests Claussen could be trying it. We need to decide whether each possibility should be taken seriously or discarded."

"Er... By 'possibilities' you mean has he already sunk, has he been delayed by mechanical trouble, has he somehow found out that we're looking for him and diverted? Stuff like that?"

"Exactly like that," said Winn. "My aim is to sketch it all out, to build a tree of logical deductions, to prove what works about each theory and what doesn't fit."

Winn felt confident that with no new plan having emerged in the hours that the navy had been waiting for news of Claussen, he would not now hear a challenge. Out of respect for the massed naval experience before him, virtually all of which outranked him, he waited for no longer than a second before continuing.

"Right! For the next few minutes our motto is this: 'If it *can* happen, then sooner or later it *will* happen.' Gentlemen, we've had the first three possibilities. Let's hear some more... And remember, even if it's only a remote possibility, it is not therefore either a wrong or a stupid one. Speak up. Let's hear them."

≈

With little stage management, Winn found himself working with Peter Kemp. However, he already realised that he needed access to another wireless specialist with very particular knowledge. He decided to start at the top.

"Admiral Cunningham, sir... A word, please?" By now the established chain of command had taken a number of knocks. It was not so obvious who was working for whom. "I'd like to review progress in about three hours, sir. You, me and the DNI."

"Agreed."

"And I need somebody else here on my team. It's somebody I've never met, but I know this person must exist. There must be a naval signals school somewhere, or something like it... The place where our top expert on Nazi wireless transmitters is stationed. I urgently need to talk to the man who knows all about their U-boat radio systems. I need him here. Do you mind speaking to whoever can fix that for me, please sir? This man may hold the key to finding Claussen's U-boat."

Despite the chill of a November fog on the streets of London, Winn, Kemp and Chief Petty Officer Rees sat well below ground level in a muggy fug of a different kind. Kemp had talked in general terms about their need to know more about German U-boat wireless systems. Rees was explaining how he saw things.

"I wish I could give you something concrete, sir, but we've been waiting for months to get a look inside a Type IX U-boat. Jerry scuttled one at Lorient in August, but they're still fighting in the Lorient pocket. No sign of surrender. With the amount of bombs we're dropping, I doubt there'll be anything left of that one."

"What about Type VIIs? Any luck with them?"

"Better news there, sir. Toulon naval base. During July and August the US Air Force sank about eight Type VII U-boats alongside, so once the port was liberated we were able to get in and take a look. Obviously a Type VII isn't a Type IX, but we reckon the transmitters would be similar, if not identical."

"Our problem," said Kemp, "is a particular Type IX that went off the plot at the beginning of November. Up to then, we'd bracketed him with Huff-Duff, but then – *poof* – he just disappeared. No more position reports."

"Presumably he hasn't surfaced again, sir."

"Oh Mister Rees..." Whether or not the pun was intended, Kemp rolled his eyes at Rees. "He *has* reappeared, but not in the way we expected. We never heard a peep out of him on the channels we were monitoring. Then we found out he wasn't transmitting directly to Berlin but relaying through their embassy in Buenos Aires. How does that sound to you?"

"I'll talk technical for a minute if I may, so just stop me if you don't understand." Kemp gave him the floor. "His transmitter has a master crystal oscillator that, if you like, gives him a main wave band. It then has a number of secondary crystals to give him his exact channel."

"Why couldn't we hear him, then?"

"One answer is that he might have been using a crystal for a non-standard channel, operating a little way outside his normal band of frequencies, somewhere you didn't expect. But there are limits to how far outside his normal waveband he can go. He's only got a relatively simple transmitter, so he can't just open up wherever he wants, say on a completely new waveband, whenever he chooses."

"Is this where it gets technical?"

"A bit. But if I'm right, it isn't too serious from our point of view." He had their attention. "His main limitation would be trying to tune his transmitter's power output into his existing aerial equipment. If the frequency was too far one side or the other, he wouldn't be able to match his output to his aerial. He could damage his gear if he wasn't careful."

"Hang on," said Winn. "Do you mean that he's started using different frequencies to contact the embassy, but not *very* different?"

"That's exactly it, sir."

"Which means all we have to do is search a broader band of frequencies?"

"Right."

"Now, Mister Rees," said Kemp. "We're worried that this U-boat could be a long way from where we thought she was. We've got to find her and sink her. Down in the South Atlantic, we're not set up to mount extensive radar-equipped air patrols and we can't expect to get lucky and just stumble across the bugger. Huff-Duff seems to be our best bet. What would you do?"

Rees scratched his chin, skewed it to the right and angled his head to stare at the ceiling, blinking slowly.

"Well, sir... All I can think of is to link up a sort of grid of operators, all scanning for this special channel and link it to Huff-Duff. Maybe we could get lucky, as you say. Or better... What if our embassy in Montevideo could provide the trigger?"

"Meaning?"

"Meaning, if we aren't already doing so, we monitor Buenos Aires from Montevideo, non-stop. If we haven't picked up this U-boat before, the minute the German embassy transmitter starts sending – but not in a normal way like he would do if he was trying to contact Berlin, if you see what I mean – well, that's when we start a frantic search for the U-boat's signals. Presumably our embassy hasn't got Huff-Duff, so if we find the U-Boat's transmission, we need to log his frequency, then another operator sitting alongside him can radio it to the Huff-Duff people."

"In other words, a lash-up."

"Yes sir. A right old dog's breakfast."

Winn stepped in. "Could it work?"

"Only with slick operators, sir. Trouble is, I can't see another way to do it. The kit you need – I mean so one bloke could handle the whole thing on his own – well, the only place we've got it is in the Huff-Duff stations. We haven't got much alternative, but the blokes doing the searching and the blokes who can pinpoint where the signals are coming from..." Rees shook his head. "Sir, they could be a couple of thousand miles apart."

The prolonged session with Rees resulted in Winn arriving late for the review meeting with Cunningham and Rushbrooke. By the time he entered the First Sea Lord's office, the navy had made up its mind.

"I'm sorry Rodger, but there it is. We can't afford to shilly-shally about with this. Based on Dönitz's past record, he's probably done something we hadn't anticipated, so we've cooked up two options. One: in case he's tricked us by arriving early, we've split the force into two and sent a small fast-moving squadron east towards the Indian Ocean. This U-boat will probably be cruising on the surface, for speed. The plan is simple: Catch up with him and sink him."

"Or two," said Rushbrooke. "He's slow-steaming, and he hasn't reached Cape Agulhas yet. He's hoping we'll fall for it, get tired of waiting, give up and go home. But this time it's not Dönitz doing the unexpected – it's us. We're sticking around till we've got him."

"I see," said Winn. "I suppose what you're afraid of is that after a few days, while the navy isn't looking, Claussen steams past with a superior look on his face and sprints off to Penang. I can't fault it. It's an obvious strategy and I can't prove there's a more likely one."

Both senior officers looked surprised. "You accept it then?"

"Yes, but I'll still keep an open mind and look for more clues. One thing is definite. Claussen is a bloody long way away from Berlin, so it's almost certain we'll hear more via the German diplomatic wireless service in B.A. I'll keep in touch with the girl in Montie."

But it seemed to Winn that with the navy 100 per cent committed to the South African route, and restricting their options to two – slow-steaming on Claussen's part, or a flat-out sprint, they had now dismissed the idea of a South American R.V.

"Whether you're right," said Winn, "or I'm right, or neither of us is right, until he's sunk it still needs somebody on this, night and day."

Later that day, and before Chief Petty Officer Rees had been able to set up his network of naval telegraphists, Montevideo sent a message to advise that the German embassy in Buenos Aires had exchanged brief radio signals with an unknown station just after darkness fell. They had been unable to detect the incoming transmission. Things were no further forward.

Tuesday 21 November

Before Winn entered Rushbrooke's office, he made sure that his face gave away nothing. Smug self-satisfaction was never a pretty sight.

"A diplomatic telegram sent yesterday, deciphered today, sir. Naval HQ, Tokyo, to their attaché in Berlin. It's about the replacement for the I-8."

"Oh yes?"

"Giving an ETA at the pre-arranged rendezvous. Clearly it's still the same place."

"ETA when?"

"In 38 days' time, sir."

"That's a bloody long time!"

But Rushbrooke was not being quite as acute as usual; he needed encouragement.

"Which says to me, sir, that the rendezvous is unlikely to be anywhere near the Malacca Strait, unless the Imperial Japanese Navy is so starved of fuel that their submarines have resorted to using oars to get from Tokyo Bay to Penang."

"Shit!"

The much-desired confirmation arrived later from Montevideo, by courtesy of Floradora, more laziness at the German embassy in Buenos Aires, and the commitment of the young cipher clerk.

Winn paid another visit to the DNI. "Two more diplomatic despatches for you to study, sir." He opened his satchel and handed over the first translation. Rushbrooke scanned it, whilst all the time his eyebrows rose steadily towards his sparse silver hair line. He seemed not to take in the contents all at once. He flicked a glance at Winn, then started to re-read the message. When he had completed his second inspection of the text, he picked up one of his telephones and spoke to the First Sea Lord.

"Rodger and I need to see you urgently, sir."

Out of respect for Winn's semi-paralysis and his likely speed on crutches, Cunningham came to Rushbrooke's office.

"What's this?"

"Rodger reckons there's a panic in Berlin because the replacement for the I-8 is going to take so long getting to the R.V., sir. That was earlier, but this has just come in." Rushbrooke handed over the translation of the latest telegram. "Have a look at this."

Cunningham began to read. Shortly he let out a string of foul lower-deck oaths. When he had exhausted his breath, if not his naval vocabulary, he brandished the translation page.

"Puerto bloody Santa Cruz. Where the fuck's that?"

"Southern Argentina, sir."

"Getting hold of a fishing boat?" Cunningham shook with fury. "Ferrying out a load of *Graf Spee* sailors so Claussen can meet them at sea? It's fucking outrageous."

"So much for parole, sir... So much for neutrality."

"Well at least now we know something about his cargo, don't we? At least they think it's worth sending out these bastards from the *Graf Spee* to guard it."

"Yes sir."

Another implication hit Cunningham. "So he's not going via Cape Agulhas after all?"

"That's the way it looks now, sir. Have a dekko at this second one." Rushbrooke pushed the signal across his desk. "This is their helpful embassy clerk again. Unless this is a trick, he's given the game away."

"This position," said Cunningham, now calmer. "Where is it?"

"I'd guess somewhere in Tierra del Fuego, sir. But you'll notice the embassy is telling Berlin that Claussen is already past Puerto Santa Cruz and he doesn't want to turn round and pick up these extra matelots. ETA 24th. He's nearly there, sir."

"Captain Winn, you'll be the death of me," said Cunningham. Then with disguised joy (for with this new information perhaps they might yet find and sink U-1226) and a theatrical air of defeat (for Winn's benefit, an admission that he had proved the navy wrong under its own roof) he took control. "Let's go down to the submarine plot and see where this position actually is... Then I'd better work out what I'm going to say to Winston."

Friday 24 November
U-1226

Oberleutnant zur See Claussen felt he had timed things perfectly. At dawn, two days before, they had rounded Cape Horn. 'First trip to sea,' he thought. 'And already I've done something many sailors spend a life on the oceans and never do.'

It was now an hour before noon on a clear, bright, spring morning in the southern hemisphere. The visibility along his line-of-sight well exceeded his horizon at sea level. The coastline stood out, as did the forested hills behind and the mountains beyond, most still capped with winter's thawing snow. This vision held him and the lookouts spellbound, as only another man can appreciate who has spent nine weeks and three days at sea (and the majority of that time beneath it) with never a sight of land.

One of Claussen's lookouts gave him a wink, then screwed up his features and nodded as one sailor does who wants to show another that he appreciates his skill – skill that in this case had brought the boat safely to its landfall. For such seamen, open praise would seem unmanly and inappropriate, or even give the impression that, at the start, the task had seemed too much for one simple navigator to handle.

The weight of emotion was too much for Claussen.

"We made it!" Cries of exultation – fists in the air – handshakes all round. "Helmsman! Five degrees starboard rudder. Bring her round nice and steady. New course – oh-nine-oh."

"Due east it is, Herr Kapitän ..."

"Lookouts! Keep a special watch for breaking water, whirlpools, shoals and Englanders."

They all enjoyed the joke.

The western entrance to the Estrecho de Magallanes is twelve miles wide but by the time they reached their destination it would have narrowed to less than two. In confined waters, the last thing anyone wanted to encounter was a cargo vessel bearing down on them, under pilotage between the Atlantic and the Pacific. Or a warship flying any God-damned ensign at all.

The Admiralty

Rushbrooke had the latest signal in his hand in case Cunningham actually wanted to see it. He hoped he wouldn't. The few words it contained would be better spoken.

"Message via the embassy in Montie, Admiral. 'Noon 24th, U-1226 abeam Cabo Pilar, course 125 degrees, ETA

Caleta Notch 20:30 local time.' Rodger is being most gracious about it. He says he doesn't care if you sink the bugger in the Malacca Strait, the Magellan Strait or the Menai Strait. It's all the same to him."

"Caleta bloody Notch. Well at least it's not in Tierra del effing Fuego."

"No sir. Not quite."

Part Two – Marchesi

(I)

Wednesday 7 April, 1982
Foreign & Commonwealth Office, London

"Good afternoon, Ambassador. I'm glad we were able to squeeze you in, but as my private secretary has already mentioned, I'm afraid we shall have to be brief."

"I'm grateful, Foreign Secretary, but nevertheless I hope you will permit me to congratulate you on your appointment before I get to the purpose of my visit."

"Er... Most kind, Ambassador."

"It appears clear from reports in the newspapers that Mrs Thatcher intends to recover the Falkland Islands and that she considers the possibility of not achieving her objective to be non-existent."

"You are reliably informed, as one might say, as to her resolve, Ambassador."

"So one could say that with the sailing of the Task Force, and with the current failure of the Argentines to withdraw from the Falkland Islands in compliance with Security Council Resolution 502, the United Kingdom is in all practical respects on the point of an undeclared war with that country?"

"Her Majesty's Government prefers to seek a peaceful solution, Ambassador."

"Whilst preparing for war."

"Whilst exercising the United Kingdom's legal rights under International Law. Britain has not threatened the security of Argentina in any way. There is no excuse for that country's invasion of our sovereign territory." Slight creases appeared at the outer corners of the Foreign Secretary's eyes, perhaps showing signs of pleasure at his mastery of the tactful response. Pleasure indeed; he was still only two days into his tenure of that great office of state.

The Swedish Ambassador inclined his head towards Mr Pym. "Exactly," he said.

Pym peered over the top of his spectacles. "I understand that the Falkland Islands are seven thousand miles away. It will take time for the Task Force to get there – time perhaps for General Galtieri to realise the error of his ways and withdraw. A military confrontation is not inevitable."

"Be that as it may, Foreign Secretary, Stockholm has asked me to enquire whether you would be prepared to divulge – in confidence of course – to divulge your war aims to us."

The Ambassador's far-from-diplomatic request took Mr Pym completely by surprise. He filled his cheeks and puffed, not in rage, but from an emotion unknown to most politicians – the discomfort of not having a ready answer to the question. Perhaps after all, his mastery of the diplomatic arts was as yet incomplete; he re-phrased his previous statement.

"Ambassador, Her Majesty's Government's objective is not to have a war in the first place. Our aim is to achieve a peaceful solution to this crisis, in line with Resolution 502."

"But if it comes to military action, Mrs Thatcher has already made her first war aim clear. She intends to restore the Falkland Islands to British rule and to remove Argentine troops, flags, military equipment and so forth from your territory."

Mr Pym blustered again. "Well, if you put it like that... If Her Majesty's Government is forced to –"

"– Because my government would like Mrs Thatcher and the War Cabinet to consider a particular war aim. Only by completely humiliating the Junta, only by inflicting a military defeat on them, only by exposing their incompetence and brutality can there be any chance of a popular rising against this evil regime."

"Ambassador, I –"

"– Only by the return of Argentina to democratic government can the regime's war upon its own citizens be terminated." The Ambassador took a deep breath which caused him to grow in height by a good two inches. "Britain stands alone among the major nations in never having condemned the generals for waging this dirty war on their own people. Sweden understands your country's former unwillingness to stand up against these criminals for fear of provoking a backlash against the Falklands, but that eventuality has now overtaken you. You don't have to stay silent any longer."

"Ambassador, I –"

"– Foreign Secretary, I wish to bring to your notice the case of an eighteen-year-old girl holding dual Swedish and Argentine nationality. She has been missing for a long time, and is probably dead – murdered by the regime. But justice must be done and both the Argentine people and the Swedish people must see that it is done, and done fully. I don't know whether your Ministry has been counting, but we have. The Swedish Foreign Ministry estimates that by now there are probably as many as eleven thousand people missing in Argentina – the so-called *desaparecidos*. The regime's death squads must be stopped and the truth must be told. And despite your Ministry's long-standing reluctance to utter a restraining word, Britain is now in a position to bring about justice faster than pressure from the United States, the United Nations – faster than anyone."

"Ambassador, I –"

"– Foreign Secretary, Mrs Thatcher's second war aim must be to bring down the Junta. To accomplish this, her diplomatic stance must be to acknowledge the 'Disappeared' and to bring up the subject in private at every meeting that she will undoubtedly have with the leaders of foreign governments in the next few weeks."

The Swedish Ambassador opened his attaché case and extracted a file. "May I present you with our indictment on behalf of Dagmar Hagelin?" Fired with energy, the ambassador practically burst forward to place the file on Pym's desk. Then, with his arm fully outstretched, he noticed a second file already lying on the corner of the desk; he halted. The file bore the words *République Français*, the image of a red, white and blue flag, and three names. The Ambassador was aware of all three – firstly the military officer named as being implicated in the arrest and disappearance of many victims, and secondly the names of the two French nuns, the other subjects of the file. Despite the fact that he had been compelled to read the file's title upside down, he smiled at the speed with which the French, too, had acted.

Gently, the Ambassador placed his file on top of the French one, stepped back a pace, bowed from the neck in the Germanic fashion and said, "I do hope you will find a few minutes to look at *both* these files. Thank you, Foreign Secretary. I must take up no more of your time."

Thursday 8 April, 1982
Ministry of Defence, Navy Department;
Merchant Shipping Intelligence Desk
London

On the Thursday immediately after the Argentinean invasion, Rear-Admiral Rennie summoned Daniel Rook into his office. The Admiral's desk was not yet a literal mound of paperwork, but it was, unusually, strewn with clutter. He didn't exactly have his head in his hands either, but it was clear that he needed help.

"See this lot?" He waved a hand over a small pile of correspondence smoothed out in front of him, then continued the gesture to take in a larger heap of envelopes, already slit open and their contents stuffed back inside. "The great British public would like to let the Royal Navy into a few little secrets about how to beat the shit out of the Argies." Danny gave a curt nod and looked the Admiral in the eye.

Rennie continued. "I haven't got time to sift through all this stuff. Most of it looks like rubbish anyway." Danny could guess what was coming but the Admiral made a brief tack on a different course. "Are you on top of that missile thing yet?"

"Well, our naval attaché in the Paris embassy says the Argies have definitely taken delivery of the first five, but we don't yet know if any of them got used for test firing. Still trying to establish that sir, but it's extremely unlikely. Even the Frogs don't do live-firing exercises."

"Costly."

"Must be. Apparently, they've rigged up a simulator instead."

With this small diversion out of the way, Rennie returned to his previous heading and sailed straight on. "You couldn't give me a hand with this, could you? Just take them away and give 'em the once-over, so we can say we've done it. Just in case there's some war-winning gem hidden away in here."

Danny could see that Rennie's mind was already made up. But it never paid to say yes straight away. One needed to put up a bit of a fight to avoid getting overwhelmed in the future with everybody else's tedious or unglamorous cast-offs.

Danny shrugged. "I don't have any spare time right now. I mean – this whole thing hasn't been going for a week yet and there must be at least fifty letters there. What if there's a hundred tomorrow and another two hundred by Monday morning? How urgent is this, sir? I thought the priority was the Exocets."

"Yes, of course it is. But just have a look through this stuff, and give me an idea how much of it's nonsense. Three piles, Danny. 'Rubbish', 'Could Be Useful' and 'Action Required'." The Admiral glanced up at Danny with an expression in which trust and pre-earned gratitude figured equally. "Some of it's technical, Danny. I'd feel happier if you did this, rather than old Tommo or one of the new boys." This was a disreputable trick, but it worked.

"Hand them over then," said Danny. "I'll see what I can do." He wondered whether it was a mark of Rennie's confidence in him that he hadn't thought to specify a fourth pile – 'Haven't Got a Clue'.

Rennie shuffled the loose letters together into his left hand, engulfed the larger bundle of yet-to-be-examined envelopes and held them out towards Danny. At the same time, he twisted in his chair and reached towards the floor. His right hand reappeared, gripping a cardboard box in which lay a six-inch stack of letters.

"Forgot about these," said the Admiral. "Came in an hour ago..."

By early evening, Danny had disposed of three-quarters of Rennie's unwanted post. He had just laboured through a detailed description of an aerial dog-fighting manoeuvre that the writer claimed to have invented in the late 1940s, and which he now offered to the navy with accompanying diagrams. Did warplanes commit to dogfights any longer? Danny didn't know, but suspected not. Surely it was all button-pressing and air-to-air missiles, now? He put the letter on the pile for further investigation by the Fleet Air Arm.

He was initially relieved that the next letter contained only a single hand-written sheet. That would not take too long to struggle through. For no reason other than the mechanical way in which one handles a letter, Danny flipped the page over and was astonished when his eye alighted on the signature.

Victor A J B Marchesi, (Lt-Cmdr Retd.)

Danny remembered meeting a fellow with the same name several years before. He reckoned the odds on there being two naval officers called Victor Marchesi must be close to zero. He recalled a short voyage on a freezer ship between home-waters discharge ports. Vic had been the relief first mate, by then making his living in the Merchant Navy.

A memorable man – retirement age, craggy-faced, kept himself to himself, posh accent. When Vic spoke, it was with a curious combination of gruffness in the throat and sibilance through the front teeth. It might have been the endless cigarettes... or the gin.

Danny had felt sorry for the guy. Two oddly superior coastal second mates had frequently been rude to Vic behind his back. He remembered imagining how he might have felt if he had known that two smirking oafs were making fun of his own father, ignorant of his past and enjoying the gratification that comes from getting away with dumb insolence and half-hearted compliance with orders.

Vic Marchesi... Danny wondered what he might have to say about the South Atlantic or Argentina. He turned to the front of the letter again and noticed that it was written on headed notepaper – The Army & Navy Club, Pall Mall, no less...

Sir

Having spent the latter years of the Second World War in command of HMS William Scoresby, on station in the South Atlantic, I believe that I have a special insight into the type of weather to be expected in that region, how swiftly it can change, the signs to look out for and, in particular, the risks from ice. I would very much welcome the opportunity to make my experience available to a meteorological officer in the hope that it may be of some assistance to the Task Force.

I would also welcome the opportunity to speak with an ABCD officer in relation to an operation in which I became involved in late 1944. At the time I was unaware of the greater significance of that operation. However, unfolding events and growing awareness of the potential political impact of the operation have troubled me increasingly over the years. This business in the Falklands could offer the opportunity to prevent future embarrassment at the highest level. In open correspondence such as this, I must refrain from going into greater detail.

I hope that I shall hear from you shortly on both accounts.

Yours faithfully

Victor A J B Marchesi, (Lt-Cmdr Retd.)

Danny gave a near-silent whistle of amazement. Vic Marchesi; what a surprise. It just showed – you could never tell what a person had been up to in the past. A brief but intriguing letter offering help but with the underlying menace of something nasty. 'ABCD'... Danny had never heard the term before but he supposed it was more than simply an alternative to a series of asterisks denoting something obscene or secret. Atomic, Biological and Chemical 'something', maybe? They called it 'NBC' now. Vic had obviously retired from the Royal Navy and joined the merchant service a good while before, so perhaps he wouldn't be up to date with all the latest terminology.

But Vic had mentioned a political angle too. Danny reached across to put the letter on the 'Action Required' pile, but noticed the clock on the wall: 6:40 p.m. He withdrew his hand and replaced the letter on his desk. The notepaper's printed header included a phone number. It was irresistible. Danny lifted the handset and began to dial. After several seconds the switchboard operator answered.

"I've got a letter in front of me from a Commander Marchesi. Do you know how I could get in touch with him, please?"

"We have a guest of that name, sir." A guest... Danny had not suspected that the Army & Navy Club might also be some sort of hotel. "Who shall I say is calling?"

"My name's Daniel Rook. I'm a Scientific Officer with the MoD. – Navy Department."

It took the operator a little while to locate Victor. During one of the interludes, she informed Danny that the gentleman had not answered his room telephone, but asked him if he would care to hold a little longer. Eventually a steward found the Commander in the dining saloon.

"Marchesi here."

"Sorry to intrude on your meal, sir." Danny detected a 'harrumph' from the far end of the telephone line. Life on board ship consisted of an interlinked series of interruptions that frequently arose five minutes after one had sat down to a meal. Vic would be used to such disturbances. "Daniel Rook here, sir." He wondered whether Vic might remember the name; it was a slim chance. At least six or seven years must have elapsed. "It's about your letter."

"Yes, I'd hoped so." No familiarity; Vic must have forgotten Danny's name.

"From what you said, you probably don't want to go into details over the phone."

"No, that's right. Where are you? Whitehall, or somewhere?"

"Close... 55 Broadway."

"Ah..."

Danny smiled. So much understanding conveyed in a single syllable. He had hoped the address might mean something to Vic.

Marchesi continued. "Say no more, dear boy. If it suits you, why don't you pop round? Expect you in about half an hour?"

Any prospect of closure on Danny's much-extended working day expired in front of him. But he was curious about Vic's letter, and keen to meet him again.

"As quick as I can, sir."

55 Broadway sits directly above St James's Park tube station. Danny descended to the street, emerging into the relative

calm that follows the frantic six o'clock rush to the public houses and the railway stations. He reckoned the Army & Navy Club lay a mere ten minutes' walk away. The Mall was still busy with cycles, taxis and Mercedes limousines opposite Marlborough Gate, so it took a couple of minutes to get across. Danny didn't want to race to the meeting and arrive panting and perspiring, so he ambled along, and mounted the Club's steps well within Marchesi's allotted half hour.

Danny entered the building and stated his name at reception. He had already spotted Vic sitting with a newspaper on his lap, craggier and more weather-beaten than he had remembered, and now rather red-faced. Being inside one of St James's elite clubs made Danny a little self-conscious. Moments after he had started speaking to the concierge, Marchesi strode up and interrupted to introduce himself, somewhat interfering with the essential order of things.

Out of courtesy, Danny turned to greet him. "Good evening, Commander... Danny Rook."

"Forget the rank, dear boy. It's just plain old Victor, these days." With due deference and without any officious undertones, the concierge re-established control and invited Vic to sign his visitor into the institution. "I thought we could go and sit in the reference library," said Vic. His voice had lost none of its refinement, gravel or power, and took Danny back to their few seaborne exchanges before he, too, had come ashore. "There'll be nobody about, especially at this time of day." They took the stairs.

Vic offered Danny a seat. Danny thanked him and decided to play the acquaintance card straight away. "You're looking a lot happier than the last time I saw you." It was hardly true. The poor chap looked worried. However, the tactic seemed to work because Vic's expression changed to astonishment.

"Oh! When was that?"

"Must have been about seven years ago. Coastal voyage on one of Port Line's finest."

"Good Lord! What were you? Deck?"

"Radio."

"Sorry, Danny. That must have been just about my last voyage. Had a lot on my mind. Not a happy time. I don't remember much about it. Sorry."

"No reason to apologise. Hung up your sea-boots now, though. Hope it's all going well."

"Tolerably, old boy, but the sea gets into your blood, doesn't it? Never lets you alone. Always something crops up and stirs the memory. Happy or sad. Now this Falklands business."

"Yes; nasty," said Danny. Time to break a little more ice. "We've had a whole sackful of mail from the public about the Falklands, but I was surprised to find your letter buried amongst the others. Total piece of luck that it came to me first. I remembered you, so I knew you weren't some time-waster – excuse me – but with you being so close to where I work..."

Danny paused to cast his eyes around the room, taking in the paintings of be-wigged nineteenth century mariners and scarlet-coated soldiers. "...I hoped you might be able to tell me, face to face, what it's all about. I agree it wouldn't have been right to discuss it over the phone."

Having been reminded for the second time that he was talking to an old acquaintance, even though he had managed to forget the circumstances, a change came over Vic. He mumbled something about showing Danny the proper degree of hospitality, then excused himself and got to his feet, but immediately he sat down again.

"I've had a better idea. Let's go and find a quiet corner in the smoking room. We can always come back here if it gets a bit noisy later."

The benefit of the smoking room was clear from its name alone; Vic relaxed and lit a cigarette. He sucked in the first lungful and held it before exhaling. The room also had a bar. Vic ordered a large gin and a small bottle of tonic water. Clearly, the passage of time had not affected his appetites. "*Burra peg*," he said to the steward, then turned to Danny.

"Er... *Chota peg*," said Danny, falling in with the Imperial atmosphere and Vic's choice of both language and refreshment. Vic and the steward smiled. Vic made a reference to Danny's command of Hindi, which Danny waved away, saying he probably knew no more than ten words in total. The steward brought their drinks and left the pair talking about sailing with Indian crew. Any remaining ice had not only broken but melted away. Shortly, Vic appeared ready to begin, so Danny took out his notebook and Vic's letter.

"I seem to have created a slight domestic problem for myself," said Victor. "The Memsahib would rather I hadn't written to you. Her opinion is that what happened in the past needs to stay there."

"Oh... Well, it's a bit late for me to ignore your letter now, sir." What was this about a domestic problem? Danny grinned, attempting to make light of Vic's revelation. "But I promise I won't sell your story to the Sunday papers..."

Vic gave a puff through his nostrils and glanced towards his gin and tonic. "Oh, it's nothing like that. No hint of impropriety, dear boy. Just that a few years ago we both decided not to mention it again. Sleeping dogs, you know. Official secrets."

Danny had not forgotten the problem implied in Vic's letter. This wasn't going to be an easy chat between old shipmates about bygone times. "Sorry," he said. "Just tell me as much as makes you comfortable."

Vic gave a grunt, then took a final draw from his cigarette and stubbed out the butt in a heavy glass ashtray. After clearing his throat, he leaned forward in his armchair, crossed his arms in his lap and looked at Danny from beneath lowered eyebrows. "Nineteen forty-four," he said. "Got involved in something I'm not so proud of now. Men died because of me." Perhaps he thought this disclosure might shock a peacetime ex-mariner like Danny.

Danny dropped his gaze for a moment and nodded. "I guess that's war," he said. He couldn't know the circumstances, but Vic's apparent discomfort over what he had done, and the ensuing silence, showed his need for sympathy. "I expect you had your orders. Actions and accidents. The fog of war. I reckon it all comes down to the same thing."

"Oh yes. Had to be done. At the time, I don't suppose I thought much more about it. Another six months and the war was over anyway. But things carried on unfolding – a bit here, a bit there. The more time went on, the more I pieced together. It all began to fit in." He took a deep breath before revealing his next bombshell. "The Memsahib was involved, which I pretty much knew already. But she takes all this hush-hush stuff seriously. She didn't want to tell me. Sworn to secrecy, you know. But, years ago, I kept pestering her. Wrong of me, I know. I'd basically figured out most of it, but I needed confirmation, if you follow me."

"I think I understand. I'd be the same. Not knowing – that's what gets you. You can't let it rest. It eats away at you, doesn't it?"

"Hmmm," said Vic. "And as you get older – I mean, you'd understand if you'd been responsible for someone's death – but I needed to know there was no alternative for me... That I had to do it." He looked across at his glass of gin again, but this time he reached out and swallowed a good half-inch of the contents. "It's a mortal sin, of course. No matter whether you've taken one life or a thousand. I've confessed... More than once. But it never goes away."

Danny let it lie – the business of responsibility for the deaths of other people. But now he felt a twinge of disappointment. He had lengthened his day, influenced by what an old acquaintance had written. He had believed Vic's contribution would amount to something more than the agonies of a retired officer's conscience. Still, now that they were drinking together, it would be rude to cut the visit short and walk away.

"How did it all start?"

Vic screwed his face up and stared at the ceiling. He opened his mouth to speak, then closed it and pondered for several more seconds before deciding where to begin.

"I was mostly brought up by my widowed godmother, you see? She – I suppose I should say 'we' – lived in a converted chapel in Belgravia. She'd always been a bit eccentric, but then she got involved with a wretched pack of spiritualists. Séances all the bloody time. No place for a youngster, I can tell you." Vic seemed more comfortable now, and Danny relaxed too.

"Well, she had a gentleman friend, a minor peer, and not long after this chap's first wife died, she married the old bugger and became Lady Caillard 'Two', so to speak. Looking back, I suppose a lad like me just got in the way of the happy couple. But rescue was at hand... She had a son by her first marriage, who was in the navy. It was him who persuaded her to let me join HMS Worcester as a cadet. So off I went and very glad too. That's how I ended up at sea."

Danny now knew the origins of Vic's upper-class accent. He grunted to show that he was awake and still following the thread.

"But it was the thirties, Danny, and jobs at sea were hard to come by – specially for a brand new snotty, all wet behind the ears. Well, I got to sea eventually, and one thing led to another. I managed to get on an Antarctic expedition – Fourth Mate on the research ship *Discovery*, which is where I met a chap called Jimmy Marr. 'Scout', they called him, though he wasn't fond of the nickname. He'd actually been south with Shackleton in the twenties. He was a bit older than me, but we became friends. Anyway, when we got home it was clear which way things were going, so I transferred from the reserve and into the navy proper."

Vic's story seemed to be heading in roughly the right direction without plunging into too many irrelevant asides, so Danny made an encouraging noise and his host started off again.

"Well, look. What with my cadet training, and a start with Brocklebank's, then this voyage down amongst the ice, I'd become a pretty shit-hot navigator." Danny smiled inwardly at the contrast as Vic's cultured accent descended into maritime slang. "So the navy trained me up as a hydrographer and stuck me on a minesweeper. I mean, whether you're laying your own mines or clearing a channel through somebody else's, you need to know where you are."

"Essential," agreed Danny.

"HMS *Gleaner*, it was. Now, she'd had a pretty interesting war already, first searching for one of our submarines, the *Thetis*. Then, early in 1940, she sank a Jerry U-boat, U-33, up on the Clyde. In no time, the Intelligence boys were swarming all over the ship, swearing everybody to secrecy, and nobody knew why." Vic paused for another gulp of gin.

"We'd picked up the survivors and frisked them for weapons and so forth, but one of the prisoners had what looked like a couple of 3-speed gear sprockets off a bicycle wheel. He'd been given them as they abandoned ship, I expect, and told to drop them in the water as soon as he floated clear. I suppose he just stuffed them in his pocket while he used both hands to climb out of the boat. But then when he hit the water it was freezing cold and he just went numb with shock and forgot what he'd been told to do. But it turned out –"

"– They sound like they were rotors out of an Enigma machine," said Danny.

"Quite right." Vic acknowledged with a smile. "I realise that now, of course. But back then we didn't know what they were. And Naval Intelligence didn't damned-well tell us anything either. Just told us to keep our mouths shut. But it was... it was fate, I suppose. When you're a lot older, dear boy, you'll look back too, and you'll realise which were your life's turning points. And like I say, this one never fell into place for bloody years."

"But this was 1940, not 1944. These weren't the people who lost their lives?"

"No. Not them. Nearly half of them got off the sub before she sank." Vic settled back into his seat. "Eventually I found myself as First Lieutenant on HMS *Franklin*. Another minesweeper. But by then I'd passed the next stage hydrographer's course and realised I was stuck in the tramlines. 'Once you're in, you'll never get away from *Droggie*', they say in the navy, and it's true. I was never going to get away and make a name for myself. I was going to spend the whole war as a two-ring hydrographer, and maybe the most excitement I was going to get would come from making charts of the invasion beaches – wherever and whenever that was going to happen.

"Safe though."

"Yes, but when you're a young bloke of twenty-six or seven, unattached, and there's a war on, and chaps are bragging about what they've done – you know – you want something to brag about too."

Danny tried to keep Vic in contact with the subject. "But you got your chance?"

"Yes, but not the way I might have expected." There seemed to be a moment's danger that Vic would become introspective again, but he overcame it. "By now it's springtime, 1943, and who should pop up but Jimmy Marr? Says they're going to bump him up to Lieutenant-Commander and put him in charge of a secret operation down in the far South Atlantic. And he wants me for his second in command. Ice experience, you see? Partly why I wrote to you. Of course, I nearly agreed straight away but I had the sense to ask what it was all about first. Operation Tabarin. Heard of it?" Danny shook his head. "No. Nobody ever has."

"What was it then? Hunting U-boats that might be hiding up fjords in South Georgia?"

"Not on the face of it. Writing letters. That's what we were going to do. We'd act as tender to ferry supplies out to some new Antarctic bases, and we'd write hundreds of letters."

For the first time, Danny was surprised. "Letters?"

"Yes, letters. Sounds dull, doesn't it? Of course, it turned out to be only half the story. But you see, Jimmy had asked for me in person, and to tell you the truth I wanted to see the ice again, even more than I wanted to get away from *Droggie*. So I agreed."

Danny felt he could now afford to be a little more familiar. "You're going to have to help me here, Vic. But I can't see how writing letters turns into people dying or how it's going to help throw the Argies off the Falklands."

"Stick with me, dear boy, I'm coming to it." Vic coughed, then lit another cigarette. "The Argies, you say? Well back in '43 they were starting to be a problem. I mean, the Jerries and the Argies were like this." Vic clasped his hands together to show how close they were. "Their troops wore coal-scuttle helmets, just like Jerry. The whole regime spouted Nazi propaganda, and as far as I can see they've been Fascists from that day to this..." By now, Vic's theme was simmering nicely. "And here's the problem... With Britain's eye off the ball because of Herr Hitler, Argentina had laid claim to the Falklands again, plus every bit of land lying below sixty degrees south." Vic raised a finger and wagged it in humour at Danny. "But not so fast! The Foreign Office and the Colonial Office had put their heads together and come up with a plan. Slipped it past Churchill while he was at Casablanca, I think."

"And this was Operation Tabarin?"

"Yes. What they wanted was this: Jimmy's outfit would set up permanent bases on remote islands and sections of the Antarctic continent. Then we'd write letters from there to our embassies in India or America or wherever..." He smirked. "Or aunts and uncles in bloody Switzerland. Then here's the clever bit... You stick specially-minted postage stamps on them and if any of your letters actually get delivered, you raise a cheer."

"Why?"

"Why? Because you've shown that another country accepts that you're conducting proper government procedures from Penguin Land, or whatever you've decided to call it. And one of the best, easiest and cheapest ways to demonstrate that is to have an international post office operating from there."

"And they needed the navy in case of trouble with Argentina?"

"Yes, although what we could have done against a neutral country, I don't know." Vic then added darkly, "...Or trouble with Hitler's navy."

"So then, presumably you headed south, complete with your envelopes and writing paper and enough fags and whisky to last through an Antarctic winter..."

"And a rather parsimonious supply of ammunition, plus several sheets of newly printed postage stamps and so forth, all crammed into the least seaworthy vessel it has ever been my misfortune to meet." By then, Vic was clearly enjoying re-living the experience. "Unfortunately, by the time we'd left the Thames, we'd already fallen behind our convoy. We pulled into Pompey to make some repairs, then set off again down the channel, but we only got as far as Falmouth. She was taking in water so fast that we had to pelt straight through the minefield or lose her offshore. When we got alongside, we had to use all her engine power to pump her out, or else she'd have sunk at her moorings."

"Good start to the operation," said Danny.

"Which left us with just one option. Trans-ship the stores to another vessel, and try again." Vic heaved a great sigh of frustration. "So, what with all this buggering about, we didn't leave for Port Stanley until about a fortnight before Christmas. That meant it was practically the end of January '44 before I boarded HMS *William Scoresby* again. Bloody planners! The *Scoresby* was already down there in the Falklands and she'd have been a much better bet for us in the first place. Not ideal, but a damned sight better than the death-trap they wanted us to take."

"You said 'again'. You already knew the ship?"

"Yes, I knew her from when I'd been on the *Discovery* with Jimmy. Circles, Danny. Life just seems to go round and round in circles, till..."

"What sort of vessel was she?"

"A research ship, no bigger than a deep-sea trawler, requisitioned by their lordships, fettled up a bit and re-branded as a minesweeper. But then, any old tub that can tow a paravane can do the job of a minesweeper. All you need to do is cut the underwater mooring ropes and take pot shots at any mines that bob to the surface."

"Did she have any armament?"

"Nothing of any use. Officially one of His Majesty's warships, and her only protection was an obsolete 12-pounder pop-gun welded on the fo'c'sle like an afterthought." Despite Vic's negative appraisal of the *William Scoresby*, his words then took on a wistful quality. "But even though I was now stuck on the navy's strangest minesweeper, and technically at war, I was thrilled to be on the fringes of the Antarctic again."

Vic slapped both hands down on his knees as if he intended to rise out of his chair and set off somewhere. "Anyway, there we were, eight thousand miles from home, and no time to lose if we were going to establish our first bases. So, we sailed out of Stanley and set off southwards together with the Falkland Islands Company's own ship, the *Fitzroy*. The first thing we did was to make sure there were no Argies occupying Deception Island, and that's where we started building our first base."

(II)

Thursday 3 February, 1944
Port Foster, Deception Island
Latitude 63° South

A little before noon, HMS *William Scoresby* led the *Fitzroy* through the opening in the volcanic cliffs of Deception Island. Lieutenant-Commander Marr had posted lookouts to scan left and right for any signs of human life or potential resistance, and ordered the 12-pounder cleared for action. A seaman squinted over open sights through the lightly-armoured shield, a Lyddite high-explosive shell loaded in the breech. The lookout in the crow's nest thought he saw movement at one of the whalers' huts so the gun was brought to bear over the starboard bow, but it proved to be only a door blowing in the wind. Lieutenant Marchesi wondered why it hadn't already been ripped off its hinges.

Marr signalled the *Fitzroy* to anchor in Whalers' Bay, but conducted an exploratory cruise in the *Scoresby* towards Telephone Bay at the northern end of the flooded caldera, a body of water some 6 miles long by 3 wide. The *Scoresby* returned, having seen no other vessels at anchor. On the black beaches the only craft of any kind were flush-decked workboats of bleached wood, drawn up and abandoned over thirty years before, now sinking more deeply year by year into the pea-sized cinders.

Even though there were no vessels to be found, that didn't necessarily mean no inhabitants. Argentina had sent a naval transport ship two years earlier to raise the flag and declare sovereignty. The Colonial Office believed that nobody had over-wintered there for maybe forty years, but they were afraid that Argentina intended to land a party there again for the southern summer. As far as Marchesi could tell though, Whitehall's suspicions were wrong and the island remained deserted, by humans at least.

A covering of snow sugar-iced the ridges that surrounded the bay. Despite the near-freezing air, in various places steam hung in clouds over fumaroles and the whole place stank of sulphur, overlaid with the fishy reek of rotting seabird guano. And this was the place where the Tabarin expedition proposed to establish its first base, paradoxically entitled 'Base B'. This was where they planned to erect the accommodation, the radio station, the laboratories and the administrative centre, including the magistrate's courtroom and the post office. This was to be home for five men until they were relieved perhaps a year later when the surrounding waters became relatively clear of ice and it was safe to navigate again.

Once ashore, Marr inspected the existing huts. Some were in a poor state of repair, collapsed and filled with wind-blown snow that had turned to ice. The largest hut, the whalers' billet, which had lain uninhabited for over ten years was still sound. Marr decided that it could serve as sleeping quarters for the Base B party straight away, and that all available hands should be employed off-loading cargo from the two vessels. He was anxious to move on to Hope Bay to establish Base A as soon as possible. He said it would be wasting precious time to spend it erecting the huts that they had brought with them. That could wait.

So the men toiled from dawn to dusk, wrestling with cargo of every capacity and contour, dragging their own workboats onto the beach and straining the muscles that had enjoyed a holiday during the sea cruise south on the troop-carrier.

Two days passed and either the hard labour grew softer, or the men's muscles toughened up. Marr gathered a salvage party to check whether any of the kit left behind by the whalers could be re-used at Base A. He sent Charles Smith, the cook, off with a tin of red-lead paint to obliterate an Argentinean flag that had been daubed on the side of one of the rusting whale-oil tanks. Marchesi and Marr were engaged in a discussion with the expedition's meteorologist when the cook came back. Clearly he had something to say.

"Ye dinna look happy, Smitty," said Marr. "What's up?"

"Always happy, sir, you know me." They all grinned. "Only I've found something, and I thought you ought to see it, in case it was important."

"What sort of a something?"

"A sort of tube. I didn't want to touch it in case it was a bomb or an unexploded shell."

Marr frowned. "Where did you find it?"

"Over by the flagpole." Smitty pointed north along the beach, a little way beyond the huts. All eyes followed the outstretched arm to where a crisp new White Ensign stood out from the mast erected by the Argentineans. The flag rippled and whip-cracked in the breeze. Treated like that, the side opposite the halyard would soon start to fray as the probing wind tested the material, jerking it this way and that in the sudden gusts that eddied around within the crater.

"Ye'd better show us," said Marr. Then he addressed the meteorologist. "Gordon, trot off and find the Doc, just to be on the safe side." Then to Marchesi, "Okay Vic. Let's go and take a look."

Smitty led the way along the black beach. To their right stood abandoned brick-built ovens, now half buried by the action of the highest storm-surges that had flooded the beach, shuffling and compacting the cinders beneath the boilers. The rusting furnace doors hung open on broken hinges. No whale-flensers on the beach now, nor giant petrels fighting to gorge themselves on the tons of offal. No stinking cauldrons of boiling blubber, no stench of coal-fires or whale guts or decay, just the pungent igneous sulphur fumes; and the birds – many penguins, some unidentified gulls and the occasional menacing skua.

On every side lay the massive jawbones of once-majestic blue whales, their discarded vertebrae as wide as tree trunks, their redundant ribs picked clean, bleached and arching. Although the rib bones might have made some think of the rafters of a barn or a church roof, the comparison that struck Marchesi was with the upturned wreck of a wooden-hulled vessel with its keel and external planking stripped away, leaving only the frames. A wooden-hulled vessel, he mused, like the *Veslekari*, that pig of a pensioned-off Norwegian seal hunter, rotten below the waterline. Some penny-pinching idiot in the Admiralty had thought she could carry them seven thousand miles to the Falklands and then another thousand through the stormiest seas on the planet to the edges of the Antarctic continent.

Flat out, she had scarcely managed 5 knots. They had only made Falmouth by the grace of Almighty God. If they'd been farther out to sea, the whole expedition would have foundered. And in their case, their bones would never have been seen again.

Marchesi became aware that Smitty was talking about the flagpole and how the people who raised it must have tried to give it extra bracing by shovelling cinders around it to form a cone about three feet high. When Smitty had put his boot on the bank of pumice before hoisting the navy's flag, he'd nearly stepped on this green tube. Well, he reckoned it must be copper, or maybe brass or bronze, now covered in verdigris. And what was it doing here if it wasn't a shell case or something? And what if it was a booby trap?

But Marr knew what it was.

"Tisnae a booby trap, Smitty. There'll be a message inside it." Marr bent down and carefully brushed away some of the black granules from above the cylinder. There appeared to be some marks engraved on the casing, but these were indistinct. Marr flicked away more of the debris. "She's safe," he said. "Nae wires." Smitty looked as though he would have preferred to be standing farther back, just in case.

"If you say so, sir."

When Marr kicked the cylinder so that it rolled down the cone, an even more worried expression crossed Smitty's face. Marr bent down and tried to twist open the cylinder. Marchesi could see he was enjoying demonstrating his bomb disposal skills.

"The Governor's got a collection of these back at Port Stanley. If ye look around, there might be a brass plaque somewhere too. It's a trick to try to try to establish sovereignty. Tell him, Vic."

"The boss is right, Smitty," said Marchesi. He stiffened his stance slightly. "This is British territory. We're here to make sure that Britain's claim to this place is better than anyone else's. Year-round possession... Not this pathetic performance – sticking messages in metal cans and buggering off to spend the winter somewhere warmer."

However, the lower decks had long suspected there was more to it. "But that's not all, is it sir? Another reason. Something to do with the war?"

But Marr wasn't going to allow Marchesi to be suckered into disclosing their secret orders. He stepped back in. "Aye," he said. "The war. And Argentina's a damned sight closer to Hitler's side than ours, so you're dead right it's to do with the war." He jabbed his finger at the cook. "But if I hear any crazy rumours about why else we're here, I'll know who to come looking for." Smitty grinned. "Once we've left, everyone here needs to understand one thing. Unless we've sent a wireless message to say we're coming to pay a visit, the minute you or anyone else sees anything bigger than a penguin come floating through the heads over there, ye need to get Mr Layther to radio Port Stanley."

"Could be anything," said Marchesi. "Not just an Argentinean claim jumper. Could even be Jerry. Surface-raider, U-boat – anything."

"Don't worry, sir. From now on I'll keep one eye on the stew-pot and one eye on the window." The serious moment was broken when a troop of penguins waddled past the group, on their way from the rookery to the bay. All heads turned towards them. "Wonder what they taste like," mused Smitty.

"From memory, they're as salty as bloody anchovies and tough as old boots," said Marchesi. "And they peck like the dickens."

London, 1982

Danny had been flicking surreptitious glances at a clock perched on the smoking-room mantelpiece. It was a fine, brass-rimmed clock in a polished wooden case, the white enamel face reminiscent of a marine chronometer with long, slender hands and elegant numerals. Somehow it had raced round to 9:35 and Vic had not added any further details about the 'ABCD' connection or the people whose deaths he felt responsibility for, almost forty years before. Danny thought his last train was scheduled to leave at around 11:30 p.m. It was starting to look unlikely that he would be on board.

"But when we got within about fifteen miles of Hope Bay, where we were supposed to establish Base A, you'll remember..." Vic paused for effect and arched his eyebrows. "Jimmy's luck ran out." Then, in a deadpan voice he added. "All his *hopes* turned to fears, you might say."

"Oh dear." But then a sudden feeling that Vic's story might come to a rapid conclusion brightened Danny's mood, despite the morbid undertones. The thought that he might soon escape, injected a certain eagerness into his next comment. "Was Hope Bay where you ran into trouble?" However, his hopes, too, were ill-founded.

"No, dear boy. What we ran into was brash ice. Miles and miles of the stuff."

Monday 7 February, 1944
Antarctic Sound, Northern Graham Land

Lieutenant-Commander Marr had joined Captain Pitt on the *Fitzroy*, which was leading the way towards Hope Bay. However, it soon became clear that because the company vessel did not have strengthened bows, Pitt was nervous of sailing any farther for fear of getting holed, or worse, becoming stuck fast in the ice. He proposed withdrawing the *Fitzroy* northwards to open water while Marchesi steamed ahead to reconnoitre conditions closer to Hope Bay. Marr and the other Falklander, Captain Roberts, transferred to the *Scoresby*, which pushed forward and soon found much freer conditions, so that by lunchtime the *Scoresby* was able to anchor just off the beach at Hope Bay.

Marr and Marchesi discussed that morning's ice and agreed that it was unlikely to be either the previous season's sea ice or new ice beginning to form as the southern summer drew to a close. They reckoned it was probably glacier fragments from where the ice-edge had broken free of the land and tumbled into the sea, to be carried away by the prevailing westerly wind and the northerly current. From their experience in the *Discovery*, they felt confident that the debris should all fetch up on the other side of the channel and that Hope Bay, somewhat sheltered, should be fairly safe from glacial ice. Marchesi could see that underneath his

Scottish reserve, Marr was delighted that they had made such an easy passage and was anxious to get back to give the good news to Captain Pitt. Roberts kept his own counsel.

To give further confidence to the Falklanders, Marr sanctioned a quick trip ashore to check the ground on which they would build their main base camp. The party returned in good spirits, one or two of them performing comic walks in imitation of the Adelie penguins that were clustered on the foreshore.

By mid-afternoon the *Scoresby* was ready to haul up her anchor and head out to sea. Behind them, to the southwest, the Depot Glacier ice-edge lay grey-green and fissured in an apparent straight line where the ice cliff met the sea. On each side of the glacier, a lateral surface moraine curved gently down to the ice-edge from the crumbling rock slopes higher up the valley. To the right of the glacier, the afternoon shadows accentuated Blade Ridge, sharp as a shard of obsidian, and coal black.

Marchesi felt real joy to be down south again, glorying in the contrast between the dark ridge and the glaring white glacial river of ice. In places the glacier was flecked with pale pink and that strange shade of green, somewhere between weathered copper and cloud-grey. To Marchesi it felt as comfortable and familiar as home.

Marr and Roberts were bent over the chart. "Look, it's ideal... No more than a three-mile haul to the top of the glacier. Reach the col between the two peaks. Maybe we should call it 'Fitzroy Pass'? Then not much more than three miles down the glacier on the other side and there ye are." He rapped the chart with his forefinger. "See? Close to sea-level, in the lee of the mountains and on the ice shelf itself." Now Marr was talking more like an Antarctic explorer than the commander of a military operation. "We should be able to sledge a considerable way along the coast." But Roberts was already unenthusiastic, reluctant to endanger the *Fitzroy*.

That night, they managed to rendezvous with the *Fitzroy*. Roberts rejoined Pitt, but by the morning the Falklanders had decided to refuse permission for their vessel to proceed into Hope Bay. They said that if the wind swung round and blew from the east it might fill the bay with the brash ice seen the previous day and imprison their ship. Marr and the others who were familiar with the Antarctic thought the excuse a feeble one. But neither Pitt nor Roberts would risk it so late in the season, hinting at what had happened to Shackleton. Besides, they said, it was obvious that there was no Argentinean or German presence at Hope Bay. Maybe they should come back next season?

For the whole of the 8th and most of the 9th a thick sea-fog enveloped both vessels. Because of the presence of ice and the fear of drifting too close to the coast and striking submerged rocks, they headed gingerly out to sea, but lost touch with each other. It was not until late on the 9th that the *Scoresby* found the *Fitzroy*, having homed-in on the plaintive blasts of her ship's whistle.

By that stage, Marr's disappointment had turned into anger. Marchesi knew this was more likely to be worry than bad temper. With the military mission again uppermost in his mind, the leader of Operation Tabarin would be conscious of his orders. True, these had been formulated by people eight thousand miles away with only a marine chart to look at – people whose experience of ice probably extended to nothing more challenging than a village pond in January. But 'orders is orders' and Lieutenant-Commander Marr was a stickler for playing by the rules. He announced that he would cross over to the *Fitzroy* for a final attempt to persuade the men from the Falkland Islands Company. On returning, nostrils flaring, he told Marchesi that Pitt and Roberts had stuck resolutely to their decision.

"Tried to sell me some ridiculous scheme for trans-shipping all the stores into the *Scoresby* but I said that'd take weeks – mauling everything by hand. They knew it too."

"Listen, Jimmy, you'll make yourself ill if you don't stop worrying about it."

"Aye, but..."

"Commandeer their bloody boat then, if you feel that strongly about it. There *is* a war on, you know."

"I cannae do that. If anything happened, the whole damned island would be after my blood. They'd never co-operate ever again. Live with sheep – think like sheep; that's their problem."

"Well, let's find another location. A safer anchorage, so it won't upset the bloody Kelpers. Somewhere with a nice beach and a flat ledge above high water where you and your scientists can spend the winter doing your perishing research." Marchesi rooted around to extract the appropriate charts.

By the evening of the 10th, the two vessels had spent all day paralleling the Antarctic coast. Along the entire coastline, the mountainous land to the east descended sharply to the unbroken ice-shelf, a treacherous shore that offered no sign of a suitable site for their main base. Marr had grown increasingly despondent. Now, running short of both fuel and time before the close of the season, he and Marchesi could only see one option – the abandoned Port Lockroy.

London, 1982

The Club's handsome clock now registered 10:10 and Danny had almost resigned himself to spending a night on the floor of his office in St James's. He was on his third gin and tonic, whilst Vic was ahead of him by one large glassful.

"I seem to recall it was the following day, late afternoon, when we dropped anchor at Port Lockroy. I think we stayed for the best part of a week, sawing and hammering and off-loading stores and such. And a damned good job, too..." Vic leaned forward and tapped Danny on the knee. "We found another of those Argentinean copper cylinders – or maybe more than one – I can't quite remember now. And we had to paint over more of their flags."

"They'd been busy, then?"

"Yes, but no sign of Jerry, which was a blessing. Then, of course, Pitt and Roberts started grumbling about the onset of winter and the risk of getting crushed by the ice, so Jimmy gave us the signal to bugger off. I hoisted the anchor and we left him and his party there to get on with it." Vic leaned back again. "No sense in hanging around. In theory, the *Scoresby* could have stayed and done some hydrographic survey work, but she'd been laid up in the Falklands for too long and all the sounding gear had seized up. No point risking her down south, you see?"

"Was Commander Marr happier? I mean, to be starting on his experiments, and to be doing his best to fly the flag and so forth?"

"Well, he said so, but I wasn't so sure. When we got back to Stanley I had a word with the Governor – lovely man – what a sense of humour his parents must have had."

"Why?"

"Family name 'Cardinall' so they christened him Wolsey. Sir Wolsey Cardinall, see? Anyway, he agreed it might do Jimmy and the lads good to see my friendly face before the winter set in, so I sailed down again – twice, I think. I mean, like the Governor said: 'somebody had to empty the post box'".

With time against him, Danny wanted to move matters forward. "What date was this?"

"Mid-April, I think. A bit lucky with the final passage through the ice that year. But after that, everyone knew there'd be no more visits for six months, at least. Maybe seven."

"I'm guessing you spent the next six months carrying out patrols farther north?"

"Not straight away... Sailed to Montevideo for a refit."

Still knowing nothing about whatever tragedy festered at the back of Vic's mind, Danny prompted him again. "Oh... I thought you were about to tell me that was when you had your encounter with fate." But either Vic was unwilling to expand on what he had said, or he wasn't listening.

"After four and a half years of war, imagine what that was like – being in a city where the lights were on at night, where the Luftwaffe didn't come calling, where you could get a prime steak for under a shilling and dance all night for even less."

Nothing Danny had done or said so far seemed capable of hurrying Vic along, so he moved his right hand towards his left wrist and, with false unobtrusiveness, snatched a peek at his watch. As he had hoped, Vic noticed.

"Also," said Vic, "did I mention there was a *secret* aspect to Operation Tabarin? If I'd stayed too long down south, my old tub wouldn't have been available for that side of things."

(III)

Tuesday 2 May, 1944
Montevideo, Uruguay

Dressed in his 'going ashore' whites, complete with crisp collar and blancoed canvas shoes, Lieutenant Marchesi strolled into the British Embassy, duty-bound to offer his most courteous thanks to the staff for their help in soothing local sensibilities over the small matter of a depth charge that had rolled from the deck of the *Scoresby* and into the harbour.

The Embassy had only recently been elevated from the status of a mere mission or legation and, thereupon, the British Minister, Mr Gordon Medlicott-Vereker, had been raised to the rank of Ambassador. Marchesi, now clean-shaven, and with his oil-stained naval duffle coat stowed away for as long as he could comfortably get away with, cut a dashing figure. A naval uniform does something for a man.

In contrast with its southern neighbour, under military rule and suffering press censorship, Uruguay felt like a free country. Consequently, the place had become the focus of much Axis plotting, largely directed from the opposite side of the River Plate in Buenos Aires. Indeed, Montevideo had moved on from being a city in which German sailors from the crippled *Graf Spee* could mingle (on their best behaviour) with Jolly Jack, ashore from His Majesty's Ships *Ajax* and *Achilles*. The city was now, at least in part, a crucible in which spies, agents, envoys and bogus trade delegations from both sides bubbled to the surface, swilled around in the currents, and submerged again to allow their plots to ferment.

As Marchesi left Medlicott-Vereker's office and crossed the lobby, a young lady, perhaps not yet 25, stepped forward.

"You must be Captain Marchesi," she said.

"Hardly a captain," said Marchesi, pointing at the two bars on his epaulette. "Just a lieutenant, I'm afraid."

"Still, you're captain of your own ship, aren't you?"

"That's true, but it's stretching a point." Marchesi had already noticed her slight accent. Conscious that, in the words of the posters that had been plastered everywhere in Britain six months before, 'CARELESS TALK COSTS LIVES' he was determined to remain polite but reserved. It was a pity. He had not managed to meet many young ladies since arriving in the Falklands in January. "Are you here to see somebody?"

"No," she chuckled. It was immensely attractive. "I work here."

"Oh!" He recovered in a second. "Doing what?"

"Now, now," she said with a grin. "Careless talk costs lives." Then she turned and disappeared towards the Embassy basement, clearly on some essential errand.

The following day, Marchesi reappeared at the Embassy having cobbled together a despatch for transmission to the Admiralty. He and Marr had earlier agreed that the 12-pounder gun was more a liability than a necessity. His message asked for permission to remove it, together with its ammunition and most of his arsenal of depth charges. The signal explained that it made more sense to deny the South Atlantic's secret harbours to enemy shipping, especially if those harbours were on British territory. The proposal was to replace the weaponry with as many mines as could be carried – or at least the capability of doing so. By chance, Marchesi also managed to re-encounter the young lady. It was just after midday.

"Hello again, *Lieutenant* Marchesi."

"How nice to see you. The advantage is yours. I don't yet know your name."

"Nancy."

"Nancy." He smiled. "It's a beautiful day, Nancy, and it's lunchtime. I'm hungry, but my ship is a couple of miles away. I haven't the faintest idea where to find a decent restaurant in this town. May I buy you lunch?" That had probably been Nancy Hobsbawm's plan all along, so she accepted.

Victor talked about his early life in Belgravia, whilst Nancy spoke of how, two generations before, her forebears had arrived on the opposite side of town, in the East End. With one set of ancestors coming from Poland and another from Austria, and with Jewish blood warming her veins, she had every reason to detest the Nazis. In 1914, trade had taken her parents from London to Egypt, and when that enterprise failed, they moved to Vienna, where she had been born. When their father died, Nancy and her brother had moved to Berlin to stay with an uncle. But by 1933, and having always spoken English within the family, it became clear that it was time to leave for a city in which they would feel safe again. That meant London.

"Yet here you are in Montevideo. How? Why?

"Well you must have guessed from my accent that I also speak German."

"It's beautiful. Just a trace of Marlene Dietrich but not so husky."

"Vell, sank you," she replied as thickly as she could manage. "Let's just say I work as a translator."

Friday 9 June, 1944

The work of removing the 12-pounder gun had proceeded slowly, faltering under countless protestations of difficulty, and promises of *mañana* or *semana próxima*. That suited Marchesi. It was good to spend his free time with Nancy –

and anyway, whilst it was relatively balmy at Montevideo, the far southern hemisphere would now be locked fast in the bitter conditions of midwinter. Consequently, any thought of a re-supply voyage to Deception Island or Port Lockroy could be dismissed as impossible madness.

Following the Normandy landings, the war had taken on a new aspect. A different atmosphere prevailed in the Embassy, too; Uruguayans simply appeared off the street to wish Britain and the Allies well.

British newspapers arrived at the embassy sporadically, often grouped in bundles of several weeks at a time, but with frustrating gaps. With no schedule and no pressure, Marchesi enjoyed skimming through *The Times*, once key embassy staff had gleaned from its pages all that seemed relevant. Then an article attracted his attention. He asked for a meeting with Medlicott-Vereker.

"Just thought you ought to see this. *The Times*. 24th of April."

The Ambassador reached out and took the newspaper which Marchesi had folded to display the report. Under the heading of 'Antarctic Research', the report stated that '*The research party and administrative officials have already arrived...*' and that '*The party is expected to remain in the Antarctic for a long time.*' The article even named the leader, along with Marr's naval rank and also an outline map of the region.

"Politics and diplomacy aren't my strongest subjects, Ambassador," said Marchesi. "But any hopes of keeping Tabarin secret now are blown sky-high, aren't they?" Medlicott-Vereker appeared to be deciding how to respond. "What's happened? Has the censor been away on holiday or something?"

"No, Lieutenant, I doubt it. I think it's more likely to do with the franked mail that you landed a few weeks ago. If anything blew the existence of the expedition, that was it – letters to here, there and everywhere. They'd have found out about it in B.A. very quickly, and Berlin very soon after that."

"So this disclosure is deliberate?"

"Almost certainly. I imagine the Colonial Office must have decided to take the bull by the horns and just announce it... And be damned to what the Argentines think about it." He smiled. "And probably be damned to what the Foreign Office thinks about it too."

"I see." Marchesi would have felt happier to have been briefed with this information by the navy, rather than to have it interpreted by a diplomat.

The Ambassador handed the copy back to Marchesi, a potent way of signalling that the matter had been dealt with and the short interview could draw to a close. But not quite. "Are you worried about this? Is there anything I ought to know? As far as I've been told, Tabarin is a legitimate exercise in confirming British sovereignty, with a secondary mission to count penguins and that sort of thing. 'Possession is nine points of the law,' as the saying goes. Is there more to it?"

"If the navy hasn't told you anything, I don't think it's my place to say."

"I see." The Ambassador mused for a few seconds. "I'll get Nancy to look into it. Don't want to queer your pitch out of ignorance, do we?"

"Nancy? Look Ambassador, there's a top-secret angle to all this," said Marchesi, for the moment forgetting his obligation of silence. "Is she cleared? I mean, she told me she was just a translator."

"Fooled you, has she? She's rather good at her job, is our Nancy."

A couple of weeks drifted by. Willingly accepting the dockyard's excuses, and temporarily hindered from progressing either the war or British sovereignty in the South

Atlantic, Marchesi sought out Nancy. Together they would amble from the Playa Pocitos to the Playa Ramirez, or take a longer stroll west to the Playa de los Ingleses. Sometimes they headed north to jump aboard a tram to Independence Square where they could admire the palm trees and avoid thinking about the future.

Then, one day the Ambassador asked Marchesi to take a stroll with him around the Embassy gardens.

"Just in case my office is bugged, Lieutenant..." Marchesi appreciated the Ambassador's discretion. "I think I now understand the idea behind the other half – if I can put it like that – of your Operation Tabarin. And that report in *The Times* seems to me to have killed two birds with one stone."

"More clever than careless, then?"

"Yes – it should keep Argentina from misbehaving for a while. After all, if they turn up at one of your bases and start trying to muscle in, it could easily provoke the sort of incident that could put them at odds with one of the Allied Powers. In the middle of a war, that might lead them somewhere that they might wish to avoid."

"That's true. I hadn't thought of that."

"Then, there's the other angle. I've received a sealed, enciphered despatch, by courier." He coughed politely and raised an eyebrow. "I understand we may be reading one or two of the Nazis' coded messages. And I gather this may allow you to be, er... *accidentally* in the right place at the right time."

"If that's what you've been told, Ambassador."

"Yes. So, if it should become necessary, I've been alerted to give you every assistance."

London, 1982

10:40 p.m. Vic was making slow progress. In the diminishing hope of catching his train south, Danny had mentally paced out the walk to Victoria station. Maybe 20 minutes.

"September and October saw us back on station at Port Stanley," said Vic, "running in and out of sheltered inlets, ferrying the Governor about to visit remote settlements and so forth. Might have made the odd voyage out to South Georgia too, I think."

"But no enemy contact?"

"No, nothing. And of course, the weather and the ice down south were still against us, so the two bases just had to sit it out. Rather a shame. We'd started getting radio reports of one or two sickness problems and the odd personality clash. But like I say, there was nothing we could do about that."

The staff in the smoking room had begun to empty ashtrays and generally to clear up after their departing guests. One of the stewards came within a few yards of Danny's table and was polishing surfaces to remove the marks left by damp glassware. Danny was distracted for the moment, and now accepted that he would be spending the night in London. Time had ceased to have much relevance for him. Diverted, he strayed from the germane into the mundane.

"Did you get back to Montevideo again?"

"You mean, did I see Nancy again? Yes, dear boy. I proposed to her."

"Sorry, I wasn't prying..."

"And she turned me down. She'd had a bad time, poor girl. Lost both parents, always on the move, school in Germany. Brother more interested in history and politics than watching out for his sister. Not to mention all her hush-hush work in a couple of different embassies. No wonder she wasn't ready to tie the knot." Vic grasped his glass of gin, held it aloft to signal for another, and cast his eyes up to the ceiling. "She had this theory... Obviously she'd had more than enough of fleeing from megalomaniac fascists in one place, only to land in the middle of a bunch of communists in another. She reckoned she'd be safest in England – the one decent-sized country where she said a dictator could never take over."

It sounded like a curious proposition. Danny knew enough to steer clear of anything tainted with political controversy or religion in conversations with people of slight acquaintance. "I've never heard that one before," he said.

Again, clearly, Vic was not listening for he failed to expand on Nancy's theory. "That's when I asked her if she'd let me take care of her for the rest of her life... I forget how I phrased it. And she said something like this: 'When all this is over, I shall go back to England. When I get there, I hope to find a man with a safe job, who goes to work wearing a bowler hat. I shall forget that I'm Jewish. I'm going to pretend I was born into the Church of England. I shall become a member of the Conservative Party and wear white gloves and a hat with a veil. I shall drink tea from a china cup in the afternoon and...'."

Danny couldn't tell whether Vic had paused to enjoy a wistful memory or whether he was temporarily unable to speak. Each looked away from the other for a few moments before Danny prompted Vic to continue. "And?"

"And that's when she burst into tears, old chap. Did me no good at all."

Danny searched for something to say but the best he could manage was to make an observation about the way war prevents people from living normal lives. It was an obvious and unnecessary comment, but Vic seemed to be spending a few moments in a world of his own and hadn't noticed. Vic's reverie was broken by the arrival of the steward who announced that because they were just about to close the bar, he had mixed an extra-large gin and tonic. Fortified by this, Vic pushed his personal life to one side and continued.

"Well, things had started to get a bit dicey at Port Lockroy. In Port Stanley the Governor was already reading between the lines. For one thing, Jimmy was drinking more than was good for him, probably still stewing about not being able to set up the base at Hope Bay... So by the middle of November, Sir Wolsey suggested I should sail south in the *Scoresby* to see if I could bring in some fresh supplies and some mail from home – always cheers the lads up to get a letter or two, let alone six months' worth."

Danny grunted in agreement and Vic continued. "It was still a bit early in the season really, but we had to try... Then we encountered pack ice and had to turn back. That's when I got an urgent signal from Sir Wolsey saying I had to sail the *Scoresby* back to Port Stanley, full speed ahead, because he had orders for me... No other details, so I knew it was serious."

(IV)

Wednesday 22 November, 1944; 05:50 a.m.
Royal Naval Base, Port Stanley, Falkland Islands

Marchesi awoke to the voice of the *William Scoresby's* cook, whose left hand was shaking his shoulder and whose right hand held out a mug of tea. Behind him stood a uniformed Navy Regulator who stated that Lieutenant-Commander Martin and the Governor sent their compliments, and requested the urgent attendance of Lieutenant Marchesi at Naval Headquarters. Commander Martin had the privilege of being the Naval Officer-in-Charge of this backwater, perhaps the Admiralty's smallest overseas shore Station, HMS *Pursuivant.*

Lieutenant-Commander Martin had been on the retired list for six years, before re-enlisting at the start of hostilities. His small contingent of officers, telegraphists and medical staff largely went about their work without needing much direction from him. Until then, Martin had been happy for Marchesi also to go about his business in any way he liked – an arrangement which suited them both.

When Marchesi arrived, both waiting men wore grim expressions. Martin handed over a signal form and waited in silence while Marchesi read it. It didn't take long. Victor reversed the sheet of paper, found no further information printed on the back, then moistened his lips, and wafted the signal in the air, unintentionally demonstrating how flimsy he felt it to be, both physically and in content. The orders were clear enough. A German U-boat would be anchored at a given position for one week, starting in two days' time. His orders were to destroy the submarine and prevent its crew from making a rendezvous with any other vessel or person. That was as far as the orders went. He shrugged.

"Doesn't tell me much, does it, sir?" Martin clamped his jaw shut, as if to avoid agreeing. He matched Marchesi's shrug with one of his own. Victor pressed on. "I'll need to know a bit more than this if I'm going to come up with a reasonable plan."

Martin had no option but to respond. "Believe me – I see your point."

Marchesi noticed that Commander Martin had avoided eye contact, making him suspect that more lay behind this telegram. Perhaps the station commander had known about this potential operation for a number of days. If so, he should have appreciated the situation back then, and not left it to stew for four days without trying to find out more. He felt disappointed in his senior officer.

"Sir... That message you sent me on the 18th..." He brandished the present form. "Is this the reason you recalled me from down south?"

"Quite possibly, Victor, but I didn't know anything about any submarine back then. I was just told to get you back here straight away." He pointed to the paper in Victor's hand. "That message has only just arrived. Hence the panic."

"There's nothing else is there? You're not keeping anything from me?" Martin and the Governor exchanged glances.

"My dear chap," said the Governor. "Please believe me. We'd tell you anything we could."

"Could? What if you'd been ordered to keep something under your hat?"

Sir Wolsey appeared to realise he had strayed into someone else's territory and might be displaying too little respect for security. Torn between explaining what he really meant to have said and clamming up altogether, nevertheless he kept digging himself into his metaphorical hole. "Speaking personally, I'd at least find a way to give you a hint. My dear Victor, there aren't many of us on these islands, so we enjoy a great sense of family here. You, your ship, your crew – you're here to protect us. The islanders respect that. I know I speak for everyone when I say that we look on you as part of our family. And I wouldn't lie to my family." Sir Wolsey appeared to find this revelation somewhat stressful. He spread his arms and splayed his fingers, his palms facing Marchesi. "I'm really sorry. That signal... I don't know any more than Commander Martin."

"Well, there's one fundamental problem, sir," said Marchesi. "Why the *Scoresby*? Since our re-fit in Montevideo, we don't have any armament – not unless you count my Webley revolver – and not even John Wayne would attack a submarine with that. What makes my vessel their Lordships' first choice for this operation?"

"I'm afraid it's rather simple," said Martin. "Because you're here... Other than that tug lying alongside, there isn't another naval vessel to the west until you get to Kiwi. Or to the east until you get to Simonstown. It's you or nobody."

An idea appeared to occur to Sir Wolsey. "I expect the garrison would step forward with a platoon of riflemen, if that would help."

Marchesi still felt aggrieved. Although he could no longer accuse Martin of delay in passing on the message, the odds currently favoured Goliath rather than David. He needed a way to swing them in his favour. For a start, more information was needed.

"Thank you, Governor. I'll think about it. But I'm going to need a lot more to go on."

"Don't think we haven't tried, Lieutenant," said Martin. "If it was me, I wouldn't want to go steaming in there without knowing more. You're entitled to enough information to make a proper plan – something that has at least a chance of success. As soon as this came in, I asked, but I haven't had any response yet. Maybe it's a bit soon to expect anything, but I tell you – I've no idea what it's all about." He turned his head towards the Governor.

"Well, I suppose I could send one last cable to Montevideo and ask if they've got any more information. Cable from the Governor... might carry some weight."

Marchesi was well aware of the traditions of the service and was not about to question his orders – or at least, not too closely. At the same time, he didn't want to become famous for leading the navy's own Charge of the Light Brigade. He felt that he had placed an obligation on Martin and Sir Wolsey, and consequently was more in command of the situation than he had been when he first read his orders. It was also clear that despite the time pressure, much planning needed to be done. "Where is this bloody place, anyway? Have you had a look at the charts, Commander?"

Somewhat grumpily, Martin indicated that he wasn't so much of a novice that he couldn't handle the basics. He led the two over to a table in the corner of his office where he had laid out one of the broad scale charts of the Magellan Strait. "The position we've been given is roughly here." He jabbed a finger onto the chart. "Somewhere called Caleta Notch. North side of the Strait; Chilean waters, of course." He lifted his finger and allowed Marchesi half a minute to appreciate the overall location. "But I can be a lot more specific than that." A more particular chart had lain underneath the general one; he slid it out and placed it on top.

Marchesi craned forward over what was a composite chart showing several bays, inlets and other features in far greater detail. He also noted that the chart included an inscription to say that the original hydrographic survey of Caleta Notch had been carried out by HMS *Sylvia* in 1883. He bit back the comment that it was good to see that the Admiralty was keeping nicely up to date with its surveys. "What's a 'caleta'?"

"Spanish for 'cove', I think you'll find." Martin picked up a pair of brass dividers and indicated a point on the chart, where *Droggie* had printed a tiny anchor. "And the exact position that we've been given is right here, at the head of this blind inlet... or cove, as the locals would have it."

The word conjured up a vision of Cornish smugglers lurking in some hidden creek, waiting for dark before portaging their contraband inland. This romantic vision was quickly swept away by the growing list of issues. Marchesi could see from the symbols on the chart that Caleta Notch was shallow and riddled with kelp-beds. The angular passage in or out was so narrow that it would require many tight turns.

"...Not a job for a cruiser squadron, is it?"

This was not the Governor's field of expertise. "What do you mean, Victor?"

"Not much room... One of the earlier, shorter types of U-boat could make it. And so could the *Scoresby*. But anything much longer than about 200 feet might not have room to manoeuvre."

Although Marchesi ought to have been thinking about tactics, he couldn't stop himself wondering who or what could be important enough to bring a Nazi U-boat all the way to a concealed inlet in the bleakest and most uninhabited part of South America. With whom might any rendezvous take place? And why was this so significant that the Admiralty would order an unarmed ex-whale-marking research vessel – admittedly re-painted in grey and dignified by the letters 'HMS' – to destroy this enemy submarine? It felt unlikely that he would find out any time soon. He wondered how much Martin or the Governor knew about the covert side of Operation Tabarin. He also realised that to go further might end up with him breaching his own security, but if the matter was as serious as he believed, he needed to persuade them both to support him. There was no time for anything except a direct approach.

"Obviously you're both well aware of how Operation Tabarin was set up to resist Argentine claims here and in the Antarctic..." Rather than framing his words as a statement, Marchesi was inviting a response. He paused, receiving a nod from Sir Wolsey and a grunt from Martin. "But there was another aspect to it, too. I just wanted to know – how much did Jimmy Marr tell you about the secret side – the intelligence angle, if I can put it like that?"

"Oh, he dropped a few hints," said the Governor. "But I don't think he expected it to come to anything. And anyway, he said he'd be iced-in for seven or eight months and unable to do very much at all. I think he felt that any secret stuff was more likely to land on your plate, dear boy."

"How very generous of him," said Marchesi. "And accurate."

"Commander Marr did say your mission had something to do with being able to react to anything the intelligence boys might come across. Anything affecting our forgotten corner of the globe, I mean."

"Which is what's worrying me." Marchesi lit a cigarette, inhaled deeply and flapped the signal form again. "This position is so precise that the boffins must know a lot more than they're telling us. They absolutely *must* know the identity of this submarine, simply from call signs and intercepted position reports. That means they also know what type it is and how well-armed it is. They probably even know the name of the captain – and they're keeping quiet about the whole damned thing. Why, gentlemen? Why?"

"Honestly, I don't know."

"But you can see how important it is for me to know what I'm up against. If I'm to carry out these orders, I need to attack the bastard where he's weakest."

"Yes, Victor, of course."

"And this business about a rendezvous... How am I supposed to stop it if I don't know what I'm looking for? Is Argentina about to enter the war on Hitler's side? Is it some senior Nazi going into hiding to save his own skin? I need to know."

"Maybe they don't think you do. Maybe it's all bound up in that one word – 'destroy'. If you destroy this sub and everyone in it, I suppose they think it'll solve the problem."

"Maybe so, but I'd still like to know as much as possible about that U-boat."

"I think we've got to stop worrying about that." Martin's assessment was timely. "Assume we're on our own and they aren't going to tell us anything. Have you had any thoughts about how to sink this bugger?"

Progress! Martin had started using words like 'we' and 'us'. Given time, he might even ask to tag along. "Well obviously gunnery is out. We haven't got one. And the *Scoresby* can't launch torpedoes..."

"Which can't negotiate round corners anyway..."

"So that means I'm pretty much stuck with either an overland attack, or mines. That was the whole idea behind removing that useless 12-pounder – to carry enough mines to deny the enemy access to coastal waters and anchorages around British dependencies." Marchesi noticed that at the word 'mines' Commander Martin had started fiddling with papers on his desk. "I was just wondering... Have you received that shipment of mines that they promised to send?" He failed to stop it sounding like an accusation.

Martin shook his head. Never was there a clearer illustration of the maxim that one is forced to fight the current battle with what is available at that instant, rather than what might become available a week, a month or a year into the future.

"So, what you're trying to avoid telling me is this: There are no magnetic mines... No acoustic mines... Not even any limpet mines... Just your dwindling supply of pre-war Mark XVII contact mines, complete with – to coin a phrase – horns, lines and sinkers."

"I tried. 'Other priorities,' they said."

Marchesi turned his back on the Commander, hung his head and sighed.

The Governor allowed a few seconds to pass, as if waiting to see who might start shouting first. "Shall I contact the garrison then, and see if they can find us an infantry platoon?" No doubt he meant it as the most peace-making intervention in the present predicament.

Marchesi rounded on Sir Wolsey. "No, you bloody won't." At least this outburst would avoid the certainty of a charge of insubordination from Martin, for whom his next words were clearly intended. "I'll tell you who to contact. I want to speak to C-in-C South Atlantic at the Cape. If you can't get hold of him, try the America and West Indies Station in Bermuda. I want to speak to their expert on Mark XVII mines. I want whoever-it-is to appreciate I've got to blow a submarine to blazes, along with everyone on it, as the damned thing comes out of a shallow inlet at whatever time of day or night or state of the tide. I want him to tell me how to lay a trap with the entire stock of sea mines at HMS *Pursuivant* – what was it? Just half a dozen the last time I looked – so I can blow this U-boat into nothing but nuts and bolts."

For the second time that day, Martin and the Governor exchanged significant looks.

"I'm afraid that won't be possible, Victor," said the Governor.

"Why not?"

"Because neither of us has a direct link to anywhere." Emphasis on 'anywhere'. "There used to be an undersea cable to Uruguay years ago, but Cable and Wireless lifted it and re-used it somewhere else." He tried to smile. "The Empire rubbed us off its map a long time ago. All my messages, in and out, are sent by hand – dots and dashes, via the embassy in Montevideo. You'll appreciate it's not so easy to have a conversation in Morse code."

"Same procedure for naval signals," admitted Martin.

"Bloody hell... So, if I understand what you're telling me, there's no chance either of you can get me a telephone call to anywhere, let alone naval headquarters?"

"I believe there's a signals detachment with the regiment, Victor. But even then, I think all their messages are Morse as well. No radiotelephones as far as I know."

Marchesi breathed out with a hiss, forced to accept that with the deadline collapsing around him, his only hope of gaining some advantage lay in messages relayed through the embassy in Montevideo. He felt bad about his outburst at the Governor. "I'm sorry, sir. All the same, will you try for me?"

"Certainly, Victor. As hard as I can."

Martin had crossed the floor of his office and opened the door. He called out. "Hodge! Come in here a minute."

A few seconds later, from outside, a hand grasped the doorframe for support, followed by the head and shoulders of a Petty Officer Telegraphist, as he canted his body round the woodwork. "Sir?"

"Hodge... Lieutenant Marchesi has an urgent signal for Vice-Admiral Burnett at the Cape. Let him dictate it to you. Code it up and radio it as fast as you can. Highest priority. And make them understand you're keeping the circuit open for an urgent answer." Martin turned to Marchesi. "For all of 1941 and into '42 Bobby Burnett was Rear-Admiral in charge of minelayers. He's been promoted to C-in-C South Atlantic now. If he can't help or can't find anyone who can, I don't know what to think."

Returning from the relative luxury of Commander Martin's office to the severe austerity of the *Scoresby*, Marchesi mooched along the main deck and climbed the external ladder to his chartroom, deep in thought. But one thought would not leave his head. It was not about the submarine or its precise position, or even how to get there and what to do when he arrived. His attacking options were very limited indeed, and consequently rather simple. No; it involved a far bigger picture. Marchesi knew enough about the handling of naval intelligence to realise how imperative the whole escapade must be. Because if HMS *William Scoresby* turned up at the exact same time and place as a secret German submarine mission, a place so remote that it might as well be on the moon, there would be consequences. It would confirm to the enemy that none of his encrypted signals were safe. The Kriegsmarine would know as an absolute certainty that their codes were broken. And in that case, they would surely implement their Plan B, whatever that was, and the Allies would remain in the dark for weeks, months or possibly years until the cryptanalysts cracked the way back in again. That could only mean that it was so utterly crucial to the Allied war effort to prevent the rendezvous, that to achieve success they would risk revealing their ability to read Hitler's encrypted messages. Whatever it was, he feared it must be something that lay beyond his imagination or experience. He shivered as though the blade of an ice-cold razor had sliced from the nape of his neck to the base of his spine. Enough. He shook his head to snap himself back to reality.

Marchesi unrolled the Caleta Notch chart, placing brass weights on the corners to prevent it curling up again. Idly, he wondered about the name. 'Notch.' It sounded like the sheltered bay took its name from some jagged slice set into a local hillside, perhaps visible as vessels crossed the bar at the entrance to the cove. And, noticing again the reference to HMS *Sylvia*, the hidden truth of a saying that he had heard countless times before, tumbled into his mind.

Though alone, he announced in his normal speaking voice, "Victor, no matter how hard you try, it seems you'll never get away from *Droggie*."

Hydrographic surveys... Some spent their lives carrying them out. Others inched across a chart, straying from one side to the other of some grimy pencil-line, relying on the accuracy of work carried out perhaps sixty years before. It was simple. You sailed to a spot where fate lay waiting for you. There, in a moment of terror and confusion, you and a whole boat-load of your mates either got blown to bits, or tried to inflict defeat on others. If with luck you managed to cling to life, there was a chance that one of *Droggie's* surveyors would have had a hand in some aspect of it.

"Well, orders is orders, dear boy," he added and, oddly, felt better for it.

Marchesi went back to the general chart covering the tip of South America and east to the Falklands. Placing his thumb and middle finger at the side of the chart, he opened them up to span two degrees of latitude – a hundred and twenty nautical miles – and roughly stepped off the distance from Port Stanley to his destination. Six spans. Allow a little extra for a bit of rock-dodging to get from the open ocean into the Magellan Straits, maybe 750 miles. They would be lucky to make 10 knots; 75 hours. They'd also have the current against them. Best estimate – three and a half days on passage.

Marchesi called his officers together in the chart room.

"Pilot," he said to the sub-lieutenant in charge of navigation, "We've got a job to do." He placed his finger on the plan of Caleta Notch. "Plot me the fastest course to this position. I want to come south round Cape Horn unless it's blowing worse than force nine and as long as we haven't got a short, steep swell on the beam. I suggest we use the cover of this southern pass, Canal Cockburn, to close with the enemy."

"Aye-aye, Number One." A disciplined response and no questions.

Marchesi looked up from the chart into the faces of his officers. "I did say 'enemy'. We've been ordered to stop playing postman for a few days. This is real." He turned to the engineer. "Chief, I want you to go to two hours' readiness. Sound the whistle every five minutes until everybody's back on board, then come down to an hour's readiness. I'm going over to see the Governor again." Addressing his radio operator, "Sparks, you're coming too."

At Government House, Sir Wolsey introduced Marchesi to an infantry lieutenant who offered an armed section of eight volunteers, under a corporal. Victor accepted, hoping that the soldiers would all have strong stomachs.

"Thank you for fixing that, Governor. You probably know the saying, 'know your enemy'. So anything you can find out from Montevideo about that submarine or its mission... You will get Commander Martin to pass it on, pronto, won't you?"

"I've given you my word, Victor. I meant it. I'll do my best to persuade the embassy that you need to know every bit of information that they've got."

Victor nodded. "Understood, sir."

If the vessel's departure had not been so urgent, an awkward silence might have descended as Governor and naval officer tried to find ways of avoiding the obvious issue that they might never see each other again. But Sir Wolsey merely assumed an encouraging expression and, as if the only danger that Marchesi faced was equivalent to missing a train, he brought matters to a close.

"You'd best be off now."

Marchesi took one pace to the rear, saluted, added a formal "Aye aye, sir," and left.

At HMS *Pursuivant*, Marchesi and Martin were making arrangements with the Chief Petty Officer (Supply) in charge of naval stores, for his entire stock of mines to be loaded immediately aboard the *Scoresby*. Marchesi had been right. There were only six. The talk turned to radio communications.

"You'll need to maintain radio silence, I suggest," said Martin. "Petty Officer Hodge is probably working out a blind-broadcast schedule with your lad right now. Anything we receive, we'll bang it out to you several times a day."

"Thanks. My sparks is pretty keen. But if necessary I'll glue his headphones to his ears." A second thought: "Anything you send, you'd better code it up on my one-time cipher-pad."

"I expect Hodge has already thought of that..." But the opportunity to check Hodge's plans occurred within the next half minute, when there came the sound of running feet and cries to attract their attention.

Hodge arrived breathless. He handed a signal form to Martin. "From Vice-Admiral Burnett, sir..." Martin took the page and motioned Marchesi alongside him. The two stood shoulder to shoulder to read the message, as if sharing a hymnbook.

Marchesi finished first and turned to the CPO (Supply). "Well Chief, the admiral wants to know if you've got any remote detonator units to replace these Herz horns?"

"No sir. None of that fancy kit here."

"In that case, I think you'd better add at least two miles of half-inch steel cable, enough shackles and bulldog grips to fill a couple of 50-gallon drums, and as much timber as you can lift aboard before I leave in half an hour... If you'd be so kind." The CPO looked at Martin.

"You heard the officer. Make it so, Chief. And make it snappy."

"I'll have a rummage and see what we've got, sir."

(V)

Friday 9 April, 1982
London

Victor had excused himself for a few minutes, giving Danny the opportunity to move around the smoking-room, encouraging the blood to flow properly again in his legs. It was after midnight and the stewards had departed, leaving the bar's shutters lowered but with the lights glowing dimly behind. Danny ambled to a window overlooking Pall Mall. London was still relatively busy, mostly with taxis. There had also been a sprinkling of rain, leaving blots of reflected orange light spaced along the street.

The panelled door made a drawn-out squeak as Victor returned. He came halfway across the room and called out, "Where had I got to, dear boy?"

"You'd just left Port Stanley heading for Cape Horn."

"So I had." Victor mused for a moment, then stepped forward to stand at the window with Danny. "When you were at sea, did you ever sail round the Horn?"

"Only once. As a first-tripper, actually. The lads had built it up – trying to scare me. I suppose they thought it'd be a laugh, the buggers. Only the laugh was on them. It was flat calm. It snowed, though. One of the few times I ever remember it snowing, actually out at sea."

"Well if you've been round the Horn, Danny, that makes you a proper sailor." Victor grinned and gave Danny a playful slap on the back. "Officially allowed to put your elbows on the table." Danny gave a weak smile. Putting one's elbows on the table was a maritime myth, a playful saying only understood by people who had spent some time at sea. However, having started on nautical jargon and traditions, Victor returned for a few moments to old habits.

"We needed to crack on. I told the Chief to pull out all the stops, and sit on the safety valves to stop them blowing."

Danny bounced back with another long-standing sailors' joke. "Did you tell him to be careful not to break the elastic band?" It made Vic chortle. Once he had Vic's attention again, Danny drew him back to the subject. "Did the message from the Admiral tell you anything new?"

"Not at that point, no. Just a load of hints. Meant to be helpful, but I'd already worked out what I was going to do. I mean, I'd been a subbie, RNR, since 1935, and promoted lieutenant in the navy-proper since January '38. I was nearly 31 by then, and pretty much on top of my game."

"In your prime."

"I suppose you could say that, dear boy. Like I told you, I'd spent a few years on minesweepers. I knew what it was all about. What I wanted from Bobby Burnett was some insight into why I'd been ordered to sink that bloody submarine – some titbit that might give me an advantage. What I didn't want was him telling me how to lay a few vintage mines. It was stuff every two-ringer should have known anyway."

"Presumably he didn't come up with anything useful?"

"Not right away, so I got busy planning. For one thing, I knew I ought to land the soldiers as close as possible so they could march overland and outflank any Jerry sailors that might have been put ashore from this U-boat. I reckoned I'd identified the ideal spot."

"After you'd landed the soldiers, what then?"

"What Burnett wanted me to do was to mine the entrance to Caleta Notch, leaving Fritz either bottled up or blown up. I seem to remember the navy changed the plan a bit at the last minute. My job was to buy some time – to stop Fritz escaping while Burnett sent a proper force to deal with him. Not too many other options. It was either that or nothing."

"Did it stop you asking questions?"

"By then, pretty much. Ours not to reason why... And he was an admiral, after all."

"I can see why you might have wanted to hold back." Danny noticed that his host had started patting his pockets – probably searching for his cigarettes. "Tell me about laying your minefield then, Vic."

Distracted, Victor leaned forward, his palms on the windowsill, and peered through the raindrops on the windowpane, out into the night. "First thing I did was to get busy with my ruler and the chart and measure the exact width of the entrance channel. I remember it was very narrow, probably only about 350 feet between the rocks on either side. The chart showed six fathoms over the bar, I think. Obviously, with the channel shelving at either end, I probably only needed to mine the middle section – say 200 feet – to be safe."

"I'm with you so far."

"The whole thing relied on spanning the channel with a net, with my mines attached to it, and the sinkers resting on the bottom, maybe only a fathom lower. If he tried to leave, I hoped Fritz would snag the net with the hydroplanes or his rudder, drag it over the mines and bend one of the horns. Or maybe bump one of the shallower mines along the bottom till one of them blew. The idea was for it to set off a chain reaction."

"You didn't mention getting hold of a net from naval stores at Port Stanley."

"No, dear boy. We were going to make one. That was what all that steel cable was for."

Danny might have expected the Royal Navy to show some ingenuity in wartime, but had not anticipated a project on this scale. He asked Vic how one went about making a steel net. Vic explained that the first stage was to chop the wire into ten-foot lengths. Next, for each length, you would clamp the two ends together with a six-inch overlap using a couple of bulldog grips. This made a loop three feet across, and by inter-linking the loops the net would grow.

Eventually the crew had daisy-chained over 400 steel circles, constructing a net 65 to 70 loops wide by 6 deep. Although the process was simple, it was time-consuming too. Vic seemed proud of his net, some 200 feet in length and three fathoms from top to bottom. His design then called for the dockyard timber to be lashed to the top of the net for buoyancy to keep it upright, with the whole assembly weighted at either end to keep the bottom on the sea bed. Vic said that if the chart was still accurate and if he had done his sums correctly, the top of the net should have come to rest a mere 5 feet below the surface.

"And the mines? These were contact mines, right? Things with horns?"

"Ah, the mines, dear boy. That's a bit of a specialist subject." At that moment Victor found his pack of cigarettes and took a moment to light up, drawing in deeply. "You see, in a normal minefield you don't want to lay your mines too close to one another. If you aren't careful, they tend to countermine." Danny looked puzzled. "What I mean is, if one goes off, they all go off. If that happened, say in the Channel or a North Sea minefield, some poor sailors would have to go out and re-lay the whole thing. It's a bit of a bore because if the enemy spots them, he shoots at them with everything he's got. It's not popular with the men."

"I can understand that."

"About 120 feet between mines is a reasonably safe distance to stop the whole minefield blowing up in one go. Only what I was going to do was string five of them to my net, maybe thirty or forty feet apart. The first mine that got triggered would set off all the others. One hell of a big bang. And because of the shallow water, the explosive pressure would be reflected off the bottom and do even more damage. Throw the U-boat about a lot; cracked skulls, broken legs – hard to escape."

"Yeah," said Danny. No response could properly reflect the mental image.

"Five mines, dear boy. I reckoned that should just about have settled Fritz's hash."

"But you said you had six..."

Friday 24 November, 1944; 07:37 a.m., local time
HMS William Scoresby

Marchesi needed to leave one watchkeeper free to assist with general duties, and supervise the net-making. His solution was to split the bridge watchkeeping into a regime of six hours on and six off. He took the 06:00 to 12:00 and the 18:00 to midnight watches.

Cape Horn (actually the southern tip of an island) lay a bare two miles to his north on the starboard side. When Marchesi felt the Cape was abeam and at the closest point of approach, he directed the helmsman to apply a touch of starboard rudder to bring the course around to 276°. The sea was choppy and confused. There appeared to be two swells, one from the southwest and another from the southeast. With that to handle, plus a strong current from the west, he reckoned they would find it difficult to make even as much as nine knots.

The pencil line on the chart continued to the next course alteration, 70 miles ahead, followed by a final run of 127 miles which would bring the *Scoresby* to the difficult but time-saving passage into the Cockburn Channel. Marchesi had already worked out that they should arrive at the mouth of the channel as the next day began. Luck was on his side; they would benefit from daylight for the whole of Saturday to worm their way between the rocks and headlands, a thing he would not have attempted in the dark, no matter how urgent the task.

The Yorkshire corporal seemed a good sort. His view was that he needed to keep his men busy – 'there's nowt so gawky as an infantryman wi' bugger all to do' – so he had volunteered his squaddies to help with the net-making. They all seemed happy enough with this pastime and probably regarded the sea cruise as a bit of an adventure.

The *Scoresby's* assistant steward appeared on the open bridge with a mug of tea and a couple of rounds of toast for Marchesi and the helmsman. Cape Horn never looked very special, even in the best of weather. However, that morning, soldiers, able seamen, the cook, and the stokers from the engine room found time to lean on the starboard rail watching this rarely-seen landmark slip astern.

Saturday 25 November, 1944;
The Admiralty

In view of the drama that might unfold in Chilean waters at any moment, none of the significant naval officers felt it right to be anywhere other than the U-boat plotting room; nobody had much appetite for food. At around lunchtime a signal, with the accompanying translation, arrived by messenger. It appeared that Claussen had declined to enter Caleta Notch until daylight.

"I'd do the same if it was me," said Cunningham. "I'd want a bloody good look inside before I'd risk my ship in a place like that."

Winn held out his hand for the signal. "Floradora again," he said after examining the preamble. "If it wasn't for Montevideo, we'd be up the creek." He thought for a few seconds. "This still means we haven't found the radio frequency of Claussen's new crystals."

Rushbrooke leaned over and gripped the corner of the signal form to read for himself. "And the timing still means we're maybe 15 hours behind the action."

The admirals put their hands in their pockets and wandered away, shoulders hunched.

A tray of tea and biscuits arrived in mid-afternoon. At almost the same time, the messenger appeared again with another Floradora signal, this time from Berlin. It directed Claussen to lose no time in landing the copper cylinder, the passengers and a party of sailors to act as guards. Berlin ordered Claussen to then leave Caleta Notch, and to advise the date and time for a rendezvous at sea, when he could pick up the party of interned crewmen, survivors of the late *Graf Spee*.

"Confirmation," said Rushbrooke. "I don't think we're going to get any better clue as to what the cargo is, or was. If it's contained in a copper cylinder it's got to be dangerous." He tried to catch Cunningham's eye. "I think we guessed right. Hitler's getting desperate. This is Nazi Germany resorting to chemical warfare. What's behind this is a filthy scheme to transfer the whole manufacturing and deployment process to the Japs. We were right to act."

"I agree," said Winn. "Though I'd argue it was more detective work than guesswork. I suggest we need to spend a few minutes working out Claussen's options and what we're going to do about them."

"No." All eyes turned towards Cunningham. "This doesn't need a ruddy committee. It's quite clear. One – I don't want Jolly Jack messing with that cylinder and trying to open it, or shooting off bullets anywhere near it, otherwise we'll have a lot of dead sailors to worry about. Two – I don't want the damned thing brought home, otherwise we'll have a whole lot more explaining to do. I want it dropped in the 'oggin, forgotten about and our chaps out of there faster than greased weasel shit off an icy shovel. Three – I want Caleta Notch mined just like Bobby Burnett recommended. And four – if there's any explaining to do I want all the fingers pointing at Jerry, and no sign that we've been anywhere near the bloody place."

And it was quickly apparent from the lack of alternative suggestions that this was exactly what everyone else wanted, too.

"Captain Winn... Be so good as to signal the *Scoresby* to that effect," said Cunningham.

Sunday 26 November, 1944; 02:45 a.m.
HMS William Scoresby;

Marchesi had stayed on the bridge beyond the end of his watch. With great care, and a leadsman standing on the main deck of the *Scoresby*, calling out soundings from just below the bridge, he had conned his vessel through Canal Cockburn and Canal Magdalena into the more open waters beyond. The problem was that it had taken all day and now darkness had fallen. In the confined channel leading northwest, and under thick cloud without a hint of moonlight, farther progress seemed foolhardy.

Marchesi had selected a long, narrow, fjord-like inlet, hoping to land the corporal and his men as close as possible to its head. Although the chart of the inlet showed adequate depth, he was worried about being observed from any habitation, as well as the natural fear of navigating in restricted waters with outdated charts. Landing the soldiers would have to wait until dawn. Nobody slept.

The wireless operator appeared at Marchesi's elbow. "Coded signal, sir. Blind broadcast from Port Stanley."

“Thank you, dear boy.” It could be urgent. He turned to the officer whose watch it rightly was. “Keep a sharp lookout. I’m going below for a few minutes.”

Fifteen minutes later, Marchesi had deciphered the message. Urgent indeed. The Admiralty was panicking because the Nazi U-boat was about to put to sea; there was no time to lose. To hell with night time caution. The *Scoresby* would have to mine Caleta Notch first and land the soldiers afterwards. There was, however, a curious postscript to the signal.

> IF CAPTAINS PROPOSAL REMAINS AS
> PREVIOUSLY STATED COMMA KINDLY
> CONSIDER OPERATION BOWLER HAT
> CANCELLED STOP

Marchesi had decided to brief the whole crew and the soldiers all together on the main deck. He emphasised that, despite the risks that currently kept them drifting in the middle of the Magellan Strait, circumstances had changed and the plan must change with them. Each man had an important part to play. From the leadsman taking soundings, to the doubling of the lookouts, to the stokers keeping the screw turning, every man must attend to his duty, as Nelson would have expected. The men made affirmative noises.

Collectively, the officers and crew had worked out a plan. The derricks would now be rigged, the mines and their sinkers would be attached to the net, the net would be suspended beneath the derricks and swung out on the starboard side, and the spare wire that had not been used in making the net would be used at each end to weigh it down and anchor it to the sea bed amongst the kelp.

“Is every man clear about what he has to do?” There came a chorus of aye-ayes. “Then get to your stations, and it’ll be ‘Slow Ahead’ as soon as you’re ready, Chief.”

Marchesi beckoned the corporal towards him. "I'd like your best bren gunner on the bridge with me, if you'd be so kind."

But despite his show of confidence, Victor felt the timings were against him. The *Scoresby* had stopped engines for safety at a place where the strait was 8 or 9 miles wide. However, Caleta Notch still lay some 40 miles ahead. Even if he dared to surge along in the dark at 5 knots until dawn and then a reckless 10 knots until they reached the entrance to the cove, they could not arrive before, say, 7:30 in the morning. His best hope was that the Germans might stop to enjoy a leisurely breakfast before gingerly manoeuvring their vessel out of Caleta Notch. It was, after all, a Sunday. Perhaps Jerry might rig church in the open air and sing a few hymns before putting to sea.

The difficulty of navigating in the Magellan Strait, with its heavily-indented coastline and lack of buoys marking the channel, was soon apparent. A wide inlet to port or starboard might easily be mistaken for the main waterway. It was only Marchesi's skills, gained from feeling his way around the Antarctic peninsula, coupled with his hydrographer's qualification and a considerable amount of dead reckoning, that kept the *William Scoresby* moving in the right direction. His 7:30 estimate proved to be a good one.

The morning mist that dulled the focus of the land to the west, on the Pacific side of the strait, also muted the colours of the coastline to the east, on the *Scoresby's* starboard side. By then, Marchesi had brought his vessel close to the landward side of the strait, with its precipitous terrain. Everywhere, patches of exposed and fissured grey rock burst through the low vegetation of ferns and tussock grass.

The bren gunner offered his assessment. "It's just like fookin' Scotland," he said.

Crossing the wide opening of an inlet running from north to south gave Marchesi confidence that they were where he hoped they were. He turned to the steward, deputised to act as his messenger.

"Pass the word. All hands to standby. Silence all round. Five minutes to the objective. It's just around the next headland."

A strangled expletive rose from the main deck. The leadsman scurried aft tugging at his line, then reappeared below the bridge, shrugging, holding up the coil of rope, minus the weight.

"Must've got snagged up in the kelp, sir!"

Marchesi cursed, knowing he should have made sure there was a second line handy; now there was no time to make a replacement. He would just have to rely on the soundings printed on the chart. "Lend a hand with the net, then," he called. He looked down at the chart and had a moment to read the legend again. Through his teeth, he hissed what might yet become his epitaph. "You'll never get away from *Droggie*." In 1883 on HMS *Sylvia*, Captain Wharton's leadsman must have either fixed his weight with a more seamanlike knot or encountered less kelp.

Marchesi ached to take over the ship's wheel, but he knew he couldn't do everything himself. He couldn't take bearings of the rocks on either side of the cove, transfer the data into a position on the chart, read off soundings from it and choose the right moment to begin lowering the net into the water. He rang 'Dead Slow Ahead', then ordered 10 degrees of starboard helm to bring the *Scoresby's* head round to the north, aiming to place his vessel closer to the shore before laying his mines across the rocky jaws of the inlet.

The steep angle at which the coastal hills plunged into the water gave Marchesi confidence that he could make a close approach to the shore. Looking ahead over the bows, he estimated his vessel was now only 300 feet from land. He ordered 20° of port helm and waited for the rudder to bite. From his time on the *Scoresby* he felt that, like many shallow-draft vessels, her rudder was too small; at Dead Slow she always took her time to start turning. He placed a hand on the engine room telegraph, hoping he had not misjudged, reluctant to order 'Stop Engines' and then 'Half Astern'. He craved a cigarette. Then she began to swing.

"Bring her back to port ten." The bows continued their lazy swing to port. A low islet lay off the port bow, perhaps 800 feet distant. Now the *Scoresby* seemed to be moving to port less quickly. "Midships." The islet became clearer, with its covering of yellowy grass and a sparse green ground-cover of stunted bushes and brushwood. From the chart, the 20-fathom line lay perhaps 300 feet to the seaward side of the islet, but Marchesi needed to bring the *Scoresby* closer. The ten-fathom line lay only 150 feet to seaward, yet they needed to come even closer than that.

Marchesi spoke to the bren-gunner. "See anything?"

"Nowt as I can see, Captain. Happen the buggers ain't up yet."

Marchesi leaned over the canvas side of the open bridge and called down to the sailors gripping the ropes and other implements on the main deck. "All hands, stand by. Thirty seconds." Then to the helmsman. "I'll take the wheel." He had studied the chart until an image of the entrance to Caleta Notch was burnt into his mind. Everything had been worked out to lay the net on the 5-fathom line that ran from near the tip of the grassy islet, across the mouth of the cove, and then to seaward of a bank of mud and gravel.

With everyone clustered on the *Scoresby's* starboard side, coupled with the weight of the net and the mines hanging out beyond, the vessel had taken a gentle list to starboard. But everyone standing there had a perfect view into the bay behind the headland: a perfect view of the multiple peaks, still with patchy snow at their summits, smudged in low cloud. A perfect view of the grey rocks and the moorland colours, and of the landslips where the gradient of the escarpment was just too sheer to allow the thin soil to cling on. In the bay there were further, bigger islets, probably moraines left perhaps ten-thousand years earlier, after the glacier had retreated. Taller bushes and wizened trees fought for life on those mounds, sheltered a little from the winter wind and daily squalls that whipped through the Strait.

"Where the hand of man has never set foot," said the bren gunner in a stage whisper. "Not a Jerry nowhere to be seen."

Marchesi leaned over and called out loud to the men below. "On my command, lay on." A five second pause. "Lay on!" He desperately hoped that the reason no Germans were to be seen was not the obvious one, that the U-boat had left already.

The hands jumped into action. It had been impossible to rehearse what needed to be done, but each man seemed to know his part and be dedicated to playing it. The first coil of wire rope slipped into the water. They lowered the derrick, so that the first mine, still tightly fixed to its sinker, touched the water. It bobbed twice before descending from sight. The drag as pleats of steel net began to peel away from their fixings worked as Marchesi had hoped, helping the net to unfold. He eased the wheel to starboard to follow the curve of what he hoped would be the 5-fathom line. For a second or two, the baulks of timber remained afloat until the weight of net and mines carried them under water.

Now the *Scoresby* had arrived in mid-channel. Midships, the wheel; nothing to starboard. The central mines – those to be laid more deeply – hung from longer tails of steel net. Bloody Bobby Burnett. The admiral had made sure of getting his spoiler in. Back at Port Stanley, his message had said:

DUE SHALLOW DEPTH ESSENTIAL
YOU LAY MINES THAT REMAIN SUNK
AT SLACK WATER STOP DO NOT LAY
MINES IN POSITION THAT RISKS
THEM SURFACING AT SLACK WATER
WHEN CABLE WILL DIP AND RENDER
THEM VISIBLE AND AVOIDABLE
STOP

Marchesi had done his best, but with the sounding gear seized solid, a chart that could be 60 years out of date, a one-fathom tidal range over a 5-fathom bar, and the fact that he was laying mines on the coast of a neutral nation, he rather wished the admiral had kept his comments to himself. They seemed less designed to be helpful than to shift the blame if things went wrong. He eased the wheel to port, noticed the proximity of the gravel bank ahead, and made it port 15 degrees. On the bank a pair of long-beaked wading birds concentrated on picking their way along the shoal probing for molluscs, and ignored the *Scoresby*. Smaller birds scuttled along like clockwork toys, pecking at whatever might help them survive.

The final coil of wire slid into the water. Marchesi gave it a few seconds to avoid fouling his propeller with his own net, then spun the wheel further to port to bring the *Scoresby* into deeper water. He looked back at the entrance to Caleta Notch and saw not a trace of net or timber; no mines had broken free. He rang the telegraph for 'Half Ahead' and invited the helmsman to resume his labours.

"Keep her in the middle of the channel, heading southeast." Then he turned to the bren-gunner. "You'd better get back to your mates. You'll be going ashore in about 90 minutes."

London, 1982

Danny had ceased caring what time it was. "Vic... You glossed over something and it's been worrying me. What happened to that sixth mine? Was it just a dud?"

"Oh, don't worry about that, dear boy."

"If you say so... But this Nazi U-boat hadn't left Caleta Notch at all, had it?"

"No, it hadn't."

"What were you going to do if you met it?"

"Well, I hoped we wouldn't. But you know what they say – 'hope for the best, prepare for the worst'."

"If the worst had happened, what would you have done?"

"Oh, for a start we were flying a Chilean courtesy ensign, which we were obliged to do, being in their waters. Naturally these U-boat chappies might be a bit surprised to see us, all painted grey. But we didn't look like a warship. We looked like a survey vessel, which is what the *Scoresby* had been. And of course, we weren't armed."

"But they were."

"And they had no more right to be there than we did. I hoped they'd spot the courtesy ensign, feel a bit guilty and ask themselves how it might look if they opened fire on a Chilean survey vessel operating in home waters. Germany and Chile weren't at war. There'd be no point in provoking a diplomatic incident, possibly forcing Chile to declare for the Allies."

"Weren't you flying a white ensign at the stern as well? Wouldn't they have seen that?"

"Well it was certainly... er... on view, so to speak. But I seem to recall it might have got a bit knotted up in its halyard and tangled round the staff. And there's red, white and blue on the Chilean flag too, so... Hard to tell them apart if they've got a bit wrinkled."

Danny smirked. "You tricky old devil..."

Victor turned away from the window and looked back at the comfortable armchairs. "I think I need to sit down for a bit."

Danny stood aside to let Victor go first and added, conversationally, "I guess you still had to get the troops ashore?"

"Yes. I mean, that bit went without a hitch. A place called 'Canal Condor' just round the corner, so to speak. I remember thinking, as we said goodbye to them, 'Condor'. A name like that – it must have been hard for Hitler's planners to resist using the place as their rendezvous. You know – they were great ones for calling some secret base the 'Eagle's Nest' or the 'Wolf's Lair' and nonsense like that. The trouble was that you could see most of the way into that side-channel. If they'd anchored a U-boat up at the far end, they'd never have been able to keep it secret."

"Caleta Notch was far better then."

"An absolute beauty. God never designed a better hideaway."

Sunday 26 November, 1944; 11:45 a.m.

The *Scoresby* had returned to stand guard, a little to the south of Caleta Notch. Marchesi brought the vessel close in, obscured from view from within the cove, hove-to behind the peninsula lying immediately to the south of the entrance to the bay. He telegraphed 'Dead Slow Ahead' and brought her bows round to stem the east-setting current, close enough to be able to row the assistant steward and one of the older seamen inshore. He had ordered the two men to climb to a point that enabled them to look into the cove to see any vessel that might be moving. They were also to choose a spot which (without too long a trek between positions) gave them the ability to use semaphore flags, unseen from inside the heads, but visible from where the *Scoresby* held position. The seaman had assured Marchesi that he was well versed in semaphore, his daughter being a Girl Guide. On board, Marchesi directed all remaining crew to wear life jackets. He also ordered the ship's boat to be streamed out astern at the end of a hundred feet of stout rope.

The boatswain presented himself on the bridge and gestured over his shoulder in the direction of the *Scoresby's* forecastle. "Do you want to come up and inspect it, sir?"

"Are you happy with it?"

"Oh yes sir, I'm happy with it, right enough. It'll work just like you want. But I'm not so happy about the idea. Nor the lads, neither. Our place is here. General request from the ship's company to remain on board, sir. This is our ship too."

"Nicely said, chief. But permission denied. If it comes to it... Well, it'll be an order."

There was not long to wait. Shortly after two o'clock in the afternoon, frantic flag-waving from the top of a grey rock, up amongst the ferns, gave notice that a U-boat had appeared between the islands in the cove, not much more than half a mile distant.

Marchesi spoke to the Engineer Officer. "Chief, in a couple of minutes I'll be going from 'Stop Engines' to 'Full Ahead'. When she's giving all she's got, I want you and everybody else out of there. Okay?" The Engineer gave a grunt that could have meant anything.

Because the *Scoresby* had earned a previous living with the whaling fleet, she still benefited from a good old-fashioned crow's nest, perhaps 20 feet higher than the bridge. Marchesi had sent a lookout up there to act as his early warning, whilst keeping, as far as possible, the hull and superstructure hidden behind the peninsula. He glanced up at the Chilean ensign, then behind him at the funnel, hoping not to see a sudden billow of black smoke or a cloud of steam vent itself from down below.

On the hillside, the able seaman's semaphore signals seemed to have descended into gibberish. The only thing that was clear was that he had become extremely excited.

Marchesi cupped his hands around his mouth and called up to the crow's nest. "Lookout, ahoy! What do you see?"

"Nothing yet, sir."

"Then shin up a bit higher, dear boy. Your mate up on the hill is almost pissing himself." The lookout gripped the wire stays above his perch and hauled himself up so that his boots rested on the lip of the crow's nest. "Anything now?"

"Bloody hell! I mean, yes sir. He's just behind that first little island, sir. I can see the fin. He's coming out... taking care... making maybe two knots, sir, if that."

"Right! Down you come – and get your lifejacket on." Marchesi turned to the boatswain by his side. "Your last chance. I'm ordering you to muster everybody down aft ready to abandon ship."

"With the greatest of respect, sir, I can't hear what you're saying. I think my ears must have got a bit bunged up. Maybe I'm coming down with a cold, sir."

Marchesi pushed the telegraph lever to 'Full Ahead', and swung the wheel to port.

Sleek. Marchesi always thought that a U-boat on the surface looked sleek. He raised his binoculars for a look. There seemed to be two people at the top of the fin, both wearing caps, with perhaps two lookouts standing behind them, gripping the rails. The person wearing the white cap was peering back through his own binoculars. Victor gave him a cheery wave. It couldn't last.

"You know what to do?"

"Definitely do, sir," replied the boatswain.

On board the U-boat, things had escalated rapidly. Now both of the officers in caps were giving the *Scoresby* a closer inspection, and gesticulating wildly, though seemingly not at the Chilean ensign, nor at Marchesi on his bridge, but at the *Scoresby's* waterline. However, problems at sea never arrive singly. The U-boat's whole deck line was now visible beyond the small island and there appeared to be a second distraction. Officers and lookouts leaned out, port and starboard, looking down into the water.

"He can hear the hull scraping across the net," said Marchesi. "We've got him in the trap. He thought he was safe. He might have had lookouts posted on the forward part of the hull on the way in, but he got away with it then, so he hasn't bothered on the way out... Sloppy."

"What'll he do?"

"If it was me, I'd go astern right now and just hope not to suffer any nasty surprises." But the U-boat kept right on going.

"Shouldn't we have heard a big bang by now, sir?"

"I'd say give it a few more seconds for the trap to work." And still the U-boat kept right on going. Only now, a hatch had opened and a handful of sailors had appeared on the foredeck and were making their way towards the gun. "How far, do you reckon?"

"No more than two cables now, I'd say, sir."

"Set your sights to 400 yards then, and cut down that deck party." Marchesi gripped the wheel and began to wind it to starboard.

"Aye, sir." The boatswain flipped up the rear sight and wound the knurled wheel to bring the vee up above the bottom stop, up to the '4' mark on the left of the frame. Then he folded the bipod, knelt down and rested the gun on top of the canvas screen. He squeezed the trigger and fired off a burst of three to check the range.

"Didn't see any splashes, so you're just a bit too high, I think. But they're worried... Again." The boatswain adjusted his aim, took up the pressure again and squeezed off a burst of five. Two men fell. "Again." Another two. "Go for the fin. Two bursts, boatswain. Then change the magazine."

Problem: the mines had not blown. Marchesi spun the wheel a little more to starboard and pulled the whistle cord to give three short blasts, the signal that he had told the crew to expect: Abandon Ship!

"Bugger off boatswain now, there's a good fellow." But the man stayed where he was.

A bark from the U-boat and splashes in the water 50 yards ahead of the Scoresby; they had found a machine gun of their own.

"Well, if you're going to stay, I'd like you to keep that man's head down... Or blow it off. One or the other; doesn't matter which."

The boatswain rattled off another burst and the German gun fell silent. 250 yards ahead, the U-boat kept right on going. But now it was clear that she had begun to dive.

"We're not going to get there in time, sir. We're losing her."

"Empty your magazine into the aft end of her hull, below the waterline."

And then, an almighty fountain of water erupted at the stern of the U-boat, followed half a second later by the sound of an explosion. And in another half second a ripple of explosions, raising a curtain of seawater, discoloured ochre with mud and yellow kelp, reaching perhaps 200 feet into the air. The reverberations chased themselves around the cove and the hills on the starboard side.

At the first spout of water, Marchesi had wrenched the wheel to port and spun it as far as it would go. With plenty of way on her, the *Scoresby's* rudder bit instantly, showing contempt for the tide, heeling the vessel over to starboard, flattening the sea on the port side and leaving an area of dark blue water with the occasional eddy surging to the surface.

A cheer from down aft. Clearly the crew had not abandoned ship, for now they were whooping and hollering, each man exalting with both arms in the air, jigging and carrying on as if it was a Saturday night and they had just spilled out into the Commercial Road from a favourite Portsmouth dive like the old 'Mighty Fine'.

And not a sign of the U-boat.

"You were actually going to do it sir, weren't you? Ram her?"

"Yes, I damned well was."

"Fuck me!"

"Thank you for the kind offer, but I feel I must decline. And now, boatswain I would be very much obliged if you would round up those defiant, insubordinate apologies for seamen on the poop, those loafers, the very worst of King George's Hard Bargains, before I come to my senses and charge the whole lot of you. I want you to get that ghastly thing off the bows of my vessel, with the utmost care. I want to see it float away, and then, boatswain, I'd like to have a go with that gun of yours and see if I can hit one of its horns.

London, 1982

"Blew her arse end clean off, I expect," said Victor. "She'd have gone down like a stone. Then I remember wondering if we still had anybody down below, so I rang 'Dead Slow Ahead' and she responded, just like that." He snapped his fingers. "Bloody mutiny." He smiled. "Great bunch of lads."

"Wreckage?"

"Wreckage, bodies, oil – the bloody works. Right away. No tricks. Not like they were okay really, sitting on the bottom and blowing odd floaters out through the torpedo tubes. Dead and gone."

"As ordered."

"Yes..." It appeared that Victor had wanted to say more, but after a sharp intake of breath he choked up. He looked away at nothing, covered his mouth, then looked down. He managed a stifled, "I'm sorry", then leaned forward with his head in his hands. "Oh God! I'm sorry." Then he began to sob, shaking with emotion. Danny leaned forward too, putting an arm round the old gentleman's shoulders. He felt his own eyes filling too.

Through the windows, the London skyline had begun its subtle change from stark sodium orange to a backlight of pale dirty blue.

"Sorry about that," said Victor, sniffing a little. "All these years... I've never said anything to anybody – and Nancy had more sense than to ask."

Danny didn't know what to say. "You'll be fine," he said, but realised it was inadequate.

"Not much more to tell." Victor dabbed at his nose with a khaki handkerchief. "We sent the boat to recover the observers off the hill. I thought of grappling to see if there was any of the net near the surface, but then I just thought, 'Bugger it. It's somebody else's problem now.' We sent the boat up to the far end of the bay to see how the Pongoes had got on, and it seemed they'd had a bit of a ding-dong. No Jerry prisoners – all of 'em dead, including two in civilian clothes, and a couple of our blokes in a bad way."

Victor had come over all matter-of-fact. He had exhausted his supply of cigarettes, and with them had gone his humour. "I thought at least I should give the Jerries a burial at sea, so we brought them on board. They'd all come round the Horn at least once. They were all proper sailors, so once we got clear of the land that's where we let the ocean swallow them up. Then it was back to Stanley as fast as I could. I'd got customers waiting down south, you see."

Danny was struggling to see the point, and struggling also to find a polite way to ask why the hell any of this mattered. He took out Victor's letter. Fortunately, it provided enough prompts.

"Tell me then... What's an ABCD officer?"

"Atomic, Biological and Chemical Defence, dear boy. Or maybe 'Damage'; I can't remember now. Thought you'd know that."

Danny let it pass. "And what about 'future embarrassment at the highest level'?"

"Ah, well... After the shooting stopped, the Pongoes went over to make sure all the Jerry sailors were dead. That's when they found this copper cylinder. 'Heavy', they said. But you see, what with all the people in the boat and most of the bodies, they thought it might sink if they tried to bring everything back in one go. They reckoned I'd want to go back and have a look at it anyway, so they left it on the beach. When I got to hear about it, something clicked and I thought, 'This is what it's all about... Better go and have a look... This could be what the navy wanted me to destroy... This might be the thing I'm not supposed to touch'. So back I went."

Danny leaned forward. "If it was that heavy, it doesn't sound like one of those territory claim things the Argies left at Deception Island."

"No. It was a monster by comparison. It had some engraving on it – one of those huge long German words made up of lots of smaller words. I wrote it in my notebook so I could put it in a report if they asked me for one. I'll always remember it – *Lecksicherewasserdruckdichtekupferflasche*. And I thought, 'this means trouble'. And to cut a long story short, we fetched it off the beach, stuck it in the boat and brought it back to the entrance channel. I took a rough bearing, then we lashed some rope round it and lowered it down to the bottom in about thirty fathoms."

"And the embarrassment"?

"Look, for all I know the cylinder is still there. And what's inside it, of course."

"Go on. What do you reckon it's got inside?"

"Well, after the war, the navy thought I'd be the ideal chap to go and have a look at some German kit – Arctic clothing and suchlike – in Kiel Naval Dockyard, to see if it was any good. Most of the stores had been looted of course, but I noticed one thing that was either unattractive or too heavy to carry – another one of those copper cylinders. I had a look and bugger me if it didn't have that same word on it. So I asked the fellow what it was for, and he said it was for carrying poison gas. Bold as you like. Poison gas. That's what had been inside the cylinder. That's the potential embarrassment."

"And what's '*Leck*-something-or-other' mean?"

"Something like 'leak-proof, water-tight copper pressure vessel'. But hold on... Not long after that, they made me up to Lieutenant-Commander. Next thing I know, I've got a whole load of the bloody things on board my own ship! Like I told you, life just goes round and round in circles."

"I don't understand."

"I guess it was about 1948. The germ-warfare chaps must have liberated the whole stock of these cylinders. I got command of a converted LST out in the Caribbean – a tank landing ship, the *Ben Lomond*. We ran a series of biological warfare tests. Operation Hornet, or something, I think. Bloody frightful."

Danny lifted Victor's letter by a couple of inches. "And that's why you wrote this letter..."

"Yes. I mean, as I said – it took me years to piece it all together. But once I'd found out what Nancy knew – she told me what the Jerries were really going to do with this stuff – well, I felt cold. I've been fretting about it for years. And as far as I know, the navy still thinks that cylinder got destroyed in a bloody big bang in 1944. But of course, as I told you, I just followed orders, gave it the deep six and left it there."

"But it's in Chile, not Argentina."

"That's true, but I thought... well I thought, shouldn't somebody try and get it back? I mean, what if one of these bloody nuisance round-the-world-yachtsmen takes shelter in Caleta Notch one day and dredges it up with his anchor? You keep hearing more and more about Sunday sailors who've got the bug, sold up everything and bought what they think is an ocean-going yacht."

"It's only a trend... And it's not very likely, is it? Sheltering in exactly that bay, anchoring in exactly that spot, snagging your bit of rope – it would have rotted away by now anyway."

"It's still possible."

Danny shook his head. "All I know is you wouldn't catch me putting to sea in an overgrown bathtub and heading for Tahiti or somewhere."

"Nor me. I suppose Francis Chichester made it look too easy."

"Maybe... I guess they reckon it beats the nine-to-five rat race, though."

"But it's still possible for somebody to haul that thing to the surface by accident. Maybe not a yachtsman but a trawler might be dragging the bottom for prawns or something."

"All right. One chance in a million. But the cylinder might just as easily have corroded away to nothing."

"Yes, perhaps." But Victor had not voiced all his worries. "But look – what if the cylinder is still in one piece and something happens to it, like a leak or something? What if it poisons all the fish and the Chileans try to find out what's going on? What if they find it? The story would be bound to come out. The newspapers never give up these days, they just keep digging. Anything with a whiff of scandal... The Jerries, the Yanks, the Chileans, they'd all have a go at us."

"Bloody hell, Victor. You never give up either."

"No."

"How many more reasons are you going to come up with?"

"Maggie can't afford to upset the Yanks, Danny. She's going to need them on our side pretty soon. If the peace talks fail, she's going to counter-attack. She'll need a lot of kit. There'll be dozens of ships down there. Wouldn't it be better if one of them quietly nosed in and recovered the cylinder? Couldn't you mention it to the right people – pass it up the tree and see if the admirals could find a way to mount a side operation and steal the bloody thing back again? After all, it's the navy's reputation they'd be protecting."

Both men fell silent for several seconds, then Victor gave the problem a final nudge. "We ought to destroy it properly this time."

(VI)

Friday 9 April, 1982
London

All the bonhomie had drained out of Victor as he reached the end of his story. The mantelpiece clock showed a few minutes before 5 a.m., and he announced that he needed to head for his bunk. This left Danny with a dilemma. He reckoned that he had been on the go without a break for about 23 hours. He felt gritty-eyed and vaguely unclean. With his sponsor gone away, he also felt uncomfortable in the Club. Having no wish to be discovered snoozing alone in the smoking-room and to be ejected as a vagrant, his only practical course was to leave. Returning to 55 Broadway just as the building was about to grind into another day of action would allow no time for rest. Accordingly, he skirted the old Admiralty buildings, crossed Horseguards, entered Westminster tube station, bought a ticket to St James's Park, descended to the platform, and climbed onto the first Circle Line train heading in the wrong direction. He was soon rocked into a bottomless slumber.

By 10 a.m. Danny was at his desk; he took a telephone call, confirming what he had expected. A small team of naval weapons officers, artificers and aerospace engineers had also been working late. The experts reckoned it was feasible to convert a sea-launched Exocet into an air-launched variant.

"I'll need to ask for permission for you to carry on," said Danny. "I'll get on to it – top priority. But I'll want to know about every hitch you come across."

"Such as?"

"Well... The need for a special component – a detector of some kind, or a transistor that's only made in France for this one purpose. The sooner we find out about anything like that, the sooner we can turn it against the Argies."

"How?"

"Maybe we could buy up the whole world stock and sit on it to stop them getting their hands on it."

"Crafty!"

"Denial of resources to the enemy, that's all. You just get busy at your end. Come up with a workable plan. I'll feed your latest findings back up through my boss."

Danny spent the next two hours trying to check historic details about Operation Tabarin. By midday, he felt that several of his most promising avenues had turned into blind alleys. He phoned Rennie's secretary to ask for a few minutes of the admiral's time and was surprised to be told they could meet right away.

Once inside the office, Danny figured it was better to remain standing, to give an impression of intended brevity.

"What's it about, Danny?"

"Those letters you gave me to look at yesterday."

The admiral interrupted. "Ah, good – I've got some more here."

"No sir. Like you thought, most of them were time-wasters but one of them got me really worried." Rennie had the grace not to interrupt for a second time. "I spent all last night listening to an old naval officer's story. Parts of it sounded heroic, and other parts seemed barely credible, so this morning I spent a couple of hours checking it out... But I can't seem to find the crippler that kills it stone dead."

"And why should I be worried about it?"

"I came to give you a condensed version and ask if it was all right to carry on with it. Like I said – personally, I'm worried."

"You'd better tell me what it's all about – but I haven't got much time. Is this relevant to Argentina and the Falklands?" Danny compressed his lips and nodded, emphasising his opinion with a serious look. Rennie was almost on the hook. "Who's this ancient mariner?"

"A Lieutenant-Commander Victor Marchesi, sir."

"Never heard of him." But the admiral seemed willing to grant Danny a hearing. "What did he get up to – some secret operation or something?"

"Yes... Something called Operation Tabarin."

"Never heard of it. Where did it happen?"

"The Falklands... And Antarctica, sir. 1944."

"Oh... Right." Like everyone else, Rennie was a sucker for the inside track on a secret operation. "I'll give you five minutes," he said. "What was it all about?"

"Marchesi's story happened – if it happened at all – at a time when Argentina was an undeclared ally of Nazi Germany. A threat to the Falklands could have been useful to Hitler, diverting British resources that were needed elsewhere. It led to what we'd call 'an incident' these days, but it probably went unreported at the time."

"They're always up to some monkey business, the Argies. Most of the time we manage to keep it out of the press."

"Well, in '44, obviously, people had other things to think about, and – if it's true – good reasons to brush this particular engagement under the carpet."

Danny feared he had already introduced too many ifs; he knew that more were just around the corner. "Whether this episode just got forgotten about or whether there was a cover-up isn't the main issue. It's the fallout that's the problem. Right now, with Lord Carrington gone, his replacement is going to be busy trying to find friends in the UN and Washington. If Marchesi is right, and if this story leaks out, friends in Washington might be really hard to find." Danny's choice of words had given him a bonus. "In fact, 'leaks out' is appropriate in another sense. Marchesi reckons there could also be a big potential pollution problem."

"Just sit down a minute, Danny." Danny did as he was told. "Now, cut to the chase."

"Right. Commander Marchesi says that in 1944 he was given the exact location of a Nazi submarine, hiding in some bay or other, and told to destroy it, along with everyone on it. But he wasn't told why it was important. Okay – maybe they thought he didn't need to know – nothing unusual in that. But he says that afterwards he kept coming across bits of information that made the whole thing seem more and more suspicious. What he reckons now is that Hitler was trying to pass either a biological weapon or, more likely, a chemical weapon to the Japanese."

It was clear from the change in Rennie's expression and the way he leaned forward across his desk that Danny had got the admiral's total attention. "Keep going."

"Okay. Marchesi says he followed his orders and destroyed the submarine. He's pretty sure there can't have been any survivors. But he also says they left a copper cylinder in shallow water. They didn't destroy it – just lowered it to the bottom and abandoned it. This bay is an inlet off the Straits of Magellan, and if you're on a small boat it's a perfect anchorage for sheltering from adverse weather. With the number of amateur yachtsmen selling up their homes and setting off to see the world, he's afraid one of them could take refuge in this bay, foul his anchor on the cylinder and dredge it up. He's got a point. If the thing is still full of Hitler's bugs or nerve gas or whatever, Marchesi's worried about potential deaths. In the aftermath, any follow-up investigation could spell trouble for Britain."

"And – let me guess – he wants me to sanction a secret mission to find this cylinder and make it safe?"

"In a nutshell, yeah. Marchesi reckons Maggie's already committed to going to war over the Falklands. If so, there could be an opportunity to right a wrong... Under cover of some side action, perhaps."

Rennie narrowed his eyes. "Is this just a case of senile dementia or do you believe him?"

"Well, he's not clear about a few things – but you'd forgive him for that. Like I said, it was all half a lifetime ago. For instance, he mentioned that after the war he'd been in charge of some biological experiments in the Caribbean, 'Operation Hornet', he said. I tried to look it up, but there was no such thing. Then I traced him back through the Navy Lists and I found the ship he was on, and through that I found an 'Operation *Harness'* which did exactly what he'd been telling me about. Infectivity tests with anthrax, plague and nasty stuff like that. Now, maybe I didn't hear him right. Hornet or Harness; could be either – he's got a sort of lisp. But here's the other thing. I know this guy. I'm used to the way he speaks. It's a complete coincidence, but I've sailed with him. Okay, maybe his memory has started going fuzzy, but I'd trust him...."

"Why's this Operation Harness important?"

"Because he said the containers the navy used for these tests were identical to the one he dropped in the water in 1944, and identical to others that he found at Kiel naval dockyard after the war. That's my worry. It's an unbroken link from Operation Harness in 1948 to Kiel in 1944, and back out again to this cylinder that the navy just dumped in some shallow water in Chile. What if it's still full of whatever-it-was? Sarin or something."

"Anything else? What ship was he on in 1944?"

"She was called HMS *William Scoresby*. He was supposedly First Lieutenant, in command, but the Navy Lists just show a blank against that ship; no names. From other things he said, Tabarin was supposed to have a secret angle to it, so maybe they didn't want to give anything away. Then I thought of asking for the log books." Danny cocked his head to one side. "But the ones dating back to that period have been destroyed. There's some stuff covering December 1940 to January '41, but that's no good to me."

"Any known witnesses or people who'd vouch for his story?"

"He mentioned an admiral – Bobby Burnett – but *he* died in 1959. And the governor of the Falklands... He died even earlier – '56. I mean, at the time we're talking about, Victor was a young man, but now he's heading for 70. It's no wonder if the people who were senior to him are all dying off." Danny felt he knew Rennie well enough to get away with a wry comment. "I suppose you could have asked Karl Dönitz what this U-boat was up to, except that he's dead too... But in his case, only eighteen months ago. A near miss."

"Ha! He only escaped the noose by a whisker. He'd never have told us anything. He'd be afraid we were going to put him on trial again." Clearly, Rennie had taken Danny's comment seriously and had not finished evaluating possibilities. "There might be some Kriegsmarine officers lower down the chain who are still alive and knew what was going on, but if it was germ warfare, they'd be unlikely to er... remember, wouldn't you say?"

"Agreed," said Danny. But he had more to say about the people involved. "There is one other person who's still alive – Marchesi's wife. Interesting angle on her."

"What?"

"She must have had some connection with Bletchley Park or code-breaking or something. She worked in the Embassy in Montevideo. I've checked; it's definitely true. He implied she knew the background to this. Except she doesn't approve of him breaking silence on it, so you might only get one-word answers out of her. But if the trail of intercepted signals still exists – if there's an archive of de-crypted wartime telegrams somewhere – you might find what you're looking for."

"What *you're* looking for, not me, sunshine. I haven't got time for this. What about the Jerry submarine? Did Marchesi identify it for you, at all?"

"Not actually by number, but he seemed very clear about the dates. The reason he remembers it is because he was waiting for an ice-free passage down to the Antarctic bases, so he was able to be very specific. This all had to have taken place in November, 1944."

"And?"

"I got lucky. Nailed down an expert in one phone call. Only one U-boat even remotely fits the bill – U-1226. But if I'm going to marry up the submarine and a cargo of biological or chemical warfare products – if I'm going to prove any basis for this story, I'm going to need clearance to delve around in the records."

"What else have you got on your desk?"

"You'll remember the priority was the Exocets? Bad news. The techies in the feasibility group reckon it's got to be possible to convert a sea-launched missile to an air-launched missile, so I told them to get on and prove it as fast as possible. If they highlight a difficulty, it might enable us to make the same problem worse for the Argies."

Rennie skewed his jaw to one side and took a deep, noisy breath, a picture of sudden, profound concentration. "I shouldn't worry about that."

"Why not? And there's something else I just thought about. The Exocet must have some sort of 'kill circuit' inside it. Imagine if the frogs sold the missile to some tin-pot regime and then found themselves at war with the same crowd. They'd want a way to zap any incoming missile, wouldn't they? If they don't tell us, we should get onto that."

"Leave it Danny. John Nott and the French Defence Minister, a Monsieur Hernu, had a meeting a week ago, just before all this nonsense kicked off. Apparently, they got on like a house on fire, and it's paid dividends already. The French take as much exception as we do to foreign dictators invading their colonies, so they're supporting us as much as they can. If Galtieri wants any bits and pieces for his Exocets, he won't be getting them from the French."

"What a turn-up!"

"Believe me, Danny, I'm as amazed as you are."

"What about my experts? Do you want them to stop work?"

"No – in fact I wonder if we could send them over to work with the French... I'll handle that. But I'm relieving you of any further worry over the Exocets. What else are you running with?"

"Well, there's the potential problem about British or Commonwealth merchant ships in South American ports and any that are on their way there. We need to plan for a diversion to neutral ports if the emergency gets any worse."

"Hand it over to Tommo and get the Shipping Intelligence people at Lloyd's to vet what he's doing."

"Sir?"

"Danny, I've never met anybody quite like you." Rennie leaned back in his chair. "You've got this gift for being in the wrong place at the worst possible time, haven't you?" He didn't wait for an answer, nor did he sound particularly vexed. "Or maybe it's the other way round – I don't know. Things just seem to happen around you, like you're some sort of magnet for trouble. All I did was give you a handful of letters and before the day's out, you uncover a crock of shit."

It sounded more like an irregular commendation than an admonishment. "It's my own fault. I asked and I suppose, knowing how you go about things, half an answer was never going to satisfy you." He pondered for a few moments longer, before adding, "I hope you hadn't got anything planned for the weekend because I want all this sorted by Monday."

Danny stood, ready to leave. "Then I'll be needing that clearance, sir."

Rear-Admiral Rennie took out a clean sheet of paper, uncapped his fountain pen and began writing: '*To whom it may concern...*'

And so, Danny Rook spent the whole of Saturday and most of Sunday trawling through assorted boxes of vintage telegrams, and the records of the Submarine Tracking Room from 1944. However, around dusk on Sunday he teased out a tiny nugget that, if he was right, might make Victor's story significantly more credible, and several shades worse than a mere crock of shit. He wrote three German surnames in his notebook, spent a few minutes selecting a number of others at random from the German Embassy's staff list, then phoned the Army and Navy Club to confirm that Marchesi had not checked out; he hadn't. Danny said he would arrive in reception in fifteen minutes.

"Just a couple of things, Vic. I know it's a long time ago but I want to ask you about the German shore party – the people that the soldiers killed."

"I'll do my best, dear boy..."

"You said there were two civilians, I think? Just two – no more?"

Marchesi nodded. "Just two."

"Presumably the German sailors were in uniform, so that's how you could tell these other two were civilians?"

"Yes, the way they were dressed. And they were obviously a bit older than the other crew members. Clean hands as well."

"Did you identify the bodies – I mean, name, rank, serial number?"

"Yes, where we could. The navy had ordered me not to leave any evidence so, like I already told you, I decided to weigh them down and bury the dead at sea."

"Did you keep the dog tags? The Jerries must have worn some sort of ID, I guess?"

"Yes, I handed them over, but I wouldn't bank on the navy having kept them, or gone back to the relatives after the war."

Danny saw it straight away. "Secret operation. Couldn't afford to leave any evidence, like you just said."

"That's right. But I thought the least I could do was to record the names in the log book." He tilted his head back with a faint air of knowing more than he should. "You could ask for the log to be taken out of storage if you're interested."

"I'm afraid your log books have been destroyed, Vic."

Marchesi raised one eyebrow. Clearly, he was not surprised. "May not be as fishy as you think. By the end of the war, with the size of the navy, they'd have needed a place as big as Wembley Stadium to store all the log books in. It wouldn't just be the capital ships. It'd go right down to individual D-Day landing craft as well. Back then, people weren't so fussy about hanging on to tons of useless paper."

"All right, Vic. What about the civilians? What can you tell me about them? Can you describe either of them?"

"No, dear boy. All I can tell you is that it looked like they'd taken cover when the shooting started. But our chaps dropped a couple of two-inch mortar shells right on top of them, so they weren't a pretty sight."

"Can you remember any of their names – or maybe anything they had with them?"

"Well neither of them was wearing an identity tag, which was another reason we suspected they were civilians."

"Was there anything on the bodies? Maybe they'd come ashore with papers or instruments or stuff like that. Can you remember writing anything about them in the log?"

"I think I remember a few scrappy notebooks, as if one of them was writing a text book or his memoirs or something. One body had a few letters in his jacket pocket."

"Let me read you a list of names. It might it jog your memory."

"You could try..."

Danny reached for his notebook, glanced at the surnames he had written down, then looked into Marchesi's eyes and spoke each of them in turn. "Ackermann?" No reaction. "Althaus?" The same. "Fischer?" Marchesi shook his head. "Fuhrmann?" Marchesi closed his eyes slowly and shook his head again. "Lehmann?"

"Sorry – this isn't doing any good is it?"

"Just keep trying. There's no-one else I can ask... What about Linden?"

"No. It doesn't ring any bells."

"Neumann?"

Marchesi scratched his chin. "Possibly."

"Nagel?"

"No."

"Teufel."

"Ha! The devil! No – I'd have remembered a name like that."

"And the last one – Thiessen?" Marchesi caught his breath. A reaction. Although he was anxious to know more, Danny had the sense not to force his man until he was ready to speak.

Marchesi didn't wait for long. "How do you spell 'Thiessen'?" Danny told him. "I'm not sure... But that could have been the name written in the front of those notebooks."

"Interesting... And Neumann. Was that the name on the letters?"

"After all these years, I can't be certain. But maybe."

"No idea about the others? Fischer, for example."

"No – but if I think of anything..."

"Just one other thing," said Danny. He unfolded a photocopy of the relevant section of a marine chart. "If you can remember, I want you to show me where the bodies lay. And I really need to know exactly where you dropped that cylinder into the 'oggin."

Monday 12 April

"So you see," said Danny, "it all hinges on Doctor Fischer. He was the practical one, the engineer. If we could prove he never left the U-boat, there wouldn't be a problem. He'd have drowned with the rest of the crew when the mines blew it up."

"But...?"

"But the orders were to land all three passengers at Caleta Notch... And the Germans weren't known for disobeying orders. Just suppose Fischer had taken himself a little way up the hillside for a crap behind a bush. Then the shooting starts."

"I see where you're coming from," said Rennie.

"He sees his mates blown up and all the sailors killed in a gun battle."

"Then there's a bloody big bang from the other end of the inlet."

"Yes, so he's worried that the U-1226 is wrecked. Eventually the *Scoresby's* boat chugs up to the head of the inlet and loads up with a handful of British soldiers, along with the bodies of all his mates. That makes him pretty certain the U-boat has been destroyed. Then this British boat sails off, leaving some smashed-up bits and pieces and, crucially, this copper cylinder."

"Right," said Rennie. "I'm beginning to see why you're worried."

"Yes. Now, suppose the cylinder is too heavy for Fischer to move on his own. He's worried the British are going to come back for it. But say amongst the wreckage there's a briefcase or a box full of important documents... He whips that away up the hillside and finds a place to hide."

Rennie joined in again. "Then after a while, Marchesi comes back in the boat, with a load of matelots to manhandle this cylinder on board and tidy away the rest of the evidence."

"And I can't prove," said Danny deliberately, "whether at the end of that day, Fischer was dead or alive."

"Yeah, but even if he *was* alive –"

"– Exactly. What happens next? He sees Marchesi's boat load up and set off for the second time."

"Yeah. So, there's Fischer, sitting on the hillside thinking he's lucky to be alive, and wondering how far he's going to have to walk until he finds a friendly face."

"Remember what happened next."

"I can't believe I'm going to say this..." Rennie put on a look of pain. "Blow-me-down if he doesn't see these stupid idiots dump his precious cylinder in the water farther down the bay. And then they bugger off."

"Yeah, well, they were only following orders."

"Yes, but it's the daft bastard who dreamed them up in the first place... That's whose balls I'd like to be crushing right now."

Danny ignored Rennie's desire for retribution. "Leaving us with two fundamental questions. Is the cylinder still there? And if it isn't, who's got it?"

"And three. Is Fischer still alive?"

"Bringing endless possibilities."

"Such as, if Fischer hasn't got it," said Rennie, "and somebody else has, do they know what's inside it, and what have they done with these germs or nerve gas or whatever?"

"Or, I suppose... What might they be about to do with that stuff?"

Both men paused for a few seconds to mull over the implications. Rennie spoke first.

"Danny... This isn't going to make me popular."

(VII)

Thursday 13 May,
55 Broadway

Danny and Admiral Rennie had not spoken for at least a week. Relieved of responsibility for the projects to find a 'kill-switch' and a way to prove whether ship- or land-based Exocets could be re-jigged to fire from the air, Danny had been spending a lot of time at Lloyd's.

An Argentine Boeing 707 had been keeping a sporadic watch on the Task Force but at the end of April, with this becoming a far more hazardous undertaking for it, the aircraft had switched to monitoring the sea lanes south of Ascension Island. Neither the Argentine Navy nor their Air Force had any real capability to harass shipping so far from their own country, but there had been rumours that they were intending to improvise a bombing solution by equipping a C-130 Hercules with long-range fuel tanks and then rolling bombs off its tail ramp, should the 707 discover a suitable target. Whilst the majority of the British merchant fleet was not caught up in the hostilities, they were nevertheless British.

The War Cabinet felt that with innocent vessels liable to be attacked as targets of opportunity by what was clearly an unprincipled military junta, something needed to be done. They had therefore directed Rennie's Merchant Shipping Intelligence Branch to record and plot all shipping (British and foreign) transiting the South Atlantic. Hence Danny's temporary home at Lloyd's, assessing the risks and attempting to maintain an up-to-date plot of ships' locations, particularly the British ones. Whether the cargo was several hundreds of thousands of tons of crude oil from the Gulf, or a lesser quantity of molasses from Mauritius to Liverpool, the risks needed to be assessed – and if necessary, vessels re-routed farther out of the reach of makeshift bombers, aiming with more hope than science.

During the afternoon, Rennie called Danny into his office. Danny arrived just as Mrs Mullet and her tea trolley were leaving. Since Rennie's meetings were normally brief, Danny didn't see any point in stopping the lady to ask for a drink for himself.

The rear-admiral's feet rested on his desk, ankles crossed, not far from a china cup and saucer and a plate on which lurked a tab-nab, smeared in a bright red, jellied substance. His hands were clasped behind his head and his chair was tipped back on two legs.

"You asked me to come up, sir."

"Danny... 'Lucky Rookie', they probably call you. Have you any idea what a narrow squeak you've had?" Danny shook his head. "A month ago, we were going to send you off with the Task Force to look into this poison gas nonsense, but somebody said it was odds against the Argies either having it or using it."

"Well... I suppose I ought to feel grateful for small mercies then, sir."

"Seen the paper?" Rennie swung his feet off the desk and pushed a copy of that morning's *Times* towards Danny. "That article about an Argentine prisoner. Seen it?"

"No. Not yet. I've been a bit busy."

"Read the middle column."

The report concerned a naval officer, a Captain Astiz, ex-commander of the garrison on South Georgia, captured when the island had been re-taken by the Royal Marines. Apparently, the French Foreign Minister had asked Britain to delay repatriating the gentleman concerned, because he was implicated in the disappearance of two French nuns and a Swedish girl.

"Sounds a bit of a bastard," said Danny.

"Yes, I thought so too. Out of curiosity I asked if there were any further details. Apparently, we've got him in solitary confinement on Ascension. Just arrived. There's a Fleet Street hack based there. He stumbled across the story and that's why it's only just come out."

Rennie's ways were no secret to Danny. Something – possibly unwelcome – was coming. He twitched the left side of his mouth and allowed the beginnings of a frown appear. Let the admiral play his little games, but the way Danny saw it, he would be unlikely to make a fortune as a poker player.

"Go on."

"No, no. It's nothing. You're getting too suspicious in your old age, Danny. It turns out that the Foreign Office has a list of Argies that – if we were to capture them – might be of interest to our few remaining friends." Rennie smiled but Danny was not convinced. "Just thought you might be interested in looking at the list and seeing what Alfredo Astiz has been up to, that's all." Rennie flipped open a document wallet to show the contents. "It's all here, look. Murder of Dagmar Hagelin; murder of two nuns, Sisters Alicia and Léonie; list of aliases; infiltration of the Mothers of the Plaza de Mayo."

"Okay," said Danny. "I'll have a flip through it."

"Listen, I don't want this getting farther than my outer office, but you're welcome to sit out there for a few minutes and have a read. Pop back in when you're done."

"Yes. All right, sir."

Danny had got as far as the door when Rennie added, "And you might want to look at a bloke calling himself Adolpho Anguilla, as well."

≈

Adolpho Anguilla had first appeared in Argentina in 1945, calling himself Luigi Pescatore. Although the only language Pescatore spoke proficiently was German, he soon learned Spanish well enough to take on the task of teaching chemistry to Argentinean teenagers in the south of the country.

He gained a certain notoriety as a man with a past – a past which he always attempted to belittle, dismissing all curiosity with a cheery wave, or scoffing at the more lurid fantasies. But his reticence only fuelled the rumours and so, in order to give the slip to growing numbers of inquisitive people, he decamped one day during the school holidays and re-emerged in Buenos Aires calling himself Adolpho Anguilla. Doubtless he took some satisfaction in calling himself after the eel, the slipperiest of fishes, although Pescatore had always been the more appropriate (if rather obvious) alias for a man who had been born with the name of Fischer.

In the richer culture of the capital city, soon señor Anguilla began to meet fellow Germans and in time he came to the attention of senior officers in the Argentine Navy who had given themselves a particular mission – that of arresting those whom they classified as subversives, and questioning them. In return for promising Adolpho a degree of protection, the naval officers asked him to synthesize small quantities of truth drugs which could be given to those being interrogated. Adolpho had been provided with a clandestine laboratory and a couple of young assistants at ESMA, the *Escuela Mecánica de la Armada* and, in time, the navy approached him on the subject of manufacturing nerve agents.

After some twenty minutes, Danny returned to Admiral Rennie's office. He replaced the document wallet on the desk, and a devil rose inside him. He half turned as if to leave.

"Sir, I was thinking it was about time I visited my folks in New Zealand."

"Come on... Don't try that one on me, Danny."

"Well?"

"Funny old thing, the Exocet... For years there were rumours it didn't work. Then, a week ago, boom! HMS *Sheffield.*" Rennie looked away. "Could have been a whole lot worse, although nobody's calling it a blessing in disguise." He fell silent for the length of a deep breath. "Tit for tat, I suppose. First the *Belgrano*, then the *Sheffield.*"

"Very sad, sir."

"Listen Danny, the more gold rings you get on your sleeve, the more you realise there's no point having a navy if you're not prepared to lose a ship or two. That's why we'll beat the Argies now; Anaya will be afraid to let his ships out of port – afraid to lose another one."

"I hadn't thought of it like that."

"No. But it's serious. The Task Force is in position now and we can't afford to lose many more ships. Especially not assets like the *Hermes* or the *Invincible.*"

"I can see that, sir."

Rennie seemed to notice that he was looking up into Danny's face. He coughed and waved Danny into a seat on the opposite side of his desk.

"Mrs T.," said Rennie, apparently changing the subject. "For the past six weeks she's had that SAS brigadier filling her ears with all the clever things his bandits did at the Iranian Embassy."

"I expect they're all pretty proud of that."

"Doubtless... And reminding her what the Israelis did – you remember – the Entebbe Raid? Apparently that sort of thing is part of their repertoire as well."

"Yeah."

"So now she thinks the SAS is the answer to everything." Another pause; another deep breath. "Anyway, at today's War Cabinet, Lewin ordered the brigadier to draw up plans to eradicate the Exocet threat." Rennie leaned forward and looked Danny in the eye. "You probably don't realise you had a hand in that."

"Me?"

"Yes Danny. Two hands, I suppose. That business about being able to tinker with the guts of a sea-launched missile. You scared them witless. If you're right, instead of only having three air-launched missiles left, there's a chance the Argies could convert the others and turn three into twenty-three..."

"Well, I never thought –"

"– And then there's the threat of poison gas."

"What?"

"Oh yes. First somebody said, 'With that many missiles they could hit us from all sides'. Then another silly sod said he dreaded to think what would happen if they replaced the explosive head with a couple of gallons of nerve gas. Still, it shows somebody was listening. It shows they're taking Operation Tabarin and your Commander Marchesi seriously."

"Not just on my say-so, surely? Somebody else must have verified it somehow."

"Hopefully..." Rennie's tone suggested little faith that this step would have occurred to those in charge. "But I tell you, once that nerve gas genie got out of the bottle, she wasn't going back in again any time soon. And because nobody wants the epitaph '*It Will Never Happen*' carved on his tombstone, Lewin told the SAS to make his little problem go away."

"I never –"

"– Oh don't worry about it, Danny. Whatever happens won't be your fault. Want to know why?" Rennie didn't wait for the answer. "The brigadier suckered Lewin into it. The word is he's been planning this for a while. He wanted to have a plan all revved up and waiting to go as soon as the War Cabinet fired the starting gun. Now he's desperate to use it."

"Do you know what he's planning to do?"

"Pretty much... Technically we aren't at war with the bastards so we can't invade sovereign Argentine territory – and for the same reason there's no way we'd dare bomb the airfield. The least worst option is some sort of infantry raid on this Rio Grande airbase, where the Super Etendards are flying from." Rennie passed a hand through his hair and cast his eyes up to the ceiling. "But he wants to go for a full-scale commando raid... On the South American mainland, for God's sake... Blow up the planes, blow up the missiles, shoot the pilots. Then after the fireworks have finished, any SAS blokes who are still left alive just make a mad scramble for the Chilean border. We won't have a friend left anywhere on the planet."

Danny knew this was not the time to say anything like, 'You're joking' or 'Why are you telling me all this?' In any case, he suspected that he already knew the answer. So he asked, "Is there no way of stopping this?"

"Well, there's one way. The Argies have established a grass airstrip on Pebble Island at the top end of the Falkland Sound. We think they've stationed a squadron of ground-attack anti-personnel aircraft there. But it's our territory not theirs, so if we want to bomb it, we can bloody well bomb the hell out of it. Legally, I mean. No come-backs."

Rennie paused, as if waiting for Danny to see the point, but much of Danny's attention was focused on looking unenthusiastic, hoping not to become a reluctant conscript again, pressganged into action. Rennie was forced to continue.

"Anyway, these SAS cowboys have landed a reconnaissance patrol on Pebble Island. If they find the planes there, they're supposed to report back, then the main force can launch a full-scale attack. If they pull it off on Pebble Island, they'll get the go-ahead for this anti-Exocet raid on Rio Grande. And if they bugger it up, the Cabinet won't risk the second operation."

"What's the likelihood of that? Buggering it up, I mean."

"Small, I'd say. So the raid on Rio Grande is likely to go ahead." Rennie shifted position in his chair; 'squirmed' would not have been quite the right word. "It means I've got to ask you something."

"Oh no, sir... You and I agreed after the Kola. No more secret squirrel stuff for Danny Rook."

"Yes," said Rennie. "I remember. But the picture has changed a bit. If Pebble Island is a success, the big raid on Rio Grande won't go ahead without an SAS reconnaissance on the mainland – Argentina." He swallowed hard. "What I want is for you and a bodyguard to go in with the recce troop. While the SAS head for the airbase, you and your minder head west, have a look into this Caleta Notch place and see if you can find Marchesi's lost cylinder... Just like he wanted."

Danny had no hesitation. "Forget it."

"Come on Danny. You're the guy who uncovered this in the first place. You're the guy with all the info – you know how much I rely on you. And it isn't only me. What about your shipmate, Marchesi? Don't you owe it to him?"

"He hadn't remembered me. He's probably forgotten about me again by now. I haven't seen him for a month."

"We need to know, Danny."

"Know what?"

"Come on – you've just read the file. We think we've found your missing Doctor Fischer, alias Pescatore, alias Anguilla. He's the Argentine Navy's secret war chemist. There's probably nothing he can't manufacture for them. Our War Cabinet can't take the risk – or at least if we're facing potential chemical weapons, it's a risk we need to know about."

"The War Cabinet! Half of it's just shit-for-brains politicians. I don't see *them* taking any risks. A month ago they didn't even know where the Falkland Islands were."

"They're still the people in charge though."

Elements of the counter argument began to filter into Danny's mind. "All right," he said. "If nerve gas is the risk, it's still nothing to do with you or me. Whether or not the Argies are about to engage in chemical warfare, the stuff in that cylinder is a Porton Down problem, not ours. Even if it's not gas but anthrax or plague in that cylinder, it may be different people but it's the same outfit. It's Porton Down's responsibility."

"No it bloody isn't. It's the navy's balls-up from start to finish and what we're trying to do is save our reputation."

"And what's the navy going to do with a cylinder full of bacteria or nerve gas – a cylinder that's been sitting in salt water for the last forty years? The navy hasn't got the facilities to open it up and have a crafty look inside – or has it?"

"No, of course it hasn't. But if we find it and haul it up, and it's safely in our possession, that's the time we'll probably decide to hand it over to the CBW blokes. I expect we'll say it got fished up in a trawler's nets, or something, and landed at Grimsby."

"They won't be fooled for a minute. It'll have southern hemisphere weeds and shellfish growing all over it."

"There won't be anything growing on it. It's a copper cylinder, remember? Ever heard of copper-bottomed warships?"

"The answer is still no, sir." Danny realised the danger of going too far; he tried to calm down and regain some self-control. "With respect, sir, no. The reasons are too unconvincing. If Pescatore-Anguilla is really Doctor

Hermann Fischer, it doesn't matter a damn whether the cylinder is still sunk in Caleta Notch or not. He was the guy who invented the manufacturing process. He doesn't need the stuff in the cylinder. He can reproduce all the industrial vats and valves and boilers and pipes and condensers any time he wants. He could hook it all up and make a batch of nerve gas every bloody day of the week if they asked him to."

In the face of Danny's earlier outburst and now his attempts to state a logical case, Rennie remained silent.

"Dredging up the cylinder would only prove one thing," said Danny. "If we've found it, nobody else has got there before us."

"You're forgetting one thing, though."

"What?"

"We don't want the Yanks to find out how close the Japs came to getting their hands on German nerve gas technology and changing the war in the Pacific." Rennie raised his voice. "Because in 1944 we cocked it up completely and it was only by the skin of our teeth that we stopped the Japs getting their hands on it." Then, regaining his normal tone, "So, before some amateur sailor accidentally discovers the cylinder, we need to get in first, grab it, and make sure it vanishes for good, just like Commander Marchesi told you." Rennie exhaled, somewhere between a hiss and a sigh. "It turns out he and his wife had pieced it together pretty accurately."

"But I'm a bloody civilian, sir. If I get captured, they could shoot me as a spy."

"Not in Chile. That's where you'd be – Chile. They're no friends of Argentina. They're secretly on our side."

"I don't care. A deal is a deal. I've done with all that. Find somebody else."

"There *is* nobody else. There's hardly a special forces section left in the country.

"I told you. No sir."

Rennie appeared to think for a few moments. "All right, all right. Well look, if you won't do that for me, how about a trip to Ascension Island?"

"What for?"

"Because, Danny, you insubordinate bastard, that's where Astiz is. And in case you missed it, Astiz was based at ESMA, the naval engineers' college. So because Astiz probably knows Pescatore-Anguilla-Fischer, he might be willing to talk if he thinks it'll save his skin. See?"

In such situations timing is always fundamental, so Danny waited for a few moments, with every one of his facial muscles locked into a disapproving glare. "For you, Admiral, all right. One more time. But no tricks..."

"I'm grateful."

Danny relaxed. "Sorry if I was rude."

"I understand."

Danny felt that some sort of explanation was necessary to account for his swift change of heart. "It's that list of wanted men that did it. I mean, if the Argies are happy to treat their own people like that, they might not worry too much about gassing our lads. I'll see if I can think up some sort of yarn, and maybe charm something useful out of him for you."

"That's more like it."

"Yes. Like I say, I'm sorry if I –."

"– It's all right." Rennie held up his hand as if to stop any further apologies, so Danny began to rise.

"Only you'll need to be at Brize Norton before breakfast time tomorrow. You'd better go home and pack."

"What?" Danny stifled his rising anger. "Well, in that case, since I could be meeting Astiz tomorrow or the next day, I'm going to need to photocopy that file with all the wanted men in it, aren't I?"

“Oh, take it Danny.” Rennie waved a hand dismissively, then performed a creditable impersonation of the Cheshire Cat. “It’s yours. I had it printed especially…”

Part Three – Tillotson

(I)

Friday 14 May, 1982
RAF Brize Norton

A Ministry of Defence car collected Danny and took him to Brize Norton. At the gate it was clear that even though the fighting was 7,000 miles away, security stood at high alert in that part of Oxfordshire. Twilight was past, the sun was up, but there was nothing sunny about Danny's welcome. The sentry asked him and the driver to step out of the car so they could be patted down for – well, for what exactly? Another sentry poked long-handled mirrors under the vehicle. Then they searched Danny's luggage before allowing access to the base. Danny's driver took him as far as a brick-built guardroom, then hurried away.

Some brickwork can appear warm in sunlight, but from the outside this military block looked pale, cold, damp and cheap – like a forty-year-old air raid shelter. Inside, behind the counter, the RAF corporal's face showed no emotion. With little doubt, this fellow livened his days by operating an unofficial contest over who would speak first. Ignorant of this challenge, Danny lost by wishing the fellow a good morning, giving his name, and stating that he had been asked to report there for a flight to Ascension Island. Creases appeared on the corporal's forehead. He stepped sideways and picked up one of several clipboards.

"Rook?"

"Yes," admitted Danny.

"Not today."

"Well I must be on some sort of list. They let me past the gate."

"You're not on today's passenger list."

Danny was finding it hard to imagine a frostier spring morning. He thought of a way to warm it up a little.

"Perhaps you'd like to take it up with Admiral Rennie? What's the time? Let's see." Danny flicked aside the cuff of his anorak. "5:35; we could give him a shake. I'm sure he'd be delighted to help." He reached into an inside pocket. "I've got the phone number of the main Navy Department switchboard somewhere, and they're bound to have an emergency contact number for him."

The mention of a significantly exalted naval rank produced a change of attitude. "Sorry sir, I thought you looked a bit like one of the blokes from the BBC." He became confidential. "Not so welcome round here, sir. Let's have another look." The corporal moved sideways again and began leafing through the contents of his remaining clipboards, but without success. "Sorry sir. There's nothing. You aren't on any of my lists."

"Maybe there's a message for me?"

The corporal's head twitched to one side and he blinked as if he had heard those words somewhere before. "A message, sir..."

"If there was a message for me, would it be in one of those pigeonholes behind you?"

It was. Apparently, the SAS reconnaissance troop had chosen the wrong location in which to land on Pebble Island. Consequently, they had been late in confirming the presence of Argentine aircraft. Lacking timely target information, the attacking vessels, HMS *Hermes*, *Broadsword* and *Glamorgan* had been obliged to turn away to avoid being observed in daylight. The whole operation had been postponed for another 24 hours.

Without evidence that the SAS could mount a covert reconnaissance on the Falklands – British territory – and follow it up with a successful raid, someone was wisely withholding permission for the follow-up recce and raid against the Rio Grande airbase on Argentine territory. Danny's instructions were to stand down until the next day. The VC-10 would be staying on the ground, there being no point in flying to Ascension with a special forces troop, only to be ordered to turn around and bring them back again if the Pebble Island thing proved to have been a total cock-up.

Saturday 15 May, 1982
Dakar Airport, Senegal

The forward doors of the RAF VC-10 stayed closed, confining the aircraft's twenty-or-so passengers to the cabin. In truth, the occupants were better off with the doors shut tight – a precaution during refuelling. Outside, the air smelled less of tropical Africa and more of JP1 jet fuel. Worse, with the sun beating down from directly overhead onto acres of airfield concrete, the temperature had risen to well over 40 degrees.

Danny, who had long since achieved the status of full-time civilian, was dressed for comfort. The rest of the travellers wore civilian clothes too, but they did not all have the bearing of city dwellers. A group of men had set themselves apart at the rear of the cabin. Each man occupied a bank of three seats with the armrests pushed up. Most had slept during the four-and-a-half-hour flight from Brize Norton. A couple of them now moved about the cabin, stretching their legs. Danny rose too and strolled forward to peer at the airport through a different window. A wiry fellow with ginger hair appeared alongside, narrowed his eyes and addressed him.

"You from the press?"

"Me? No. People keep asking me that. I get the impression the media aren't so popular."

"Some of 'em need a kick up the arse. Giving stuff away to the Argies all the time. What outfit you with, then?"

"MoD Navy Department. You?"

"Don't ask, don't tell. That's my motto."

But Ginger *had* asked... Danny ignored the shattered motto. "I should have thought you blokes had a regimental motto more like 'Who Keeps Quiet Survives'."

The fellow cocked his head to the left and raised one eyebrow. "Very good," he said. "Must remember that one. The lads need a bit of a laugh right now." He seemed to think for a few seconds. "Anyway, what brings you down here?" Asking again.

"They've brought a prisoner up from South Georgia. I've got to interview him."

"Heard about him. He's lucky to be alive."

Danny nodded towards the rear of the cabin, where the majority of Ginger's mates still remained horizontal. "How many in your troop? Six?"

"Eight."

Since Ginger had not already thrown Danny to the deck, dislocated his major joints and disabled him in a throttling headlock as punishment for penetrating his special forces cover, he figured he could extract a little more information through a calculated disclosure of his own. Curiosity had always been one of his vices.

"They knocked me back for 24 hours over this Pebble Island thing," said Danny. "Any idea how it's gone?"

"You too, eh? Yeah, the lads done good." He flicked a glance towards the cockpit. "Got the nod from the boys up front."

"Good luck then... with your recce, I mean. I'm only guessing, but... Rio Grande?"

Ginger made a noise, more of a sneer than a sniff. "Recce? You mean fookin' 'Operation Certain Death'." He put on a glum expression. "Shouldn't of minded if you *was* the fookin' press. Some fooker needs to know. All the lads feel the same."

"I see," said Danny. "But you couldn't have told the papers anything about your mission."

"Who said anything about that? It's the stupid bastards we're doing it for. That's what somebody needs to hear about. That's what's getting to us. Haven't even got any proper maps. All we've got is what looks like a page torn out of some poor kid's school atlas. Fookin' ridiculous."

"Oh."

"And the Argies aren't stupid."

"No."

"They'll be expecting us."

"I suppose so."

"They'll have worked it out. But our stupid bastard planners haven't worked out that the Argies *must* have worked it out too. Either that or they don't care."

"I think I followed that. You're saying both sides ought to have come to the same conclusion... But you doubt it."

Ginger sighed and made an exasperated face; not his fault if this civilian hadn't appreciated his tactical appraisal. "All right; it's like this... What's the big threat right now? It's the Exocet, okay? 'Fix it,' says the brigadier. So the planners had a think. 'We know what it is,' they said, 'and we know what aircraft it's launched from.' So before long they'd worked out that if they found where these froggie-built jets were, and if that just happened to be pretty close to the Falklands, they were on to a winner." He shrugged. "Turns out it's not a big secret. A couple of phone calls to the local cafés and bars down in Patagonia and they'd verified it. Easy. Like I say, *we* worked it out. It's got to be this base in Tierra del Fuego – like you said – Rio Grande. Only we need to credit *them* with some brains too. *They* know we've got to take out the Exocets. So, they'll know we're coming."

"Right," said Danny. "I see what you mean." He wanted to steer clear of any fatalistic expressions, and also to avoid referring euphemistically to any Argentine preparations, such as 'organising a reception committee'. "But you're saying our planners hope the Argies haven't worked out there's likely to be a special forces raid, or what to do about it."

"Faint hopes. Operation Certain Death. I told you."

"Do the unexpected, then. Someone told me that a long time ago."

"Was that person sitting in freezing sleet in the middle of winter on the bare pampas? Was he half a mile from a thousand trigger-happy Argie marines, and no hope of getting pulled out? Was he trying to hide himself, his mates, a week's rations and a radio behind nothing bigger than a clump of tussock grass?"

"He was somewhere a bit warmer, I think."

Ascension Island

As Danny descended the aircraft steps, although it was only about half-past-six in the evening, the sun had sunk to the breadth of three fingers above the horizon and would probably be gone in ten minutes. The passengers filed away from the VC-10 towards a large tent, where a queue formed.

Formalities completed, a naval lieutenant stepped forward, introduced himself to Danny and said that he had been sent to accompany him to the *Dumbarton Castle*. Danny felt pleased, assuming the name belonged to a passenger ship owned by the Union Castle Line that had perhaps called into Ascension on her way to Cape Town; or perhaps she was anchored there to provide accommodation for the hundreds of people in transit. An image of sleeping that night in a comfortable cabin swam into his mind; he had spent a long day in the air and felt he deserved a shower and a decent rest. In the morning, he might enjoy breakfast in the dining saloon waited on by a steward in a starched white monkey jacket. He might even fit in a quick visit to the wheelhouse and radio room to stir his seagoing memory. But assumptions frequently nudge a fellow in the wrong direction.

The lieutenant led Danny to a Lynx helicopter with its rotors already turning. They both climbed in. The vibration and noise level rose quickly to a pitch that made conversation impossible. The lieutenant pointed to where a lifejacket was stowed, and that gesture completed the safety briefing. Full darkness had by then marked the end of another day, so Danny knew there was no point in peering down at the anchorage trying to spot the distinctive lavender-coloured hull and black-topped red funnel of RMS *Dumbarton Castle*. The helicopter soon descended, to land on the after deck of a small warship. Presumably the rest of the journey would be by boat. After all, merchant ships like the *Dumbarton Castle* were rarely built with helicopter landing pads.

"Welcome to HMS *Dumbarton Castle*," said the lieutenant. "I've got to take you straight down to the Captain of Marines so he can let you interview the prisoner." Silently, Danny kissed goodbye to the idea of a comfortable cabin and a silver-service breakfast.

The Royal Marine officer introduced himself as Paul, and told Danny that the prisoner was proving difficult. He had already assaulted one of his guards. Astiz also had a list of demands – and the Royal Navy's corresponding shortcomings – in relation to his treatment under the Geneva Convention as a prisoner of war.

The reference to the Geneva Convention was no surprise to Danny. "I know what the navy *hopes* we'll get out of him," he said to Paul. "But from what you say, it doesn't sound like we'll be lucky. What do you know about him?"

"The word is he's a kidnapper and a mass-murderer. Dozens of missing civilians."

"More like hundreds," said Danny, "so it's rather ironic for him to try hiding behind international law."

The officer snorted. "Yes. It's a pity he didn't think of the Convention back in South Georgia. We ought to charge him ourselves. He tried to lure a bunch of our lads into a minefield while he was waving a white flag. He's a grade one scumbag."

"I don't think the government wants to hang on to him, Paul. They don't want to give the Argies an excuse to delay repatriating any of our guys who've fallen into their hands."

"That's bollocks though, isn't it? How many of our blokes are wanted in three or four countries for human rights violations?"

"I expect you're right." Danny sighed. "Let's have a look at him, then."

Danny waited in a cabin that had been set aside for interviewing the prisoner. It was bare except for a table and two chairs. Shortly, two Royal Marines entered with Astiz. One guard removed the pair of handcuffs from the captive's wrists, then left the cabin and closed the door. The other guard stood adjacent to the door with his hands behind his back, his face blank and his mind unreadable.

Danny had already seen photographs of Astiz, but was unprepared for the handsome man who sat before him. His instant impression was that the fellow had the looks, complexion and hair style of what used to be known to plain (but resentful) men as a lady-killer. But if there had been some conspiracy to combine in human form the reality and metaphor of that description, then he doubted that a person existed anywhere else on earth who scored so highly on both accounts.

"Who are you?" Astiz glared at Danny. "What rank? Under the Geneva Convention I may only be interviewed by an officer of equivalent rank. Also, this is not an appropriate time. It is night. I want to go to sleep."

Danny greeted Lieutenant-Commander Astiz in Spanish, apologised for keeping him from his bed, and added that the interview shouldn't take too long. He nodded at the guard. "Also, I don't expect the Marine speaks Spanish, so this need only be between the two of us."

Astiz, clearly surprised to be addressed in his own language, folded his arms across his chest. "I have already told you people that I have nothing to say."

"Commander," said Danny, leaning forward. "I haven't come here to accuse you of anything. I haven't got time to taunt you with a list of your aliases or your alleged victims."

"What do you want, then?"

"It's about somebody who's turned up in the South African embassy in Montevideo, asking for political asylum. He says you can vouch for him."

"If I've done all the things everybody says, I don't think my word would count for much."

"They don't want to bring your name into it. They just want to know if he's genuine."

"They can ask me themselves, then. You have to free me and repatriate me. I'll be home in a couple of days."

"No sir. You're going back to England. It could be a long time before you're free."

"Fuck you," spat Astiz in English. Danny knew of several equivalent Spanish expletives. He assumed Astiz intended the words as much for the marine guard as for himself.

He continued in Spanish. "It's not me, sir. The French and the Swedish are preparing charges. Britain has to examine the indictment and act under international law." Danny noticed that Astiz deflated slightly. "You'll be going to England on the first homeward-bound vessel that calls here. You could be at sea for a couple of weeks. That's why I needed to see you before they put you on board some filthy old tanker or something."

"Britain hasn't charged me. You can't hold me or hand me over to a third country."

"It's a grey area." Danny waited for a moment, glanced at the Marine, then lowered his voice. "From what I hear we could charge you ourselves."

"What with?"

"South Georgia. The white flag and the minefield. Look – don't make it difficult for me."

"You don't frighten me."

"You're lucky you surrendered to the Marines. If you'd tried that trick with the Gurkhas, they'd have sliced you and diced you, and done the same to any of your men who happened to be near-by."

"Now who's talking about war crimes?"

"The Gurkhas don't leave witnesses, Commander Astiz..." Astiz appeared ready to ponder for a while so Danny decided to add a little more pressure. "You need to think about the mess you're in: Dagmar Hagelin, Alicia Domon, Léonie Duquet."

When Astiz spoke again, it was on a different subject. "Your Spanish is good, Mister Rook. But I can't exactly place your accent."

"I learned Spanish from working with some Cubans."

"In Cuba?"

"No. Free Cubans. In the Congo. Supporting the *Makasi* pilots. We were fighting Guevara's communists. Deep down, I've got the same interests as you, Alfredo."

That kept the Argentinean quiet for a little longer.

"South Africa, you say. Why would an Argentine citizen want asylum in South Africa?"

"I didn't say this person was from Argentina. But maybe he can see what's going to happen. Maybe he'll feel safer in

South Africa. You know what it's like there. It's no secret that you were there for a couple of years as assistant naval attaché. Our records say you only left last December, to avoid a scandal. You see? We know everything about you." Astiz looked away, not quite managing to appear aloof. "Come on, Alfredo. You know the country. Maybe you even told your friend it was a good place to go."

"None of my friends has any reason to leave Argentina. This asylum story – it's a trick."

"Get real, Alfredo. You've got the dubious honour of being the first to surrender, but you won't be the last. If you gave your conscripted soldiers a choice – fight and die, or surrender and go home to a warm bed – which one do you think they'd pick?" Astiz lowered his gaze for an instant, then changed it to a slow, disdainful blink.

"It's too late now," continued Danny. "Costa Mendez can't talk Argentina out of this hole you've dug for yourselves. You've lost this war."

"Argentine troops in the Malvinas will fight to their last drop of blood." At the word 'Malvinas' the Marine guard broke his stance and looked angry. "It is sacred to us. You English will die needlessly, thousands of miles from home."

"No, Alfredo. Surrender is your best option. And when your troops come home and start telling their stories, Galtieri will be finished. The junta will fall."

"Never."

"How does the idea of a democratically elected government strike you? Maybe this person wants to get out of Argentina before a People's Government takes over and starts investigating *Los Desaparecidos*. Run and hide. Maybe you'd like to do the same?"

"Huh! Who is he anyway? I assume it's a man?"

"Yes, it's a man. Calls himself Doctor Pescatore. I'm told he showed the South Africans the front of a German identity card, but he wouldn't hand it over for them to look at. Is he genuine?"

"I don't know anyone of that name." Astiz assumed a haughty air and looked away.

"He told them he's an industrial chemist. I expect you know him under another name."

"Describe him to me."

"Do I look like an idiot? You know that's not the way this works. If you want to help your friend to get into South Africa, either tell me what name he's using now or tell me something about him so I know we're talking about the same person. If he's fighting communism, I'll try to open some doors for him."

"You're British. You people bare your arses trying to avoid upsetting anybody, then end up pleasing nobody. You're weak – led by a woman. You never commit to anything. Your government isn't interested in helping the South Africans to fight communist infiltrators."

Danny hoped he had managed to avoid letting any signs of anger show on his face during Astiz's calculated insults. "You're wrong," he said. "I told you – I was fighting communism in the Congo when I was still a teenager. I'm committed – same as you."

Astiz fell silent, perhaps not broken – but stuck in a hole. He yawned once, but for most of the time Danny could tell from watching the way his eyes moved, yet noticed nothing, that he was thinking. Danny hoped he was thinking about his options, weighing up every move, deciding what he could divulge without incriminating himself. Eventually:

"This is between us, right?" Danny nodded. "What do I get out of it?"

"Remember I said it was a grey area? Maybe I could have a word with some people – you know, make it a little less grey where you're standing."

A thoughtful pause, then, "I do know an industrial chemist. But he's quite elderly."

"Yes?"

"He could be the person you're talking about. When he speaks, he sounds as if he could be German – or maybe Austrian or Swiss. Germans never lose their accent, do they?"

"Can you remember a name?"

"Something like one of those Caribbean Islands, I think." Astiz sucked his teeth and cast his eyes up towards the deckhead. He was certainly trying his hardest to make it look good. "Anguilla, or something... Adolpho Anguilla?"

"What makes you think that's the right name? It doesn't sound German – more like Italian, the same as Pescatore."

"It's the name he's using now."

"How do you know?"

"Because he's shown me that identity card, too. Only it says 'Fischer'..." Astiz stood; the marine stepped forward as a precaution. Then, reverting to English Astiz said, "You've got what you came for. Please don't forget what you promised."

Once Astiz had been handcuffed and taken away to his cell, Danny wrote out a short message for Rennie, confirming that Anguilla and Fischer were definitely the same person. He headed for the officers' wardroom to find Paul and ask how to get his signal transmitted.

"Here, give me that," said Paul, taking the note. "You look pretty whacked. I'll just go and get Commander Wood to check it." He looked down at the paper. "Urgent? I'll see how soon we can get it sent off." Then he bought a pint of lager for Danny and sat him in the corner of the wardroom.

Paul returned at around 22:00 to find Danny asleep, and the lager hardly an inch below the top of the glass. He touched Danny's arm to wake him.

"Helicopter waiting, sir. Got to get you back to Wideawake airfield."

'Good,' thought Danny. 'A flight home. I'm off...'

(II)

Ascension Island

By the time the helicopter returned Danny to Wideawake airfield, it was after 23:00 and he was very hungry. He had survived on a sporadic diet of uninteresting sandwiches for the previous eighteen hours, during which so much had happened. The Fleet Air Arm pilot landed close to the RAF airhead operations tent and pointed out where to go. Many people were about, some wearing their shirts open to the waist; it was a sticky night. Danny wondered whether this amount of activity was normal for so late an hour. He announced himself to the clerk in the tent and innocently added that he was expecting to fly home to Brize Norton.

An RAF squadron leader sprang to his feet. "This way sir." He led Danny behind an internal flap that divided the tent in two, and conducted him into a well-equipped communications centre. "The minute you arrived, sir, I was supposed to put you through to your boss."

"Rear-Admiral Rennie?"

"That's him. Half a mo'." The squadron leader picked up a telephone, consulted a hand-written note and began to dial. Danny was not certain whether he was using a satellite link or the undersea cable, but within seconds, or so it seemed, the squadron leader said, "Here – it's ringing," and gave him the telephone handset. Seconds later Rennie came on the line, full of praise.

"Brilliant bit of trickery Danny," said Rennie. "That Astiz interrogation must have gone like a dream. Well done."

“Thanks, yes. Better than I expected. He accepted what was true and fell for what wasn’t. It was just as if I was telling a four-year-old about the tooth fairy. I couldn’t believe it.”

“And there’s no doubt in your mind – Fischer and Anguilla are one and the same?

“Definitely. He mentioned Fischer without me prompting him. He’s seen the guy’s old ID card.”

The admiral became more business-like. “That’s better than I’d hoped. On the strength of that, we’re moving fast to get the SBS to start searching for that cylinder in Caleta Notch.”

“Okay. I suppose everything would be nice and tidy if they could find it.”

“One thing... It means I’ve got to ask you something, Danny.”

Danny experienced a sudden familiar twisting feeling, down where the ribs divide. “Oh?”

“Sandy Woodward has asked if you’ll give him a personal briefing.”

Was that all? Danny felt surprised but knew the success of the operation could depend on his knowledge. There he sat in a communications centre with a telephone in his hand. Presumably, in a matter of moments, the squadron leader could hook him up via satellite to the Royal Navy’s most senior man in the South Atlantic, the commander of the carrier battle group, Rear Admiral John Forster Woodward, aboard HMS *Hermes*.

“All right, sir. I’ll be happy to tell him anything he needs to know.”

“Good man, Danny.” Rennie sounded more pleased than Danny had ever known him to be. “That’s the spirit. Er... just put the squadron leader back on the line, will you?”

Danny returned the handset. “He wants a quick word.”

There followed a brief conversation, of which Danny could only catch half, but it ended with the words: "I expect we'll be able to find something sir," after which the squadron leader cut the connection.

"Do me a favour," said Danny. "I'm starving. Any chance of a couple of rounds of sandwiches? A banana? A packet of crisps. Anything? My stomach thinks my throat's been cut."

"Certainly. No problem at all," said the officer, and took Danny back into the other half of the tent. He beckoned to an RAF sergeant who wore the insignia of the eagle's wings above his stripes. "Mike, fix Mister Rook up, will you? Get him a pie and a pint before he flakes out."

The flight sergeant seemed to understand Danny's needs very well because he took him to the mess tent, treated him to a pint of lager and a micro-waved steak pie, and had the same himself. For a few minutes, they talked. Mike proved to be an air loadmaster, currently serving on a C-130 Hercules squadron.

"Bloody noisy," said Mike. "Most of us air crew are half-deaf already."

"I remember the row," said Danny. "I had a few flights on the Hercules in the sixties... in the Congo."

The two were becoming the best of temporary acquaintances when Mike suggested that they needed to make a start. Keen to get home, Danny tagged along. Mike led Danny to a store room where a quartermaster sergeant held sway.

"First man for the special flight," said Mike.

The quartermaster peered at Danny, sizing him up by eye. "What do you weigh, sir?"

"About thirteen stone. Why?"

"And your age, sir?"

"Thirty-six. What's this all about?"

"Just checking you're fit, sir. Do you do any sports – football or jogging maybe?"

"Not too much running around if I can avoid it. I try to have a swim once a week and I play cricket for the village second eleven if they're short-handed."

"I see. Swimming... good. Cricket... Do you bat or bowl, sir?"

"Whatever they want." Danny felt this all seemed very odd.

"I see. All-rounder. Anything else – weight training, kayaking maybe?"

"I enjoy a long bike ride occasionally or a walk in the country. Why is this important now? Nobody at Brize Norton asked me anything like this."

"Cricket... That's good for strength and co-ordination, I'd say. Swimming, cycling... They need a fair slice of endurance as well. Would you say you're generally fit? No heart problems or anything?"

"Fit enough. I could be fitter but I'm not about to collapse. What's the problem?"

The QMS disappeared for about two minutes, then returned carrying a pillar-box-red one-piece neoprene wetsuit. "This looks about your size sir," he said. "Try it on for me."

Danny was truly astonished. "What do I want that for? I thought I'd be flying out of here in a VC-10."

"No sir." Mike seemed quite amused. "A Herk. You're lucky. You're first in the queue. Best chance of copping a suit that fits. The poor sod at the back of the queue will have to take pot luck."

The thought of flying all the way from Ascension to Oxfordshire in the cargo bay of a non-soundproofed aircraft like the Hercules held no attractions. Still less appealing was the idea of resembling some sort of crimson amphibian while doing so.

"So all this is a sort of survival precaution, is it?"

"Exactly, sir."

"How long is the flight?"

"Thirteen hours." Mike looked at his watch. "Take off in about two hours."

Danny halted. "Can I delay putting this thing on then? Even if I lie flat and don't move a muscle, I'll probably sweat a gallon an hour in this heat." He smiled. "Don't want to drown." Mike and the QMS guffawed and said that would be perfectly all right.

Sunday 16 May

Danny had been sitting in the waiting area for about ninety minutes when a couple of people arrived and started trying on wetsuits. He took his cue and tried to watch what the others were doing so he could imitate them and dress with the minimum of fuss. A little wiser, he began to put on his own suit. Over the next fifteen minutes, more people arrived in ones and twos. Danny lost interest until he felt a nudge from behind; he turned round.

"This is a turn up for the book," said his sandy-haired partner-in-conversation from the VC-10. "Don't tell me you're on this flight, as well. They said there was a civvy, but I never thought it'd be you."

For several seconds nothing made sense. "What's happened?" asked Danny. "Are you going back home? Have they cancelled your operation?"

"What? Operation Certain Death? No mate, more's the pity."

"I don't understand."

"Hey, listen. You could do something for us... The whisper is that you're going to meet Sandy Woodward. When you meet him, tell him 6 Troop said bye-bye and could he sack the planners, or better still send them out on a no-hoper so they know what it feels like."

"Meet the admiral? I'm supposed to be flying to England."

"Not dressed like that, matey."

Danny could think of no suitable response. He stood, and, given the restrictions imposed by his wetsuit, hurried across to speak to Mike.

"I think there's been a mistake. I'm supposed to be flying to England, aren't I?"

"No sir. Admiral Rennie told me directly. Get you togged up for a flight to the South Atlantic so you can give Admiral Woodward his personal briefing, like you agreed."

Until Ginger spoke, Danny had half-forgotten about the briefing. He had been expecting to be called to the telephone at a time when the admiral found it convenient to speak to him. He said so to Mike.

"No sir. Personal, as in 'in person'... face to face."

Danny swore softly, calling Rennie by every obscenity that he knew. It occupied several seconds. "So all this..." he tugged at the collar of his wetsuit; "all this means I'm expected to parachute into the southern ocean just to save a rear admiral the bother of getting on the R/T?"

"Well you told the quartermaster you could swim, didn't you sir?" Danny gulped. "Then there's the SBS boys," said Mike. "They're bound to have a whole list of questions that won't have occurred to the admiral. You can't let *them* down."

Danny wasn't stupid. He recognised that he had been Shanghaied. But he also knew he had a real obligation to the people who would be going out to look for Doctor Fischer's cylinder; he could hardly back out. "But I've never parachuted before... never."

"Don't you worry, sir. Nothing can go wrong. I'll be on the flight with you. And there's two RAF parachute instructors –

the best there is; and two army dispatchers. And best of all, you're jumping into water... a soft landing."

Danny set his lips into a straight line. "Right. But the day I get home is the day I quit." He went back and sat next to Ginger.

"Just heard," said Ginger. "Not a nervous flyer, are you?"

"Didn't used to be. Why?"

"Heard the pilots having a chinwag. Apparently the Herk is so choc-full of fuel for the flight that she's six thousand pounds overweight. She's right off the end of all Lockheed's safety graphs."

"You're joking."

"No. Straight up." He pointed at one of the pilots, dressed in flight overalls and wearing the epaulettes of a flight lieutenant. "That's him," said Ginger. "He reckoned it was touch and go. 'When we get to the end of the runway,' he said, 'and pull back on the stick, don't blame me if it's only the wings that soar off into the sky and the rest of us carry on along the ground till we shoot off into the bloody ocean.' Straight up, he did."

"Great story," said Danny.

"It's the way I tell 'em."

All the same, Ginger might have been telling the truth, for when the Hercules started its takeoff roll, the aircraft stayed on the runway far longer than Danny would have expected. Once he felt her lift off, she gained height at a very shallow angle. The reason for the pilot's caution was obvious to all those in the cargo bay. Almost the whole internal space had been taken up by four extra cylindrical fuel tanks, fixed to the deck. Danny learned that these added another twelve and a half tons to the aircraft's take-off weight.

Several hours into the flight, the Hercules began to descend. The moment for Danny's first parachute jump could not be far away, making him feel very nervous. Ginger and the rest of 6 Troop appeared to take no notice of the descent, continuing to sleep wherever they had managed to find a place. Mike had rigged a few stretchers above the fuel tanks, which the soldiers seemed to regard as an ideal sleeping place. Danny went to ask Mike whether the parachute drop was about to take place. This conversation was held by yelling alternately into each other's ear at close quarters. Mike led Danny to one of the circular windows where he was surprised to see that they were flying in close company with a Victor refuelling tanker, perhaps only a hundred feet away. By gesture and bellowed explanation, Mike told Danny that the C-130 was still very heavy. Consequently, the fuselage was sagging so far beneath the normal position of the wings that these were canted upwards, and fuel couldn't flow into the outer wing tanks.

The only way to counteract this was by making a shallow descent. Danny carried on watching until the Victor detached and the surface of the sea could be clearly seen, not so very far below them. The Hercules droned on and began to climb again, very gradually.

After twelve hours in the air, the Hercules started to descend again. Within minutes, Mike came and had a word with the SAS troop commander; the soldiers shrugged themselves into their parachute packs. One of the RAF instructors strapped Danny into his pack and explained everything he needed to know. The aircraft sank from the clear blue stratosphere into a layer of cloud three miles thick, covering the drop zone. Buffeting and turbulence increased. The smell of fuel sloshing around in the internal tanks started to make Danny feel nauseous; he swallowed to equalise the pressure in his ears.

Eventually, the C-130 emerged below the cloud base and the upper tail door began to open, locking into position in the fuselage roof. The army dispatchers opened the side 'para-doors' and the tail ramp lowered into the horizontal position. Everyone craned, hoping to catch a glimpse of the ship that they hoped soon to be aboard – the RFA *Fort Austin* – but all they could see was the sea itself, deep dolphin grey and flecked with white, beneath clouds the colour of car park concrete. The soldiers checked each other's parachutes and static lines. 'Red on'. Then, 'green on' and, as calmly as one might cross a road, 6 Troop trotted out into the winter air. Mike, the instructors and the dispatchers checked each man all the way, from parachute opening to splashdown.

The plan was for Danny to jump in a second wave. First to go would be the two packages of SAS equipment, polythene-covered, taped and netted – then his big moment. The Hercules flew on, turned 60° to port for several seconds, then made a similar turn to starboard to complete the circle and fly back down its course line on a reciprocal bearing.

There seemed to be a problem. The *Fort Austin* was there, but the men and their parachutes were still in the water, with the ship's boat struggling to cover the distance to pick them up. (Ship's boat? Had nobody thought of using a helicopter to pick up the men in the style of a NASA moon mission?) Mike, the dispatchers and the parachute instructors, all attached by safety lines, peered down to try to understand the difficulty. Danny felt sure he could see the *Fort Austin's* boat being propelled by oars. If that were true, he wondered why the navy felt it was a good idea to maintain practices that seemed not to have altered much in a hundred years. And he wondered whether, when he arrived on board the *Hermes*, he would indeed be meeting Rear Admiral Woodward or perhaps a small gentleman sporting an eye patch and wearing a gold-trimmed bicorn hat worn athwartships, whilst carrying a telescope under his remaining arm.

The Hercules had no option but to fly in wide circles, waiting for the signal that the drop zone was clear and that it was safe to release the equipment – and Danny of course. Danny could tell that Mike and the army dispatchers had become agitated by the delay, huddled together consulting their watches. He felt that their hand gestures betrayed deep concern either for being able to make it back to their mid-ocean refuelling rendezvous, or for avoiding detection by Argentine radar systems; probably both. His utter helplessness in this situation added to his unease. It seemed an awfully long time, too, that 6 Troop had been in the water. If things could go so badly wrong for the professionals, what chance did he stand? He tried to adopt a nonchalant air, and largely failed.

When the signal came, over thirty minutes had elapsed since the first parachutist had left the aircraft. The RAF instructor gave Danny a brief reminder of what to do. The army dispatchers let go the SAS equipment and Danny followed it down beneath his own 22-foot canopy, trying hard to follow the advice to disregard the steering toggles. A soft landing, as he had been promised, and the parachute canopy sank harmlessly onto the sea surface, downwind. His one fear had been that it would come down over his head, get wet, stick to his face, and prevent him breathing; he might even drown.

The aim had been good. Within five minutes, Danny and the SAS stores were safely in the boat, making their way towards the looming grey bulk of the *Fort Austin*, her blue ensign spread proudly in the stiffening breeze. With a professional eye Danny noticed the number of aerials festooning the vessel's bridge deck. After a few moments he turned his gaze back to his companions. Ginger was shivering and had turned blue-grey. Through chattering teeth, he was stammering a terse criticism of the planners' choice of wetsuits over dry. Seawater was trickling out of both bales of equipment. Everybody looked pissed-off.

≈

On board the *Fort Austin*, an officer led Danny and the SAS troopers aft to the helicopter hangar. The chief steward met them there with a great pan full of chicken soup. He handed out mugs to the men and told them to help themselves because a Sea King helicopter would be landing in twenty minutes to ferry them to the *Hermes*.

Danny wanted to ask why it could not have been there an hour sooner to help rescue them all from the gut-chilling sea. Instead, he asked how far south they had now flown. The escorting officer told him that Port Stanley lay only about seventy or eighty miles southwest of them. Then Danny asked why the Hercules could not have dropped them alongside the *Hermes*. 'Understandably' (as he was told) Sandy Woodward couldn't risk stopping the *Hermes* dead in the water to pick up the men because this risked an Exocet attack without the freedom to manoeuvre; that was why. He was right, of course, but that didn't stop Danny wanting to give the jumped-up, one-ring, supercilious prick a smack in the mouth.

A couple of the men were now wrapped in thermal insulating blankets to prevent further heat loss. Danny felt the whole caper could have been, and should have been, better organised. Through the open hangar doors, the rhythmic thud of approaching helicopter rotors penetrated his thoughts. Ginger dipped his mug into the pan again, then shuffled along, sipping as he went, bent like a ninety-year-old. Before stepping onto the heli-deck he took a last sip, then deliberately threw the mug over his shoulder onto the steel deck where it shattered in a pool of creamy-grey liquid. Everybody still looked very pissed-off.

In the Sea King's cabin, the troopers had recovered sufficiently to feel able to contribute some blunt views to the general discourse. Their commander was attempting to assure his men that neither brigadier generals, rear admirals, God, nor Mrs Thatcher herself would shift him in the direction of Tierra del Fuego until his rations, weapons, radios, explosives, clothing and toffee tin had all thoroughly dried out. ("And been tested," shouted one.) To unanimous approval Ginger recommended adding a beer, steak and chips and a good sleep to the list of pre-requisites.

On board HMS *Hermes*, her captain hardly needed a strategic appraisal from the SAS. He could see that the men could not be landed near Rio Grande in their current condition. News of thick fog on the mainland made up his mind for him. He ordered that the reconnaissance operation, officially known as 'Operation Plum Duff' (and certainly not as 'Operation Certain Death') be postponed for 24 hours. He set off to tell Woodward of his decision.

(III)

Monday 17 May, 1982
HMS Hermes

Word reached Danny that Rear Admiral Woodward was too busy to speak with him straight away, the 17th of May being Argentina's Navy Day. Clearly, if the country intended to mount some spectacular operation against Mrs Thatcher's Task Force, this was the day they would choose to do it.

Sadly, a night's sleep in the lower decks of the *Hermes* had not improved Danny's temper. He had reached his temporary bunk by descending stairways, then ladders, and by squeezing through kidney hatches. These openings, measuring about 24 inches by 18, had rounded ends and were pinched in the middle. They were set into the larger alleyway doors that divided the vessel into watertight compartments, these doors being clamped shut due to the vessel's state of wartime readiness.

Only one man could pass through a kidney hatch at a time, and only then if he wasn't carrying too much flesh around the waist. Danny was sure there must be a technique for getting through unscathed, but he had already found that one had to suffer the bruises first before learning which parts of the body went through the aperture at what angle and in what order.

He understood perfectly that the Argentine Air Force knew roughly where the Task Force was. He was well aware that there could be an Argentine periscope squinting in his direction at that exact moment. He appreciated the need for precautions and for the vessel to be at the highest state of preparedness. Yet he was angry with the navy. He was angry about the incompetence of some of the planners and he was angry about the minor contusions already sustained due to the kidney hatches. But this was no mood in which to meet a rear admiral. He took a deep breath, smiled at his escort and made some comment about a rabbit warren.

Danny's escort leaned past him and knocked on a door, above which an engraved label read 'Nuclear Biological and Chemical Warfare Office'. Apparently, now Danny couldn't even be trusted to rap on a door for himself. He had been told to prepare a personal briefing for the admiral, but when he was admitted to what he hoped would have been the right place, he found himself faced with an unsmiling, under-height, pale fellow, wearing on his navy-blue jersey the epaulettes of a full three-ring commander. It seemed that Danny's briefing had been delegated to a minion.

"Well... Why do you think you're here?" asked the commander.

The commander had the petty, impatient air of a martinet. Clearly, he was not only a very busy minion but it was debatable whether he or Danny was feeling the more liverish that morning. Danny thought from the tone of the commander's question that he would be unlikely to appreciate a philosophical debate about physical existence and the human condition. This left two main possibilities. It was either a silly question or a trap.

"How long have you got?"

Back came the instant response. "I haven't got time to fuck about."

Along with everything else, Danny had also been brooding on the way Rennie had tricked him in small but clearly deliberate steps. First, he had been duped into flying to Ascension. Then, owing to a difference in their individual interpretations of a single word, Rennie had hoodwinked him into a 13-hour flight, ending with a dunking in the South Atlantic. The navy had not improved matters with that mug of lukewarm soup on board the RFA supply ship, followed by his damp arrival on Woodward's flagship, the *Hermes*. He had had enough.

He sniffed. "Don't then."

That seemed to sting the officer. He raised a finger and brandished it at Danny. "Now you listen here..."

Danny's hands had been resting on the table across which he and the commander were now exchanging very similar facial expressions. Without warning he snapped his right hand up and grabbed the offending digit, twisting it enough to cause shock, pain and the clicking sound of cartilage under strain. The commander's arm had not been tensed for more than the hand gesture, so there was no resistance as Danny continued the movement. He swept the commander's hand backwards and used it to deliver a self-administered slap to both the officer's cheeks. Danny still had hold of the finger; he shook it.

"You wave that thing at me again, and next time I'll break it off and shove it up your arse." The officer looked shaken. "I'm here to speak to *your* admiral because *my* admiral is a lying bastard and he's fucking-well Shanghaied me." The officer had still not snatched his finger away so Danny shook it again. "I suspect your admiral needs to be told what he thinks I know – if that's not too complicated for you to grasp – and I think I might also need to brief some boys from the SBS. That's why I'm here." Danny had had enough of holding hands so he slammed the commander's arm back on the table. "But there's a fucking big 'Why?' sitting behind all this... So, if you need to know more... HOW LONG HAVE YOU GOT?"

Rear Admiral Woodward could probably be a bit of a bastard too if he wanted to be. However, his weapon of choice at that moment seemed to be charm.

"I need to know three things," said the Admiral. "One: do you have any information to suggest that I face a biological hazard from the Argentines?" He smiled. Danny noted that he had avoided calling them 'Argies'; he respected that. Woodward seemed content to take his three things individually; he opened his hand towards Danny, inviting a reply.

"No sir, I don't. As I understand it there's little point in bio-weapons at sea. Rapid dilution of the agent and slow-acting effects are one thing, but we think this copper cylinder that the Nazis left behind never contained –"

"– Hold on," said Woodward. "What cylinder? What Nazis?"

The admiral's questions knocked Danny off course. "I don't understand, sir. I thought you knew all this. I thought I was here to update you about Doctor Fischer's new identity and where we think the nerve agent might be now, and –"

"– Mister Rook, all I know is that I've been asked to mount a covert insertion of SBS personnel into Chile. Admiral Rennie agreed that you would tell me why, and that you would then brief the personnel involved."

Danny blinked hard and shook his head in disbelief. "I'm sorry sir. I thought you'd know all the background."

"Not about this operation, I don't. Don't be too surprised. The Russians are listening to everything we send and receive. It's all encrypted, obviously, but whether it takes them one year or ten to crack our encryption, they'll carry on until they do. Somebody somewhere must have decided that whatever information you're acting on was safer in your head than being sent over the satellite link."

"So you don't know anything about documents captured in Paris, or U-1226, or –"

"– None of it. Perhaps you'd like to give me an outline?"

So Danny tried to summarize what he knew about Doctor Fischer's survival in 1944, the likely cargo of U-1226 and the cylinder's location. He went on to mention the error of judgement made by Admiral Cunningham, moving on to Doctor Fischer's alias and likely employment since the war, and one other factor of fundamental importance – the need to preserve the United Kingdom's 'special relationship' with the USA. Only by finding Doctor Fischer's copper cylinder (if it was there to be found), recovering it and destroying both it and its contents for good could Mrs Thatcher be sure of keeping the details of this wartime naval cock-up buried in the archives, together with its narrowly-avoided consequences.

Since Woodward did not follow up Danny's briefing by asking his two remaining questions, Danny assumed with some pride that he had covered them already. What the admiral then went on to say came as no shock to Danny.

"Mister Rook, I'm cross-decking you over to the *Invincible* as soon as possible. The raid is going in tonight, and I think it's essential you brief the SBS in person, as soon as possible."

By now Danny knew what the navy meant by the term 'in person'. "Yes sir," he said.

In maritime jargon, the day had turned out 'partly cloudy, fine and clear', which was better than would normally be expected in those latitudes. But the crew of the *Hermes* had not been relaxing, filling their lungs with bracing sea air and glorying in the fine weather.

The good visibility also favoured the Argentine Air Force. For anyone wanting to mount an Exocet attack, the conditions were as good as they were going to get, so every sailor with a view of the horizon and a distrust of radar systems was scanning the surrounding ocean for incoming warplanes or sea-skimming missiles. Danny noticed how focused they were and admired their sense of duty – even if it was also self-preservation.

His belongings, including the Astiz file, had remained behind at Ascension in a secure lock-up. This meant he had become dependent upon the pusser's slop chest on the *Hermes* for a change of clothing. Consequently, apart from having no badges of rank, he had now become indistinguishable from the rest of her crew. Because he had never expected to be required to brief anybody about the geography of Caleta Notch, Vic Marchesi's mark-up of the 1883 chart lay even farther away; it had never left 55 Broadway. However, Danny's memory of where Victor said he had consigned the cylinder to the depths was good, partly because the location was so well-chosen as to be obvious. He hoped the SBS had access to an identical chart so he could point out exactly where they should start searching.

The admiral's word being law, before lunchtime a Lynx helicopter ferried Danny on the short flight to HMS *Invincible*. He enjoyed the experience. The navy had laid out below him a tableau, a veritable naval review of the carriers with their screen of destroyers. The Lynx pilot gave a wide berth to a fleet auxiliary nuzzling up to replenish one of the destroyers under way, the pair steaming parallel at 18 knots so as not to waste a precious mile or minute. There was something rather glorious and confident about the whole performance that cheered him immensely and wiped away his earlier irritability. He hoped the NBC Officer's finger wasn't hurting too much – but hell... too bad if it was.

Aboard HMS Invincible

There was something tantalisingly familiar about the officer of the day, who met Danny on arrival. Temporarily unable to put a name to a face, it was the unexpectedness of the encounter that defeated him. By the time he had worked out that he had been welcomed aboard by the person standing second in line of succession to the British throne, thankfully, he was on the mess deck, shuffling in line to receive a hot meal. Once he was seated, out of curiosity he thought he would try to confirm his deduction.

"Any idea who's the officer of the day today? I've got to find him after I've finished this plate of stew..."

"Randy Andy, I think," said the marine sitting opposite him.

"Oh okay," said Danny. "Maybe you can point me in the right direction later."

"You from the press?"

In classical mythology, Hermes is the messenger of the Greek gods. But because he is also the god of boundaries and the transgression of borders, there could be no more fitting name for the flagship of a naval expedition sent to deliver a message to a military dictatorship concerning their unwelcome infringement of British sovereignty. By some accounts, Hermes also has a daughter, Tyche, the goddess of luck, chance and the unpredictable... It seemed that Tyche had not yet finished toying with Daniel Rook.

The officer of the day led Danny, now somewhat subdued, slightly over-awed, and highly respectful, to the hangar to meet the SBS team who were to infiltrate Chile in search of Doctor Fisher's cylinder. Although the hangar was primarily the space where Sea Harrier aircraft and Sea King helicopters were kept and maintained, it was also the only place large enough for Royal Marines to lay out kit and weapons for inspection prior to an operation. It had therefore become a second home for Britain's sea soldiers needing a bit of space.

"Here's your man," said Prince Andrew. "See you later." And he marched importantly off.

The man in question knelt amid a jigsaw puzzle of varnished wooden laths, odd tools, stout cord, and what appeared to be canvas sheeting. He looked up in the direction of the departing officer, twitched his right arm to perform a half-hearted salute, mumbled his thanks and transferred his attention to Danny. His face transformed in an instant as his eyes widened and his mouth opened still more. An intake of breath came next, followed by a traditional sexual expletive, not normally taken literally, but rather denoting extreme shock and surprise. He was not alone. At that exact second, the same two words came to Danny's lips, so that the two men spoke in a chorus of profanity. Two seconds of gaping silence, then:

"What?"

"You!"

The marine leapt to his feet and both men threw themselves into the manly embrace beloved of presidents and prime ministers world-wide – the firm right-handed shake with the left hand grasping the opposite man's right shoulder, bicep or elbow. Any display of deeper feelings would have been unseemly; one never knew who might have been watching.

"Carlisle!"

"Danny!"

As if responding to some telepathic cue, there came a second chorus, "What are you doing here?" Then a sudden release of emotion – laughter.

"Carlisle Tillotson... Don't tell me you're off to Chile tonight."

"Danny Rook. I don't believe it. Go on. Spill the beans."

"I'm supposed to be briefing some poor sod who's off on a mission." A thought hit him. "I guess I shouldn't have mentioned Chile in case it's not you. Careless talk. Is it you?"

"Yep. Drawn the short straw. As usual."

"What's all this?" Danny passed his arm over the assortment of wood and canvas. "Looks like some sort of tent or something."

"It's a Klepper canoe. German-made, I think. Two-man job. You can break it down into bits to make it easier to transport. I'm just making sure I've got all the pieces and they all fit."

"What time are you off?"

"Midnight."

Danny grinned. "Like Cinderella."

"Hardly... Hey, it's good to see you, Danny."

"You too."

There was so much more to say that neither knew where to start. Carlisle necessarily had his mind more on the job in hand and broke the silence. "Here – help me put this bloody thing back together, will you? We need to go and see my boss about this briefing." He looked down at the kit-form canoe. "I can't leave these bits lying about or Jolly Jack will have 'em away."

"Just show me what to do."

Carlisle's boss proved to be a Royal Marine major. Although he had no information about what part of Chile his man was expected to infiltrate, and so did not have the appropriate chart to hand, it took very little time to get hold of the right one from the *Invincible's* South American chart folio. Together, the three of them pored over the chart of Caleta Notch and the larger scale charts of the Magellan Strait. Danny explained why the mission had taken on its sudden importance and Carlisle filled in a few details for his boss about his and Danny's brief acquaintanceship. Carlisle had started talking about some of the specialised equipment he would need when there came a knock at the door. A marine sergeant with a chest like that of a cart horse entered.

"Beg pardon sir," said the sergeant. "But the Bear has fallen off a ladder."

Nothing could now surprise Danny. However, the mental image that this news conjured up posed two principal questions. If in the first place this bear performed some mysterious but invaluable service aboard the *Invincible*, what could that be? And, given the importance of this animal, why was it permitted to risk its life by climbing ladders? His second thought – that this reference to a bear and a ladder was some form of tactical code – brought temporary relief. It was all right; he probably didn't need to know...

The major nodded at Carlisle. "You'd better go and see." Carlisle left with the sergeant. Danny and the major filled in time talking about Vic Marchesi, life in the Merchant Shipping Intelligence Branch and the duplicity of admirals. After about ten minutes Carlisle returned.

"Corporal Bearwood has broken his leg, sir," said Carlisle.

"He's WHAT?"

"Broken his leg, sir."

"Well, it's not rough today, is it? We aren't shipping it green or anything. Bearwood's been a marine for how bloody long and you're telling me he can't go up and down a ladder safely. What the bloody hell was he doing?"

"Carrying a keg of beer, sir." Carlisle glanced down then slowly raised his head again. The corners of his mouth gave the suspicion of a twitch. "He said he didn't want to drop it in case it went all frothy inside. It left him hanging upside down on a ladder clasping this barrel to his chest and hooked up by a broken leg... He's in a lot of pain."

"He'll be in a lot more when I get hold of him."

"Trouble is, it leaves me with a problem," said Carlisle. "He was my number two."

"Shit!" The major turned around to face the bulkhead, his neck bent and his head shaking slowly from side to side. After a moment, he turned back again. "Who else have you got?"

"Nobody now. The rest of the lads have been allocated for covert observation posts. Most of 'em are due for insertion shoreside tonight."

"You're sure – nobody?"

"Nobody, sir."

"Well, we can't cancel the operation. You'll just have to go single handed."

Carlisle shrugged. "It's a *two*-man canoe sir. If you try to paddle it on your Jack Jones it just goes round in circles. Added to that we reckoned we'd need two men to make proper headway against the current through the Strait."

The major appeared to think hard. "I don't suppose we could find an SAS bloke hanging around, doing nothing..."

Carlisle shook his head. "I doubt it. And of course, the other reason Bearwood came top of the pile was 'cos he speaks Spanish..."

Both men turned slowly to look with slightly raised eyebrows at Danny.

(IV)

Midnight, Monday/Tuesday 17/18 May
HMS Invincible

Danny, Carlisle and the SAS troop sat in the flight deck operations room, hushed and introspective. For most, the time for talk or nervous jokes had passed. Now each man had retreated into his own silent space to be alone with his thoughts. Thoughts of what he was being called upon to do, of course. In all probability, thoughts too of family or a favourite whore house; thoughts of death or hopeful survival; thoughts of a scar or two and another bragging session with the lads back at the barracks; thoughts of spitting in an admiral's eye.

There had been talk, plenty of it, and argument too. The soldiers had not been so clannish or security-conscious as to keep their concerns to themselves. Danny had tried to see past the men's body language, to listen beyond their tone and choice of words. He already knew they had no confidence in their mission or the motives of the politicians and officers who had sent them there. But there was something else. Did they also lack faith in their leader?

The SAS troop commander entered the operations room with a Royal Marine loadmaster, whom he introduced as Pete, a member of 846 Squadron. The SAS soldiers were familiar with the reputation of those who flew in the 'Junglie' squadrons, so fell silent.

"You're going to find this Sea King a bit different from usual," said the troop commander. "With our two extra passengers," – he turned to acknowledge Carlisle and Danny – "the pilot has asked for even more kit to be stripped out of her. It could be a bit uncomfortable. All the seats have been taken out, and the soundproofing. The *Invincible* is about to go to emergency full ahead to get maximum wind speed over the flight deck so I'll let Pete add a little more technical detail."

The air loadmaster explained that the Sea King would be operating well in excess of its maximum all-up mass due to the full fuel tanks and heavy payload. Some of the avionics had been de-installed, cargo equipment unbolted, life raft and fire extinguishers removed. The winch, flotation gear and machine gun mountings were all gone. He explained that the Sea King would take off at the optimum point that combined range, arrival in darkness at the dropping zone, and the need for the *Invincible* to get clear of Argentine waters before dawn. He emphasised that the aircraft was being sacrificed; this was a one-way flight. Once the SAS troop had been inserted, the helicopter would fly into Chilean air space and ditch in a spot where it could be sunk in deep water, leaving the crew to make their way inland. There, they would conceal themselves for a week, before giving themselves up to the Chilean authorities.

Danny heaved an internal sigh, doubting that the aircraft would remain undiscovered for long once the pilots had given themselves up. There would be some explaining to do.

Pete finished his talk by inviting his passengers to dress in survival suits.

"In case you hadn't heard," shouted Ginger, "this was already 'Operation Certain Death'. Now you're telling us there's no life rafts in this chopper, no survival gear, nothing. For me, if I'm ditching in the drink with no hope of rescue, I'd rather freeze to death in five minutes than live for twelve hours bobbing about in rough seas in a Michelin Man suit and getting sea sick. Stuff it!"

Most of the troop then made it known that they shared this opinion.

"Well, it's up to you," said Carlisle, "but I'm having one. It'll be brass monkeys in the back of that chopper and just in case we don't plunge into the ocean, I'd rather arrive on land feeling toasty-warm in my immersion suit than freezing my nuts off in my combats." This proved to be a persuasive intervention; the SAS then opted for warmth too.

Ten well-insulated, orange-suited and not very happy people trudged from the operations room onto the blacked-out flight deck. The Sea King's rotors were turning, but against all regulations a fuel hose was still attached, keeping the tanks topped up at the same rate as fuel was being burnt.

Danny had been silent and subdued. "You're very trusting," said Carlisle to him.

"You've kept me safe before. I just hope these Marine pilots will do the same."

"They're the best." Carlisle put a hand between Danny's shoulders to help him step up into the Sea King's bare cabin. "What I tell myself every time I climb into any sort of aircraft, military or commercial, is this: They'll be careful – they don't want to die." He scanned the stripped-out cabin and non-existent seating arrangements. "Flying… I bloody hate it."

Ginger turned to the loadmaster. "What's the weather like up ahead?"

"A bit of fog. Nothing to worry about."

A perceptible change in motion signalled that the Sea King had become airborne. The familiar pitch and roll of a ship at sea, with the occasional judder as her bows struck a bigger wall of water, had gone in an instant as the helicopter lifted into the hover. The pilot banked to port at a very shallow angle to clear the flight deck. Danny assumed that the overweight aircraft would handle like a pig, forcing the pilot to make any transition up or down, port or starboard, gently. Carlisle was probably right. If the pilot wished to stay alive, he wouldn't want to strain the moving parts any more than conditions dictated. Danny managed to look at his watch; it showed a quarter past midnight. He had no sensation in his lower stomach of any change in height, and realised that the plan would be to fly close to sea level, below the horizon of any Argentine radar systems.

An hour into the flight, in the dim red glow of the cabin lighting, Danny noticed the SAS troop commander haul himself to his feet, swing towards the cockpit and brace himself against the forward bulkhead. Danny presumed he briefly plugged into the aircrew intercom system because he began to make gestures of speech and understanding. When he returned to the main cabin, he was carrying an object shaped rather like an electric hand tool. It had a pistol grip; perhaps it satisfied some internal soldierly need to be holding a weapon. The SAS captain stood first at a starboard side cabin window and pointed the device in a slow arc to the north, then repeated the process to the south through a window on the port side. When he sat down, he showed the apparatus to the man next to him and by gesture and exaggerated lip movements the word passed around that the gadget was a hand-held signal detector, designed to indicate whether the aircraft had been illuminated by enemy radar. The troop commander was on his feet every few minutes after that. From his position, Danny could see one of the pilots. The night vision goggles attached to his flying helmet shed a faint green glow, giving him the appearance of an alien.

Confined on the cold, hard, bare deck of the Sea King, Danny's bottom had become numb. Shuffling around only provided temporary relief, so he and others had begun to stand and move about. The SAS officer seemed happy to let his troops try out the radar detector. There was some doubt as to whether or not it was working properly because it had indicated nothing since leaving the *Invincible*.

Nearly three and a half hours into the flight the pilot unexpectedly banked to starboard. Though the turn was not steep, it surprised everyone. After a few minutes one of the troopers noticed something through one of the port side windows. All took a look – Danny too. It was obvious that the weather had closed in. Ahead, about thirty degrees to port, a tall flickering orange glow could be made out, diffused in the mist. Danny felt it could only be one thing – an Argentinean drilling rig, burning off a pocket of natural gas. He hoped it had only recently taken up position, because if it had been there for some time there would have been notices to mariners to advise its position. Uncharted, the thing would be a hazard to navigation. As bad as everyone supposed the Argentines to be, they had every interest in preventing ships from colliding with rigs in their waters, so they would have issued corrections for marine charts – and issued them to all international navigation authorities. It had the makings of yet another naval cock-up.

Really, it seemed so fundamental... Somebody ought to have checked to see whether there was anything shown on the charts between *Invincible's* position and the coast of Tierra del Fuego, anything that might prove a hazard to a helicopter flying at fifty feet above the waves. Fortunately, the night vision goggles had enabled the pilots to see the flame well before it became visible to the eye alone, and in sufficient time to avoid the rig. Now the hope was that nobody aboard the rig had heard the Sea King and reported it to the authorities.

When the glimmer of the gas flare lay directly to port, the SAS captain gave a grunt. He had clearly reached the limit of his patience. He got to his feet with the air of an intolerant schoolmaster, annoyed with some unfortunate child who still failed to grasp a rudimentary mathematical or linguistic principle. Once again, he wedged himself into the opening between the cockpit and the cabin; conversation ensued. The captain sat down again and cupped a hand to the ear of the man next to him, so he could relay what he had discovered. When the word passed down to Danny, now considered 'one of the boys', he learned that the officer had been annoyed that the helicopter had flown so close to the offshore production platform. He seemed to think the navigator was not keeping on top of his job.

To further prejudice the mission (in his view), he had found out that the radar altimeter had developed an intermittent fault. Added to that, the inertial navigation system needed such regular updates to correct its calculations – some story about the magnetic variation changing wildly – that the SAS captain reckoned the navigator was mentally overloaded. His belief in the professionalism of the helicopter crew had evaporated. He doubted that the navigator knew where he was, and consequently (he said) it was unlikely the troop would be landed in the right place.

To Danny, it all sounded like a grubby effort to establish an excuse in advance of possible failure. He had felt puzzled when the helicopter began to fly a northerly loop around the rig, but when he thought about it a little more, it seemed logical. By now, they must be close to the coast of Tierra del Fuego. If the navigation system had drifted slightly, perhaps a southerly loop risked bringing the helicopter too close to Rio Grande and possible radar detection. He realised that by flying to the north, the crew would have to make their landfall in a different place from that initially intended. However, the pilots knew that too. Benefiting from their night vision goggles they would soon be looking out for different coastal features to re-establish their position. It seemed to him that the crew had adapted flexibly to an unexpected circumstance. There was nothing wrong with that. A few minutes later the pilot banked to port. Danny felt safe in assuming they were now clear of the rig, with the helicopter crew still committed to the mission and intending to drop the squad where they had originally planned.

Danny stretched his arms and rolled his neck so he could take a peek at Carlisle. The SBS marine did not appear to be in any way anxious about what was going on. Danny felt reassured. The helicopter banked to port yet again. It felt like a ninety-degree turn, as if they had made landfall and turned south. Danny noticed that the captain and his men had given up using the hand-held radar detector. He wondered if the pilot knew. If they were close enough to have crossed the coast, the likelihood of being picked up on Argentinean radar must have increased markedly.

He flexed his wrist to look at the time; the luminous hands of his watch showed 4:25 a.m.

The troopers had now become intent on getting first sight of the land below them, and were taking turns to peer through the side windows. This was practically futile, since dawn was still hours away. The aircraft lurched from side to side or up and down as though the pilot was avoiding hillocks or rocky outcrops; he had also reduced their air speed. Danny guessed that they were flying almost at ground level. Within minutes the Sea King's nose tilted up, like a reined-in horse. She settled on the ground with a bump and the throb of the rotors subsided to a mere growl. Pete, who had been clinging to chromium-plated grab rails at the cockpit bulkhead, turned round, stepped over the pile of kit and flung open the main starboard doorway. He turned to the SAS captain.

"This is as far as we can take you, sir." He held a map in front of him, clamped to a clipboard. He tapped a particular spot. "We're just here, Captain."

"I don't agree." A vehement, almost aggressive response. "We've been flying in ever-decreasing circles for half an hour now. I'm not prepared to accept that your navigator knows where we are." Two or three soldiers were already out of the aircraft and were stacking bergans on the ground. The captain ordered them to stop. "I want to speak to the pilot."

There was nothing to be gained by arguing. Pete and the captain squeezed into the cockpit.

"I don't trust this position," said the captain to the Marine pilot, avoiding looking at the navigator. "Convince me why should I believe you."

"Okay, fair enough. That rig was a problem we didn't expect. Right on our nose, so we had no option – we had to go round it. Bit of a detour but we got a good landfall north of where we'd intended. We're confident we identified the place. There's a north-south spit of land with a sandbar at the southern end – the only one of that size on this stretch of coastline. Through the goggles it was pretty obvious where we were."

"Well even if you're right, any fool can see we're still way short of our objective."

"Seven miles, give or take. I wouldn't call that 'way short'. This fog's the problem."

"Your navigator's the bloody problem."

"No, Captain. The fog's getting thicker with every mile we fly inland. I can fly above it and take you right above your landing site if you want. But first, once we're above about fifty feet we'll get spotted by the Argie radar at Rio Grande... And second, another five or six miles from the coast this fog could be as thick as pea soup – visibility at ground level down to five or ten yards, and no visual reference points. I can't let down through fog as thick as that. Even if my rad-alt was working, so I knew my height above ground, I'd still need clear sight all around. You know that. I need to see if I'm going to foul my rotors on a tree or a cliff. It wouldn't be safe... At least you're down now."

The captain was saved from having to admit that he could see the sense in what the pilot was saying by the arrival of his sergeant.

"Boss, Corporal Myers has just come back from a bit of a recce." It was an irresponsible thing to have done and the sergeant didn't want to take any blame. "I didn't tell him to, but he just hopped out... He says there are lights maybe three hundred yards from where we are, like some rancho or something. And he can hear traffic."

"Well there we go," said the captain. "I'm aborting this landing site. It's five o'clock in the morning and we've woken up every Argie for three or four miles in every direction. Everybody knows there's a big helicopter sitting here in the tussock grass, and pretty soon somebody's going to have enough wit to wonder why. By the time it's light this place will be alive with dogs, choppers and God-knows-what all looking for me and my boys." He turned to his sergeant. "Make sure the lads get all that kit back on board in the next minute. Do a headcount. We're off."

"You could still make it," said the navigator. "The position I gave you is accurate to within maybe half a mile. In two hours you could tab five or six miles from here – maybe even reach your O.P. before dawn."

"No. I told you. I'm not happy that you know exactly where we are. We could be miles away. This location is now aborted. On top of that we're compromised by the civilian population and a nearby road. Forget Argentina. Take us to the alternate in Chile."

≈

Carlisle had been keeping quiet, but it was obvious from his face that he disagreed with the SAS captain's appraisal of the situation. Now, the pilot had to make a fast exit from the Argentine half of Tierra del Fuego and head for Chile. Although the frontier was close, a mountain range lay between their present position and the emergency landing site over the border. The navigator had taken back the radar detector and plugged it into the intercom system.

Within a minute of lifting off, still rising through the fog, the detector sprang to life. Every ten seconds there came a warning chirp as a pulse bathed the Sea King with energy from an air-search radar scanning at a constant six revolutions per minute. The monotonous chimes continued as they climbed, bringing the realisation to all that now they faced a new danger – that of interceptor fighters from one of the nearby Argentinean Air Force bases. The troopers became tight-lipped, knowing that there was no hope of evading an incoming missile. Or if there was a mobile anti-aircraft artillery unit based on the western side of the mountain range, the Argentineans might not even need to launch fighters.

In the feeble, red cabin lighting, Danny could tell that the soldiers were worried. He imagined that being self-reliant, they disliked having to depend on the competence of others – and their officer had already labelled the helicopter's navigator hopeless. For almost twenty minutes, the relentless pings continued their subtle torture. Danny tried to time the interval between each buzz so that he was ready for the next one, but inevitably the noise arrived either a fraction of a second early or late, bringing a nervous shock that he could feel with an abrupt, more powerful heartbeat in his neck. But after what felt like a day's hard labour, the Sea King began to descend. A full ten seconds passed, fifteen, twenty and no tooth-gritting clang from the detector as the aircraft crossed the mountain ridge and sank into the radar shadow, now screened from the Rio Grande search system. One by one, SAS men raised their chins or blew out their cheeks and leaned back against the sides of the helicopter in relief. Chilean air space meant safety. Danny glanced across the cabin and met Ginger's eyes. The soldier was making a thumbs-up gesture at him.

A faint gleam of moonlight competed with the red cabin light. Although it was well short of dawn, the troopers were on their feet again, breathing on the cabin windows and wiping their sleeves over the perspex, hoping to get a better view. The pilot angled the nose down, perhaps anxious to be rid of his charges quickly. His thoughts would now be turning towards his own task of ditching the Sea King and taking his crew into hiding. Ahead and below, Danny thought he could see water, glinting through the cockpit window in the moonlight. He looked at his watch again; 05:50. The pilot, still wearing night vision goggles, must have been able to pick out a landing site because he banked the helicopter to port and began a wide descending turn.

Touch down. A minute before six o'clock, local time. The air loadmaster flung open the doors and the commandos sprang out onto the beach. Carlisle and Danny followed, setting themselves slightly apart, gathering their own kit. Danny's eyes had been adjusted to night vision for almost six hours, so he could see that the helicopter had landed on a spit of sand and large pebbles that protruded into a wide bay.

A little way to the right of the helicopter, Chilean *terra firma* began with a six or eight-foot, flat-topped earth bank, overhung with coarse grass. The bank and lack of light hampered his view into the hinterland so he was unable to form a better impression of his surroundings. Carlisle was already busy unpacking the disassembled Klepper canoe. On the floor of the helicopter, the SAS captain and Pete sat with their legs dangling outside. They pored over the available maps, disappointingly lacking in useful detail. After his previous doubts, the captain now appeared willing to agree their location. Danny was close to the helicopter, fetching the last of their belongings and heard the captain repeat, '70 miles'. He then heard Pete add for emphasis, '*Nautical* miles... 70 *nautical* miles'.

"That'll be more like 80 statute miles and a mountain range, then," muttered Danny, as he walked away with his and Carlisle's black lifejackets.

The troops wasted no time. The captain took a sighting through his compass and the whole patrol set off, with only one backward glance. Ginger raised an arm. Danny stood and mirrored the single wave, lowering his arm slowly, hoping they would make it and that Operation Plum Duff would not, as prophesied, prove fatal.

Danny became aware that Carlisle was standing behind him.

"Go and see how much of the framework you can fix together," said Carlisle. "I need a quick word with the crew."

Danny nodded and stepped over to the Klepper. Carlisle had been using a shielded torch to begin construction work, so Danny took it over. As requested, he began putting together some of the parts that he had last seen in the *Invincible's* hangar. Pete was still sitting in the helicopter's doorway. Carlisle stood outside, consulting the map. In the faint backlight from the moon, struggling to break through the semi-overcast sky, Danny could see the two men apparently agreeing. Carlisle plunged a hand inside his combat jacket and pulled out a notebook, into which he wrote briefly, then stepped away, tipping his fingers to his forehead in a mock salute.

846 Squadron dared not waste any more time. Pete slammed the cabin doors shut. The Sea King left the ground straight away, transitioned into forward flight and then began a rising turn to the west. Seeing no navigation lights, Danny was unable to follow it into the sky for more than a minute.

"Could do with a hand here," he called to Carlisle, who had also been watching the departing helicopter. "Some of these bits need two hands to hold them and a third hand to tighten the fixings."

"I hoped you'd have finished it by now," said Carlisle. "We need to be off and gone before the chaps in the local *estancia* decide to come a-looking."

(V)

Dawn, Tuesday 18 May
Bahía Inútil, Chile

Carlisle had taken the rear seat in the Klepper canoe. Danny accepted that the SBS marine probably wanted to match paddle strokes with him, expecting him to tire quickly from the exercise. Having glided easily away from the beach, they were now a thousand yards off shore, heading a fraction south of west. Ahead and slightly to their left, the first headland lay some six or seven miles distant, a continuation of the Land of Fire on which they had arrived only an hour before. The headland sloped down and dipped into the sea below the horizon. Sitting in the canoe with their eyes no more than two feet above the sea surface, their visible horizon was probably only about three thousand yards away. Clearly, the headland would reveal more of itself as they progressed. To the north, if there were more distant features, a fog bank obscured them all.

"No fires that I can see," said Danny. "Magellan should have called this place '*Tierra del Viento Frió*' – Land of the Cold Wind."

"That's Spanish, isn't it? Magellan was Portuguese." Carlisle sounded gloomy.

Danny didn't want the conversation to founder so early in the day, so he feigned a degree of ignorance, hoping to draw Carlisle out. "I wasn't much good at history. I remember hearing about Vasco da Gama, though. He was Portuguese, I think. But if Magellan was Portuguese too, why would he give this place a Spanish name?"

"Dunno... Follow the money – that's always good advice. Maybe Magellan was working for the Spanish."

Danny took the hint and occupied himself by trying to find a way to grip his paddle that minimised the trickle of cold water which ran down over his gloves at each stroke. After about fifteen minutes, the first wisps of breeze began to drift towards them over the surface, rippling the calm water in patches.

"You shouldn't have mentioned the wind," said Carlisle. "It's bad luck." Danny kept quiet. A Magellan Strait without wind would have been like a lion without a roar. Their landing in broken moonlight and windless conditions had been an uncharacteristic exception. "See if you can increase your stroke rate a bit. We need to make the best use of this flat calm while we've still got it." Danny dug in his paddle. Carlisle was silent for another twenty minutes before asking Danny how fast he reckoned they might be travelling.

Danny was glad that Carlisle had begun involving him. The Marine had seemed very withdrawn on board *Invincible*. "A good bit quicker than walking pace, I'd say. Four knots – maybe even a bit faster."

"How are you feeling? Tired?"

"Not yet. Maybe we can breathe a bit more easily once we've made it round the headland..."

"Hopefully." Carlisle's tone suggested there might be more. "I don't know whether to worry or not. I mean, if there was, say, a bloody alpaca farm within a couple of miles of where we landed, the point is, it was dark. Added to that, the Sea King was only on the ground for five minutes, so any ranchers wouldn't know exactly where we'd landed."

"Less, than five I'd have thought... Three minutes at most."

"Right, so if we woke up any locals, they'd most likely dismiss it as a military exercise – training in making night landings, maybe. Once the chopper had flown off there'd be nothing to see. No point coming down to the shore, so only a small risk of us being found out."

"And even if somebody was looking at us right now, wouldn't they want to keep themselves to themselves and not bother the authorities?"

"That's the part that worries me. The boys across the border are at war, so it's likely this lot would be a bit more vigilant. The Argies and the Chileans have never been best of pals."

"That's true." Danny longed to change the subject and learn more about Carlisle's plan. He felt he could make a significant contribution to it but, not wishing to seem too eager, he let their conversation settle for two minutes, then said: "I'll be interested in how long it's going to take us to paddle to Caleta Notch."

"Let's get beyond this headland first. Then if it looks safe, we'll beach her, have some breakfast and I'll show you what's what."

With the canoe drawn up on the beach, Carlisle unpacked a dried substance, which he announced to be 'oatmeal block'. He added a little more information concerning its nutritional value and other beneficial effects, then broke out the central one of four charts that had been rolled up in a waterproof tube.

"Here we are then," said Carlisle. "Pete gave me a starting position that located us close to this place..." He indicated a point on the chart, on the south side of a wide bay. "So, if he was right, we should just have rounded this headland, '*Punta Cameron*'."

Danny flicked a glance at the chart. "*Bahía Inútil*," he said. "Useless Bay. I wonder why it deserved such a lousy name." From his time at sea, Danny had been used to seeing the vessel's planned course marked out in pencil on a chart, complete with compass headings. Carlisle's chart gave no indication of how he intended to reach Caleta Notch. "Give us a clue. What's our route? Where are we going next?"

"I'd like to make it to this next promontory, then cross this stretch of water..." Carlisle tilted his head over to one side to read the legend which was printed vertically... "If we can make it across before the weather starts getting rough, we'll have covered a healthy distance – a good day's work." He jabbed the chart again. "We can lay up for the night somewhere like this." He leaned forward to make out the name printed on the chart. "B. Harris."

Danny lowered his eyebrows and leaned over the chart. "B. Harris. That'll be *Bahía Harris*. And I notice it says '*Isla Dawson*' underneath."

"Funny – all these British names..."

"Not so funny. We need to give that place a wide berth."

"Why?"

"The day before I set out, my Admiral..." Danny turned to his right and mocked the action of spitting to show what he now thought of his boss. "...Rennie, the bastard, gave me a report to read. Most of it was about Argentineans that were wanted for crimes against humanity. But there was a paragraph or two about Chile."

"Go on."

"Comparing the two countries, you know. A completely different scale, but when Pinochet deposed Allende, he accused half the ministers from the previous government of being communists, rounded up a few trades unionists and professionals like lecturers and lawyers, and packed them all off to prison. There was already a prison on Dawson Island. Pinochet had a new wing built and turned it into... well, I suppose you'd call it a concentration camp."

"Oh."

"The Chilean Navy ran it. They already had a base at somewhere called *Puerto Harris*, so it's a fair bet that *Puerto Harris* and *Bahía Harris* are close together."

Carlisle gave an immediate, powerful puff through his nostrils. He looked angry. "It's happening again, isn't it? It's the same sort of planning balls-up we had on the Kola."

"We can't worry about that now. If those places were the same, we'd probably see some buildings or a harbour wall or something on the way in, and be able to do a quick about-face. But if they were running a radar, they might pick us up before we cottoned on, and they might come out looking for us – especially if we suddenly turned and fled."

Carlisle uttered a tirade of curses before his ability to speak in calmly constructed sentences was restored.

"Cock-up after cock-up. It just keeps getting worse." He picked up a stone the size of a tennis ball, sprang to his feet, and flung the rock into the sea. "A naval base. A bloody naval base, and nobody thought to mention it."

"Sorry." It was a conditioned response and didn't help.

"Don't be sorry. And don't be too hard on your Admiral Rennie, either. That report... if you hadn't read it and remembered it... well, the good thing is it's stopped us blundering into trouble before the operation has hardly got under way. Not your fault." He tutted. "Planners!"

"What do you want to do, then? Steer clear and carry on down this side of the channel till we're past *Bahía Harris*?"

"It's the only safe thing to do, isn't it?

The next headland lay ten sea miles beyond *Punta Cameron*. When they set off again, the muscles in Danny's shoulders, upper arms and across his chest had begun to ache. Also, his stomach muscles and lower back were feeling tender, all of which made for slower progress. However, a benevolent sea seemed happy to break them in gradually, though it had now turned from calm to mildly choppy. The fog had receded, allowing first sight of a series of mountain peaks – the endless jagged kind that a child might draw. The peaks on *Isla Dawson,* perhaps twenty miles ahead, were tinted a pastel shade of blue-grey, whilst those to their left, the coastal mountain range of Tierra del Fuego, stood out thundercloud grey and snow-streaked, sweeping down to the rocks and narrow beaches.

By the time they arrived abreast of their next waypoint, a sharp headland, Carlisle's watch indicated that it was past midday. Mindful of the energy they were both using, he allowed a break for lunch and a rest. They moved in closer to the shore, hoping to spot a beach that offered a soft landing – one that would not rip the bottom out of their canoe.

They were out of luck. The coastline consisted of low unbroken cliffs and rock-strewn beaches all the way. There was nothing to do but carry on hugging the shore in the hope of sighting a safe place to land. The only half-suitable site, a narrow beach no more than twenty-five yards wide, was occupied by a couple of South American sea lions, young bulls just sprouting their furry manes. Carlisle preferred not to dispute ownership with them.

Around two o'clock in the afternoon, Carlisle took them in closer to inspect the mouth of a minor river. They probed the bottom with their paddles until they located a softer, muddier section of the sea bed, whereupon both Danny and Carlisle climbed out to lighten the canoe and waded ashore, towing the craft through the low waves. Carlisle examined the chart.

"I reckon we're here," he said, pointing to a place on the chart where the hydrographer had marked a river flowing straight from the mountains into the channel. "I don't want to stay too long. See what's on the other side of the channel?" Sure enough, they were virtually opposite *Bahía Harris*. "It'll start getting dark soon, so I'd like to get away as soon as we've had a bite to eat. I'd like to make it a bit farther down the channel. There's another river mouth about five miles south and the chart shows a shallow bar jutting out. My guess is it'll be more suitable for beaching the canoe. If it's deserted, we'll spend the night there."

That evening, Carlisle thought it best not to light a fire. With the Chilean naval base lurking diagonally across the channel only ten miles away, he didn't want to risk showing a light and attracting attention. He and Danny, now encased from toes to armpits in Arctic-grade sleeping bags, had eaten cold rations and talked of inconsequential things. They were both tired. Danny knew the sleeping bag would keep him warm and dry, and let his painful muscles relax, but even though he wanted to fall asleep for nine or ten hours, he couldn't. Carlisle had told him little about how their journey would progress; he needed to know.

"How far do you reckon we've covered today?"

Carlisle had a ready answer. "Twenty-seven miles."

"Nautical miles?"

"Yep."

"Is that good? Are we on schedule?"

"Well, it's hard to say," said Carlisle. "There aren't many examples to rely on. The best guide we've got is a couple of kayakers who circumnavigated the UK a couple of years ago. As I understand it, they did it in eighty-five days."

"Seems a long time."

"Maybe so. But out of every five days, they lost one day either through bad weather or needing to rest. And they did it in summer, too, so it would have been warmer... easier."

"All right. What sort of average does that work out to?"

"Start to finish, twenty-seven miles a day."

"So we're bang on!"

"But on the days they were able to paddle, it was more like thirty-four miles."

"Oh," said Danny. "Was that sea miles or land miles?"

"Dunno... I'll make a note to ask them when we get back."

"What I'm trying to get you to tell me is how long before we get to Caleta Notch."

"Danny, my friend... At this rate, a week from now we'll still be paddling."

Wednesday 19 May;
From Rio Yartou; 53°53'S, 70°08'W

Carlisle had set an alarm for six o'clock in the morning, no doubt planning to get farther south before the Chilean Navy decided it might be the day for a pleasant cruise around the bay. He handed Danny another chunk of oatmeal block. Given a choice, Danny might have opted for something with a little more variety or colour, but the substance was sweet, palatable and didn't require a knife, fork or spoon. He ate carefully, not wasting a crumb. They had a short debate about filling their drinking-water containers from the mountain stream, and whether or not to break into their supply of water purification tablets. After weighing up the relative risks and merits of either sustaining some vile form of South American gut rot or gagging on the taste of chlorine, Danny proposed a solution.

"Tell you what," he said. "Let's fill the empty bottles from the stream. Then you drink what's left of the *Chateau Invincible*, and I'll drink a pint of *Côtes de Yartou*, and if I haven't come down with a dose of the squits by lunchtime, we'll know it's safe."

Carlisle had no desire to slake his thirst with a liquid tasting of diluted bleach either, so Danny's selfless act was approved, and they repacked their sleeping bags into the canoe. The pair squeezed into their neoprene dry suits and then launched the craft into the gloom of a late autumn, southern hemisphere morning. Straight away, every muscle from Danny's thighs to his shoulders warned him that wielding a twin-bladed paddle for another minute, another hour or, far worse, for the rest of the day was foolish. He groaned with every stroke.

"That was quick," said Carlisle. "I've never known a bloke come down with a dose of the Egyptian two-step so fast in my life."

"It's not my guts, you slave-driver. It's a massage I need – not kaolin and morphine."

"Steady, Tiger, I know. Just take it easy for a while. I'll do the work, and you get into a rhythm. Your old bones will warm up and you'll be okay before long."

"It's all right for you bloody bootnecks," said Danny. "A ten-mile run before every meal; fitter than a butcher's dog. What you forget is I've been stuck behind a desk since the last time you saw me."

"Getting fat and flabby, I know," teased Carlisle. "Don't worry though. Another week of this and you'll be wanting to sign up and join Her Majesty's Corps of Royal Marines."

Danny made a comment which could be taken to indicate that such a change of career was an unlikely outcome. At the same time he appeared to misjudge his next paddle stroke, sending a sheet of sea water aft, in Carlisle's direction, for which he failed to apologise. Carlisle smiled; Danny was not yet a dead weight, nor likely to be. Seeing no sign of dangerous shallows, he steered the canoe across the sandbar to the south of Rio Yartou. He then altered course to stay close to the land, but safely to seaward of the rollers beating onto the rocks.

Every twenty minutes or so, Carlisle exchanged a few words with Danny, remarking on the many shades of grey to be seen in daylight, the direction of the wind, a passing seabird and, each time, enquiring after the state of his strained muscles. His earlier assessment had been correct. Danny was beginning to find that his body could accept the regular circulating motion of inserting the blade of his paddle first on one side, then the other, and gently dragging it through the water. Whilst he couldn't contribute as well as he had on the day before, it wouldn't be long until the pain had gone and his power would return, hopefully all the greater.

By around ten o'clock, Danny could see from the front seat that the southerly run of the coastline was interrupted by a sharp turn to his right. Carlisle had seen it too; he said it would be a good place to stop for a rest. As they came nearer, there looked to be a wide area of sharp rocks at sea level, as if there had been a recent cliff fall, so they abandoned the idea of landing and turned right to pass clear of the point. A low islet emerged from behind the point, maybe half a mile off shore. But again, beaching the canoe appeared to be too dangerous. Thwarted, they followed the shoreline, still hoping to find a landing place.

After not much more than a mile, a narrow inlet came into view offering better prospects. Carlisle probed again with his paddle and once he was confident that they had arrived in waist-deep water, he passed the paddle forward to Danny.

"One paddle each side, touch bottom and steady the canoe while I slip over the side," he said. "Then I'll tow her ashore." A minute later, Carlisle held the canoe in shallower water so that Danny could disembark over a patch of peaty-looking coarse sand.

Carlisle's first action ashore was to unpack the chart and announce that with *Puerto Harris* just over twenty miles behind them, he would permit a hot meal. He showed Danny what kit was needed, inviting him to make a selection from their ration packs and finally instructing him in how to reconstitute the chosen substance into something edible.

"How are your guts?"

"I think you'll find *Côtes de Yartou* to be a zesty aromatic number that's at its best right now. Eminently drinkable, it travels well. There is no lingering afterburn..."

"...Perfect," said Carlisle, before adding a culinary comment of his own. "It sounds just the right thing to turn beef curry briquettes into a wholesome, though pale, imitation of Bombay's finest."

Carlisle didn't seem too anxious to spoil the meal by gobbling it down and hurrying back to the canoe. Danny thought the welcome break might be a good opportunity to fill in the first of many gaps in his understanding.

"How long have you known I was coming?"

"What do you mean?"

"Your reaction. When Randy Andy brought me down to find you on the hangar deck of the *Invincible*, you did a double-take."

"Huh?"

"Like this..." Danny tried to imitate the movement that he had seen Carlisle perform, such a short time before. It consisted of a double jerk of the head from side to side, whilst his face wore a look of total bewilderment. "I've never seen a real person do that before."

"I'm not following you."

"Come off it, Carlisle. It was an act, wasn't it? The only time I've ever seen a double-take like that, a cartoon character did it – Bugs Bunny, I think."

"What are you talking about? It was just surprise. I'd totally forgotten about you. You were about the last person I was expecting to see. What was I supposed to do?"

"Well, you aren't much of an actor, Bugsy. Just don't give up the day job, that's all." Carlisle shook his head and sighed in what he probably hoped was an exasperated fashion. It didn't convince Danny. "And that major of yours is an even worse actor. 'the Bear' was never real, was he?"

"Nice curry..."

"I mean... Hanging upside down from a steel ladder by one leg – a broken leg, mind you – all the time clutching a barrel of beer to his chest. Really... What a story."

"Be nicer with some chutney and a few poppadoms..."

"And that last little act about needing a Spanish speaker... Entertaining, but total garbage."

"Some geezer in the corner twanging away on the sitar..."

"Don't piss about, Carlisle. When did you know?"

"All right. Three or four days maybe; I can't remember. I wasn't expecting the Spanish Inquisition."

Danny tutted. "I told you Rennie was a bastard."

"You didn't have to agree. You could just have asked to see the chart and drawn a cross. 'X' marks the spot. Nazi treasure lies here. You could simply have told us to get on with it. But you didn't. It's not my fault if you can't say no."

"Okay, okay. I just wanted to hear the truth, that's all." Danny scooped up another spoonful of food, and turned it over slowly in his mouth to soften the parts that the Yartou water had not fully penetrated. After a while he continued.

"I did say no, actually. Only when I did, old Rennie started playing games."

"He caught you easily enough, didn't he?"

Danny ignored the jibe. "There was always just one more hoop to jump through. Go to Brize Norton; fly to Ascension; question a prisoner; talk to Sandy Woodward. That was his knockout punch. Bloody parachute jumps, getting soaked in the freezing ocean, cross-decking from one ship to the next to the next. Always just one more hurdle... Then you."

"Well, I'm glad you're here. Truly I am."

Danny had not anticipated such an obviously heartfelt response; it silenced him for a few seconds. "Thanks, Carlisle." He took a deep breath, then sighed. "You might have been expecting *me*, but I wasn't expecting to find *you*."

“I could tell *you* weren’t acting.”

“If it had been anybody else, I’d have told them to sod off. I was remembering the Kola. Loyalty, I guess.”

Carlisle hung his head. “We ought to think about setting off again. Dunno about you, but I need to find a bush and commune with nature. I suggest you do the same.”

Impressed by Tierra del Fuego’s finest river water, and aware that daylight was running out, Carlisle selected another river mouth for their overnight bivouac. It lay across ten miles of the inland sea, directly to the south, close to a feature marked on the chart under another British-sounding name.

Half an hour before reaching their objective, and just before darkness might have made locating the river impossible, Danny sighted white water cascading over rocks on the mountainside. It was sufficient to give them the direction that they needed. The pair followed what was becoming a practised procedure of approaching a river mouth, feeling for the bottom, stabilising the canoe between two paddles while they got out in turn, then carrying the craft up above the strand line before making camp. It was a great relief and comfort to be ashore again for the night.

Thursday 20 May;
From Cabo Rowlett River Mouth; 54°15'S, 70°04'W

Danny heard Carlisle moving about and asked, somewhat muffled from inside his sleeping bag, whether it was time to set off. It was. Government-issue oatmeal block graced the menu again, to his concealed delight. He asked how many miles they had covered the day before.

“Twenty-three.” A pause. “How are you feeling?”

“The sleep’s done me good,” said Danny. “I don’t feel so stiff.” Carlisle had not directly accused him of causing the fall in daily mileage, but the implication was clear. He felt able to offer a little encouragement. "I think if I can warm up properly I ought to be able to pull my weight a bit better today."

"That's the key – warming up properly. We don't want any pulled muscles."

"Let's have a look at the chart... See where we're going."

Carlisle unrolled the chart and, by torchlight, pointed out their starting position. The plan for the day took them northwest along a tapering channel on the south side of *Isla Dawson.*

"It's a long way from *Puerto Harris,*" said Carlisle. "We should be safe." They both bent lower over the chart. "It shows open water, here at the narrowest part." Carlisle read out the name printed on the chart. "Here... '*Angostura Gabriel*' – part of this Gabriel Channel. It looks less than half a mile across. We should be able to get through in a canoe."

"I hope so. We don't want to waste time carrying everything overland. Personally, I'd be more worried about any current squeezing through a constriction like this... It could be flowing against us faster than we can paddle."

"Shit."

"So we might end up carrying everything anyway."

Carlisle sighed. "Well as long as we know, we can be ready for it. No surprises. We can't turn round and go back."

Now rather subdued by the thought of what Angostura Gabriel held for them later in the day, they both turned their attention to packing away their overnight kit and dressing in their waterproof suits. With growing proficiency at climbing into a floating canoe, Danny had made himself comfortable in the forward seat and was ready to leave when Carlisle spoke.

"Gabriel," he said. "He was God's messenger, wasn't he? All these messengers... I'm just hoping that between him and Hermes, we might get a slice of good luck today."

"Me too."

"Just one other thing. I always thought Angostura was something you dribbled into a glass to make a pink gin. Does it mean something different in nautical Spanish?"

"It just means 'narrows', that's all."

They passed a relatively uneventful morning. Danny spotted gulls picking titbits from the surfaced branches of a kelp bed early enough to avoid getting tangled up in it, but the main difficulty came from the wind. In the exposed part of the channel the prevailing westerly blew into their faces at a rising force 5. Later, spray from the frequent white horses began to get troublesome for Danny, numbing his face.

Because Danny partly shielded Carlisle from the spray, Carlisle decided to play fair, abandoning his course along the centre of the channel and making for the lee of the high land to the south. This proved fortuitous, because the southern shore contained more frequent small bays and the occasional open beach. They were able to stop for a warm drink without difficulty.

When they stopped again for a midday meal, Carlisle unrolled the chart and confidently stated that by relating to a promontory standing out on the opposite shore and an obvious inlet lying behind it, they had covered fifteen miles. Angostura Gabriel lay nine miles ahead, so he was keen to finish the meal and resume their voyage while they still had the advantage of daylight. The narrows, however, were not yet visible. It seemed to them that the channel led to a dead end under glowering grey mountain peaks. Danny peered at the chart. On the far side of the narrows, he read the words '*Canal Magdalena*'. He knew that name. That was the way Vic Marchesi had entered the Magellan Strait in 1944.

If all went well, he would soon be travelling in the old gentleman's wake. As Carlisle rolled up the chart again, Danny realised that his shoulders didn't hurt any more.

≈

During the afternoon session, Carlisle became more apprehensive. They were now canoeing between two fjord-like mountainsides, either one of which (he said) could harbour a military patrol or a sheep farmer who might report their presence.

After two hours, the wind direction became confused and the air noticeably colder. Rather than nosing into the suspected head current they found themselves buffeted by random gusts which seemed to swing around on a whim. Carlisle steered the canoe towards the southern shore, having a theory of his own.

"It's these mountains," he said. "A couple of thousand feet up, the air is a lot colder. The mountains block the way of the cold, moving air. Then it just rolls down the mountainside till it reaches sea level and escapes horizontally as a wind."

"How do you know that?"

"Arctic warfare school. How to avoid freezing to death, lesson two, sub paragraph, 'why some valleys are colder and windier than others'."

"Why did you bring us over to the south side?"

"To prove it. If we cross to the north side, the wind should swap over and come from the right. Shall we see?" So they did; and it did.

Nearing the narrows, surface fronds from submerged kelp beds could be seen extending from either shore. Danny felt more confident, telling himself that kelp would never grow in places where a strong current might carry marine growth away. On the northern side, the shore re-formed into cliffs, whilst on the southern shore, the steep, scree-peppered mountainside simply dipped into the water.

Anxious not to be caught out by Danny's theory about a counter current, Carlisle called for extra effort. But it was unnecessary. In the narrows, the headwind died away for a few minutes, then switched around to their rear, helping to whisk them out of the channel and prove Carlisle's theories. When it became clear they would have no further trouble from adverse currents they relaxed.

"Steady as she goes," called Carlisle.

"Aye-aye number one," answered Danny.

"You're a real pessimist, you are. You really wound me up with all that rubbish about finding an impossible current in the narrows and having to carry the canoe through the undergrowth."

"Or maybe we came through at slack tide. Good timing."

"Or perhaps Gabriel was kind to us."

Carlisle steered the canoe back towards the southern shore. Putting their exciting day behind them, they began to look for a landing place that promised a safe camping site for the night.

Ashore, and after examining the chart one last time, they decided to sample the lamb stew for their evening meal. Because they had made better time and camped a little before the light faded, the cubes of meat had longer to absorb the liquid and consequently had a far softer texture than the previous night's curry.

"You know I said you were the last person I expected to find," said Danny.

"Uh-huh."

"Well it's still got me puzzled. I mean – you're a Russian speaker, not Spanish. What were you doing with the Task Force? Or was it a case of sending everybody we'd got?"

"A bit of desperation, I think. The government keeps cutting armed forces numbers, so we're short-handed more often these days. It won't be long before we'll be hard pushed to find enough blokes to march past the Cenotaph on Armistice Sunday."

"I know what you mean."

"The thing is, on the voyage down to Ascension and then on into the South Atlantic, there were always Russian trawlers hanging around on the horizon, passing info to the Argies. I spent a lot of time listening to them nattering away between themselves... My brief was to pass on anything useful to Northwood and keep Sandy Woodward informed. They really needed me and my Rusky language skills, Danny. I felt I was doing a good job."

"You didn't want to do this side operation though, did you?"

"No. Solo or duo, I didn't want to get sucked into something like this."

"Why not?"

"I'd had my thrills on the Kola. That's what I'd been trained for – infiltrating Russia through the northern flank. I'd pitted my wits against Ivan, used the lie of the land, found somewhere for us to hide, moved us forward and not left any signs. You know – endurance at forty degrees below. Survival. Completing the mission. It all seemed like a great game. Maybe the best game there is. Primitive. Relying on your instincts, your senses, your intuition."

"I never thought of it like that. You paint a fantastic picture. You should write a book."

"I don't think so." Carlisle used his spoon to draw idle patterns in his stew for a few moments before continuing. "Then after you and I got back home, when I weighed it all up, I just didn't think I'd done a very good job. I'd made mistakes. Remembering all that – that's why I didn't want to do this."

"I knew you weren't happy back then. I never realised it went as deep as that."

"I'm older too; I wasn't sure I could pull off this Caleta Notch caper. It all seemed too ill-defined, too unplanned. Until you came along, I wasn't part of any of the assault teams. I wasn't on any list to sneak in and operate an O.P. or anything. I was doing a bloody desk job, Danny. I was the closest thing to a civilian the navy's got."

"But you're here."

"Only to keep you out of trouble, you fucking nuisance."

Friday 21 May;
From Near Punta Anxious; 51°09'S, 70°19'W

Carlisle rolled up the chart and stowed it away in its tube. He drew himself up straight, legs slightly apart, and spoke a little more loudly than Danny felt was necessary.

"You'll have worked it out for yourself I expect, but from here on, there's a fair chance of sighting shipping coming through the strait..."

"...Or them sighting us."

"So we'll be sticking close to the southern side and keeping a sharp lookout."

With Carlisle in the grip of this spasm of organisation and command, Danny thought it best not to appear too smart. There was plenty of time to find a way of suggesting that it might be a good idea to invent a cover story, in case the Chilean Navy should overhaul them and ask what they were doing.

"How far yesterday?"

"Twenty-nine miles. Let's see if we can do as well again today."

But Danny knew they wouldn't. The coming day would mark the first time they met any significant currents, and you only had to read what was written at the bottom of the chart concerning currents to understand that the going was about to get tough.

An hour and forty minutes into their first stretch, they had to correct their heading; to maintain their course the canoe's bows needed to be angled a good 30 degrees towards the western shore. It was clear that they were in the grip of a current from the Pacific, sweeping into the strait through the Magdalena Channel. Danny reckoned it must be running at about two knots. For the first time, they had entered waters navigated by Lieutenant Marchesi forty years earlier. That two-knot current would have helped the *William Scoresby* save a little time in her pursuit of Claussen. They maintained their offset for another forty minutes to compensate for the powerful flow but then, quite abruptly, it disappeared.

"Let's see if we can find a place for a hot drink," said Carlisle. "I need a breather." He was puffing, which surprised Danny. Keeping close to the southern side, they didn't have far to look, and were ashore again in a matter of minutes. Danny busied himself making coffee, while Carlisle pored over the chart.

"It talks about a three-knot current," said Carlisle. "We'll be lucky to make any headway at all if it's as strong as that."

"Can I see?"

Danny held out Carlisle's hot drink, which he swapped for the chart without protest. He read the notes printed on the chart, then tried to offer some comfort.

"I think it means three knots out at sea, 'setting south-easterly', it says. But there'll still be some current in the straits. It just means we'll have to stick close to the land and stay out of the main stream. The wind might be a worse problem for us." Danny cocked an eye at the sky. "With clouds as black as that, there could even be a snowstorm."

"I've been watching that. Still..." Carlisle found a happy face from somewhere. "...it might keep the Chilean Navy tucked up in their bunks for another day."

And so, by keeping close to the rugged shoreline and maintaining one eye on the land and one eye on the compass, the pair made good progress, turning, in the late afternoon, into a broad inlet, almost two miles wide. A second inlet opened off the first, pointing southwest. Driving rain had turned to sleet and although it had reduced visibility and their risk of being seen, these were morale-sapping conditions. They needed to get ashore for the night, have a hot meal and warm up.

They decided to try the beef curry again, to check whether it was naturally as tough as timber, or whether careful cookery could improve it.

"Twenty-six and a half miles," said Carlisle. "Not bad – considering."

Ashore, time was never a pressure so Danny let it lie for a while. He was curious about something else. After a few minutes he said, "How do you think Operation Sudden Death will be going?"

"Plum Duff? Doomed from the start." Carlisle uttered an ironic kind of huff. "I mean, if you were a high-up officer in SAS Headquarters, and you had this critical operation to prepare, and they allocated a name with the word 'duff' in it, wouldn't you tell 'em to get you a better name or look for another planner?"

"I see what you mean."

"How do I think they're doing?" He gave that scornful huff again. "They haven't got a snowball's chance. Total failure."

"Dead?"

"No! Alive and in big trouble. First thing, they'll be just about to run out of rations, and second thing, I don't think they'll be anywhere near Rio Grande yet." Danny stayed silent, obliging Carlisle to add more – something he seemed happy to do. "Okay, this is our fourth day, right? Theirs too, obviously. We're carrying fourteen days' rations. They were carrying four – that's all."

"Why so little?"

"Because the planners probably gave them a couple of hours to get into position from the first landing site, and a max of about two days observing the airfield. Then, day three, if the Plum Duff blokes said it was okay, they were planning this mighty raid, Entebbe style, company strength, a couple of C-130s, a big shoot-up. After that, anyone left alive had two days' rations left to chew on while he made a run for it. Head for Chile. Give yourself up."

"But the Sea King flew them to the wrong position."

"The Sea King took them to the *right* position, only they didn't trust it. Me? I knew both the pilots. I'd trust them to fly me blindfold to the dark side of the moon in thick fog and still be no more than half a mile off target." He raised one eyebrow and gave Danny a devilish look. "You'll notice the SAS didn't argue about the position when we all hopped out on that sand spit four days ago."

"But they're still alive, you reckon?"

"Oh yes. But nowhere near Rio Grande. Good thing too."

"Why?"

"Cheezus, Danny. You heard that radar warning device. I don't suppose we were fifty feet up before it started bleeping. Even if they'd dropped off the SAS patrol at that first landing site, once the Argies clocked us on their radar, they'd have flooded the place with troops as soon as it got light. If our blokes didn't get captured, they'd have all been dead; no escape."

Clearly, Carlisle felt he had to continue defending 846 Squadron. "And anyway, the Sea King pilots had no alternative. They needed to gain height to fly over the mountain so they could get to the place where they were going to ditch the chopper."

"You mean they could have flown us all in, under the radar, without being detected, then given it all away when they flew their escape route?"

"Great bit of planning from Hereford."

"And what about us? What are our chances?"

"Pretty good, I'd say."

"Really?"

"Well, nobody's looking for us. We're in Chile all the way and getting farther from Argentina all the time. Provided we can avoid getting spotted in the main strait, we should be okay."

"We managed all right today, didn't we? I didn't think it would be very busy."

"Why not?"

"My job in Merchant Shipping Intelligence... The Cape Horn route and the Magellan Strait route are never too busy at the best of times. But the war's been going for six weeks now. Most ship owners have had time to re-route through Panama. It might mean a few days extra steaming in the odd case, but when you set that against the extra insurance for being in a war zone... And the risk. They're staying well away."

"That's good."

"But the Sea King pilots... If they get captured, they could give us away."

"No. They weren't involved in the planning for this little sideshow. They don't know anything except there were two of us... and where they dropped us off. Their job is to sink the chopper and go into hiding for a week. They're trained. They're special forces. They won't give us away."

"But Chile must have patrol boats in the strait – police or navy – somebody could stumble across us by accident and demand identity, or answers to a few questions. What's our cover story?"

"This all happened in a bit of a rush, I'm afraid."

"So you're saying we haven't got a cover story. Just hold our hands up and say 'fair cop'."

"Chile is on our side in all this. If we get caught, Mrs Thatcher will look after us. She and Pinochet are the best of buddies right now."

Saturday 22 May;
From Seno Lyell; 53°59'S, 71°27'W

Sleet, borne on a near gale from the west, both helped and hindered progress. Reduced visibility provided a reassuring cloak but the sea had heaped up. Wave tops had begun to break and even half a mile from land, though there was no spray, the windward side of the waves showed white streaks. Carlisle said he was confident that the waterproof apron covering the canoe's cockpit would keep out the seawater but when Danny said he was afraid of an upset or damage, they headed closer inshore.

Around midday, they started traversing a wide inlet leading south. Faced with a two-mile stretch across open water, with the wind more or less dead ahead, both men were grateful to find a sheltered bay on the other side and very pleased, too, with the qualities of the canoe. Carlisle got out the chart and they both peered at it, noting that the open water leading south actually led into the Pacific. The pull across the channel had left them both exhausted so they rested for a longer time than they had on previous days.

"You realise it's the cricket season back home," said Danny.

"I thought I recognised the weather. Time to press on."

Sunday 23 May;
From Near Mount Pond; 53°52'S, 71°51'W

Saturday had added a mere twenty miles to the total. Carlisle's prediction was proving to be accurate; they would still be paddling after a week had passed. But Danny could see that his protector, neither impatient nor fretful, was wanting to get on with the mission.

"We need to set an objective," said Carlisle. He pointed to the chart. "Here – 'B. Choiseul' – that'll be '*Bahía Choiseul*' I expect, will it? That's where I want to be tonight."

"How far?"

"Twenty-five or so."

"Better get cracking..."

But they never made it to *Bahía Choiseul* that day. The westerly had turned into a full gale, flinging salt spray in their faces all the way. It not only rendered progress slow but also somewhat nauseating from the taste of seawater. Before the end of the afternoon, they made their way into a west-oriented bay. Both would have preferred a more favourable direction, offering better protection from the wind, but exhaustion proved to be the deciding factor. Like Carlisle, Danny wanted an end to the monotony of paddling and camping, but when they first beached the canoe, a glance at the chart told him their destination still lay two days ahead; three if the weather worsened. He craned over Carlisle's shoulder while the marine worked out their daily mileage.

"How far?"

"Seventeen and a half today, that's all. Bloody cold, isn't it?"

"Not surprised." Danny knelt down and pointed to a lighter shape engraved on the chart. "There's this ruddy great glacier five miles away. A couple of days ago you were the one telling me about cold winds rolling down the mountainside." He pointed into the wind. "This lot is blowing straight off an icefield. We need to find somewhere sheltered to pitch the tent."

"It's pretty thickly wooded," said Carlisle. "We'll be all right."

Monday 24 May;
From Ensenada Smyth; 53°50'S, 72°15'W

Over the much-appreciated oatmeal block, Danny persuaded Carlisle to get out the chart, hoping to plan a more achievable target for the day's paddling. Late the previous afternoon, he had noticed from the chart that farther to the northwest the main channel split, to pass round an island. One branch was very much narrower than the other and he was concerned about the strength of any opposing current, squeezing through the *angostura*. But Carlisle seemed to be losing his approachability.

Danny suspected that a confrontation would only make his companion's mood worse, so he avoided making too many suggestions or appearing to want to take control. It was difficult. The best plan was probably to pass on the other side of the island, but he wanted it to appear to be Carlisle's decision. A passage in the wider strait should be safe. Up until then, they had come across no settlements of any kind, no deep-sea ships cutting through the straits and no smaller naval vessels or police launches.

Carlisle worked his way through the pros and cons, weighing up the risks: Though the island was nine or ten miles long, it was likely to be uninhabited, purely because of the difficulty of getting to it from anywhere. He latched onto what Danny had said about coming through the *Angostura Gabriel* at slack tide, saying he was keen to avoid contra-currents now they were in the main strait. The conclusion proved to be easier than Danny had feared; they would need to cross to the north side of the strait at some time, so why not today?

During the day, the wind moderated to a force 6, then to a 5 as they began their northerly crossing towards the island. Carlisle rated it as the first piece of good luck they had had for several days. That evening they camped at the end of a line of cliffs, opposite a small grassy island. They saw cormorants, making Carlisle wonder about catching fish for supper. With a day's run of twenty-one and a half miles, his mood had improved.

Tuesday 25 May;
From Islas Carlos III; 53°35'S, 72°20'W

The examination of the chart at dawn on the seventh day revealed how close they had now come to their objective. Danny asked about the other charts rolled up in the tube, prompting Carlisle to look at them, seemingly for the first time. They discovered a larger scale chart of the north-western end of the Magellan Strait, and two detailed charts, one of which included an enlarged plan of *Ensenada Smyth*, where they had camped two nights before.

"Pity we didn't dig it out."

"It didn't change anything."

They joked about the legend on the chart. *Ensenada Smyth* had been surveyed by a Royal Navy vessel in 1829.

The larger scale chart of the straits was welcome because it suggested a plan to Carlisle. If the north side of the channel proved too exposed to westerly wind and waves, they could cross into the shelter of the mountainous land on the southern side. The main advantage, however, was that although Caleta Notch was reachable in the day, an inlet lay on its eastern side where it would be prudent to camp for the night. The following morning, Carlisle could climb to the top of the peninsula that separated the two inlets. From there he could inspect the bay. Having got so far without mishap, it seemed a wise precaution.

That evening they dined on reconstituted chicken stew, and celebrated with a tinned pudding that they had been saving in honour of their former colleagues – plum duff.

"Nineteen and a half miles," said Carlisle. He nodded at Danny. "Not bad for an ageing amateur."

(VI)

Wednesday 26 May
Bahia Guirior

By chance, certainly without a great degree of forethought, the navy had provided Danny and Carlisle with a one-man tent each. For the past week they had come to appreciate this, since at none of their overnight refuges had there been space to pitch a two-man tent. Wedging two smaller tents in amongst the low bushes had been possible, albeit after some hacking at the undergrowth. In the early hours of Wednesday morning, the wind rose to storm force.

Danny lay awake inside his sleeping bag. He realised that, while half asleep, he must have been listening for hours to the wind whipping through the bushes and the slap of driving rain. He wondered how much rest he had lost. Knowing he would be unlikely to doze off again soon, he tried to characterise the external sounds. Every comparison seemed to have been used already. Yes, the wind roared, but not like a wild beast – more like the continual cry of a football crowd whose blood had been roused. And it whistled too, rising and falling like a siren, as streaks of salt-laden air darted amongst the matted twigs and thorns of the squat coastal rain forest. Pebbles clattered on the beach, thrown up and sucked back at each surge. The frantic brushwood scratched and scraped at the outside of his tent. With help like that, it might not be long before the rain found its way inside.

"Are you awake?"

"What a bloody stupid question," replied Danny, half-shouting.

"How about a recce to the top of the peninsula?"

"How about waiting for an hour or two for this weather front to pass over?" Danny felt that his next comment was well-justified. "And it's dark. I'm bloody well staying here."

"Mutiny, huh?"

At around 6 a.m. the wind abated noticeably. Carlisle called out again to Danny, telling him it was time to get his boots on and prepare to carry out their reconnaissance to the top of the peninsula. He sounded anxious to get his first look into Caleta Notch. Danny protested, but saw the point when Carlisle told him that he needed him to come along – first, in case he, himself, slipped and fell, and second to make connections with the memories that Vic Marchesi had shared.

With no reasonable excuse now to stay in his pit, Danny accompanied Carlisle on what appeared from the chart to be a trek of only half a mile, but which felt ten times as far because of a change in altitude of perhaps a thousand feet. Both men soon became breathless with the effort of forging their way ever upwards, stumbling over spongy hummocks of moss in the half light, and amongst ferns and gnarled, scrubby branches.

Dawn was still cloaked under a dismal overcast when Carlisle and Danny arrived at the crest of the peninsula. Carlisle wanted to be in position well before the sun, if it ever appeared, had risen clear of the mountains. They approached the summit on their bellies as a precaution, though Carlisle admitted there was little likelihood of any human presence in Caleta Notch, and consequently little risk of revealing themselves on the skyline to whoever or whatever might be sheltering there. Nothing stirred. At the summit of the peninsula, the wind was in a dying phase, a lilting diminuendo, whilst down in the cove the water looked to be free from wind waves and as black as a marine bandsman's parade boots. The nearest other humans could have been fifty miles away, but when Carlisle spoke, he whispered.

"It's beautiful."

"To you, maybe." Danny was still panting. "But I'm knackered." A moment's reflection. "You bring me to the nicest places."

"It looks pristine. As if we're the first to come here... Unspoiled – you know?"

"Yeah, but forty years ago, it was a killing ground. Must have spoiled somebody's day." But Danny had to admit that Carlisle had summed up their target destination well; he tried to sound less negative. "Calm after the storm. If only some of our other stopovers could have been so sheltered."

"Plenty of places to pitch a tent down there, too..." Carlisle inched forward to get a better view over the convex slope down to the water. "Whereabouts did Marchesi say they'd sunk the cylinder?"

"Pretty much opposite where we are. See the final island? The big one; not so flat as the others... The last one before the shoal that leads back out into the strait... He said it was half way between that island and the mainland beyond, to the west."

Carlisle must have felt safe. He raised himself on his elbows and pushed out his lips into the shape of a kiss, sucking in a breath that whistled gently. "If the bloody thing is still there, of course." He gave the area a long stare, then looked over to his right. Perhaps three-quarters of a mile to the north, a neck of land jutted out, preventing them from seeing all the way to the end of the bay. "Did Marchesi say much about what was down at the far end?"

"He didn't say a lot. When I went back and showed him the chart, he pointed to a little anchor printed on it and nattered on about '*Droggie*' for a bit. He reckoned that's where the Jerry submarine would have anchored."

"Completely out of sight. What a place." Carlisle was silent for a generous half-minute before adding, "There could be something small, like a launch or a yacht there now at the far end. And we'd never see it until we were almost on top of it."

"It isn't likely, though, is it?"

"No, but just imagine... When news of this place finally leaks out... All the bloody sea-gypsies will flock here. The place could be choc-a-bloc full of hippies... and the bums who've sold their homes and bought a boat, all waiting for a fair wind to waft them through from one ocean to the next." He sighed, then smiled. "There'll be barbecues and beer cans everywhere."

"Like hell there will, you silly sod! It's close to freezing for most of the year."

Carlisle unshipped a pair of lightweight binoculars and started to scan the cove. "This is the eighth day. We'll have to be twice as alert now."

"Why?"

"Our chopper crew planned to come out of hiding on the seventh day. That was yesterday. Suppose they walked into Punta Arenas without being stopped, they'd probably head for the nearest bar to try and find a phone. They'd try to get a call through to the embassy, then give themselves up."

"That would take them up to about lunch time, I suppose."

"Right... Then an hour or two at the local nick before a couple of tons of excrement had had time to fly up in the air and come back down again... The higher it flies, the longer that takes, of course. If things shot up as far as Pinochet, maybe our boys would get stuck in a cell for the night..."

Carlisle stopped for a few seconds, perhaps imagining himself in the shoes of Pete and the two pilots. Then he took a deep breath and became more matter-of-fact. "But the Chileans are bound to be suspicious. They won't fall for any stories about engine failure or the gyrocompass going on the blink – not when they take a look at the Sea King and find how much kit has been stripped out of it. They're bound to suspect the chopper crew of landing a special forces patrol."

"Of course. Otherwise, why go into hiding for a week, unless you're trying to give your special forces time to get the job done?"

"Exactly," said Carlisle.

"But friends or not, no country on earth is going to just roll over and say 'Oh, that's all right then'."

"Nope... First chance they've got, they're going to come a-looking. So once there's enough daylight to see by, we've got to expect Chilean air patrols."

Danny made a disparaging remark about Rear Admiral Rennie and 'another fine mess' that he had gotten him into. Then, as if it were all of little consequence, he added merrily, "Seen enough?"

Carlisle appeared cheerful too. "Yep. Let's get back to camp."

Amongst Carlisle's kit had lain a shrink-wrapped package which he now handed to Danny, saying that he didn't exactly understand how it worked, but because Danny would understand perfectly, he could take charge of it.

"All I know is, it's a sort of cross between a mine detector and an echo sounder," said Carlisle. "And I'd like to know whether it's working or not. I thought we ought to test it."

"How?"

"Well, if Marchesi is right, there's a wrecked U-boat lying on the bottom of the strait, maybe half a mile outside the entrance to Caleta Notch."

"Rusty, blown to bits, and covered in kelp."

"Yes, but if that gadget is working, it ought to be able to detect some of the bigger chunks. If it can't find a thousand tons of Nazi steel in fifty or sixty feet of water, then we'll have to fall back on Plan B."

"What's Plan B?"

"No effing idea, yet mate." Carlisle scratched his head. "No effing idea."

"Is that why they made you an officer? Because you've got no effing idea?"

"I don't think so." He appeared to think for a moment. "I reckon it's because, like I told you, after the Kola, I thought I hadn't done such a good job, so I marched into the adjutant's office and said I wanted to buy myself out."

"Quit the Marines?"

"Yep. That's when Her Majesty realised she didn't want to waste all my training. My C/O had a quick think and told me that fooling the Russians into thinking I was one of them was something to be proud of... Full of bullshit, he was... He said being self-critical and realising my mistakes was the best way to learn." Carlisle filled his chest and looked proud – a theatrical impersonation of his commanding officer. He put on the brusque voice of a stereotypical colonel: "All those qualities make you ideal officer material, my boy."

But the act was short-lived; he paused for a moment. "After that it all happened quite quickly. And before long I was wearing my rank on my shoulders instead of my biceps, looking at a useful pay rise and drinking my soup with a spoon instead of out of a mug."

"You really should write a book – *Galtieri; My Part in His Downfall.*"

"Forget it."

With work to do, Carlisle decided that he would like to find a suitable place in Caleta Notch to cache their equipment and supplies, before venturing out into the strait to test what had become Danny's new gadget. Searching for the U-boat was, however, their second priority; the first was to paddle down to the extreme end of the inlet and check that they were alone. By the time they had travelled the first half mile into the cove, the translation of the Spanish word '*caleta*' had begun to seem badly chosen. Carlisle drew comparisons with his commando training in Scotland and reckoned the place was more like a sea loch, except that the surrounding mountains were higher, more barren and more snow-capped. Danny agreed, adding that if he had been asked to name a Scottish glacier he would have been stumped.

The calm waters, the absence of human life, the shelter from the wind and the spellbinding silence combined to retard Danny's paddle strokes to a slow, effortless tick. Carlisle matched tempo without complaint. Both men seemed equally fascinated by the small islets around which they were forced to navigate, awestruck like a pair of schoolboys, captivated by the idea of exploring new territory, of camping there, possessing the place for a brief sliver of time. All sense of urgency had evaporated.

Carlisle had been speaking in a normal tone about keeping to the centre of whatever nameless channel they found themselves in, and idly speculating about what might lie on the far side of the neck of land jutting out ahead, on their right-hand side. For a few seconds, they missed the low throbbing beat, as if it were some sort of weird echo of their voices, reflected from the steep surrounding hills. Then their thoughts connected at the same instant.

"Helicopter!" Carlisle twisted round but there was nothing yet to see. "Dig in! Let's get behind that outcrop." Danny obediently thrust his paddle into the water and levered a volume of it sternwards. Then another, and another. "Faster," cried Carlisle.

Danny had enough breath to add, "Fast? They're pretty fast off the mark, too." The sound grew louder, but they could tell that its bearing had altered. The aircraft was crossing behind them, not coming directly towards them. "How far away?"

“Shit, I don’t know. Two miles? Three? Keep digging in.”

“It’s flying north. What do you reckon? Is he this side of the strait or the other?”

“Let’s get into cover first, eh?”

The pounding of the rotors continued, nearer but still crossing. Carlisle kept twisting round to check, but the chopper remained out of sight. Danny strained to register any change in tone – anything that might indicate that the observer on the helicopter had spotted them and pointed them out to his pilot – but no such change came. Surely they would present such a tiny target, a barely man-sized speck several miles distant, clothed darkly so as to merge into the murky green and peaty earth shades of the loch’s background. Surely they wouldn’t be seen...

With the tip of the headland at 3 o’clock on their right and the sound of the helicopter opened out now to about 8 o’clock, behind and to their left, Carlisle used his paddle blade as a rudder to make a sharp turn to their right.

“I’m hopping out,” he said. He felt for his binoculars. “Take her in gently for me.”

Danny, now practised at approaching land, began feeling for the bottom with his paddle. “Two feet down,” he said. “Feels like big round stones.”

“I’m gone.” Carlisle was already over the side, surging ashore thigh-deep. He called over his shoulder, “Find somewhere close by and drag her ashore. If you can uproot some bracken, cover her over. Smear some mud on your hands and face. Stay out of sight.”

Danny had already started back-paddling but with the weight distribution all wrong, the craft handled less like the sort of upmarket canoe an expedition might choose, and more like an antiquated camel being goaded on a one-way journey into a meat market. He changed to forward motion and put in several heavy strokes on the right-hand side to bring the canoe round to the left, hoping to avoid an obvious kelp bed stretching out from the shore – a steep shore with nowhere to beach the canoe. Close by and directly in front lay a patch of drying rocks, no more than two or three feet out of the water. They offered no cover at all. It looked more inviting on the western side of the loch, but in case the helicopter returned, he didn't want to be caught in the open, crossing to the far side. He could only head round to the right, sticking close to the land, avoiding the forest of seaweed and hoping for a suitable landing site. He had built up a turn of speed on the canoe now, and she handled a whole lot better. The pulsating sound of the rotors had grown more distant.

A quarter of a mile ahead, there looked to be a narrow opening enclosing a tiny cove – a proper cove, a sight to make a smuggler's heart sing, not this misclassified sea loch. Danny headed towards it, thinking he ought to make it within five minutes. But half way there, rapidly revealing itself on his right, lay a narrow beach. He paddled towards it. Clearer water here made it easy to see the bottom – a covering of small shells and a sprinkling of sand. Quickly ashore, he dragged the canoe to the back of the beach onto a surface of flat pebbles.

Straightening up, he looked back the way he had come, and was confronted by the highly noticeable thirty-foot track that he had made across the sand. If the helicopter came right to the end of the loch, the furrow would stand out. He began to move the canoe so that it didn't lie directly in line with the track, then started doing what Carlisle had said, breaking up the craft's outline with driftwood, ferns and dried seaweed, harvested from above the tide line. Carlisle... Yes; now they were separated.

No sound from the helicopter... It wouldn't hurt to try to disguise the track in the sand so that it looked less like somebody had dragged a canoe up the beach and more, perhaps, like the flipper imprints of a sea lion returning to the water. Having no knowledge of what such a trail actually looked like and with nothing else to occupy him for a while, he bent to the task, depending heavily on his always-active imagination, and a degree of artistic licence.

Twenty minutes later, the rhythm of the rotors returned, faintly at first, then growing louder than before. Danny remembered that he had been told to mask his face with mud, but it was too late now. With the reverberations bouncing around the nearby mountainsides, he couldn't be certain where the helicopter was. He didn't think it was coming straight towards him, but he knew he mustn't take any chances. He snuggled up close to the overhanging bank of earth at the back of the beach, lay face down with his hands under his groin and waited. Presently, Caleta Notch became quiet again.

The beach felt more homely than some of the places where he and Carlisle had camped, but he felt less sure of how Carlisle might react if he recommended it as their base. Rather than take responsibility and begin off-loading some of the kit from the canoe, he scrambled up over the earth bank and wandered around in the undergrowth. A touch of sleet rode in on the wind. He suspected that by this time of year any wild berries would have withered or been consumed by whatever wildlife inhabited the area, whilst the thought of making a meal from marine invertebrates revolted him. Clearly, they must still depend on 'compo' rations until the mission ended and they returned into the care of the Royal Navy.

After his fruitless search of the ice-cold landscape, Danny returned to the beach and was relieved to see Carlisle wading out of the water.

Carlisle called out, "Saw where you went," then added with a grin, "Just hope these binoculars are properly waterproof." He continued up the beach, taking in Danny's efforts to camouflage the canoe. "Good effort," he said. "We might as well lighten the canoe and make this our camp."

"That's a good idea. Did you get a look at the chopper?"

"Yes. Curious really. It was making a lot of noise, so I suppose I'd expected it'd be a big one... Something like a Sea King, or at least the same thing with the original Sikorsky badge on it. But it wasn't."

"No?"

"No. It must have flown up the far side of the strait when we first heard it, then turned round and come back down this side."

"So, they're looking for something or somebody?"

"Yes, but I don't reckon they've got much chance of finding anyone." Danny stayed silent, obliging Carlisle to carry on. "When I spotted them, they were outside the *caleta*, flying away from me. It looked like one of those old choppers that we used to call the '*Whirlwind*'." He put his head on one side and smiled. "I always thought that machine looked rather like a tadpole... But they hadn't got the side doors open, so even if there was somebody in the main cabin, he'd have been looking through streaky perspex, covered in salt spray. He wouldn't see a lot."

"And I guess the pilot would have been too busy to take much notice, anyway."

"Most likely. And if he'd come from Punta Arenas, or even that Puerto Harris place, he'd probably be right on his range limit. He wouldn't want to stick around too long."

"So we're safe for a bit?"

"Yep. Let's crack on."

The long-legged wading fowl, and small, scurrying, brown and white birds that occupied the mud flats paid no heed as Danny and Carlisle slipped out of the loch and into the choppy waters of the strait. Danny had thought it worthwhile to see whether the gadget could pick up any return from the remains of Lieutenant Marchesi's steel net as they left the loch, but he couldn't tell whether it had or hadn't. Carlisle paddled them gently seawards on a roughly west-southwest heading. Danny's gadget could certainly tell the depth of the water which, as expected, increased as they drew away from land. However, it didn't register any stronger echoes or detect any metallic objects. Three quarters of a mile out from the narrow loch entrance, Carlisle offered the thought that the sea bed was a big place and maybe they should start looking in a different part of it.

"Well, I'm doing my best. I'm twisting this bloody thing from side to side, scanning as much of the ocean floor as I can," said Danny. "Believe me, if there's anything down there, I want to find it more than you do. This water's so cold, my hand is likely to drop off soon."

"Okay, keep your hair on. I'll see if I can widen the area and take us in a zigzag pattern..."

Which, after another fifteen minutes, resulted in an exclamation from Danny that he thought he had found something. "A hundred and twenty metres down. Big change on the bottom. Could be the wreck, maybe?"

"The shape... Can you tell what shape it is?"

"That's what I'm bloody well trying to do." He gripped the side of the canoe with his left hand and plunged his right arm and the gadget a little deeper into the water to scan fore and aft as well as side to side. "There's a chunk below us and another chunk a little way ahead, and as far as I can tell, they're both long and thin."

"Bullseye!"

"I think we've found it." Danny withdrew his arm and shook the water off. His flesh had taken on a corpse-like whiteness with a tinge of blue. He swore, then looked around.

"We ought to log this position somehow. Somebody back home might want to know."

A little way north of them, a scattering of rocky islets made it relatively easy to fix an approximate location by eye. Without the benefit of a gyro-stabilised compass and proper surveying equipment it would have to suffice. "A hundred and twenty metres," mused Carlisle. "I hadn't expected it to get so deep so quickly. Let's get back into the loch and get you warmed up again."

Danny's right hand had become so numb that he couldn't easily hold his paddle, so Carlisle had taken over and canoed them back inside the *caleta*. Both men now sat on the hump-backed island, a little way back from the shore, drinking tea and facing across the small enclosed bay under which they suspected the cylinder lay.

"This is the part that worries me," said Carlisle. "We've proved your gadget works, so – if the bloody cylinder is where Marchesi said it was, and if nobody has half-inched it – we won't have a good excuse for not finding it." Once again, Danny tried to remain silent and let Carlisle develop his argument. But this time Carlisle needed some participation. "Seen the chart?"

"Yes. What about it?"

"Seen the soundings?"

"Is there a problem?"

"Well, for one thing, they're all over the shop. And yes, there could be a problem. Some places are really shallow, but the deepest soundings are just over there." He raised his left arm and waved it towards the most open part of the loch where it widened out into a great black pool, just inside the entrance. "56 fathoms. 336 feet. Just over 100 metres."

"That's quite deep, isn't it?"

"Yeah. Just suppose Marchesi wasn't quite sure where he dropped the cylinder. If the old boy chucked it in over there, *we* won't be fishing it out. Not on this trip."

"Because?"

"Because, unless you're a professional diver, it's close to the limit in any circumstances, and because anybody going as deep as that would need a buddy to go down with him."

"Anything else?"

"He'd need a dive boat to give him proper support from the surface."

"Are you telling me this is another cock-up?"

"Not quite; not yet. The thing is, we couldn't muster enough specialist deep-diving gear in the whole Task Force for me to pinch it and bugger off with it on a side operation. Besides, we couldn't have carried it all in a single canoe, let alone an overloaded helicopter." He looked pointedly at Danny to emphasise his next words. "All I've got is a single nitrox bottle that won't last more than thirty minutes."

"Oh."

"And that's not taking into account the need to spend any time searching at depth, or for decompression stops on the way back up."

Danny turned his head to gaze across the waters in front of them. The feeling had now returned to his fingers. He jabbed one of them at the area half way to the mainland. "What's the depth out there – where the cylinder is supposed to be?"

"The 20-fathom line is about 150 yards off shore. At least it was in 1883, according to the chart."

"But the water could be deeper?"

"See for yourself. 38 fathoms was the maximum depth they recorded. I wouldn't dare go down that deep without a lot more safety gear..."

"No. I can see that. I wouldn't want you to."

"And a dive-buddy... And this time, I don't mean you." It seemed a long time before Carlisle added, "I suppose the first objective should be to see if we can get an echo from Hitler's vile canister of crap."

So Carlisle and Danny took to the water again, and although they spent a good hour quartering the area to the west of the big island, Danny could only find a solitary meaningful echo from the depths. The location, the depth, the single target all pointed to it being the copper cylinder – but there was only one way to find out. And of course, their luck had not changed one iota, for their goal appeared to be sitting on the edge of a submerged cliff, lying in 30 fathoms of cold, briny water.

Carlisle announced that he had some thinking to do, and called a halt to the day's events. With little sensation in Danny's right arm, which he said felt as cold as a slab of meat from a slaughter house freezer room, Carlisle canoed them swiftly back to the morning's beach for a hot meal.

After eating, Carlisle began to unpack his armoury of stores, laying out the diving gear, polypropylene rope, a float, something that appeared to be a camera sealed into waterproof wrapping, a slightly larger package shrouded in orange plastic, and a small pouch of papers. It was clear that he wanted be alone, intent on working out what to do. Left to fill an empty afternoon, Danny conceived a plan of his own.

"You've obviously got a lot on your mind..." No reply. "Well, if it's all right with you, I'll just take the canoe and paddle over to the far end of the loch... See how well Marchesi's men tidied up. Never know... Might be a crate of undiscovered documents or something." Carlisle still wasn't listening. "...A crock of gold or a grand piano, maybe."

Carlisle's head remained buried inside a book of tables. He never even looked up. "Yeah. Good idea."

≈

Danny kicked around in the undergrowth for a while, half daydreaming, half an eye open for a shepherd, a sheep or two... possibly a discarded rifle, rusty with age. After a while it seemed that perhaps his operation of the gadget, which needed to be fully immersed to work at all, had given him a chill. With little warning, he experienced an urgency below the waist and felt moved to find a spot a little higher up the valley to attend to his needs. Ordinarily it might have been a fine viewpoint, offering him a view to the mouth of the loch, a mile away. If it were not for the sleet blowing into his face from the west, he might also have enjoyed a view of the indistinct land on the other side of the Magellan Strait. In the nature of things, not wishing to hurry matters, Danny cast his casual gaze left and right, closer to home. A few feet away a glint of white, almost totally obscured by a patch of ferns, attracted his eye. When he had finished doing what was necessary and felt confident that he could move off without the immediate return of his malady, he shuffled over and parted the foliage to expose the white object. His first reaction was both automatic and, he quickly realised, rather insensitive.

"Oh shit," he said.

His second utterance was more sympathetic. "Oh dear..."

(VII)

Thursday 27 May
Caleta Notch

While Danny gnawed at his cake of oatmeal block, he began to notice signs of an overnight change in Carlisle. The marine had acquired a slightly fugitive look and was avoiding eye contact. Nine or ten days' growth of dark, piratical beard did not improve his appearance, but this morning his eyes seemed to have sunk into their sockets, and his shoulders to have sagged.

"How do you feel?" Danny asked.

"I'll be okay. Mission sickness. I just want it to end now."

"I know. A lot of crap landed on your shoulders yesterday. I'm sorry."

"I just wish I felt it was worthwhile. Never mind 'Operation Certain Death', this one isn't much better. If I was giving it a name now, I'd call it 'Operation Pointless' or 'Operation Red Herring' or something."

"Yeah, I was thinking along those lines myself. 'Operation Wild Goose Chase'."

"You too?"

Danny needed to nudge his colleague out of his depression. "I don't blame Vic Marchesi. Poor old bugger – he's had this place on his conscience for a long time. I sort of blame myself –"

"That's rubbish." There was little power in Carlisle's voice; his gloom was clear to see. "From what you've told me, Vic came across plenty of bits of evidence, all pointing one way. More pieces are starting to fall into place for us. For one thing, we think we found the bloody U-boat yesterday... And the cylinder."

"So why are we both so pissed off about it?" Danny quickly answered his own question. "It's because, us being here is totally bloody futile. And we're only just coming to understand why."

"All right, why?"

"Well there's the *Sailing Directions* for one thing. They all warn you about anchoring outside the bay. 'Foul anchorage,' they say. But I'll bet somebody revised the pilot books a long time ago just to stop trawlermen or yachties from hooking into the wreckage of that flaming submarine. Easy thing to fix. Just a few words in a book, but mighty effective at keeping people away."

"I suppose so."

"You're worried yourself, aren't you?"

"Yeah. I've been fretting about the dive all night, but I agree with you. There's something about this anchorage that doesn't add up."

"Well nobody would anchor inside the heads in that first great lagoon – 56 fathoms – or that pool where we located the cylinder yesterday – 38 fathoms. The proper anchorage is marked on the chart – it's here, right behind us – shelving up from 12 fathoms; bloody perfect. The *Sailing Directions* say so as well."

"Okay," said Carlisle. Creases appeared between his eyebrows.

"What I'm saying is Vic's cylinder was as safe as houses, where he dropped it. It was never going to get disturbed. Only an idiot would try to anchor there. Too deep; no room to swing if the wind changed."

Carlisle began to nod slowly.

Danny continued: "Think about the Navy Department. All that gold braid, and nobody smart enough to take a look at the chart and see that the cylinder could have stayed where it was."

Carlisle lifted his chin. "I suppose it could have... Well, almost."

"Until," said Danny, "some mental defective decided the Argies might have collared it and used it to make nerve gas... And that defective was me."

"No it bloody wasn't. The nerve gas angle was just an excuse – a smokescreen. This whole thing is about saving face with the Yanks. This is about never having to admit that we cocked it up, big time. You've already told me – if it hadn't been for Marchesi, Hitler would have given the Japs the kit to gas thousands of US marines. This is about naval reputations and political favours."

"But I started the ball rolling."

"But somebody else did a lot more digging, and then some admiral or general or politician somewhere thought this might give his career a boost, and somebody very senior gave the orders. None of this is your fault."

"Until they're looking for a scapegoat. Then it'll be my fault."

"Not if we finish it right."

Danny felt pleased that he had rekindled the wildfire in Carlisle's belly. "Thanks for being on my side," he said.

"We still make a good team, don't we?" The pair exchanged grins and nods, laying down a few feel-good moments, then: "Do you want to know what's been worrying me?"

"If it's a plan for salvaging that cylinder, yes I do."

"All right. It's a bit complicated, though..."

So Carlisle began to describe his plan to Danny. He explained how his bottle of nitrox-36 contained sixteen percent more oxygen and the same amount less nitrogen than normal air. He explained how nitrogen dissolves in the blood and how extreme pressure increases the amount that dissolves. He explained the dire effects of nitrogen bubbles in the bloodstream if a diver were to ascend more rapidly than his body could safely off-gas, and then he showed Danny a set of decompression tables, which he called 'the diver's bible'.

He traced a pathway through the tables and made sure that Danny understood the theory of what he proposed. The rigour of the explanation and the second pair of eyes proved to be what Carlisle needed. At the end of the tutorial, he was clearly more confident in his plan. His voice had regained its strength and he managed not only a reassuringly playful punch on Danny's shoulder but also a little teasing.

"Okay," said Carlisle. "Now you'll know how to stay safe when you swim down to rescue that cylinder."

Danny laughed and there followed a few more moments of banter before the mood returned to business-like normality. Danny needed it to. "There's something else you need to know."

"What else could possibly go wrong?"

"I found a body yesterday..."

Up on the hillside, Carlisle knelt almost reverently over the human remains. Substantial items of the person's uniform, including his boots, still clothed the body, but the skull and hands were partially uncovered.

"I suppose the clothing kept him hidden," said Danny.

"Held him together... Stopped some vulture from carrying off his bones." Carlisle tried to unbutton the tunic at the fellow's neck, but the threads were perished and the buttons came away in his fingers. No flesh remained. A grey oval dog-tag hung over the top ribs, suspended from a piece of bleached and withering string. The cord protruded through two holes above the long axis of the badge and was knotted at the front.

"Kriegsmarine," said Carlisle with no surprise. "See?"

Danny bent forward and read the word on the tag. "No name though?"

"Only 'Kriegsmarine' and his number... That's standard. And the year he enlisted. '41."

"I guess that removes any last shreds of doubt. The Nazis really were here." It was the sort of situation that called more for reflection than great haste. "I suppose his number would tell us who he was."

"Yeah, but whoever he was, I don't think he was just a hairy-arsed matelot. I don't know much about German Navy uniforms, but look at his teeth. See all that gold? He must have had a pretty penny."

"An officer?"

"Maybe." Carlisle had carried on searching the body. "But a wounded one. Look." He pointed to a small circular hole in the skeleton's left shoulder blade, no wider than a pencil shaft. "I reckon a three-o-three round did that." He snorted ironically. "Classic from the cowboy movies – a flesh wound in the left shoulder."

"Is that what killed him?"

"Not straight away. Eventually, maybe, if it got infected. Obviously there wasn't any medical help anywhere around, so it's possible it killed him... But it tells us something else."

"What?"

"At least two Jerries would have been left alive after Marchesi buggered off. Your man Fischer, and this chap... I don't know – call him'Gustav'."

Carlisle's mention of Vic sparked Danny's memory. "Marchesi gave the dead Jerries a burial at sea. We ought to give this one a final resting place too. He shouldn't stay here like this. Someone ought to say the proper words over him."

"We can't take him with us. There'd be too much explaining to do."

"Explaining would be the easy part. The navy could fix it to find his bones in a cave in Shetland, or Crete, or Goose Bay. You never know – it might suit them. A bit of mystery. Anybody looking for a lost U-1226 would start looking in completely the wrong place."

"Best they don't even start looking. That U-boat is lost already. Let it stay lost."

"It'll stay lost as long as no details about its mission leak out from their archives."

"Where are they held?"

Danny took a deep breath. "We've got them locked away," he said, then fell silent to let this information sink in.

Carlisle raised an eyebrow. "So if Gustav's body turned up 5,000 miles away from here, you're saying it's a great way to throw treasure hunters off the scent and make certain U-1226 stays lost forever."

"Yes I am, but I don't want you to think that was the plan all along." Danny flexed his fingers in an open gesture. "It's only just occurred to me."

"All right, but why bother burying this bloke? It's too much trouble. He's just a pile of bones now."

"Because Hitler's dead and gone. We're friends with the Germans now. This bloke is just the same as you and me. He wasn't forced to join the Kriegsmarine in 1941 through fear of the Gestapo. A couple of years later it might have been different, but he probably joined up out of a mixture of patriotism and testosterone. I remember Marchesi said something – 'wanting something to brag about'. Gustav was as committed to the country he grew up in as you or me. Wrong, according to us, but when you think about it, he deserves a war grave now. I just think he ought to have a proper headstone."

"Danny Rook. Always full of surprises."

"If it was one of our men, you'd agree to it."

"All right. But there isn't a spare seat in the canoe. He'll have to be parcelled up in bits."

"Carlisle Tillotson. The killer with a heart."

A familiar low throbbing sound caused them both to stop and listen.

"A bit earlier than yesterday," said Carlisle. "But that means the Plum Duff guys must still be at large, otherwise that helicopter wouldn't still be sniffing around."

"We'll just wait till he's gone, then?"

"Yeah. Here's a cam-stick. Smudge some grease on your face and hands, like I told you yesterday. Officer's orders!"

"Yes sir!" Danny started to camouflage his face. "You're not worried?"

"Worried? No. Pleased. Once the chopper's gone, it won't be back till tomorrow. It gives us a free hand to float around undisturbed all day if necessary, trying to fish that cylinder out."

While Carlisle changed into his sub-aqua gear, he gave Danny a friendly lecture about planning, although Danny appreciated the value of a good plan as much as he did. However, in the same way that he had explained the decompression tables as a means of being absolutely certain of his calculations, the explanation of what needed to be done to recover the cylinder clarified his own thinking. He finished by telling Danny that it was a good idea to think about your mistakes before you made them.

Incoming sleet, borne on a force 5, brought elements of both good and bad fortune. Certainly, it virtually guaranteed that the Chilean helicopter would not return that day. Even so, labouring against the constant wintry weather was becoming a chore, sapping their energy and worrying away at their spirits. The wind direction had altered, allowing Magellan weather inside the heads of Caleta Notch. Carlisle's current task was to counteract the wind and maintain the canoe on station by responding to Danny's positioning commands.

They had tied several pounds of beach stones inside a dirty T-shirt together with a couple of empty food tins to improve reflectivity, then attached the makeshift weight to the end of a polypropylene line. The other end was secured to an eye-bolt in the bow of the canoe. Danny had allowed his paddle to float away on the end of a length of cord so that he could co-ordinate two tasks: With his left hand he was paying out the weighted end of the line. With his right he was operating the echo-sounder-cum-metal-detector equipment.

The hope was that having got used to his new toy, Danny would be getting skilled enough to distinguish the cylinder from the weighted T-shirt as it descended – skilled enough to guide the line close to the cylinder. When Carlisle entered the water, he would then be able to follow the line to the bottom, minimising the time he had to spend down below searching for Hitler's nasty surprise. He very much hoped to be able to complete his dive quickly – straight down, lash the cylinder to the line and straight back up again. By spending the bare minimum of time at depth, the number of decompression stops could be reduced to a single one much nearer the surface, at a depth of about 32 feet.

"How's it looking now?"

"The line's gone slack," said Danny, "so we've touched bottom. But I think we must have drifted a bit. There's a gap between the cylinder and your T-shirt now... could be as much as six feet."

"It's worth seeing if we can get it down to three feet or less. If there's kelp roots down there, and they're close together, I could waste time searching in the wrong direction."

And so began a process of trying to position the canoe directly above the cylinder, hauling in a couple of feet of line, drifting with the wind for a few seconds, then dropping the weights before the line could start swinging like a pendulum. Eventually, the process had become so slick that Danny reported the weights seemed so close to the cylinder that they might even have landed on top of it. Carlisle expressed himself overjoyed.

For the third time, they went over the signals to be used: two tugs to haul in about five feet of line; three tugs clear to haul to the surface; repeated tugs to stop hauling. Following this, Carlisle sluiced some seawater round inside his face mask, donned it, closed his lips over the mouthpiece of the second stage regulator and, with a wave, slid over the side. Danny noted the time.

After only twelve minutes the first signal came. Danny took up the slack, then took the strain as he and the canoe experienced the weight of the cylinder. He hadn't given its weight much thought until that moment – or the buoyancy of the canoe. The signal came to take up another five feet of line; then again, then once more. That probably made just over three fathoms, leaving the best part of thirty still to go. He hoped Carlisle was coming up now.

Soon came three tugs, so Danny heaved away. Because the weight was all on his left side, every muscle from his stomach to his groin let him know it was not happy. Too bad; he couldn't see a way of transferring the rope to the right-hand side of the canoe to equalise the strain. After pulling on the rope for at least a minute he realised he had no idea how much more line hung beneath him; he wished he had at least counted the lengths that he had already recovered. Then the weight seemed heavier and the canoe heeled over somewhat. It must mean that Carlisle wanted him to stop; he was grateful for that. He looped three or four twists around Carlisle's paddle to stop the rope slipping back and laid it athwartships across the canoe's cockpit, noticing how much closer to the island he now was; wind drift, no doubt. The right thing to do would be to paddle back into deeper water to avoid the risk of fouling the line and snaring the cylinder in the kelp forest. He did that as gently as he could; he didn't want to make any sudden movements and start the cylinder swinging.

After eighteen minutes Danny felt the signal to haul away again, which he did. At least Carlisle must still be okay. Maybe it was a decompression stop or maybe he had called a halt because he needed to make the cylinder more secure. In between puffs Danny started looking for Carlisle's bubbles, but the surface of the *caleta* had become too choppy.

After twenty-one minutes the canoe heeled over again, so Danny stopped pulling. Two minutes later Carlisle surfaced.

"It's about twenty feet below us," he said. "Can you haul it up until I say stop?"

Danny agreed, glad that an end was in sight. Carlisle made a circle around the rope with his thumb and forefinger to hold position, dipped his face in the water to watch for the cylinder, then after a few grunts from Danny he signalled a stop.

"Suggestion," said Danny as he belayed the rope again with several turns around Carlisle's paddle. "That thing is pretty heavy, but it'll be a lot heavier out of water. I'll never be able to lift it on my own. How about if we take it over to the mud flats and drag it ashore?"

"Good plan. Bring it up to just below the surface, then I'll swim ashore with the rope when we're a bit closer." Danny hauled for what he hoped would be the final time, secured the rope again and took up his own paddle.

Presently, when Carlisle could stand in the shallows, he slapped web-footed across the slimy mud at the mouth of the cove and lashed the rope to a bush.

"Time for a hot drink," said Danny. "I'm goosed. Are you okay?"

"Yeah, fine. Went like a dream." Carlisle began to gabble. "No weeds growing anywhere near it down there. It's copper, see? No weeds, no clams – nothing. You'll see in a minute. It still had a rope strop on it, but I didn't want to trust it."

A lighter patch appeared in the sky and within moments the sleet died away.

"We've done it then," said Danny.

Carlisle flopped back into the herbage and exhaled with relief, almost a sob. The wind dropped as if some minor god had been appeased, or as if perhaps this recovery of the cylinder was the final atonement for the evil act that had brought it there in the first place... and the deaths that came about as a result.

"I'm cold now. Are you cold?"

"Relieved more than cold. Anything could have happened to you down there."

"Yeah – but I'd love a mug of tea, seeing as you offered."

When they had both rested, Carlisle crossed the mud again to ease the cylinder safely out of the water, while Danny pulled from just above the waterline. Rather than roll it, Carlisle had said they could try to sledge it across the mud; that would be faster and take less effort. He re-joined Danny. They both sat and stared at the thing. Danny was on the point of asking what should happen next, when a strange sound occurred, a soft sound, not at all a threatening sound, but an out-of-place one.

"What was that?"

"Over there, I think..."

"The cylinder?"

... Glug ...

As they watched, a dribble of liquid issued from a narrow outlet at the neck of the cylinder. 'Glug' it went again.

"Oh fuck! It's leaking." Carlisle's training kicked in as he leapt to his feet. "Gas gas gas!" One finned foot stood on top of the other, tripping him so that he fell backwards. "Get away," he screamed, scrambling up the bank.

Breathless, neither Carlisle nor Danny broke stride until they had gained the high ground on the western side of Caleta Notch.

"Let me look at your eyes," said Carlisle. "It's supposed to be an indication. If you've had a dose of nerve gas, your pupils shrink."

"I thought they dilated. Do you feel okay?"

"Winded, but okay I think."

"How did it suddenly spring a leak?"

"Dunno. Maybe we did it ourselves with the T-shirt full of rocks. Maybe we dropped it on the valve or something. They're only brass. One good clout and it might have fractured."

"Or maybe Marchesi did it when he gave the cylinder the deep six," said Danny. "Maybe that bit of pipe snapped off when it hit the bottom in '44." He sat and pondered.

"What are you thinking?"

"Suppose they didn't lower it – they'd have needed a long line to reach the bottom." Danny stood up and peered in the direction of the cylinder. "Suppose they just chucked it in. It'd go down with a hell of a force, wouldn't it?"

"Yeah." Carlisle's tone encouraged more.

"And suppose that brass nozzle got broken forty years ago... Well over all those years, wouldn't the gas have leaked out and seawater filled it up?"

"Oh right... So you're just going to walk up to it and give it a kick? Bend down and have a sniff? Dip your finger in the stuff that's leaking out and see if it tastes salty?"

"No. I'm going to do a spot of bird watching. I'm going to wait until one of those shite-hawks down there shimmies up to it. I'm going to hope he sticks his beak in the mud close to the cylinder and pulls out a nice juicy jelly worm, and when he doesn't drop down dead, I'm going to start cheering."

"Bloody birds? They're different from us. They can eat all sorts of berries and seeds and crap that would poison you and me. Who says nerve gas would be any different? What if they can swim around all day in gallons of the stuff and still no ill effects?"

It was mid-afternoon before a sufficient number of waterfowl had sampled the lower lifeforms in the mud near the cylinder, allowing Carlisle to change from outright opposition to mere scepticism. Perhaps he had become motivated by a desire to reclaim the canoe and return to their camp near the inner anchorage. And possibly the thought of a hot meal and a change of clothing also influenced him.

Danny volunteered to go first, crossing his fingers in the hope of reaching the canoe alive. The leakage from the pipe had stopped. It seemed a safe guess that the contents were now nothing but brine.

(VIII)

Friday 28 May
Caleta Notch

Conversation the previous evening had drifted around the subject of getting the cylinder back to Britain for destruction, as ordered. Like the tide, Danny and Carlisle flowed in and out of the topic, whilst also speculating on how Plum Duff might be going and the story behind the body on the hillside. Lacking information of any kind, they also wondered how any actions against the Argentineans had gone, and indeed whether the Prime Minister had managed to stay in office. A mental tiredness had settled over both men. Consequently, their discussions lacked focus and no great insight could be brought to bear on any issue.

By the morning, with the benefit of a night's sleep, a solution to one of their problems had occurred to Danny. He crawled out of his tent to find Carlisle brushing a light dusting of frost off the top surface of the canoe. Carlisle, too, had something on his mind.

"Today's the eleventh day," said Carlisle. "With all the excitement, I clean forgot a piece of mission administration."

"What was that?"

"We were supposed to go on reduced rations yesterday so we could stay out longer than fourteen days if we needed to."

"Is that going to be a problem?"

"Hopefully not. We've done what we came for, so any time now I reckon we can break radio silence and shout for a taxi. If necessary, we could probably eke out the rations and go 16 or 17 days without much hardship." He glanced at Danny, as if to gauge his opinion. "We ought to do it – just in case... But it shouldn't take us as long as that to get outside coastal limits and get picked up."

"Sounds good to me." A pause. "That's a secure satellite phone you've got tucked away in the orange packet, then?"

"Yep..."

"You might have mentioned it me... I wouldn't have told anyone." Carlisle flicked him a gesture that said, 'Now you know. What's the problem?' Danny crossed that issue off his mental list and allowed a moment or two in case Carlisle had something else to bring up.

"Don't forget we need to visit the hillside again," said Danny. "We've got to pop Gustav in a bag with some bits of his uniform and his dog tag."

"No, I hadn't forgotten. There's no rush. I just thought the timing worked well yesterday. You know... When the helicopter appeared for a few minutes and then was gone for the rest of the day. If we pack up everything here, we can deal with Gustav last thing before we move off. If the chopper turns up, we'll just hunker down in the bushes again."

And so it proved. Danny placed the body's larger bones directly into a plastic sack. To keep the smaller bones together, Carlisle wrapped the hands and feet in his own unwashed undergarments. Finally, for padding, he added some threadbare remnants of clothing taken from the skeleton. In his notebook he recorded the German's identity number, then dropped the tag into the bag. Danny twisted the neck of the bag into a hank and tied a knot in it. Then, as if on cue, the sound of a helicopter brought a smile to their faces.

"The Plum Duff boys must be getting really hungry by now," said Carlisle.

With fifteen or twenty minutes to wait before the helicopter was expected to pass again on its southbound leg,

Danny was in no hurry to talk about his solution. After a period of comfortable silence, he said, "I've had an idea."

"The way you said that... You think it's a pretty good idea, don't you?"

"Well, yes. I'd been worrying about our buoyancy. Yesterday with that cylinder dangling underneath me, I didn't have very much freeboard. Later today, with you sitting in the canoe as well, the cylinder hanging underneath it, the weighty stuff like the diving equipment, plus Gustav and all our dirty washing, it's going to be even less. I was thinking there must be another way... In fact I'm surprised neither of us thought of it last night."

"Thought of what?"

"Leaving it behind. It's no use to anyone now. There's obviously nothing in it, so no chance of the Argies getting hold of anything more lethal than salt water. Vic won't have to worry either – no pollution danger."

"We can't just leave it lying about on the mud."

"No. I suggest we drop it just beside U-1226. Even if nobody found it for another hundred years it wouldn't be unreasonable to find it in amongst the wreckage. It'd look as if it had been flung clear when the U-boat blew up... So there'd be no cause for anyone to jump to any awkward conclusions." Danny wasn't sure whether Carlisle looked convinced, so he added. "And it'd be deep enough so no yachtsman would be likely to drag it up with his anchor."

"You'll take responsibility for not bringing it back?"

"Sure. We'll just take a few photos to prove we did what we were asked to do. Then we'll put a strop around it, tow it out, and unless the strait is already too rough, we'll cut it free and kiss the damned thing goodbye."

"All right. Suits me."

Buenos Aires

The previous day's newspapers had gloried in Tuesday's sinking of what turned out to be HMS *Coventry*, and the damage done to a merchant vessel, later confirmed as *Atlantic Conveyor*. However, the Argentine news agency had reported so many ships from the Task Force sunk (some more than once) that some folk had learned to wait for a few days to be sure of what harm their Air Force had inflicted. For accurate intelligence, they depended on the Ministry of Defence in London to inform them, via the British press or the BBC.

Though he had carved out a life for himself in Argentina, Señor Anguilla was able to spare himself much of the Latin euphoria. He took a more sceptical view of what was published in the newspapers. Many years before, under a different name, he had noticed that reports of extensive sinkings and shootings-down by one side or the other didn't always accord with the truth. Although he knew enough to keep his thoughts to himself, in his experience, such exaggeration was often a prelude to defeat.

At the same time as the public was in raptures over the sinkings, Señor Anguilla, due to his position at ESMA, knew that Argentina's Navy was essentially bottled up – redundant as a fighting force – and its Air Force had lost a third of its most capable fighter aircraft. The Junta had admitted, too, that 1,500 British troops had landed in the Malvinas at San Carlos. There was no cause for alarm, they said. The landing was being contained.

The year before, half a million people had thronged the Plaza de Mayo and the surrounding streets to celebrate National Day. This year the junta had called for sobriety, and had swamped the city with heavily armed police. But of course, like Anguilla, the military hierarchy was in a position to know how bad things really were. Fortunately, only a few thousand people turned up in the square, so any fears that Galtieri might have had about a popular uprising were premature.

Adolpho Anguilla now harboured genuine fears about the survivability of the regime. A more liberal, democratic government might spell trouble for him. There were a lot of people like *El Asociación Madres de Plaza de Mayo* – the Mothers of the Plaza de Mayo – who already wanted to know where their loved ones had gone. But he didn't feel compelled to stick around for the final act. He wasn't part of the junta, struggling to hold things together. He didn't need to carry a loaded pistol in his pocket, whilst dreading the moment when the mob broke down the gates. He wouldn't have to decide how to use that last bullet, after carefully counting his shots.

But Adolpho was not as young or dynamic as he had been forty years before. He fluttered around inside his house, trembling a little, unable to settle, rubbing his thumbs and fingers together distractedly as if he were massaging a tiny rubber ball in each hand. Occasionally he would open a drawer and flick through the contents, but rarely did he take anything out. Rather, it seemed, he was putting his possessions in order. He sat on his bed and picked an identity card out of his jacket pocket.

"Goodbye old friend," he said, and placed the card on the skew, poking out from beneath a neat pile of handkerchiefs. Anyone opening the drawer would be bound to find it. From the same pocket he took two passports and placed one underneath the identity card. He flicked through the second one, noticing the occasional immigration stamp with a smile.

And though there was nobody to hear him, "Time to go," he said.

Caleta Notch

While the helicopter was away to the north, Carlisle suggested that because they probably had about a quarter of an hour to kill, they ought to widen the search in case Fischer or Gustav had concealed anything of importance nearby. They performed a fingertip search on hands and knees for the first two or three yards around, glad to stay out of the sleet, then stood and beat at the ferns, bending to look beneath bushes. But they found nothing.

"I'd have thought we'd have found something," said Danny. "It reminds me of the funeral service. Gustav brought nothing into the world and left nothing behind."

"No surprise."

"You mean Fischer, must have cleaned the place up before he left?"

"You've got it. No weapon. No tins of food. Not even his mess tin or mug. Nothing."

"Not quite nothing," Danny reminded him. "What about the dog tag?"

"Yeah. He may have been a shit-hot chemist, but your Doctor Fischer didn't think of everything, did he?"

When the helicopter could be heard heading south, shrouded in sleet and sea fog, and invisible to Carlisle and Danny, they broke cover, trudged back down the hillside to the canoe and, like Fischer, left not a trace of their having spent any time in the *caleta*.

Suspecting that the sea state in the strait could be getting rougher, Danny and Carlisle returned to the island in the centre of the cove from where they had launched their diving expedition the day before. Each wearing his dry suit as protection from the cold, they began to unload everything from the canoe. The job was almost complete when, with no warning, Danny gave a sharp sigh, then turned downwind and threw up his breakfast.

"Are you okay, buddy?"

"I'll be all right in a minute."

"How are your guts? You're not coming down with food poisoning, are you?"

"No. I said I'll be all right. It's just Gustav. He suddenly got to me."

"You weren't squeamish on the hill. Why now?"

"Not squeamish exactly." Danny spat, rinsed his mouth with salt water, then spat some more. "I just suddenly thought, 'what a horrible way to die'. Not like a bullet in the brain and you're dead before you hit the ground."

"You can't afford to have morbid thoughts, matey. Especially not about wars that ended before either of us was born."

"I know. But it made me think about the Congo – about my war. It's one of those things that lurks in my shadow all the time – the memory of that Chinese bloke... Just when I'm least expecting it. I can't control it. It's like he creeps up and taps me on the shoulder. He would have taken a while to die too... if somebody hadn't finished him off for me."

Carlisle cast his eyes down. "You never say much about that. These days they tell us to let it out."

"It's gone too far now."

"No, okay. I get it." It was clear that Danny would be broody for a few moments longer and needed Carlisle to say something understanding, or utter a pithy, comic profanity that would snap him back to reality. "I keep forgetting you've done something I've never had to," he said. "Maybe I'd feel the same. But most of the time it comes down to kill or be killed... I know which I'd rather."

"Yeah, but it's the old story. Gustav might have been a family man, just doing what he saw as his duty for his country. He might have been innocent of anything else, anything evil. But he's the one who died on the hillside and the real guilty one – Fischer, the one who was going to give this chemical technology to the Japanese – he's the one who got away."

Although Carlisle's first attempt to make Danny feel better had not ended the discussion, but had widened it instead, his next reaction was instinctive as he switched into song – the chorus of a music hall refrain, adapted for barrack room ribaldry:

"It's the same the whole world over,
It's the poor what gets the blame.
It's the rich what gets the pleasure,
Ain't it all a bleedin' shame..."

Danny coughed. A tear had clouded his eye. He wiped it away. "Yeah," he said, with a sniff that had the beginnings of a laugh beneath its surface. "I feel a bit stupid now."

"No. Not stupid. You're right about Fischer. But I told you. You can't go round feeling guilty about casualties from other people's wars. Gustav must have died nearly forty years ago. That was before we were born. It's nothing to do with us, except this – we're the ones who are trying to make it better – taking him home for a proper burial." Carlisle put his hand on Danny's shoulder and squeezed. "Okay now?"

"Yes. I'll be all right." Danny rinsed out his mouth again, spat, then splashed water over his face, rubbing away the embarrassing tear.

"Let's paddle over and photograph that cylinder, then." Carlisle nudged Danny. "I expect you'll want to see if it's still got that big German '*Leck*' word written on it."

"I couldn't give a flying fart about the damned thing any more," said Danny. "I just want us to get away from here as fast as we can."

≈

Danny lifted his hand out of the chilling water, placed the detector on his lap, then leaned to the left as Carlisle slid out of his seat and slipped over the right-hand side of the canoe. The Marine had already sunk his nitrox bottle in a deep part of the *caleta*. All he carried was his knife, sheathed and secured by a cord attached to his wrist. He took a breath then plunged below the surface, but was gone for a mere fifteen seconds.

"Job done?"

"Job done."

Rather than upset the canoe by trying to climb back into it afloat, Carlisle hung on to the side whilst Danny turned it around and pointed it towards the cove. With the wind behind them, Danny paddling strongly and Carlisle kicking with his fins they were back on the island in under fifteen minutes. Carlisle wanted to share a last look at the charts with Danny, to confirm the fastest way to get into international waters.

"What I'd do," said Danny, "is cross the strait and head northwest, then cut into this *Canal Abra* and through to *Bahía Otway*." He used his thumb and middle finger to roughly span a whole degree of latitude at the left-hand side of the chart. "It's a lot nearer than the southern route out into *Bahía Stokes*."

"All these English names. I can't get over it."

"Are you happy to take the northern route?"

"Yes, but half the day has gone already," said Carlisle. "We probably won't make more than ten miles before needing to camp for the night." He gave Danny a concerned look. "And you need something in your belly after chucking up your breakfast."

"Cold rations is fine. I told you – I'm sick of this place. Let's be on our way."

Ezeiza International Airport, Buenos Aires

The flight to Rome via Madrid was only half full. Some serious-faced passengers attempted to conceal a fear of flying, while others assumed a haughty air, playing the part of the experienced international traveller to whom a Boeing 747 was simply a necessary evil – an interruption in their executive lives. A smiling Aerolíneas Argentinas steward held out his hand to inspect the boarding pass gripped by the elderly, apprehensive-looking gentleman. The steward leaned forward to peer at the details.

In Spanish: "Welcome aboard Señor Thomas. Madrid, sir? 31C is an aisle seat down here on your right." He held out his left arm to show the way. "Have a pleasant flight Señor."

Dilwyn Delgado-Thomas managed a weak smile of his own in response, thanked the steward and shuffled down the port-side towards the cheaper seats, confident that the steward would have forgotten about him already.

Saturday 29 May
53°23'S 73°02'W

Carlisle had set his watch for 5:30 in the morning. He and Danny had paddled without a break during the previous afternoon, covering their ten miles in one hop, there being no practical alternative. They needed to cross to the western side of the strait and find shelter for the night, but they found its coastline both steep and exposed. Carlisle had picked out an inlet (or 'cove') for their evening camp which narrowed to about 300 yards. It wasn't ideal. They both knew they were taking a calculated risk because the cove opened directly off the main strait. However, the chart showed nowhere else that they could reach until well after dusk. They had both analysed the risk the same way. One: the search helicopter needed to wait for daylight to make its activity worthwhile. Two: because it had never appeared before nine o'clock, and had almost immediately returned in the direction from which it had come, it must be at the extreme limit of its range, so its base must be relatively far away. Therefore, as long as they left very early, they should be safe from detection.

That Saturday morning, Danny got moving as soon as Carlisle shook him awake, but it couldn't be said that he looked happy about it. "Of course," he said, whilst kneeling down to stow a bundle in the forward part of the canoe, "what we don't know is how far north the helicopter went... Or if he only stuck to the main strait. He might even have flown up this *Canal Abra* for some way before turning round."

"Well this channel was your suggestion. I'd have happily gone for the southern escape if you'd chosen that one."

"All I'm saying is, I can see there's no alternative to an early start. I'm cold, tired and hungry, fed-up and far from home. When I see Rennie, just before I spit in his eye, I'll try to remember how I'm feeling now."

For the past few days both men had been growing steadily more embittered with their mission. Carlisle made a sympathetic face, understanding why Danny's feelings needed an outlet. "Ready to go?"

"Yeah, let's go. But I vote we stop around ten o'clock and have a proper meal. Speaking personally, I'll probably feel quite tired by then."

"Good plan."

They both knew they would be tired once they turned off the main strait and entered *Canal Abra* because it faced almost directly west. That meant canoeing into both the prevailing wind and waves, and yet another counter-current entering the Magellan Strait from the Pacific.

As soon as they stopped for their morning rest and the meal that they had promised themselves, Danny got busy with the cooking while Carlisle unpacked his satellite phone. Ten o'clock, their time, would be mid-afternoon in London.

Carlisle said he wanted to speak to someone at Northwood before they all started trickling off home or thinking about a round of golf. He took himself a little way away from Danny to make the call. Danny kept flashing quick glances across at Carlisle, whose demeanour appeared subdued.

"Not good news," said Carlisle on re-joining Danny.

"What a surprise... What's happened?"

"Well, it seems there's only one conventional submarine assigned to the Task Force. Even then they seem to have sent it as a bit of an afterthought. HMS *Onyx* – a diesel-electric submarine. One good thing. It's the same sort that rescued us from the Kola – best suited to working with special forces patrols... And mongrel operations like ours, I suppose."

"What's the bad news then? Have the Argies sunk it?"

"No. Like I said – it's a late addition. It's not due in San Carlos Water until Monday, so there won't be any rescue for you and me until some time after that."

"Is there any good news?"

"Yes, in a way. San Carlos Water is in the Falkland Islands Sound, so the Task Force must have landed fighting troops ashore. They hope the Argies won't hold out for long."

"Meanwhile?"

"The pressure is off. We just make our way quietly and gently along this channel –"

"While winter draws on and the sleet turns to ice –"

"And I give them another call at this time tomorrow to see if they've managed to fix us up with a lift home."

"Pathetic," said Danny, and then swore vehemently for half a minute.

"Good job we've decided to go on half rations, I say."

Barajas International Airport, Madrid

Mr Delgado-Thomas – occupation, retired sheep farmer; residence, Las Martinetas (in Santa Cruz province, in the

Patagonian region of southern Argentina) – stepped out of the airport terminal and was immediately assailed by the heat. Although he had not lived in Las Martinetas for many years, he remembered enough about the place to have bluffed his way through if anyone were to question him about it. But the gentleman's caution was coloured by having lived in a police state for too long. Neither Immigration nor Customs seemed bothered to question him about anything. Spain appeared happy to welcome him as a tourist.

Although the climate was oppressive, Delgado-Thomas sustained himself with the thought that he should soon gain relief from it. His plan was to travel to the Pyrenees and find a cheap hotel for a few days, where he meant to rest from the flight. After that he intended to take one of the minor roads across the border into France, and from there...

01:27 Local Time
Friday 4 June, 1982
53°34'S 74°13'W

Even though they had waited for the forecast of semi-favourable sea conditions, it amounted to a significant act of trust for Carlisle and Danny to paddle from their last refuge on the coast of South America out into the open ocean, in the dark, overcast night. Without stars to steer by, Carlisle kept his compass secured around his neck by a lanyard, consulting its luminous dial every few minutes to maintain a course of 225°, as well as they were able. He had also switched on a small radio beacon to allow the submarine to find them.

From checking their watches, and having got used to the amount of distance they could cover in an hour, they both judged that they had canoed well outside Chile's twelve-mile limit of coastal waters.

"They've had long enough," said Carlisle. "I don't think they're coming."

"Maybe they're out here, but can't find us because our beacon isn't working."

"I'd have thought they'd have had enough sense to use radar to search for us as well."

"It's got a bit rougher. If there's too much sea clutter, they might not pick us out."

"Too much technology; too few eyeballs on the job."

"You're an officer now. How about a bit of initiative? Why don't you flash your torch for a few minutes? If we aren't careful, it'll be 'next stop, Antarctica'."

"All right. Five minutes. Then what do you reckon? Turn round and try to set up something for tomorrow. Maybe get them to come closer to land?"

"AHOY, THE CASTAWAYS IN THE CANOE!"

"Not before fookin' time," said Carlisle. "Fookin' sailors!"

However, once they climbed aboard the great matt-black shape and helped those same sailors to pass the Klepper canoe down through the torpedo loading hatch, both he and Danny remembered their manners and let the Royal Navy know how grateful they felt to be back on British territory.

Mid-day Local Time
Boppard-am-Rhein, West Germany

'Dilwyn Delgado-Thomas' sat under the trees outside a bar, facing the river. Technically, having already destroyed his passport, he was stateless and it was debatable what name should really apply to him. That might have been true, but there was the rest of his life to sort that out. For the moment he was fascinated. He had sat there, taking more than two hours over lunch, watching the river steamers and the barges making their way along the river. It was clear from his face that he gained great pleasure from occasionally calling, in German, for another glass of *pils*, and from listening to snippets of conversation, overheard between fellow diners and passers-by.

There was plenty of time to think about what he might do next. His current favourite was to march into the Boppard Polizeiamt, come to attention, report for duty under his Kriegsmarine serial number, then break down in tears, pretending memory loss. Tears would be easy; he felt nothing but joy.

Thursday 30 September, 1982
Heathrow Airport, London

The immigration officer was perfectly polite about it, but unwilling to answer any questions as he led Danny away to an interview room. Danny got the impression that he was in trouble. The series of connecting flights from New Zealand had left his eyes red-rimmed, bloodshot and feeling as though they had recently been blasted by a sand storm. His stomach felt pretty much the same.

"You!"

"Hello Danny. Welcome home."

"Whatever it is, the answer is no."

"Nice to see you too." Rear-Admiral Rennie put on an offended expression, then replaced it with a smile. "I've had Immigration monitoring the passenger lists from Kiwi for weeks. They spotted your name yesterday and let me know you were coming. I'd be most grateful if you'd agree to come back and work for me again."

"I've already resigned. You'll have had my letter."

"Please?"

"Why should I? I've had enough of your tricks."

A sheaf of papers lay on the table in front of Rennie. He stroked the top right-hand corner of the sheets to separate them, rotated them for Danny to read, then gestured Danny to the chair facing him.

"Grant me a moment or two for old time's sake."

It would have been impolite for Danny to refuse, and pointless to storm off; Immigration was still holding on to his passport. He sat and absorbed the details. The pages included a partial translation of data that appeared to have been extracted from German personnel files.

```
Doctor Hermann Fischer, born
1904, blue eyes, fair hair,
height 165 centimetres,
occupation industrial chemist.
Assumed to have been lost aboard
U-1226 on or about 23rd October
1944…

Obermaat (Petty Officer) Hans
Klein, born 1913, blue eyes,
fair hair, height 177.5
centimetres, occupation science
teacher. Assumed - the same…
```

Danny looked up.

"Well?"

"Well, the bones you brought back belonged to a gentleman of below average height, whose dental records – God! The Germans keep everything, don't they? – Whose dental records – It must have been those gold teeth… Whose dental records, as I was saying, seem to match those of the esteemed Doctor Fischer –"

"Wait a minute –"

"– Whilst the identity disk you brought back was issued to a certain Herr Klein when he joined the German Navy in 1941."

"There's probably been some sort of mix-up then. It'll sort itself out."

"No mix-up. You can't argue with records. *German* records. It's what they're best at"

"I don't see why that's a good reason to haul me out of the Immigration queue. It's none of my business now. All I want is to go home for a shower and a sleep."

"I don't want to deny you a few hours' sleep – not at all. I only thought you might be interested to know that an elderly gentleman of above average height turned up in the middle of West Germany a few weeks ago, claiming to have lost his memory. Well, almost. One thing he could remember was from years ago, when he was a kid. He was able to recite details of the pupils he went to school with, in a place called Boppard."

"Poor old sod."

"Yes. It all seemed to check out, too. He couldn't remember his name of course, but he kept repeating his Kriegsmarine identity number..."

"Oh, don't tell me..."

"Afraid so."

THE END

Glossary

30AU	30th Assault Unit A Royal Navy unit set up by Ian Fleming to gather German Naval Intelligence
ABCD	Atomic Biological & Chemical Defence
ACNS	Assistant Chief of Naval Staff [Royal Navy]
B.A.	Buenos Aires (colloquial abbreviation)
BBC	British Broadcasting Corporation
B.d.U.	*Befehlshaber der Unterseeboote* U-Boat High Command
B.P.	Bletchley Park (colloquial abbreviation)
C-in-C	Commander in Chief
CBW	Chemical & Biological Warfare.
CPO	Chief Petty Officer
DDO	Deputy Director of Operations [Royal Navy]
DNI	Director of Naval Intelligence [Royal Navy]
Droggie	Diminutive nickname for the Royal Navy's hydrography department
ESMA	*Escuela Mecánica de la Armada* [Argentine Navy]
ETA	Estimated Time of Arrival
FDR	Franklin Delano Roosevelt US President from 1933 to 1945
GMT	Greenwich Mean Time
Großquadrat	See *Marinequadratkarte*
h.f.	[Also, H/F] High Frequency (referring to radio transmission and reception)
HMS	[In 1944] 'His Majesty's Ship' [In 1982] 'Her Majesty's Ship'
HQ	Headquarters
Huff-Duff	H/F D/F – i.e., Direction Finding that targets High Frequency radio/wireless signals
ID	Identity

Küstenpolizei	Marine Küstenpolizei (MKP) – German coastal protection military police, controlled by the Kriegsmarine, and deployed in occupied countries
LST	Landing Ship [for Tanks]
Marinefunknamenliste	Kriegsmarine codebook containing naval radio callsigns
Marinequadratkarte	Literally, 'marine-square map' (or chart) For secrecy, the Kriegsmarine encoded all positions at sea, not by latitude and longitude, but by reference to its own specialised marine charts which divided navigable waters into 'squares' (though these were not always truly square). The major squares could be hundreds of miles across and were referred-to by two letters. For instance, *Großquadrat* AE contained almost the whole of Iceland and the waters south and east as far as the Faeroe Islands. Each *Großquadrat* was further divided, usually into a 9 by 9 grid, each resulting square being referred-to by its *Großquadrat* letters and a 2-digit code. For example, *Planquadrat* CO37 spanned the central part of the island of Crete, whilst LF51 defined the northern end of the Malacca Strait. By further sub-dividing each *Planquadrat* on a 9 by 9 grid (e.g., DH1724) an even more accurate position could be communicated, as required.
MoD	Ministry of Defence [UK]
NASA	National Aeronautics & Space Agency [United States]
NATO	North Atlantic Treaty Organisation
Naxos	Radar-detection device carried by German U-Boats in WW2
NBC	Nuclear, Biological & Chemical

O.P.	Observation post
Planquadrat	See *Marinequadratkarte*
Pongo	Derogatory term for a British soldier
QMS	Quartermaster Sergeant
RAF	Royal Air Force
RFA	Royal Fleet Auxiliary
RMS	Royal Mail Ship
RNR	Royal Naval Reserve
RNVR	Royal Naval Volunteer Reserve
R.V.	Rendezvous
SAS	Special Air Service
SBS	Special Boat Service / Squadron
Schnellboot	German fast patrol boat, (abbr. S-boot); known to the allies as the E-boat
SNAFU	"Situation normal – all 'fouled' up"
SS	*Schutzstaffel* [Nazi-German military unit, literally 'Protection Squadron']
UK	United Kingdom
U.N.	United Nations
US (USA)	United States (of America)
Vergeltungswaffen	Nazi 'revenge (or retaliation) weapon'; e.g., V-1, V-2
Wolfsschanze	Hitler's command bunker in East Prussia. Literally, 'Wolf's lair'
WRNS	Women's Royal Naval Service; also a 'WREN' – a woman serving in the WRNS
Y-Station	Wireless signal receiving station ('Y' being short for '**<u>Wi</u>**'reless)

By the same author

Re-birth

...The model, which was not attracting a great deal of interest from other delegates, had what he took to be an impracticably long barrel. This made him doubt that it actually represented a gun. Yet this was an arms fair, after all. What else could it be? The maker had constructed such a finely detailed model that it captured Danny's imagination. He and Rashid bent over to peer at the thing more closely and began to debate what was meant by the signage – '*Project Babylon*' – under which the model sat. After a couple of minutes, a North American voice spoke from behind them.

"Ain't she a beauty?"

Danny straightened up and turned to face a fellow of about sixty. The mohair suit, elegantly pressed, clearly labelled him a salesman.

"Yes, I suppose so. Fascinating. I've never seen anything like it."

The fellow stepped forward, hand outstretched, leaving Danny with no alternative other than to take it and shake it.

"Gerry Bull," said the salesman. And then, "Have you worked it out yet?"

"Worked it out?"

"What it's for. Come on, take a good look. What's this baby for?" Bull bubbled over with infectious passion, evidently convinced that the purpose of the full-sized device could be determined simply by inspecting the model.

"Er... First I thought it looked like some sort of gun, but neither of us is very sure." Danny cocked his head sideways at Rashid. "Rashid thinks it could be part of an oil pipeline."

Let's hope you didn't miss the first three episodes in the Danny Rook *Secret History* series...

Bunkeya:

Danny Rook is only 17, rather shy, and somehow, he's arrived in the Congo as a mercenary. And he's not alone. Cuba, China, Russia – they're all there, wanting a hand in the post-colonial re-domination of Africa. Naturally, the USA has a different outcome in mind.

When Danny's training exercise turns nasty and then an RAF aircraft crashes with something even more terrible in the bomb-bay, it's Red China that seems to hold all the aces.

As the song goes – "*It's the same the whole world over*" – government incompetence at the highest level, nobody really knowing what the hell is going on, and (if they want to stay alive) the 'little people' down at ground level having to dig the powerful people out of the mess they've got themselves and their countries into.

And oh yes, this is also a story about how Mao got 'the bomb'.

Pedro Miguel:

Next to Mao, Lin Biao is the most powerful man in China... and the Russians have turned him. Whilst Lin and President Richard Nixon might be on opposing sides, they sort of agree on one thing – they want to end the Vietnam War. But where Nixon's plan is characteristically devious, Lin's is drastic, secret, and not only dangerous but likely to be apocalyptic.

In the middle of the Pacific Ocean, there's a British freighter, and on board, two junior officers who don't have the full picture, but stand the best chance of preventing disaster, if only they can outwit their own Captain and hoodwink a boat-load of Chinese pirates.

Meanwhile, Lin's wife and son are plotting to overthrow Mao... And on board ship, Danny Rook, radio officer, is working on encrypting the most important message of his life.

Kola:

In the north of Finland, the forests are in trouble... trees, animals, bugs are dying off. And just across the border, inside Russia, a huge arrow-shaped structure has showed up on satellite imagery. But the photos are too oblique and too shaded by clouds for the photo-reconnaissance analysts to work out what's going on.

NATO needs to take a look at this weird arrow from ground level. But whom can they send? Someone resourceful... someone with the right knowledge... someone who isn't on a government payroll... Someone expendable? It could just be time to send for Danny Rook. But where is he?

Meanwhile, university arboriculturists think they know what's causing the forests to die back, so they want to get a look inside Russia too...

The Real Press

Come and have a look at our full range of books at **www.therealpress.co.uk**

You can also download your free book at... ***http://bit.ly/RemainsoftheWay***

FREE DOWNLOAD

Get Remains of the Way for free...

☆☆☆☆☆

"Evocative and engaging mystery story set on the Pilgrim's Way with a political twist"

☆☆☆☆☆

"This book is a fine read... read this book a couple of months ago and it has stayed with me. Highly recommended"

BARNES&NOBLE amazonkindle booktopia amazon.co.uk Rakuten kobo

Get your free copy of Remains of the Way when you sign up to the author's VIP mailing list.
Get started here: http://bit.ly/RemainsoftheWay

Printed in Great Britain
by Amazon

12123526R00222